REBELLION

THE SAINTHOOD – BOYS OF LOWELL HIGH BOOK 2

USA TODAY BESTSELLING AUTHOR
SIOBHAN DAVIS

Everything changed the night he betrayed me, and now, the game has entered a new level.

Galen did me a favor, reminding me the only person I can count on is myself, and I'm more determined than ever to avenge my father's death and avoid the destiny Sinner has mapped out for me.

Saint is used to calling the shots, but there are new rules, *my* rules, and if he wants me in his life, and in his bed, he'll toe the line. They all will, because I can't pull this off alone, and they owe me.

Sinner thinks he's in control, but forcing me into initiation plays right into my hands. War has come to Lowell as rival gangs battle The Sainthood for ultimate power, and I enjoy rebelling from the inside, placing more obstacles in Sinner's path while I exact my revenge.

But I'm not some innocent thirteen-year-old anymore—I have blood on my hands and lethal enemies on my tail.

I'm playing a dangerous game, especially where my heart is concerned, but there's no turning back. I haven't come this far to walk away empty-handed, and the more secrets we uncover, the more we realize how far-reaching the betrayal and corruption extend, and there's no choice anymore.

The Sainthood must be taken down, and we're the only ones who can do it.

PRAISE FOR REBELLION

"Siobhan hits every button – steam, intrigue, in-depth plots, and STEAM!"
S.E. Hall. New York Times Bestselling Author

"Rebellion is a thrill ride from start to finish! Five SAINTLY stars!"
USA Today Bestselling Author K Webster

"The storyline is very intriguing and like book one, will keep you on your toes."
Author Joanne Schwehm

"Thrilling. Addictive. Dark. Delicious. Magnificent. This book is an adrenaline high…"
Native Hippies Book Obsession

"This book had my heart beating wildly in my chest, my fingers itching to turn the pages and my soul begging for more. 5 delicious stars!"
Hooked on Books 11

"Absolute perfection. It's riveting from beginning to end, packed with intense action and steamy hook-ups!!"
Saucy Southern Readers Blog

Copyright © Siobhan Davis 2020. Siobhan Davis asserts the moral right to be identified as the author of this work. All rights reserved under International and Pan-American Copyright Conventions.

This is a work of fiction. Names, characters, places, incidents and dialogues are products of the author's imagination or are used fictitiously. Any resemblance to actual people, living or dead, or events is entirely coincidental.

This book is sold subject to the condition that it shall not, by way of trade or otherwise be lent, resold, hired out, or otherwise circulated without the prior written consent of the author. No part of this publication may be reproduced, transmitted, decompiled, or stored in or introduced into any information storage and retrieval system, in any form or by any means, whether electronic or mechanical, including photocopying, without the express written permission of the author.

Printed by Amazon
Paperback edition © December 2020

ISBN-13: 979-8636815853

Editor: Kelly Hartigan (XterraWeb) editing.xterraweb.com
Cover design by Robin Harper https://wickedbydesigncovers.wixsite.com
Photographer: Michelle Lancaster
Cover Model: Lochie Carey
Formatting by CP Smith

NOTE FROM THE AUTHOR

This is a dark reverse harem romance, and it is not suitable for young teens due to mature content, graphic sexual scenes, and cursing. The recommended reading age is eighteen-plus.

GANG STRUCTURE & CONTROL

<u>The Sainthood (Prestwick & Lowell)</u>
President: Neo/Sinner Lennox
Junior chapter leader: Saint Lennox
Junior chapter second in command: Galen Lennox
Junior chapter members: Caz Evans, Theo Smith, Bryant Eccleston

<u>The Arrows (Prestwick)</u>
Leader/President: Archer Quinn
Sergeant at arms: Diego Santana
Junior chapter leader: Darrow Knight
Junior chapter second in command: Bryant Eccleston (Sainthood spy)

<u>The Bulls (Fenton)</u>
New Leader/President: Marwan

<u>Ex-Lowell High School gang</u>
Leader: Finn Houston
Second in command: Brooklyn Robbins
Finn's girlfriend: Parker Brooks
Parker's bestie: Beth McCoy

<u>LOCATIONS</u>
Prestwick: birthplace of The Sainthood and The Arrows.
Lowell: where Harlow lives and where the new chapter of The Sainthood has been established
Fenton: birthplace of The Bulls

<u>SCHOOLS</u>
Prestwick High – The Arrows reigns supreme
Prestwick Academy – The Sainthood reigns supreme

Lowell Academy – A private school Harlow used to attend
Lowell High – The Sainthood reigns supreme

KEY CHARACTERS
Harlow Westbrook – 18, MC.
Giana Westbrook – Harlow's mom.
Trey Westbrook – Harlow's dad (deceased.)
Saint Lennox – 18, MC
Galen Lennox – 17, MC. Saint's cousin.
Caz Evans – 18, MC.
Theo Smith – 18, MC.
Alisha Lennox – Galen's mom.
Diesel – Harlow's friend/trainer & VERO employee
Sariah Roark – Harlow's best friend.
Emmett – Harlow's friend.
Sean – Sariah's boyfriend.
Lincoln – work associate of Trey Westbrook.
Howie Young – DEA Agent
Randall Solice – Head of VERO
Taylor Tamlin – Parker's half-sister
Ashley Shaw – Harlow's friend
Jase, Chad – Ashley's boyfriends

REBELLION

THE SAINTHOOD - BOYS OF LOWELL HIGH BOOK 2

CHAPTER 1

HARLOW

Sweat glides down my spine and plasters strands of hair to my forehead as I roll around the trunk of Darrow's BMW while he takes me to who-the-fuck-knows where. The skin on my wrists is torn and bleeding because my asshole ex bound the plastic ties way too tight, most likely on purpose, because he seems hell-bent on making me suffer.

I don't know how long we've been driving, but it seems like forever before I feel the car slowing down. We take a sharp turn over bumpy terrain, and my head slams into the side of the trunk as he drives over a pothole way too fast. I'm tossed around like a rag doll, and I hiss, as pain zips across my brow, cursing him through the rag still stuffed in my mouth.

An icy-cold chill whooshes into the cloying space as the trunk opens, and I welcome the cool balm on my overheated skin. I glare at Darrow as he roughly lifts me out by my upper arms.

He smirks, his eyes raking over me. "You're a mess."

Yeah, no shit, Sherlock.

If I could speak, I'd tell him he's not looking so hot himself. He's sporting several cuts and bruises on his face, a streak of blood is smeared across one cheek, his shirt is ripped, and mud mixes with blood splatters on his pants and dirty boots, in the aftermath of the epic gangland battle that went down earlier tonight.

Darrow places me on the ground and slams the trunk closed. My legs are stiff from being bent at an awkward angle, and I almost take a tumble when my feet hit the gravel underfoot, but I recover fast, straightening up as I drink in my surroundings.

Darrow digs his nails into my arm while dragging me along a debris-strewn path toward a derelict three-story apartment building. Sparse open fields surround us on one side, and a dense forested area is on the other. It's pitch-black out here, and the only illumination is from some large building in the far distance.

Galen told him to take me someplace remote to kill me, and it looks like Darrow is listening. He could shoot me dead right now, and no one would hear the bullet echoing through the silent air or see my lifeless body falling to the ground. He could drag me to the forest and bury me in full view, because there is no one around to witness the crime.

When we reach the building, Darrow shoves me onto the stairs, nudging a gun in my back, urging me to climb. I walk carefully up the rusted stairway until I reach the first level.

"Turn right," he commands, and I step over broken glass, crumpled beer cans, dirty cigarette butts, and evidence of drug usage, wondering what other kinds of criminal activity goes down here.

When I come to a dead end, Darrow presses the muzzle of the gun into my temple while he removes a set of keys from the back pocket of his jeans. "Move a muscle, and I'll pull the trigger."

I wonder what it says about me that I'm not scared. It's not because Dar is incapable of following through. He's a dangerous asshole, and he thinks I betrayed him, so it wouldn't take much to force his hand. But he forgets I know him, and he's selfish to his core. When he realizes what he's done, and how badly this could end for him, he will play it my way.

I'm confident I can talk him around, provided I don't piss him off in the meantime.

He unlocks the door to the last apartment, shoving me inside as he flicks the light switch on the wall. The door slams shut behind us as I walk the narrow hallway with Darrow close at my back. "In there." He pushes me forward, through an open door, into a small square room, switching the light on.

The place is surprisingly clean but sparsely furnished. There's a tiny kitchenette on the right with a table and two chairs. On the left is a lumpy-looking couch in front of a worn wooden coffee table and an empty bookcase.

He pushes me down on the couch, and I face-plant on the worn navy material, my nose wrinkling in disgust as I'm assaulted by a myriad of putrid smells. I push off my elbows, awkwardly straightening up, ignoring the chafing at my wrists and the accompanying pain.

Dar stalks to the kitchen, returning with a couple bottles of water. He puts them down on the table before tucking his gun into the back waistband of his jeans. He removes the rag Galen stuffed in my mouth, and I suck in greedy lungsful of air. In an unexpected tender move, Darrow brushes strands of matted hair off my brow, tucking hair behind my ears. "Here." He holds a bottle of water to my dry lips, and I tilt my head back, drinking as he tips the liquid into my parched mouth.

"Thanks," I say after I've drunk my fill, and he recaps the bottle.

He runs his fingers along my jawline, and an unpleasant shudder whips through me.

There was a time his touch was welcome, but now, everything about him disgusts me.

"It should never have come to this, Lo." He shakes his head while his fingers continue sweeping across my skin. "You shouldn't have stepped foot in that room. The minute you swapped sides, you signed your death warrant."

"Why am I here?" I ask, glancing around as I ignore his attempt to bring me down memory lane. "I thought you were supposed to be killing me."

He snorts out a laugh. "Eager to die, babe?"

"Eager for the truth to come out."

"And what truth is that?" He pulls a chair over from the kitchen. Placing it in front of me, he sits down, straddling it.

"You are not in possession of all the facts."

"Why else do you think I haven't put a bullet in your skull yet?" He quirks a brow.

"What deal did you strike with Galen?"

He shakes his head, smirking as he grabs my chin, gripping it painfully. "You're not calling the shots here, Lo. I'll be the one asking the questions."

"So, ask me."

He runs his thumb along my bottom lip. "Why does Galen Lennox want you dead?"

I shrug. "There could be many reasons. He's been gunning for my ass from day one, and I'm convinced there's something in the past driving his behavior. But it's probably because he thinks I betrayed them by giving up the location of the warehouse."

"The *fake* warehouse," Darrow cuts in, his nostrils flaring.

"I didn't know it was fake when I messaged you, and we both know I wasn't the one who leaked that intel first." I scrutinize his face, watching his reaction carefully. A muscle ticks in his jaw, and he doesn't refute my statement, which is all the confirmation I need.

The Arrows have a mole in The Sainthood's ranks.

Interesting.

"Did you know it was an ambush?" Dar asks, removing his hands from my face.

"I only found out late last night."

"That was still time to warn us," he hisses.

I keep my cool as I drop the first hint. "And why would I go against my own to do that? Especially when you reneged on our deal."

"I didn't renege on shit," he spits. "I was holding Johnny off until you delivered." He gets up and starts pacing. "Have you any idea the shit you've landed me in?" He pulls his gun out, stalking to my side and shoving it in my forehead. "I should just kill you now."

"If you do, you'll be signing your own death warrant."

He laughs hysterically. "I'm not afraid of Saint. He can't even control his own crew."

"You say that with confidence, but how do you know Galen wasn't acting on Saint's instructions? That this isn't part of some bigger play?"

My heart hurts at the thought it could all be a lie.

That Saint's concern was an act.

That Galen wasn't going rogue but merely following orders.

Emotions have clouded my judgment, and I don't know what to believe.

He shrugs. "Whether he was or wasn't doesn't concern me. He doesn't frighten me. As far as our prez is concerned, I fucked up big time tonight. We lost good guys at that warehouse, and their blood is on my hands. You helped set us up. Killing you will go some way toward righting the wrong."

"No, it won't. C'mon, Dar. You're way smarter than this. If you kill me, you'll bring the full weight of The Sainthood down on top of you. It will make earlier tonight look like child's play. I doubt Archer Quinn will thank you for digging a deeper hole."

"What the fuck are you talking about? You're not that important to them."

"I'm a member of The Sainthood, Dar. Sinner just approved my initiation. That's where the guys were supposed to be taking me. Galen wouldn't have pulled this stunt had he known."

He bursts out laughing. "You expect me to believe that bull?"

"It's the truth. I bear the mark. Pull up my hoodie at the back, and I'll show you."

"I've seen your back, sweetheart, and there's no mark there."

I fight the urge to roll my eyes. "Think about it, Dar. I kept my skirt on every time you fucked me from behind. Didn't you ever wonder why?"

"That was on purpose?" His voice reveals his surprise.

I nod. "I've gone to great lengths to disguise the mark, as did my father. He's the one who arranged my avenging angel tattoo."

I turn around, offering him my back. "Take a look. Lower right-hand side of my back, just above my ass."

He gets up and presses his palm into my back, shoving me into the icky couch, and I hold my breath to avoid inhaling the noxious fumes. He pushes my hoodie up to my waist and tugs my yoga pants down a little, exposing my bare back. He leans in close, his warm breath creeping across my skin like fog. His fingers skate over the exact place where Sinner branded me at thirteen. "Holy fuck."

I turn my head to the side. "Now, do you believe me?"

He fists a hand in my hoodie, yanking me back up. "If you expect this to work in your favor, you're sorely mistaken." He curls his finger around the trigger as he pushes the barrel of the gun into my chest. "It only adds to the reasons to kill you."

"Sinner branded that on my skin when he kidnapped me at thirteen. He's had plans for me all this time. What do you think he'll do to you if you eliminate me? I'm not just the first female member of The Sainthood. I'm soon to be his stepdaughter. If you kill me, it won't just mean an Arrows versus Saints war. Sinner will go after you personally. He won't stop until you're dead." I stare at his blood-streaked face. "I don't know about you, but a scenario where we both end up dead sounds like a fucking shit plan to me. Especially when there are much better plans we could enact."

"Like what?"

I force my eyes wide and deliberately inject excitement into my tone because I need to sell this if I'm to get out of here alive. If The Arrows already have a mole, my suggestion carries less weight, so I need to convince my ex this is a solid offer and something he can take to his president to get back into Archer's good graces. "Like I become a spy for The Arrows. Sinner is sending me to their training facility, and he'll assign me initiation tasks. I'm being groomed to enter the senior chapter with the guys after we graduate next year. I will be privy to all their inner workings and all their secrets. Isn't that intel worth more to The Arrows than my death? And I have more files like the one I gave you. You can get more of your guys out of jail with proof evidence was planted and witness testimony coerced." I'd given him a file Dad had on one of The Arrows, a guy named Alfred, to keep him happy and off my back. The file contained proof he'd been set up, and Alfred was now a free man.

He keeps the gun pressed to my chest, but I spot the indecision in his gaze. He's wavering.

"Why would you do that? If you are a member, why risk betraying them? If Galen could do this to you now, imagine what the organization would do if they discovered you were spying for us?"

"That's for me to worry about. As for the reason." I pause for a second, swallowing over the lump in my throat. My chest heaves as the usual pain presses down on my rib cage. "They kidnapped and tortured me when I was only a kid and they murdered my father," I say through gritted teeth.

Dar's face registers shock, so this is news to him.

"I want them to pay. All of them but especially that bastard Sinner."

He lowers the gun, tucking it back in his jeans, and I breathe a quiet sigh of relief, knowing I've won. Thank fuck. It was a little touch and go there for a while.

"I didn't swap sides, Dar," I add. "I've always been on Team Lo, and that hasn't changed. We have a common enemy. We both want to see The Sainthood taken down. I can help. We can help each other." I hold out my bound wrists. "And this way you get to save face with Archer and get your future back on track. Win-win for both of us."

"Don't make me regret this," he says, bending down and removing the knife strapped to his calf, before cutting the ties off me.

"That works both ways," I say, gently probing the tender skin at my wrists.

He sits down beside me on the couch, flipping the knife between his fingers. "How do we spin this?"

I lean in, as if I'm going to kiss him, and his eyes zero in on my mouth. I whip the knife from his hand and slam it into his thigh before he's had time to register the motion. I press down on it, twisting it for good measure, deriving immense pleasure from inflicting pain.

Bastard fucking deserves it.

A bloodcurdling roar rips through the air as blood pumps from the wound and his face pales. I work fast, stretching behind him to grab his gun before he shoots me. I put the safety on and zip it in the pocket of my hoodie. "Don't worry, I didn't hit any arteries," I confirm, reaching into the pocket of his jeans and pulling out his keys and his wallet.

"You fucking bitch," he yells, his fingers curling around the handle of the knife.

"I wouldn't remove that—not unless you want to bleed out all over the floor." I stand. "You should get to a hospital." I grin as I crouch down over him. I grab firm hold of his chin, tilting his face up as I peer into his eyes. "That's a warning. Betray me again, and next time, I'll embed it in your heart."

His face is a mix of hatred and respect as he glares at me. "Now, now, don't be like that." I mess up his hair, straightening up and slanting him a mock smile. "This explains how I escaped when Galen comes knocking."

It makes him look like a total pussy too, but I don't articulate that thought.

I saunter toward the door, humming under my breath.

"We have a deal, Lo," he yells. "And if you fuck me over again, I will slit your throat without stopping to ask questions next time."

I spin around, narrowing my eyes at him. "I'm glad we're both on the same page." I dangle his keys from my fingers. "I'll be in touch." My lips twitch. "Try not to die in the meantime."

He screams obscenities at my retreating back as I exit the apartment, steal his car, and hightail it out of there.

CHAPTER 2

SAINT

WE ARE AT Lo's house, grabbing clothes and shit to take with us to the safe house in Grenlow, when my cell pings with a message from Galen.

Change of plans. Meet me at the barn.

"What the fuck?" I stop what I'm doing and call his number, but the asshole doesn't pick up.

"Sup?" Caz asks, wandering into Lo's bedroom. He stalls when he sees my expression.

"Galen wants to meet at the barn."

"Why?" Theo asks, materializing behind Caz.

"I don't know, but I'll kick his fucking ass. I made myself clear." Galen does not get to challenge my decisions. Especially not this one. Not when it comes to her safety. I stuff the rest of Lo's things into the bag, grab my duffel, and stride toward the door.

"You drive," I tell Caz when we emerge outside, tossing him the keys to my Land Rover. "I want to keep trying the asshole." Caz puts his foot to the pedal, and we floor it out of there with Theo hot on our tail in his SUV.

I call Galen repeatedly, but he's not picking up. I go to call Lo before remembering I smashed her cell to smithereens. Couldn't risk Dad tracking it when she doesn't show at the training facility.

"What do you think is going on?" Caz asks, taking his eyes off the road for a split second to look at me.

I drag a hand over my shorn blond hair. "I've no clue. This is Galen we're talking about. His recklessness is legendary."

"Or maybe, Sinner sent a tail, and he's taking necessary precautions." It's no surprise Caz jumps to Galen's defense, because he is loyal to a fault.

"I have a bad feeling," I admit, hoping my gut is wrong. But it rarely is.

"How do you plan on keeping her away from Sinner?" Caz asks, taking the exit off the highway for Prestwick.

I sigh, kicking my booted feet up on the dash. "I've no clue," I admit. "I'm winging it here. I just know she can't undergo initiation. I don't want that for her."

"It's fucked up, dude," he agrees. "What is Sinner up to?"

"I don't know, but I intend to find out."

We don't talk again until we reach the hidden entrance at the far side of Prestwick Forest. Caz puts my Land Rover in park, hops out, and slides the gate back. I scoot over into the driver's seat and drive the car forward. When Theo is inside, Caz closes and locks the gate and hops in the passenger seat.

I drive us along the narrow dirt track for a few miles until our place comes into view.

Theo found it a couple years ago, and it was exactly what we'd been looking for. Someplace close by, under the radar, where we can disappear to when we need to regroup. Theo handled all the paperwork, purchasing it under a pseudonym, so it can't be traced back to us. We got it for a song which meant there were funds left to do some repairs, because the barn was basically a shell when we bought it. Thankfully, the structure and roof were sound, but we had to replace all the windows, and the interior was just this giant open space that needed work. Now, we've added bedrooms and bathrooms in the loft area, installed a basic kitchen, upgraded the rudimentary heating, and fashioned a living area and game room, complete with a pool table.

It's not plush, by any means, but it's home.

And Sinner doesn't know about it.

I'm sure he's figured out we have someplace we go to, or maybe, he assumes we're crashing at chicks' houses, but he hasn't asked, and we're not volunteering.

I park in front of the large wooden structure beside Caz's Mitsubishi Eclipse—the car Galen was driving—and kill the engine. Even though I'm wound up over this unexpected development, a sense of calmness washes over me like always when I'm here.

Towering trees surround us on all sides, hiding us from prying eyes. It's at the far side of Prestwick Forest, miles from the areas normally frequented by partygoers and nowhere near the section Sinner uses to bury his enemies or conduct initiation tasks.

Still, we know not to take chances, so we used the last of our change to install a few cameras on the perimeter and a wireless alarm system. Theo has it set up to activate remotely, and if anyone should happen across our place, the alarm will trigger a warning that will be sent to all our cells.

I get out the same time Caz and Theo do, and we stride toward the door together, all alert and on edge. It's fucking Arctic out tonight, and my balls are freezing. I open the door and step inside, spotting Galen standing by the window at the far end of the barn, staring out into the darkness. His spine stiffens as he hears us approaching, but he doesn't turn around.

Caz closes the door, frowning.

My eyes scan the room, but I don't see her. Theo keeps pace beside me as I advance toward Galen, his gaze growing in concern along with mine.

Galen slowly turns around, jutting his chin up and spreading his legs a little, standing tall, holding my gaze confidently as I walk up to him. A muscle clenches in his jaw as we square off.

"Where is she?" My voice betrays no hint of my escalating fear.

"Not here" is his clipped reply.

"What the fuck did you do?" Theo demands, nudging me aside and shoving Galen's shoulders.

"Something you three pussies were too weak to do." His lips curl into a snarl as my hands automatically clench into fists at my side.

Theo shoves Galen again, but I pull him back, putting my face all up in my cousin's. "Where is Lo?"

"She's with Knight. He's probably put a bullet in her skull by now."

I ram my fist into his stomach, and he stumbles back. He lifts his head, smirking. "When you remove your head from your ass, you'll see I've done the right thing. She betrayed us. She played us. And she had you all under her thumb. That shit would not end well."

I slam my fist into his face this time, and blood bursts from his nose. "You're a fucking idiot."

His laugh is bitter. "Bullshit." He spits blood on the concrete floor. "You've lost your touch. She made you weak. I eliminated the issue. Feel free to thank me anytime soon."

His arrogance will be the death of him someday and if he doesn't shut his stupid fucking mouth, that day might be today.

Caz charges past me, leveling Galen with one of his signature punches. Galen falls back, crashing awkwardly to the floor. "You're all overreacting," he shouts, losing the smirk. Anger flares across his face. "And you've forgotten the brotherhood! Forgotten what's important!"

I lean over him and punch him in the gut again. "She's one of us, you reckless fucktard." I slam my fist into his ribs, and a cracking sound reverberates through the cavernous space.

It's telling that he's not fighting back. He knew to expect this. He's taking it like a man, but he fully believes he'll be vindicated once we cool down.

"She's a hot piece of ass!" he yells. "That does *not* make her one of us." This time, Theo gets one in, pummeling his jawline. Galen spits more blood out.

"Sinner branded her with our mark when she was thirteen," I explain, thrusting my fist in the other side of his ribs. "And he ordered us to take her to the training facility to start initiation." I slam my fist into his face as Caz paces, pulling frantically at his hair, and Theo pulls out his tablet.

"What?" Galen croaks, his brow puckering in confusion.

"It happened after the ambush, when you were nowhere to be found."

"Because you were busy making plans to hand our girl to the enemy," Caz says, grabbing Galen up by the shirt and punching him.

"I didn't know!" Galen yells between punches. "And I was also responding to Theo's text. Retrieving the body."

I glance at Theo, and his expression conveys it's not important and he'll fill me in later.

Caz punches Galen again, and Galen's head whips back as blood flies everywhere.

I yank Caz back. "I want him conscious."

For now.

I glare at a bloody Galen. "Where is Knight? Where was he taking her?"

"I don't know." He shakes his head, and Caz raises his fist again. Panic flares in his eyes. "I swear! I don't know where he planned to take her." His eyes plead with me for understanding, but I've got none of that in supply.

"Where did the exchange go down?" I ask.

"Prestwick gas station," he blurts. "The one on the outskirts of town."

"Shit," Theo exclaims without looking up, fingers flying over the keypad. "They don't have any working cameras."

"Try the street cams in the area. Check all directions," I instruct. I stab Galen with a venomous look. "What car was Knight driving?"

"A silver BMW six series."

"I'm on it," Theo says.

"If anything has happened to her," I say, grabbing Galen up

and shoving him against the wall, "I will kill you."

"She still betrayed us," he protests, but his voice lacks punch.

I kick him in the leg, and his knee buckles. He falls to the hard floor with a grimace. "She wasn't the one who told The Arrows about the location of the fake warehouse. Lo only caved on Thursday after she overheard a conversation between me and Sinner, but she regretted it almost straightaway. She came to me Friday after school and fessed up to everything."

"You fucked up, asshole." Caz delivers a swift kick to Galen's ribs, and he cries out. I'm sure at least a couple are broken, and he's in obvious pain. "And I'll be helping Saint with the killing if Lo isn't okay."

"You should've told me," he shouts, clutching his stomach and rolling around in agony.

"You should've obeyed orders," I snap.

"I'm sorry!" His worried eyes dart among us, and I see the fear simmering under the surface. He knows he's fucked up.

"I've got them," Theo yells, and Caz and I race to his side, eyes glued to the screen.

"She's not in the car," Caz says.

"She must be in the trunk," Theo supplies, and I want to hit Galen all over again.

Caz darts for him, but I hold him back. "Enough." As much as I want to pummel my cousin until every bone in his body aches, I don't want to kill him.

At least not yet. However, I won't account for my actions if Darrow Knight has killed Lo.

"Can we trace his cell?" I ask, because trailing him via street and traffic cams will take too long. Also, we have no way of knowing if he ditched that car for another one.

"I'd need his number to trace it." Frustration oozes from his tone. "If you hadn't destroyed Lo's cell, I could've tracked them that way."

"You think I don't know that!" I roar, throwing my hands up.

Theo's gaze is cold as he glares at me. "This all could've been avoided if you'd just updated Galen."

I push my face into Theo's, and my knuckles blanch white with the effort involved in not hitting him. He knows Galen was with Lo today while I was running errands for my psycho dad and there hadn't been time to fill him in. I planned to, but I didn't think it was urgent because Galen usually obeys my commands. I had no clue he'd gone rogue, or I would've made it a priority. And Galen disappeared after the fight at the warehouse. If he'd stuck around, he would've been with us in the basement when Sinner revealed all. "This could've been avoided if Galen had done what he was fucking told to do!" I shout, adding, "I don't have to explain myself to you or anyone!"

Theo's gaze bounces between me and my cousin. Galen is sitting, propped against the wall, clutching his ribs, his face contorted in pain.

Good.

He deserves to suffer.

"If anything has happened to her, I'm blaming both of you." He points his finger between us, like we're naughty children, and I see red.

I grab his tablet, thrusting it at Caz before I ram my fist into Theo's face. He ducks at the last second, so it grazes the side of his jaw. He springs up, grabs the nape of my neck, and slams his head into mine.

I stumble back as splintering pain rattles around my skull. "Fuck."

"This isn't helping find Lo," Caz says, stepping between us. "And that bastard could be out there killing her right this very second, so focus, assholes!"

"I have his number," Galen rasps between long breaths. He holds out his hand. "Here."

I swipe his cell, growling at him. I show the number to Theo, and he gets to work while I press the call button. It rings out, so I try again, over and over, slamming my fist into the wall when it continues to go unanswered. "Keep looking!" I scream at Theo when he lifts his head from his tablet.

He scowls at me, but says nothing as he refocuses on his task. I keep my finger pressed to the button as I pace the room, growing more and more agitated as the call goes unanswered.

Pick up, you asshole!

"Saint, I—"

I level my cousin with a lethal look, and he instantly clams up. "Do not even attempt to speak to me right now."

"I've got them!" Theo calls out, and I rush to his side.

"Where?"

He scratches the back of his head, frowning. "At the hospital."

"That makes no sense," Caz says.

"I know," I agree, "but it's the best lead we've got. Let's go." I move toward the door.

"Hold up a sec," Theo says. "Let me pull up the cam outside the hospital."

"We don't have time to waste," I shout, hustling toward the door.

"There!" Theo shouts. Caz leans over his shoulder, his gaze darkening.

"What?" I race back to their side.

"That's Bryant Eccleston with Darrow," Theo says, pointing to where Knight's number two is helping him out of a car and into the hospital.

"But no Lo," I add, kicking the wall in frustration.

"He's injured," Theo says, glancing up at me with a glimmer of hope in his eyes. "Maybe, she got away."

"Lo has proven she's resourceful, so it's possible," I agree, hope blossoming in my chest.

"Or she fought back," Caz says, more quietly, not completing the end of the sentence.

"She's not dead," I blurt, feeling it in my bones.

"Then where is she?" Caz asks. "If she's still alive, why hasn't she contacted us?"

"Because she doesn't trust us anymore," Theo says, pinning me with a troubled expression.

The three of us look at Galen, and panic skates across his face. The reality of what he's done is fully sinking in.

"She thinks you were acting under my instruction," I growl, lunging at him and kicking him in the leg. "This is all your fault, and I will never forgive you if we've lost her."

THE SAINTHOOD

CHAPTER 3

HARLOW

I REACH THE cabin in less than two hours, having ditched Dar's BMW at a gas station and hot-wired a battered old Chevy I found lying idle. I couldn't risk driving Dar's car here in case it had a tracker. I head straight for the shower the minute I step foot inside my safe haven, properly breathing for the first time in hours.

After I've washed the blood and grime from my skin, I change into sweatpants and an oversized sweater and pad downstairs. Putting a frozen pizza in the oven, I pour a glass of water and head into the living area. I drop on the couch, leaning my head back as I contemplate one of the longest days of my life. It's after one a.m., and I should be exhausted, but adrenaline still pumps through my veins, and I'm too wired to sleep.

I can't believe Galen traded me to Darrow. That he was so cold and callous. So insistent that Darrow kill me. *What the fuck have I ever done to Galen Lennox to deserve that?* I know he thinks I betrayed them. That he believes I have the evidence proving Sinner and his buddies killed Daphne Leydon, the police commissioner's wife and the woman who was also the niece the newly elected president of the United States, and that I intend to use that to bring the organization down, but why would he make such a call without verifying the truth? *And would he go against his cousin like that?*

That's the part that has me most tied up in knots. The thought they were all in on it—that the emotional goodbye at the forest was an act. That this was their plan all along, because it honestly doesn't seem like their style.

Things were different with Saint and me last night. I know the emotion I saw on his face was real. *Why would he give Caz a Kevlar vest for me at the fight if he was planning on killing me? Surely, it would've been easier to leave me unprotected in the hope a stray bullet would do the job for them?*

I don't think Saint wanted me dead. But I'm also struggling with the notion Galen would go behind his back and do this without his knowledge.

Ugh. I bury my face in a cushion, wishing I had a crystal ball or a hotline to their minds. The timer on the oven pings, and I grab my pizza, cutting it into slices as I contemplate where I go from here.

I sit on the couch with a plate in my lap, munching on pizza, as I consider my options. I only have a short window to decide, because Sinner is expecting me to show up for training and initiation, and questions will be asked if I don't make an appearance soon.

I remove the burner cell I purchased on the way up here and tap out Diesel's number. Thank fuck, I had the smarts to memorize all my key contacts. He answers almost straight away. "I need you," I say before he has uttered one word. "I'm at the cabin. How soon can you get here?"

"I'm on my way."

Diesel shows up four hours later, and I'm roused from slumber by the simultaneous beeping of the alarm at the front gate and my ringtone. I'm spread-eagled across the couch, where I nodded off. Hauling my weary limbs up, I head to the study and grant him entry. Then, I make a fresh pot of coffee and leave the front door ajar, stifling a yawn as I wait for my badass trainer to arrive.

"Are you okay?" he asks, striding toward me and sweeping me into his arms.

"Define okay," I mumble against his chest, sinking into his warmth and his familiarity.

"Is this something to do with what went down in Landing's Lane?"

My eyes widen in shock. "How do you know about that?"

He purses his lips. "I keep an eye on you, Lo. You know that."

I'm sensing that's not the full truth, but whatever. "I was there," I confirm, because there's no point asking him to come here and then lying. "And Sinner pulled me aside after the fight ended to tell me he's claiming me. Saint was supposed to take me to their training facility to start initiation, but he wanted to take me to a safe house. Galen took me to Darrow Knight instead. Passed me off in some kind of sick exchange. Darrow was meant to kill me, but I talked my way out of it, stole his car, and came here."

Diesel's jaw slackens. "What the actual fuck?"

I sigh, shuffling to the counter and pouring two cups of coffee. "It's a fucking clusterfuck to end all clusterfucks, and now, I don't know who to trust."

"Back up there a sec," Diesel says, accepting the cup I offer him. "Sinner is *claiming* you?"

I nod. "He says they're admitting women to membership now. It's a ploy to keep the heat off the guys who are apparently coming under more scrutiny from the authorities."

"This is tied into your kidnapping."

I bob my head, sipping my coffee to avoid spilling the entire sorry story. Diesel doesn't know the part where The Sainthood blackmailed me into copying paperwork from my dad's office and handing it over to them. Or that it went on for years. Or that my father knew about it and was deliberately leaving false intel for me to copy hoping to trip Sinner up, to incriminate him.

I should tell him, but I hate the thought of him thinking less of me. It doesn't matter much in the overall scheme of things, but what does matter is Diesel's opinion of me.

"I have their mark on my back," I admit. "It's why Dad arranged for the tattoo. He was trying to cover it up and protect me."

He flops back on the stool. "Jesus Christ." He runs a hand over his cropped dark hair. "Why is he making a move now?"

I slide onto the stool across from him. "He thinks I have stolen evidence in my possession, and he was using the guys to intimidate me into giving it up. When that didn't work, he brought me into the fold." I scoff. "As if that would make any difference. If I had that evidence, the only thing I'd be doing is turning it over to the police."

Diesel sits up straighter and the vein in his neck visibly throbs. "What evidence?"

I eyeball him, hoping I'm right to trust him with all this. Not that Diesel has ever given me reason to doubt him, but I'm doubting my judgment after tonight.

This happens when you let emotions get in the way, and I'm better than that. Even if Saint hasn't betrayed me, I have opened myself up too much, and that's got to stop.

"Evidence that proves The Sainthood kidnapped and murdered Daphne Leydon."

He jumps up, spilling hot coffee all down the front of his shirt. "You need to leave town. Immediately."

I eye him curiously. "Why exactly?"

"She was the president's niece, and he's pulled out all the stops to find out what happened to her. There are all kinds of rumors circulating about how and why, and when this thing blows up, it will implicate everyone involved. I don't want you mixed up in that."

He paces, rubbing a hand across the back of his neck. "I know a guy who can get you out over the border, and I have a few safe places in Europe. I can send you there."

I walk to him, stopping his frantic pacing. "I appreciate the thought, and I know you want to protect me, but I'm not running, Diesel. I'm already in the thick of it, and I won't rest until I nail Sinner's ass to the wall. He killed my dad, but I might not get the evidence to prove it, so if I can pin Daphne Leydon's murder on him and the other board members of The Sainthood, and they go down for that, at least then justice will be served."

"Justice *will* be served, Lo." He gently cups my face. "You don't have to carry that burden. Let the authorities take them down."

I examine his face carefully. "Who are you, Diesel? Who do you work for?"

His hand drops away from my face. "I can't tell you who I work for, Lo." He has the decency to look apologetic. "But I'm the same person you've always known." He grips my face in his large palms. "I will kill every motherfucker before I let anyone lay a finger on you again." He rests his forehead against mine. "I'm on your side. I've always been on your side."

I ease back, staring into his handsome face. "So, why can't you tell me who you work for? Do you work for the government and you're sworn to secrecy? Is that it?"

"It's better if you don't know. Safer for you that way."

I don't miss how he hasn't refuted my claims, but he's still holding back, and that doesn't instill faith. "How can I trust you when I don't know why you're invested in this?"

He takes my hands in his. "I understand fully why you have a hard time trusting people. And you should trust *none* of The Sainthood. What Galen did tonight proves they are not trustworthy."

"I think he acted alone."

He rubs my hands. "I know why you want to believe that, but these guys have been brought up in this organization, molded by Sinner and other corrupt members to act outside the law. Saint is Sinner's flesh and blood, Lo." He gentles his tone. "Why do you think he'd have loyalty to you over his father?"

"Because he hates him! And he knows he's been lying to him, and…" I stop myself before I blurt about our connection, because that will just make me sound weak and immature.

"Did you ask me here for my advice? Or have you already decided, and you just want me to agree with you?"

I remove my hands from his, crossing my arms around myself. "I asked you here to help me, Diesel. I need to know there is at least one person on my side."

"You *always* have that in me, but I won't sit here and tell you what you want me to tell you. Those assholes are dangerous, and I want you nowhere near them."

"I have little choice, Diesel, because I'm not running away. Sinner will hurt my mom if I just up and disappear. She might be on my shit list right now, but I won't have that on my conscience."

He sighs, and his shoulders slump in defeat. "What's your plan, and what do you need me to do?"

I tell him about my deal with Darrow and how I intend to use it to my advantage. "As far as the guys will be aware, I got the upper hand and escaped. Whether or not this was Galen working alone, the guys will owe me. I'll be calling the shots and using them to further my aims."

The difference this time is I'll be keeping my emotions under sturdy lock and key. I'll use sex to draw them closer, to get them to deliver my plan, but my heart won't be invested. I can't afford for it to be especially where all trust is now shattered.

"I'll feed Darrow some intel, enough to keep him happy, without compromising my position. And I'll use it to wreak havoc on Sinner's plans to dominate in Lowell and crush his opposition. It'll help distract him while I use the guys to help me locate the missing evidence."

"Why would they do that? It seems unlikely they would turn on the organization for you."

I let loose a wide grin. "I think you underestimate the power of my seductive abilities."

He offers me a grin in return. "Having been on the receiving end of it, I assure you I don't underestimate you."

My expression turns serious. "The connection between them and Sinner is flimsy. From what I've determined, Galen feels indebted to him because of his family situation, Theo is sticking two fingers to his parents, and Saint shares blood. I'm unsure of Caz's motivations, but he seems committed to the guys before The Sainthood. I'm not detecting true loyalty to Sinner from any of them. It's weak enough that I can break it. My sense is their loyalty is to the organization or their idea of what they believe it should be. Right now, their faith is shaky because they know Sinner and the board is lying to them. The organization is rotting from the inside, and they need a purge. Moving product is one thing, but kidnapping and murdering females is a whole other ballgame. Letting Sinner and the board take one for the team will enable them to rebuild The Sainthood the way they want it to be."

He nods. "That's a good angle, but will they buy it when your intention is to take the organization down too?"

"They won't know that, and I think they'll buy into this. They've failed me, and this is the best way of making it up to me."

Well, that and helping me go after The Bulls, because if what Parker said is true, Ruben and his motley crew will be gunning for my ass. The Bulls are a gang who operates out of Fenton. They used to be allies, but they turned up at the warehouse fight with the opposition. Apparently, they know I was the one who killed Luke McKenzie because they somehow got their hands on a recording of the night we blew the drug house to kingdom come. It was self-defense, not that they'll care about that. They've recently moved into sex trafficking, and McKenzie was their contact, or so we've been told.

Can't say I've lost any sleep over his death.

"What can I do?" Diesel asks, extracting a silver chain from his pocket.

"Get me everything you can about Daphne Leydon and her kidnapping and subsequent murder. And let me know if there are any leads or new intel as it becomes available."

"Isn't there anything I can say to change your mind?" he asks, toying with the chain in his fist.

"C'mon, Diesel. You know what I'm like when I get an idea in my head. I'm doing this. I'll do Sinner's stupid training and initiation tasks. I'll bring the guys in deeper under my spell, using their guilt to work against them. I'll use Darrow to help distract Sinner while I work to bring him down."

He brushes my hair to one side and clasps the chain around my neck. "I need you to promise you won't take risks with your safety."

"I won't," I agree, running my fingers over the heart-shaped locket resting in the hollow at the base of my throat. "Is this some kind of tracker, or you're declaring undying love?" I tease.

"I'd declare undying love if I thought I stood any chance, but let's not go there again." He brushes his fingers along my cheek. "There is a tracker embedded in the silver. Wear this at all times so I know where you are."

"I can do that."

He presses in on the locket. "It doubles up as an audio recording device. Press once to activate it, and press again to deactivate it. It's set to copy to a secure file on the cloud I have access to."

I press down on it to switch it off, smiling at him. "You're amazing. You think of everything."

He shrugs it off, but I can tell my comment pleased him. "And you need to drive the Lexus all the time. Don't get lifts with those assholes, and don't take the Gran Turismo out. You're making enemies left and right, Lo, and you need to take precautions."

"Agreed, and I'll be more careful."

"What's your next move?"

I chew on the inside of my mouth. I've been giving this some thought, and I think this is the only game play. "I'm going to call Theo and ask for a meet."

THE SAINTHOOD

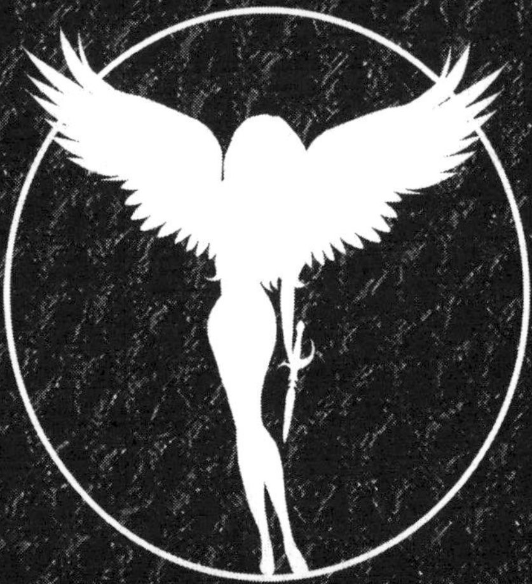

THE SAINTHOOD

CHAPTER 4

I PULL INTO the small parking lot at the front entrance of Prestwick Forest the following morning, and although I'm twenty minutes earlier than the scheduled meet, Theo is already there.

He climbs out of his SUV and hurries to my side, yanking my door open and pulling me into his arms. "Oh, thank fuck." He buries his head in my hair, squeezing me so tight I can scarcely breathe.

"Struggling to breathe here," I say, attempting to wriggle out of his iron-grip embrace.

He lets me go, scanning me from head to toe. "We've been so worried. I thought I'd have to physically chain Saint and Caz to the wall to stop them from going after Knight. They were up all night coming up with creative ways to torture and kill the asshole." He runs his hands through his long, dirty-blond hair. It's untied, swaying loose around the nape of his neck.

"I think we've got more pressing problems than Darrow Knight," I coolly reply. "And I took care of him myself."

Theo pulls me into his arms again, and I think this might

be even easier than I imagined. He hugs me tight, and I want to believe it's genuine, but I don't trust any of them with good reason. Still, I let him embrace me because I've a new role to play.

"We thought as much, but we weren't sure," he says, letting me go. I take a step back, needing a little distance. "Saint was getting ready to head to the hospital and beat the truth out of Knight when you called. Whatever your revenge plan is, it better be good."

I knew the guys would want to retaliate against Darrow, so I've had to get creative again. "You doubt me?"

"Never." His hazel eyes glisten with emotion.

"Where are the others?"

"Waiting for you." He eyes the decrepit truck I drove here. "I assume you want to ditch that?"

I nod.

"Get in my car."

I climb into the passenger seat of his SUV, watching as he removes a can of gasoline from the trunk, pours it over the old Chevy, and sets it on fire.

"We'll dispose of the charred remains later so there's no way it can be traced back to you," he says, getting in and starting the engine.

"Thanks." I stare out the window, contemplating the next few minutes.

"Lo." His voice is soft.

I turn my head to face him. "What?"

He eyes the bruise at my temple and the scratches on my cheek. "Did he hurt you?"

"Did he cut me, use a blowtorch on my skin, or stub cigarettes out on me? Is that what you mean?" It's a deliberate reminder of what his beloved Sainthood has done to me in the past. He winces, and I take pity on him. "No, Theo. He didn't hurt me. He never got the chance."

I watch with interest as Theo drives us around the outside of the forest for a few miles before stopping at the side of the road in front of thick shrubbery. He jumps out, and my eyes almost bug out of my head when he appears to part some shrubbery with his hands. I lean forward, straining against my seat belt as I inspect the strange sight. "Holy shit," I murmur to myself when I realize part of the shrubbery is actually a gate disguised to blend into the scenery. He slides back the hidden entrance to reveal a dirt road, bordered by the dark forest on both sides. I stare at him with my jaw hanging open as he drives the SUV through the small gap. His lips twitch at my reaction as he puts the car in neutral and climbs out to close the concealed gate behind us.

"What the hell is this?" I ask when he's back behind the wheel.

"I'm taking you to our place."

"It's like I've walked into a Bond or Bourne movie," I supply, as he drives the SUV forward over uneven terrain.

"Our privacy is important to us." He glances at me, and his hazel eyes dive into mine.

"What?" I'm instantly on guard.

"I thought you'd be angry."

I swivel in my seat to stare at him. "Why on Earth would you think I'm not?"

"You're calm."

"Haven't you ever heard the saying 'the calm before the storm'? Because that's a pretty apt depiction of what it looks like inside my head right now." I swirl a hand around myself. "Don't let this exterior fool you. I'm a fucking tornado waiting to happen."

"That's fair, but you should know Galen did this on his own. We had no clue."

"Of course, you'd say that," I scoff. "I've been around you all long enough to know what Saint says is law. Galen wouldn't risk going against him."

A pained look washes over Theo's face. "We knew you'd think that, but it's not true."

"I'll reserve judgment till we meet the others. I want Saint to look me in the eye and tell me he hasn't betrayed me."

The dirt track widens a few meters ahead, eventually bringing us to an open clearing housing a massive wooden barn. It's freshly painted, and the windows look new. The door is open, and Saint and Caz emerge from the inside, stopping alongside Caz's Eclipse as they wait for Theo to park.

A messy ball of emotion clogs my throat as I lock eyes with Saint through the glass. He's wearing a fierce expression, holding himself stiffly, with his muscular, inked arms folded across his impressive chest. He's not giving much away, but that's not unusual. Caz runs his hands repeatedly through his dark hair, his tongue toying with his lip ring in an obvious tell.

"Lo." Theo kills the engine and turns to me. "I know you're pissed, and it has shaken your trust in us, but please hear us out. We've been going crazy worrying about you."

"I'm making no promise, Theo." I open the door and step out as Caz jogs toward me.

"Lo." He bundles me into a hug, lifting me up in his strong arms. "Thank fuck." He places my feet on the ground, clasping my head in his hands. "You're injured. I'll kill that motherfucking ass—"

"He didn't touch me." I cut across him, stepping back despite how much I crave his closeness. "I got the scratches when Parker threw me to the ground, and the bruise happened when I was in Darrow's trunk."

"Princess." Saint's deep tone reaches a hand inside me, but I swat it away.

I turn around, eyeing him warily. He stares at me, his gaze roaming the length of my body, and tension bleeds into the air. It hasn't escaped my notice that Galen is nowhere to be seen. They are right to keep him from me, because they'll have a hard time stopping me from killing him with my bare hands. "What?" I ask, planting my hands on my hips. "Cat got your tongue?"

His lips kick up at the corners, and it pisses me off. "Don't fucking smirk at me." I close the gap between us, poking my finger in his chest. Anger rampages through me. "Not after the shit you pulled."

His gaze whips to Theo for a split second before he refocuses on me. "We didn't pull any shit. That asshole who shares my DNA lost his goddamned fucking mind."

"It's easy to point the finger of blame when he wasn't the one giving the orders." I shove at him, pushing him back a couple steps. I stretch my arms out to the side. "You want me dead, take your best shot. I'm unarmed," I lie. "Or don't you have the guts to do it yourself? Is that why you wanted Darrow to do your dirty work for you?"

He launches at me so fast I have no time to react. Wrapping his arms around me, he buries his face in my shoulder. His chest heaves, and his body trembles against me.

If he's role-playing, he's one hell of an actor.

I don't attempt to escape his embrace because I know it's futile, but I don't return his hug either, standing mute like a statue as he clings to me. After a couple minutes, he lifts his head, piercing me with no barrier between us. "If I wanted you dead, princess, I'd pull the trigger myself. I never shirk my responsibilities."

And that's about the only thing he could say that I'd believe. Because that is the Saint I know.

"He's telling the truth. I acted alone."

Blood boils in my veins at the sound of *his* voice. Slowly, I turn around and face a barely recognizable Galen Lennox. I mask my shock behind an impenetrable facial wall. He's doubled over, clinging to the door frame, his mottled face contorted in pain. His left eye is swollen and a blue-black color. His lip and nose are busted, and bruising covers most of his cheeks and jawline.

I don't need to ask to know the guys did this to him.

Warmth spreads across my chest until I shut that shit down.

All of this could be for show.

I cannot trust them.

They are still my enemy. Maybe, they always were.

Or it could be the truth, that annoying inner voice whispers in my ear.

"As if I'd believe a word that comes out of your conniving mouth," I hiss, gnashing my teeth at Galen.

"I didn't have all the facts when I made that deal with Knight. I never would've gone there if I'd known the truth. I swear."

Naked aggression blankets me until I'm almost drowning in

anger. "Try peddling that bullshit to someone who buys it!" I roar, stalking toward him like the living embodiment of the avenging angel inked on my back. My hands clench and unclench at my sides, my lips curl into a snarl, and fury pummels me from all sides. I'm shaking with rage and a multitude of other emotions as I stand before him. My chest heaves in and out as I bore holes in his damaged flesh, and I'm seething, my entire body trembling, as we stare at one another.

I could kill him.

The thought has crossed my mind a thousand times.

But then, I'd be no better than him.

And I'm nothing like that reckless, arrogant asshole.

My thoughts force me to calm down somewhat, reminding me to stick to the plan. But it's challenging, because he wanted me dead. And besides the obvious, that hurts.

Keeping his eyes locked on me, he straightens up even though it's obviously killing him.

"Who cracked his ribs?" I ask, glancing over my shoulder.

"It was a team effort," Caz says, walking to my side and lacing his fingers in mine. I let him only because it's part of my plan.

"I'm sorry, Lo. I—"

"Save it," I snap. I grip Galen's chin, digging my nails into his bruised skin. "Not so pretty now, huh, Lennox?"

"I fucked up." The remorse on his face appears genuine. But I couldn't give two shits.

I slap him hard. "You didn't just fuck up, asshole. You tried to murder me!" I shove at his shoulders, and tears prick his eyes from the pain. "Instead of, oh, I don't know, asking me to my face if I betrayed you, you deemed yourself judge and jury and decided I was guilty with no trial."

"I was wrong, I shouldn't—"

"You were more than wrong, you fucking idiot!" I shout, and I know I need to rein my emotions in, but I was unprepared for the extent of my feelings when confronted with the man who wanted me dead. My entire body shakes with rage as I bend over, grab my knife from my boot, and hold the sharp blade against

Galen's neck. Tension is thick in the air as I glare at him. "I made a promise to myself when I was thirteen," I say, pressing the blade in and drawing blood. "I promised that no one would ever hurt me again and live to tell the tale."

"Do it," he says, surprising me. "I deserve it."

"Harlow." Saint's tone is cool as he places his hand on my arm. "You don't want to do this."

"You're defending him now?"

"Fuck no. I want to gut him as badly as you do."

"I highly doubt that."

"Trust me, babe. I do. He betrayed all of us when he handed you to the enemy." Saint moves his hand lower on my arm.

I press the knife in again, slicing a thin line through Galen's flesh. A muscle ticks in his jaw, but he holds firm, and his eyes almost plead with me to do it. A dart of pain flashes across his face, hinting at immense suffering, and there is so much I don't understand.

Saint uses my distraction to grab my wrist, forcing my hand to pull away. I battle him, because no one is going to fucking tell me what to do anymore. "Lo, stop."

"You fucking stop," I hiss, crying out when he digs his nails into the tender flesh underneath my wrist, making me drop the knife.

A shrill siren rings out, and a red flashing light blares from someplace overhead.

"What the fuck?" Saint shouts, eyeballing Theo.

"Someone has breached the perimeter," Theo confirms, stabbing buttons on his phone.

"That'd be me, asshole," a familiar voice says from behind.

Saint still has a grip on my wrist, and he roughly shoves me behind him. Sharp pain shuttles up my arm, and I cry out again.

Diesel trains his rifle on Saint. "Let Lo go, or I'll gladly end you."

CHAPTER 5

"Diesel, don't." I attempt to extract my arm from Saint's grip, but his hold is tight, and it's clear he has no plan to let me go anytime soon. I bend down and bite his hand, burying my teeth deep in his flesh.

He lets out a roar, dropping my arm and staring at me like I've gone crazy.

Ignoring his expression, I step around him, striding toward Diesel. Slowly, he lowers his rifle, but the lethal look on his face remains. I stop in front of him. "What are you doing here?"

"I told you I don't trust those assholes," he says, carefully lifting my arm and turning it over. The skin on my wrist has broken again, and a thin line of blood is pooling at the site of my wounds. "You fucking hurt her." He stabs Saint with a murderous look before softening his gaze when it lands back on me. "I told you you should've let me bandage them."

"It's nothing."

"Take your hands off her," Saint says, coming up behind me.

"Fuck off, asshole, before I put a hole in your skull."

"I'd like to see you try, old man," Caz says, leveling a Glock at Diesel's head.

The flashing light and piercing siren die out, and I spy Theo repocketing his cell and walking this way. "Lo, you know this guy?" he asks.

"Yeah. I can vouch for him."

"What the fuck is he doing here?" Saint growls, scowling at me.

Diesel drops my hand, prodding his rifle into Saint's chest. "Lose the attitude, punk, and stop speaking to Lo like that."

"Listen here, grandad." Saint shoves the rifle away as if it isn't loaded and couldn't go off at any second. "You don't get to show up on our turf and start making demands."

"I could wipe you all off the face of the planet in the blink of an eye," Diesel says. "Don't fucking tempt me."

"Let's everyone cool their jets," I say, stepping between Saint and Diesel.

"Who is he?" Theo inquires, looking directly at me.

"I'm her trainer," Diesel says, and I know I shouldn't add to that, but I'm in the mood to inflict pain.

"And onetime lover," I confirm, winking at Diesel.

He arches a brow, and I grin just as Saint shoves me out of the way, lunging at Diesel. They tumble to the ground, throwing punches at one another, as they instantly get into it.

"Twenty on the old dude," Caz says into my ear.

"You'd bet against your *saintly* leader?"

"I know a crazy motherfucker when I see one, and I'm not talking about Saint. That dude is hardcore, and I'm intrigued." Caz waggles his brows, shoulder checking me.

"That makes two of us," Theo says, coming up on my other side. "What the hell is going on, Lo?"

"If they stop acting like idiots, I might get the chance to tell you."

"You fucking pervert," Saint roars, landing a punch to Diesel's nose.

Diesel rolls on top of him, pummeling his face with a barrage of punches that's got to hurt. "You fucking delinquent."

"Okay, enough." I grab the back of Diesel's shirt, yanking him off Saint.

Saint sits up, spitting out blood as Diesel presses his fingers to his nose to check for damage. They sit across from one another, both with new cuts and grazes on their faces, spewing vitriol through their eyes. Any other time I'd find it funny, but we have shit to talk about, and we're getting sidetracked.

I loom over them, planting my hands on my hips. "Stop this petty shit. It's beneath both of you. We have stuff to discuss, and it can't wait."

A few minutes later, we're seated around a large rustic table, on mismatched chairs, facing one another over cold beers. Tension is so thick you'd need a machete to cut through it.

I love the guys' place although I haven't seen upstairs yet. It's got this edgy, industrial-type vibe, yet it's homey, and I'm surprised because it's not really a guy thing. I knew their bedrooms back at our house were only places to sleep, that they had somewhere else they called home. Where their bedrooms lack personality, this converted barn has it in spades.

Framed movie pictures line the walls along with an assortment of biker pics, sports memorabilia, and the requisite naked chicks. Multicolored rugs are scattered around the vast space, taking the cold edge off the hard concrete floors. Two comfy-looking battered brown leather couches and a matching chair rest in front of a large open fire, and if things were different, I could visualize nights cozied up to all of them in front of a roaring fire, toasting s'mores and drinking beer and getting our sexy on.

But things won't be like that anytime soon, because the trust is broken, and Galen's betrayal is the colossal-sized elephant in the room.

"How did it go down?" I ask from my seat at the top of the table. Saint is on my left and Diesel on my right. Theo and Caz are seated beside their leader, and Galen is by himself at the end of the table, slumped in the chair, in obvious discomfort. He needs medical attention, but no one has offered him any. It seems fitting. His actions have ostracized him from his crew, and he has no one to blame but himself.

I tap my fingers on top of the table, drilling him with a look that challenges him to deny me.

He puts his beer down and clears his throat. "Darrow approached me after the fight ended. I was carrying Parker's body to the car when—"

"Wait." I sit up straighter. I can't believe I forgot about that. "Where is the body?" I glance at Theo.

"Who is Parker?" Diesel asks.

"It's taken care of," Theo confirms.

"How?"

"The less you know, the better," Saint says, and I slam my fist down on the table.

"No." I glare at him. "That is not how this is going down." I point my finger in his face. "There are new rules, *my* rules, and we're playing it my way from now on."

"I get you're pissed," Saint says, flipping the bottle cap between his fingers. "But I'm still junior chapter leader, and I'll be calling the shots."

"Because that's been working out so well." I sneer at him, waving my finger in his face. "I wonder what Sinner would say if I told him Galen made a deal with our archenemy and deliberately went behind your back. Or how that psycho would react if he knew his precious son was planning on hiding me away instead of taking me to the training facility like he demanded."

I sit back, smirking as I pick at the label on my bottle. "I don't think you'd be leader for much longer if I divulged all that."

"Lo, you can't go to Sinner. He's unpredictable as fuck," Theo chimes in.

I jab my finger in his direction. "Let's get one thing straight here." My gaze moves between them. "No one gets to tell me shit anymore." I eyeball Saint. "You might be the leader, but I'm making the decisions now. Cross me, and I'll have a little word in Sinner's ear." I narrow my eyes at Galen. "Betray me again, and I will take great pleasure in ending your miserable existence."

"Fuck, princess," Caz says, pinning me with a lust-drenched expression. "My cock is hard as a rock."

I grin, because I can always rely on Caz to bring some levity. And to be horny.

Out of all of them, I'm least mad at him.

Saint is seething, practically vibrating in his chair, and I'm sure he'd love to wrap his hands around my throat and angry fuck me into obedience. He'll soon learn I'm not so easily swayed with sex anymore.

"Do you have to be so vulgar?" Diesel isn't pleased, and that amuses me.

"Says the pedo," Saint snarls. He's so observant, but I don't know if he's genuinely picked up on the very thing that pushes Diesel's buttons or he's just reaching an obvious conclusion.

Diesel jumps up, but I grab hold of his arm, forcing him back down. "Ignore him. He's pushing your buttons on purpose." I lean into him and rub his arm in a soothing gesture, knowing it will wind Saint up.

Saint grabs his bottle, guzzling beer like it's water, and I pretend like the way his throat works as he drinks isn't hella sexy.

"Now that's been sorted," I continue, tossing my hair to one shoulder. "Let's get back to Parker." I turn to Diesel and explain. "Parker was Finn Houston's girlfriend. Finn used to control Lowell High until these guys took control. She put my bestie in the hospital, and she made it clear she wanted my crown."

"She tried to take Lo out at the warehouse," Theo adds. "But Lo killed her first." There's a hint of admiration in his tone, which is wrong on so many levels.

"What did you do with the body?" I ask.

"Theo messaged me to clean up," Galen admits. "I put her in the trunk of the Eclipse and Caz and Theo took it from there," he adds.

"We burned the slunt's remains," Caz says, grinning, like burning a schoolmate's body is an everyday occurrence.

"For fuck's sake." Saint rolls his eyes. "Seriously, dude?"

My brow puckers as I look between them, and then a light

bulb goes off. I burst out laughing. "Word of the day?"

"Got it in one, princess." Caz glances at the time on his cell. "Think that might be a record for me. It's not even eleven."

"Can we move this along?" Diesel says. "Some of us have work to do."

"Don't let the door hit you on the way out," Saint says, smirking.

"Where are the remains now?" I ask, ignoring the latest jibe.

"Buried in the woods," Theo confirms. "Don't give it another thought. She's gone."

I probably should feel bad for taking another life, but Parker would've had no qualms killing me, and it was self-preservation, so I refuse to feel any remorse.

"Did Darrow see?" I ask Galen.

He nods. "But he doesn't know how she died, and he couldn't give a fuck about her."

"Of course not," Saint snaps. "He was preoccupied helping you plan Lo's murder!"

Galen's Adam's apple bobs in his throat, and he grips the table hard, digging his nails into the wood. "I don't know what else you want me to say." He throws his bottle at the wall, and broken glass mixed with sticky beer coats the floor. "I fucked up!" he shouts. "*I'm* fucked up. I never should've acted so recklessly, and I regret it, okay." He leans forward on his elbows, beseeching me with his gorgeous green eyes. "If I could go back and do everything differently, I would."

"I'm done listening to your pathetic excuses. You gave me to my ex to kill me! That shit will never be okay." I hold those steel walls firmly around my heart, refusing to let his words breach the new barriers I've built. "Just answer my goddamn questions. What did Darrow say?"

He slumps in the chair, sighing, his face defeated. "He told me you were the one who gave up the location. Said you'd screwed both sides over and you'd continue to come between us if you weren't dealt with." He averts his eyes. "He suggested he could make you go away, and all I had to do was give him a ten percent cut of the next five shipments."

"Jesus fucking Christ." Saint hops up. "Are you fucking insane? On what planet would Sinner have ever agreed to that?"

"I was making it up as I went along," Galen protests, pouting a little.

"Thank fuck, *you're* not in charge," I drawl.

A red flush creeps up his neck. "He told me she was the mole. That she gave up the location and she handed over evidence which got Alfred freed. I figured Sinner would be pleased I'd eliminated the threat, and I'd no intention of giving them jack shit. They're the fucking enemy, and we're already at war. Not my fault he's the idiot who believed me." Galen's legendary arrogance creeps into his tone, and I shake my head.

"You're the fucking idiot who took the enemy at his word without any fact-checking," I hiss, enjoying watching the smug look disappear from his face.

"You're a damn fool, Galen," Saint agrees. "Your jealousy and single-minded stubbornness made you vulnerable. You let that asshole Knight use that to manipulate you. I've never been so fucking disgusted with you."

"You think I don't know that!" Galen yells. "You think I'm not disgusted with myself?!" He bites down on his lip, shaking his head, and looks away but not before I see the torment shining in his eyes.

But is it real, or he's tormented because he failed in his quest to get rid of me?

No one speaks for a few beats. Tension and emotion swirl around us, and I've no clue how any of us come back from this.

"Sinner can't know you were behind Alfred's release," Saint says, breaking the silence. From the lack of surprise on Caz's and Theo's faces, I know Saint updated them on that part of our conversation from Friday night. But it's obvious from the frown on Galen's face that he's still in the dark about all the other shit that went down between me and Darrow.

Saint's eyes bore into mine. "That was another reason I wanted you to go to the safe house."

Galen opens his mouth to offer some opinion, but he clamps his lips shut. Maybe he's finally wising up.

"And let's not forget The Bulls," Theo says, swinging back and forth on the legs of his chair.

"What about The Bulls?" Diesel asks. He's been quietly listening, taking everything in.

"I accidentally shot one of their guys. They have the video footage, and now, they're coming for me."

"Lo." Saint's tone contains caution.

"I've known Diesel for five years. He's trustworthy." Saint opens his mouth, to spew more pedo crap I'm sure, but I shut him dead in his tracks. "Unlike some."

He grinds down on his teeth, and he vibrates with open hostility.

Diesel shakes his head, fixing his gaze on Theo. "You took care of that, right?"

I fight a smile. "Is there anything you don't know?"

He slants me a lopsided grin. "Told you I had your back, but Theo wiped the footage before I got there on this occasion."

"Who the fuck are you, dude?" Theo asks, shifting uncomfortably.

"Your worst nightmare." Diesel smirks.

"I don't know what happened, because I know you have mad skills," I tell Theo, "but remember what Parker told us. She said The Bulls sided with Finn and The Arrows and they somehow had a copy of the satellite footage showing me shooting Luke McKenzie."

Theo rubs a tense spot between his brows. "It makes no sense. I wiped it clean less than an hour after it went down. How did they get their hands on the footage?"

"Someone else made a copy *before* you wiped it," I say, because it's the only logical conclusion.

"It seems unlikely unless..." Theo stares off into space.

"Unless what?" I ask, drumming my fingers on my jean-clad

thigh.

"Unless someone was watching it go down," Diesel says, continuing Theo's train of thought.

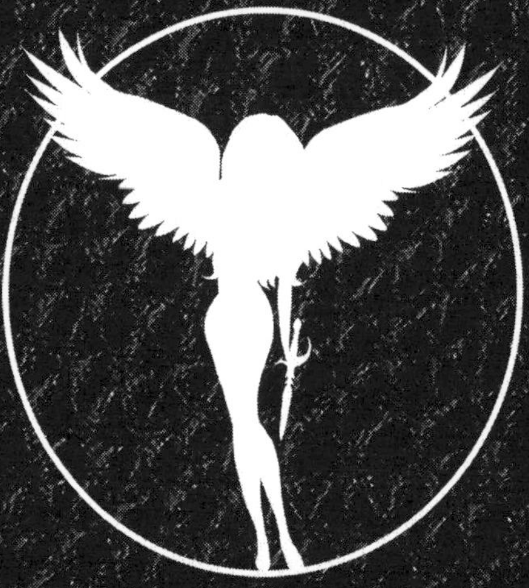

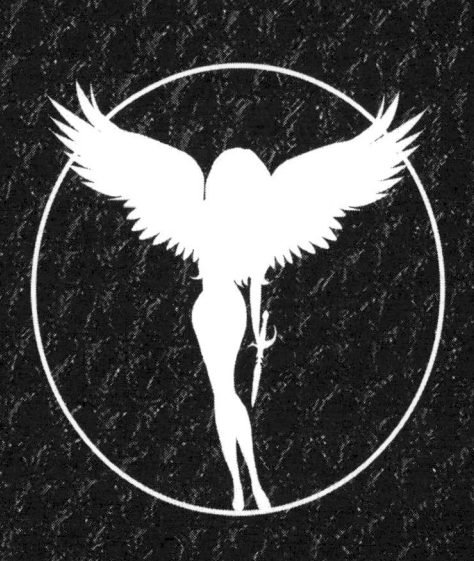

THE SAINTHOOD

CHAPTER 6

"WE NEED TO get our hands on that footage," Saint says, rubbing a hand across the back of his neck.

"And we need to neutralize Ruben," Caz adds. "With or without that footage, he won't stop coming for Lo."

"I'll see what I can dig up," Diesel says, standing. He removes a card from the inside of his jacket, handing it to Theo. "Let's coordinate our efforts. That's a private chat room."

Theo nods, sliding the card into the back pocket of his jeans.

Diesel looks down at me. "Walk me out?"

Saint snarls, and it's amusing to see him like this. With the mask down. Unable to conceal his jealousy.

I glare at Galen, as we walk past him toward the door, funneling every ounce of hatred into the dark look.

Once outside, we walk in silence for a few minutes until we've put enough distance between us and the barn. "Thanks for that," I say in a low tone, circling my arms around his neck and hugging him.

"I want to help. They need to know you've got backup. That I care about you. That I will go postal on their asses if they try anything again."

"What do you think?" I ask. "Was he acting alone?"

He runs a hand over his prickly jawline. "As much as I hate to say it, because I fucking loathe Saint, I think he's telling the truth. I think Galen went rogue."

"Not that it really matters," I say, and it's only half a lie. "Because it's a timely reminder I can't trust them anyway. I was getting too close."

He plants his hand on the nape of my neck, reeling me in. His lips linger against my forehead. "I can't believe I'm going to say this, but…they care about you. At least Saint, Caz, and Theo do. It won't take much to have them eating out of your hand, but Galen is a dangerous asshole because he's damaged goods, that much is clear, and that makes him volatile. Make him grovel for forgiveness, but never trust him."

"I don't need any convincing."

Diesel's gaze darts over my head, and his lips kick up ever so slightly at the corners as he bends down, pressing his mouth against mine. It's only a peck, and I'm guessing it was for Saint's benefit. "Stay safe, sweetheart. Call me if you need me."

I watch him disappear into the trees with fondness, glad I called him. I turn around, keeping my gaze trained on Saint's as I walk back toward the barn. He's standing in the doorway, his expression and stance like that of a strict army major. He's furious. That much is obvious.

I move to brush past him, but he grabs hold of my elbow. "Were you fucking him the same time you were fucking me?"

"I don't recall him being in the room." I'm being facetious on purpose because this shit never gets old.

"Don't get smart. You know what I mean," he growls.

"Jealous, *Saintly*?"

"Of that old perv, hardly," he scoffs.

"Then you don't need an answer, do you?" I shove his arm off and step into the room.

The door slams with a violent bang, and then, I'm pushed up against the wall with Saint's strong, tan, inked arms caging me in.

"I spent hours terrified you might be lying dead or injured, and then, you show up with attitude and that prick in tow. Cut me some slack here, princess." He presses his body against mine, and red-hot emotion rolls off him in waves.

I reach up, running my fingers along his stubbly jawline. "I haven't fucked him since you guys moved into the house."

His lips crash down on mine, and he winds his fingers through my hair, firmly clasping the back of my head. The kiss starts off rough and punishing before his lips soften and he makes love to my mouth in a way he's never done before. The rawness of the emotion pouring from him scares me, and I rip my lips from his before he sucks me back into his orbit again. He presses his forehead to mine, holding me in place at the back of my head. "I know you don't trust us, trust me, and I hate that Galen has fucked things up, but please give us a chance to put it right because we can't lose you, Lo."

"Why? Because I'm one of you now?"

He moves his hand, rubbing his thumb along the side of my neck. "Because you're our girl."

"That remains to be seen," I say, ducking out from under his hold.

"The fuck does that mean?" he demands to know, trailing me as I walk back to the table.

I reclaim my seat, and he plonks down beside me, radiating thunderous vibes. "You owe me." I glance around the table. "All of you." My eyes narrow on Galen, and I jab my finger at him. "Especially you."

"Whatever it is you want, it's yours," Galen says.

"I want you groveling at my feet," I coolly reply.

He gulps, and I bet he'd love to protest, but I have him where I want him. His brothers are pissed at him. I'm pissed at him. Sinner would lynch him if he discovered what he did, and Darrow will be out for his blood now too.

He is at my mercy, and he knows it.

"Whatever it takes."

When he doesn't move, I arch a brow and stare at him.

"What?" he asks, looking confused.

A knowing smile curves the corners of Saint's mouth, and Caz chuckles. Theo's lips twitch while his fingers fly over the keypad of his tablet.

"I meant it literally," I explain, enjoying watching all the blood drain from his face.

"You can't be serious?"

I school my features into a neutral line. "Do I look like I'm not?"

He glances at Saint.

"Don't look at him," I snap. "I'm calling the shots now." I curl my fingers at him. "Get up here and kneel before me."

Slowly, he stands, biting back a hiss of pain and clutching his upper torso as he hobbles toward me. His entire face is flushed red with anger when he reaches me, but he doesn't bother arguing anymore, clutching the side of Saint's chair as he painfully lowers himself to his knees.

"Kiss my feet," I demand, smirking as he leans down and kisses the toes of my mucky boots. "Stay there until I tell you to get up."

Saint pins me with one of his trademark amused looks while Caz is full-on grinning. Theo is oblivious, lost in technology.

"We should hit the road soon," Saint says. "It'll take six hours to reach Grenlow, and it's best to get there before dark."

"I'm not going to the safe house. You'll take me to the training facility like Sinner requested."

"Like fuck I will." Saint's heated expression and response are predictable.

"You cannot shield me from this, and I'm not running."

"Babe, initiation is hardcore fucked-up shit," Caz says.

"You think I don't know that?" I lean forward in my chair. "That I'm not capable?"

Galen hisses, and I'm guessing he's uncomfortable bent over like that.

Well, screw him.

I reach down, grab handfuls of his messy dark hair, and tug on the strands. "Stay still," I snap.

"We know how resourceful you are, Lo." Saint rubs at his mouth. "But the training process is extremely physical, and the initiation tasks usually involve violence and criminal activities. None of us want that for you."

"What we want doesn't come into this," I say. "It's doing what needs to be done to achieve our end goal."

"Which is?" Theo asks, lifting his head from his screen.

"The same one it's always been. Vengeance."

"Look, none of us have allegiance to Sinner," Saint says, pinning me with a grave expression. "Our plan was always to climb the ranks and take control as soon as possible so we can restore order to The Sainthood. Kidnapping, torturing, and murdering kids and women is not something any of us signed up for. Hell, most members in most chapters feel the same way. Sinner's new direction makes a lot of members uncomfortable, but he has powerful allies, and he's a bona fide psychopath. He won't be easy to take down."

"I know that, but I have a plan."

"Let's hear it," Theo says, closing the cover on his tablet and folding his arms.

"Get up." I grab the back of Galen's shirt. "This involves you too, so get back to your seat."

Saint helps Galen stand, propping him up as he hobbles back to his chair. His skin is flushed and his eyes full of rage as he sinks into the chair with pain contorting his face.

"Sinner thinks I have the evidence that proves he and other board members killed Daphne Leydon, but I don't. I'm sure my father didn't have it either, because he would've used it if he had."

"But someone stole it," Caz says.

"Exactly. But think about it. Who would have access and opportunity to steal it?"

"It has to be someone from within," Saint says.

I nod.

"The rat," Theo says.

"Maybe, maybe not, but I think the mole is our best starting place because this person is already snooping around, and it could give us a head start." I smooth a hand over my hair. "We need to find this person."

"There are hundreds of members in the state," Theo says.

"This person has fed intel to The Arrows, so they've got to be local," I say. "I suggest we start with the Prestwick and Lowell members."

"There are almost one hundred members between both chapters," Saint says. "It could be any of them. I've some ideas on how we might narrow it down, but I'd like to hear your suggestions."

"What about background checks? And checking camera footage? The Sainthood HQ building in downtown Prestwick is where all official business takes place, right?" I ask, and Saint nods. "Then we tap into those cameras. We might spot something that leads us to the identity of the rat. And you guys know these members. Can't you come up with a short list of likely culprits? Maybe, some newer Lowell members are behind it?"

"Those are good suggestions, but it'll take time," Saint says.

"I have another idea, and this one might generate quicker results," I say, fixing my stare on Galen. "As far as Darrow is aware, Galen still wants me dead."

"Darrow is a dead man walking," Saint hisses. "You leave him to me."

I shake my head. "Don't interrupt. I'm not finished, and no one will touch Darrow until I say so."

Saint's hands ball into fists on top of the table, and Caz winks at me.

"Darrow expects retaliation, but we can't go after him without risking Sinner discovering the truth that his nephew is a lame-ass double-crossing back-stabbing enemy-loving asshole." Plus, I need him alive so I can drip feed him intel and wreak a little havoc of my own.

Galen clenches his jaw, gripping the armrests of his chair tightly, but he says nothing, and I'm liking this more obedient version of him.

"But if we do nothing, it makes us look weak, and it'll set

alarm bells ringing in Arrow circles which is not something we want with a mole in their midst," I continue. "So, I think we can play this to our advantage."

I stand, needing to stretch my muscles. I walk the length of the table, stopping in front of Galen. "You will reach out to Darrow. Act furious that I escaped." My mouth pulls into a sneer. "Or not act, I guess." He stares at me, helplessness mixing with frustration in his gaze. "Tell him you still want me dead, but you have to bide your time because the guys are pissed at you. Tell him the deal is still on, but the terms are altered. You'll give me to him, and the cut he was after, when the time is right, provided he hands over the rat. You can say you need that to get back into the guys' good graces and it's the only thing you had to bargain with, the only reason they're not gunning for him. Explain that once things are smoothed over he can take me out."

"What if he won't agree?" Galen says.

"He will. He's in hot water with Archer Quinn, and he's already pinned the blame for the ambush on my betrayal. And his pride is wounded now. I got away. That makes him look weak in your eyes. He'll welcome the opportunity to prove he's got balls."

They don't know I have my own deal with the devil, and that is how I know Darrow will go for this. He isn't trustworthy. I know the only thing that'll keep him on my side is if I hand over decent intel that will justify keeping me alive. However, even I know there is an expiration date. There will come a time when he'll want me dead, when I no longer serve a purpose. Galen's new deal will give him a legit reason not to come after me immediately, so our deal can play out. And when Darrow decides he wants to kill me, Galen will be privy to the details, and that's when we take Darrow out.

I'm not worried about Galen betraying me, because he's seen what'll happen if he tries anything again. The guys are barely tolerating his presence right now. They won't give him a second chance. If Galen conspires with Darrow behind our backs, he is writing his own death sentence. It's against crew rules to take out a member, because they vote on such shit, pretending they're democratic and fair.

Ultimately, Galen's too selfish to risk his life, and there's his mom to consider too.

"That could work," Saint says, bobbing his head. "It's worth trying."

"You can put the wheels in motion while I'm in training." I prop my butt against the table.

"I don't like it," Saint says.

"Get over it. That's how it's going down. I need to keep Sinner appeased while we put all this in play. Where does he think I am?" He would have expected me at the training facility by now.

"I told him we stopped to eat en route and all picked up food poisoning. I said we'd camped out in a hotel and we'd deliver you to the training facility sometime tomorrow."

"And he bought that?" It's a flimsy excuse. One I wouldn't expect him to believe.

"He'll rip me a new one when he sees me. But it worked for now. He's distracted doing wedding shit with your mom this weekend."

"Where does my mom think I am?"

Saint shrugs. "Don't know. I'm sure he's told her some bullshit."

"You need to watch her while I'm gone."

"That's a given," Theo says. "We all heard his threat. We won't let anything happen to her."

"And I need you to check in on Sariah." I messaged Sean before I left the cabin, but I want someone to have eyeballs on her while I'm away. My bestie is in a coma, thanks to Parker and her bitches. I have dealt with Parker, but we still need to make Beth and the other girls pay for what they did. I add it to the mental checklist in my head.

"Consider it done," Saint says. "We'll update you daily."

"How long does this training take anyway?" I inquire.

"It depends on how skilled you are. They'll put you through several physical tests as soon as you get there to determine your skill level. Then, they'll pit you against other members in a series of challenges. Once you pass all stages, they'll approve you to move into the initiation phase," Saint says.

"You'll be able to come home for that," Caz explains. "Each chapter leader sets those tasks, and they're usually based locally."

"Great," I drawl. "The psycho will set my tasks. I can hardly wait."

Saint shares a worried look with Caz and Theo, and Galen huffs. They are freezing him out, and he doesn't like it.

"We'll help," Saint says, but he doesn't elaborate, and I don't ask.

"Okay, now that's agreed, I think I'll take a nap." Yawning, I walk to where Caz sits. "I didn't get much sleep last night." I place my hands on his shoulders and lean down, pressing my lips to the side of his cheek as I say, "Care to join me?"

"Hell yeah." The chair scrapes as he jumps up.

"Sit your ass back down," Saint barks, standing and walking toward me. He drills a hole in my skull. "I'll be your sleeping buddy." He smirks, knowing full and well there'll be minimal sleeping going on.

I loop my arm through Caz's, eyeballing Saint and daring him to challenge me. "You're not calling the shots anymore, remember?"

A muscle pops in his jaw as he glares at me. "You don't get to decide this."

I snort. "It's my body. Of course, I do." I let Caz go, putting my face all up in Saint's. "You're done monopolizing me." I pat his arm, offering him a fake sugary smile. "Console yourself with the fact you only have to share me with Caz because Theo's not into me, and I'd rather burn in the fiery pits of hell than let your asshole cousin touch me again." I place my hands on his chest, peering deep into his eyes. "Do I need to remind you of our earlier conversation?"

The vein in his neck throbs, and he's seconds away from exploding, but he knows I have him by the balls.

"Thought not." My gleeful tone matches my expression.

I lace my fingers through Caz's, tugging him forward. "Lead the way, sexy."

THE SAINTHOOD

CHAPTER 7

"YOU LOVE PUSHING his buttons," Caz says, chuckling as I walk up the left-hand-side stairs with him in front of me.

"He secretly gets off on it." I shamelessly ogle Caz's toned butt in his snug jeans.

"I think you get off on it too," he adds, tossing me a grin over his shoulder.

"You can check for yourself in a minute," I quip, reaching out and fondling his ass cheeks.

"I'm glad you're okay," he says, hauling me into his arms when we reach the top of the stairs. "I was freaking the fuck out."

"I can handle myself. And I know how to handle Darrow Knight."

He threads his fingers through my hair as his warm brown eyes dart all over my face. "I know that, babe, but it didn't stop me worrying."

I circle my arms around his neck, pressing the length of my body against his. "You're the only one I believe."

His brow creases. "Why?"

"Because you don't play games. You're straight with me."

He palms my face. "Then, believe me when I say Saint, Theo, and I had nothing to do with this."

I kiss the corner of his mouth. "I don't want to talk about it anymore." I'm exhausted from the past forty-eight hours, and I'm done thinking about all the shit that's gone down. I need a distraction, and Caz is the perfect kind.

His eyes bore into mine. "What do you want?" He grips me at the waist. "What do you need?" His hips rock against mine, his hard-on pressing against the soft flesh of my lower tummy.

I kiss him hard and fast. "You."

His hands roam my sides, his fingers brushing against my breasts, sending a rake of shivers ghosting over me. "I can take one for the team."

He smirks, and I smack his chest. "Careful or I'll kick you to the curb in favor of *Saintly*."

"Like fuck you will." His lips collide with mine in a possessive kiss that curls my toes.

I roam my hands up and down his back as our mouths slant hungrily against one another. "Fuck me, Caz," I demand, between hot kisses.

He lifts me up, and my legs automatically wrap around his waist. "It'd be my pleasure."

He keeps his arms locked around me, walking me through the first bedroom, past a shared bathroom, and into the second bedroom, with his lips latched onto my neck, sucking on my skin, determined to leave his mark on me.

Throwing me down on the bed, he kneels in front of me, prying off my boots. I sit up on my elbows, watching him remove my socks before his hands trek up my jean-clad legs. "You are so fucking sexy," he purrs, lowering his body flush against mine. I drop flat on my back as his mouth covers mine, and we kiss and grind against one another until we're both panting.

"I need you inside me, Caz." I tug his shirt up his body, and he rips it the rest of the way off. He balls it up, ready to toss it aside before a mischievous glint appears in his eye. Angling his body, he purposely throws his shirt over the edge of the steel railing which partially conceals the upper level from the lower level. Anyone looking up here now wouldn't be able to see us, but they sure as hell will hear us.

If we're loud enough.

"I'm due some payback," Caz winks, returning his focus to me, and I know he's referencing the time Saint pulled me off him mid-thrust, leaving him with a bad case of blue balls.

"How far are you willing to take it?" I murmur, popping the top button on his jeans.

His grin is so wide it threatens to split his face. "As far as you want to, baby," he replies, unbuttoning my jeans and tugging them down my legs along with my flimsy lace panties.

"That is music to my ears, stud." I sit up, yanking his jeans down, and palm his erection through his boxers. I trace his length with my fingers as he lifts my sweater and tank off me before unclipping my bra and flinging it aside.

"You're a sight for sore eyes, baby," he says, gently removing my wrist from his dick.

"And we're like cliché city," I joke.

He grins, shoving his boxers down, freeing his thick shaft. I lean forward, and my tongue darts out, lapping up the bead of precum glistening on his crown.

"Fuck yeah, babe." He kicks his boxers away.

"Louder," I command before trailing my lips up and down his cock, sucking and nibbling his warm flesh.

"Suck me, princess," he all but shouts. "Just like that!"

I grin as my fingers curl around the base of his cock, pumping him in slow, measured strokes. I want to prolong this and make it last because I need a marathon fucking session to remind me of who I am. To remember sex is just a physical act and that feelings have no place in my world.

"Fuck my mouth, sexy," I yell, opening my mouth wide and guiding his dick inside. I slide my lips up and down his shaft as he thrusts his hips at the same time. Grabbing the back of my head, he fists my hair, holding me in place as he fully takes over, rocking his pelvis into me as he rams his cock in my mouth.

When his dick breaches the back of my throat, I almost choke, and he eases his hold on my hair and gentles his thrusting.

I meet his eyes as he rocks inside me, startled to find so much emotion residing there.

There's a popping sound as I release him from my mouth, and his cock slides free. "Don't go getting all soft on me, Caz," I say in a low voice. "Don't start treating me like I'm precious." I stand, circling my arms around his neck, as his hot cock pushes against my stomach. "Fuck me hard and fast. Leave me so raw I'll feel you inside me for days after."

His lips crash against mine, and our teeth clatter as we devour one another. He breaks the kiss first, grabbing my head on both sides in his meaty palms. "Fuck, you're so perfect, Lo. Absolutely perfect." His eyes pin me in place. "I'm never letting you go. *We're* never letting you go. Tell yourself whatever bullshit you need to, but that is the only truth that matters."

He shoves me roughly on the bed, and I scoot backward, stretching my arms over my head and gripping the headboard as he parts my legs wide and lowers his tempting mouth to my pussy. He dives in, worshiping my cunt with his tongue and his fingers before his lips suck my clit hard. I'm writhing and moaning on the bed, extra loud for the audience below, and the sensations he's coaxing from my body are out of this world. The crescendo is building, slowly and steadily, and then I rocket toward the sky, shooting upward in a blazing ball of fire as every inch of my body comes alive.

My back arches off the bed as I come, and I scream out his name as wave after wave of euphoria rolls over me. I don't have any time to recover before he's lining his cock up at my entrance, and he slams into me in one hard, fast move.

I cry out as he fucks me frantically, my body jostling as he thrusts into me, over and over, in punishing strokes that leave me stripped raw. The headboard knocks against the wall repeatedly as he fucks me, and we share a conspiratorial smile. "Harder," I yell, and I'm not acting for the audience anymore. Wrapping my legs around his back, I tilt my hips up as he drives inside me, altering the angle while I grip his cock in my slick channel.

"Fuck, baby. Your pussy's like silk on my cock."

"I want on top," I demand, and he slides out of me. Pushing him down flat on his back, I sit on his thighs and face him. "Hold still," I warn, bracing my hands behind me on the bed, on either side of his legs, and lifting my body up. I move up a little, repositioning myself before slowly lowering on to his cock. I love this position because I have full control, I can set the pace, and this angle is perfect, his cock hitting me in the right spot to summon stars.

I bounce up and down on him in controlled movements as he lies underneath me, watching me with an intense lens. He trails his hands up my calves, over my knees, and along my inner thighs. I rotate my hips in circular movements as I lift up and down, and he groans. "Jesus, fuck, that feels so good." I pick up speed, bouncing up and down while his fingers find my clit and start rubbing.

I throw my head back, and messy waves of my long dark hair fall down my sweat-dampened back as I ride him.

My orgasm hits me out of nowhere this time, and I keep my punishing pace going, riding him fast and hard, as more blissful tremors tear through my body. I'm screaming and crying and whimpering, and a loud crash from downstairs has my lips curling into a smile.

"You're so wicked, baby," Caz says, quietly chuckling while he takes hold of my hips and sits up. "But I love it."

He flips me onto all fours, brushing my hair to one side and planting a soft kiss to my neck. "This will be brutal because I need to come *right now*."

"Do your worst, sexy. I can take it."

He skims his lips down my spine, and I shudder all over as his touch does amazing things to me while his cock teases my entrance from behind. Then, all the teasing is over, and he jams into me hard, slamming in and out of my pussy, his cock destroying me in all the best ways.

He roars out his release a few minutes later, and I feel his hot cum depositing inside me. Wrapping his arms around my waist, he pulls me to my side, and we flop down on the bed, still joined, both breathing heavily. "I will never get enough of that," he says, nipping at my earlobe. "Never get enough of you," he adds, and those are the last words I hear as I drift off to sleep.

I wake sometime later, still in the same position, with the black cotton sheet pulled up over our naked bodies. Caz's arms are locked around my waist, and his body heat is like a furnace behind me. I guess he didn't get much sleep last night either. His soft snores confirm he's still out for the count, and I don't want to wake him.

Like a sneaky thief, I slowly extract myself from his grip and slide out of bed. I sit on the edge of the bed, turning around to look at him in a moment of weakness.

He looks even more gorgeous in slumber with his tousled dark hair, full lips, and long, long lashes fanning sculpted cheekbones. My fingers itch with a craving to touch the light layer of stubble on his face, and my lips yearn to press against his lush mouth.

Those alarming thoughts have me jumping up, almost tripping over the bag on the floor. Bending down, I open it, finding it full of my things. I guess Saint or Theo must have dropped it here at one point. I remove the box of tampons with an amused smile, wondering which asshole is keeping track of my cycle.

Snagging my sweater from the floor, I tug it down over my slim shoulders. It hits just above my ass, so I pull a fresh pair of panties and sleep shorts out of the bag, shimmying them up my legs before I wander to the bathroom to relieve myself.

After I've attended to business, brushed my teeth, and attempted to tame my sex hair, I head downstairs.

My tummy rumbles as I hit the bottom step, and Theo lifts his head, eyeballing me. He's stretched out along the length of the couch in front of a roaring fire with his tablet propped on his lap. "Where are the others?" I ask as I move across the floor in my bare feet.

"Galen is sleeping, and after taking his aggression out on the TV, Saint is now working it out in the gym."

My eyes find the broken TV lying against the rear wall, the glass littered with splintering cracks. I smother my smug grin. "Gym?" I arch a brow as I perch on the arm of the couch.

He jerks his head forward. "That small outbuilding you can see from the back window is our workout area."

I turn my head, spotting the structure behind the barn.

"Caz still asleep?" he asks, and I nod. He clears his throat. "There's some pasta in the kitchen if you're hungry. I kept you both some."

"Sounds good. Thanks." I jump up and walk past him.

His fingers wrap around my wrist, stopping me in my tracks. His familiar touch is both comforting and troubling. We stare at one another. "I'm glad you're okay, Lo. I hope you know how much I care."

I remove my hand from his grip, shaking my head as I continue staring at him, like he's just sprouted an extra head. *Does he seriously not get it? Or he thinks his words will magically make it all okay?* "I know no such thing, Theo." Remembered pain surges to the surface. "All I know is you have a habit of not being there when I need you the most."

Hurt flares in his eyes, and his shoulders slump. "Will you ever forgive me?" he asks in a low pleading tone, and pain lodges in my chest.

I don't reply, because I'm incapable of it, so I walk off toward the kitchen, fighting my thoughts and battling my emotions every step of the way.

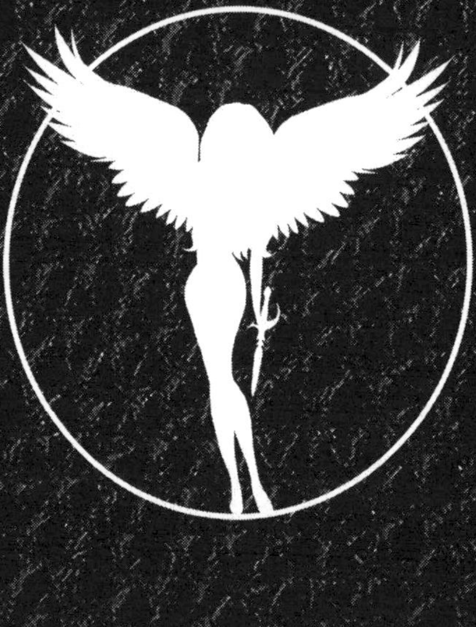

THE SAINTHOOD

CHAPTER 8

"WHAT HAPPENED TO your eye?" I ask Caz early the following morning as he strides into the bedroom with a towel slung low on his hips. His skin and hair are still damp after his post-workout shower, and he's lick-worthy in the extreme.

"What do you think happened?" He waggles his brows.

I don't even need to consider it. "He's an asshole."

"He's the definition of jealousy," Caz says. "And it won't get any easier because that's who he is, and he's off-the-charts possessive with you."

"He must learn to share because I'm not choosing."

"Saint doesn't know how to handle love because he grew up without it," Theo says, entering the bedroom I shared with Caz last night.

Saint spent hours in the gym, and when he returned, he ignored me for the rest of the night. Galen stayed holed up in his room, and Theo was immersed in his tablet, so Caz and I cooked dinner together before retreating to bed for another few rounds of wild monkey sex.

My limbs ache deliciously today, but other than that, I'm well rested, and I feel invigorated as we prepare to head out to the training facility.

"What's that got to do with anything?" I ask, packing my stuff back in my bag.

Theo sinks onto the bed beside me. "You really need to ask?" I snort out a laugh. "Please don't pretend like he's in love with me. Lust maybe, but that's all."

Caz grabs the towel off his hips, standing stark naked in front of us as he dries himself off. I lick my lips, pinning him with a sultry look, wishing there was time to fuck.

"Saint never goes back for seconds, Lo," Theo says, working hard to keep his gaze trained on me. "Yet he can't get enough of you." His eyes dart to Caz, watching him getting dressed. "What do you think that means?" he asks, swinging his gaze back around.

"I'm the best fuck he's ever had," I say, zipping my bag. "And I'm on tap. There are many reasons. Love is the last one."

"We see the way he looks at you, princess," Caz agrees, buttoning up his jeans. "He's falling hard, and it's fucking with his head."

Theo stands, taking my bag. "So, you needn't go there." He offers me his hand. "Cut him some slack."

I refuse his hand, climbing to my feet. "Why should I?"

"Because you have feelings for Saint too, and it's your dynamic with him that dictates the mood within the crew," Theo says. "Shit is gonna rain down on us soon, and we need to be united."

"Perhaps, you should've had this little pep talk with Galen *before* he tried to murder me," I hiss, snatching my bag from him and stomping out of the bedroom.

If anyone is responsible for the current divide, it's that asshole, not me.

"You'll ride with me," Saint tells me when I step outside. "The others will follow in Caz's ride."

I could argue, but I'd rather pick my battles, and I need intel on what I'm facing, so it requires a temporary ceasefire of hostilities.

"Fine."

He narrows his eyes warily.

"What?" I throw my hands in the air. "Would you rather I sassed you?"

He takes a step forward. "I can deal with the sass, but nonconfrontational is a new look for you. Screw me if I'm suspicious."

Can't fault his reasoning. "Contrary to popular belief, I don't enjoy fighting with you."

He raises a brow, and my lips twitch. "Well, not all the time," I acquiesce. "I'd like to have a civil conversation about the training facility on the drive there," I admit. "I want to be prepared."

"Why do you think I suggested we ride alone?"

"Because you're a jealous, possessive Neanderthal and you want to monopolize my time?"

"Don't flatter yourself, sweetheart." He throws my bag in the trunk alongside his, before pushing his chest into mine. "Don't confuse my desire to fuck you for anything else."

He's so full of shit. We both know it's more than that. His previous actions and words already prove it, but I'm not about to get into it with him.

"It's not me who's confused," I retort, pointing at Caz and Theo as they exit the barn. "Have a word with your buddies."

Galen appears in the doorway, and from the grimace on his face, it's clear he's still in agony and still rolling in self-pity.

"And keep that fucking asshole away from me," I add, turning on my heel and jogging to the passenger door.

"What do you want to know?" Saint asks after we've driven a few miles in stony silence.

"What can I expect from the skills test today?"

"They built the facility in the middle of Mantiss Forest and—"

"The Sainthood sure is obsessed with forests," I interject.

"It's ideal burial ground," Saint replies, glancing at me as he steers the Land Rover out onto the highway. "Perfect for disposing of enemies and annoying girls who interrupt people midsentence."

"I thought you loved my sass." I kick my booted feet up on the dash.

"I never said that, and get your feet down. Your boots are muddy." He swats at my legs, and the car swerves on the road.

"Do you have OCD?" I unlace my boots and kick them off. Planting my sock-clad feet back up on the dash, I smile mockingly at him.

"This is the first new car I've ever had. Sue me if I want to keep it clean."

Shock splays across my face. "Why didn't Sinner buy you a new car when you got your license? It's not like he's short on cash."

A sneer appears on his face. "He offered, but everything he does comes at a price. I wanted to buy it myself so I owed him nothing. So it wasn't tainted by that evil piece of shit."

I stare at him, momentarily speechless at his honesty and hurting for him. *What must it have been like to grow up with a parent who showed you no love and always expected something from you?* "So, um, Mantiss Forest," I mumble, needing to redirect the conversation to safer topics, because Saint has just opened himself to me, and I'm feeling far too much. I can't let emotion affect me because it screws with my head.

"The training facility has this massive assault course on the grounds of the forest, and that is where your skills test will take place."

"What's involved?"

"Water crossing, zip lines, tunnels, rope swings, high walls, balance beams, etcetera."

"That's doable."

"It's testing your strength, stamina, and agility mostly. After that, you'll enter the maze. It's a simulated war zone, and it'll test your combat skills against the other trainees. Then, there's the shooting range test." His lips kick up. "We know you'll ace that one and the knife throwing test."

His eyes move to his crotch, and he shivers, and I crack up laughing. "How are the itchy pubes?" I tease.

"Still itchy." He slants me some serious stink eye. "I haven't forgotten I owe you for that."

"I'm as bare as the day I was born, so you're shit out of luck."

"I know my way around your pussy, princess." He smirks, and a dark glint flashes in his eyes. "And there are other forms of payback."

I jab my finger in his arm. "You owed me that, and now, you owe me again."

"Is that why you did it?" His fingers dig into the steering wheel, and a muscle pops in his jaw.

He need not elaborate because I know what he's talking about. "I did it because I wanted to fuck Caz and you need to learn to share. You're done cockblocking me."

He grips the steering wheel tighter but doesn't reply.

"I'll have no issue passing those tests," I say, putting this conversation back where it needs to go. "How soon will I be out of there?"

"You'll stay a minimum of a week, and I wouldn't get too cocky. You'll be head to head against other members." His eyes drill into mine. "Other *male* members."

"Most all of my training was against guys," I admit, enjoying the look of displeasure that creeps across his face.

"You're still inferior physically. No amount of skill can compensate for that."

"I know men are physically stronger than women, but that doesn't mean women can't win in a physical fight. Being lighter on foot has its advantages, and it's as much about mental resilience as it is physical."

"How long have you been training with *him*?" He looks like the question pains him to ask it.

"Since I was thirteen."

His head whips to mine. "Since…"

"Your father kidnapped and tortured me. My dad wanted to make sure if anything happened to me again I could at least protect myself better."

The car slams to a halt in the middle of the highway. Brakes screech and horns blare as cars swerve to avoid plowing into us.

"What the actual fuck is your problem?" I roar, throwing my hands up. "Do you have a fucking death wish?"

He flips the hazard lights on and kills the engine as his cell pings. Out of the corner of my eye, I spot Caz parked behind us, flipping his finger up at passing cars as they blow their horns and shake angry fists in both our directions.

Turning to face me, Saint grips my face in his hands. "I need to know if he touched you, Lo." His eyes scream, and I wonder if he truly cares or if he can't stand the thought of Sinner touching what he considers his.

I convince myself it's the latter, because it's the easiest one to process and it enables me to remain detached.

"Did my father or any of those other bastards rape you?"

"What if I said they did?"

His chest heaves, and anger blazes in his eyes. "Then, they're all fucking dead."

"Killing them might seem like an easy solution," I say, "but they deserve to rot in jail for their crimes. Dying is too easy." I place my hand on top of one of his. "They didn't rape me or touch me like that although they stripped me to my underwear, and I felt their pervy eyes on me all the time." It was an effective form of psychological torture, and I spent that entire time waiting for them to take it further. It made me feel vulnerable and weak and utterly helpless.

He pulls my face to his, pressing his lips against mine. His kiss is hard and blistering with simmering violence. When he pulls back, it feels like my mouth's just been assaulted. "They're sick fucks, Lo, and I wouldn't be surprised if you'd told me they had raped you." He rubs my mouth, ignoring his cell when it vibrates again. "You're older and sexier now, and that psycho dictates what you do for initiation. It scares me."

All the color drains from my face. "You mean he could force me into having sex with him?"

He nods, and now, I get why he made the call on the safe house.

"Or it could be worse," he adds.

Understanding dawns, and I shake my head as bile swims up my throat. "There are many things I'm prepared to do to see this through, but letting those assholes have sex with me, one after another, is not one of them."

"That's not happening," he agrees. "If it comes down to it, we'll find a loophole." I'd like to believe his words, but the troubled look on his face speaks volumes, and acid crawls up my throat at the thought of what that psycho has planned for me.

For all our sakes, I hope Sinner doesn't make that a task, because if I have to resort to murder to avoid being abused by him and his buddies, I won't hesitate to take out every one of them, consequences be damned.

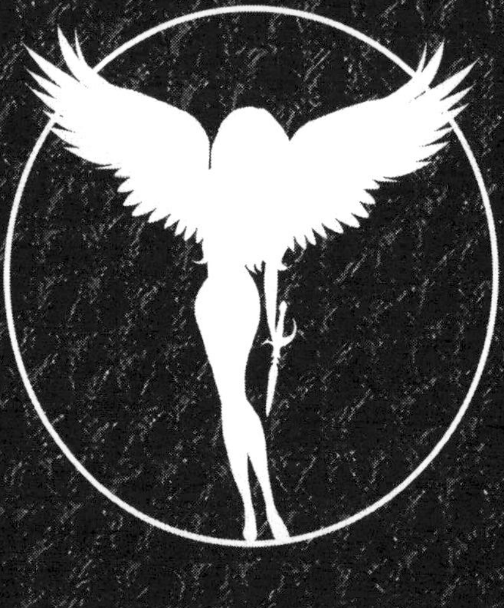

THE SAINTHOOD

CHAPTER 9

We arrive at the training facility on the outskirts of the sprawling town of Mantiss just after lunch. High wooden gates conceal the compound, and a tall gray wall borders it on all sides. Barbed wire sits atop the wall along with several mounted cameras.

Security is clearly tight, but is it to keep people out or to keep the trainees in?

Saint presses the button on the small keypad attached to the wall, and after he has confirmed our names, the gates automatically open to let us through. Saint drives along the winding driveway for a few miles, and I stare out the window at the thickly wooded area. All I can see on every side are trees and more trees. It's been raining, and drops of water drip in a steady line from the branches, adding to the soft rivers of water trickling down the gravel driveway as we advance.

The driveway gives way to a large opening, and an impressive building comes into view. Saint parks in front of the entrance, and I hop out, eager to stretch my limbs after so long in the car.

"Here," he says, rounding the car and holding out an iPhone.

"This isn't secure, so be careful what you use it for. Check in daily."

"I will," I agree, slipping it into my pocket, alongside my burner cell. "Thanks."

"They won't let you take weapons with you. I'll safeguard your knife."

"I'm not parting with my knife." I fold my arms, stabbing him with a warning look. "And I'll gut anyone who attempts to take it from me."

"Lo, you can't ruffle feathers here. Sinner will go apeshit if you embarrass him."

"You say that like it'll deter me."

"I know it will because you're too smart to be this dumb." He steps right into my face. "The quickest way you'll get out of here is to pass all the tests and keep your head down and avoid trouble." His hand lands on my hip. "If you piss him off, he'll devise the worst initiation tasks imaginable."

"He'll do that anyway."

"We don't know that for sure, and it's not smart to antagonize him."

I know he makes sense, but it'll kill me to act like some Mary Sue; however, I don't have any choice. Bending down, I roll up the end of my jeans and unstrap my Strider SMF from my calf. Straightening up, I hand it to him. "This feels like I'm handing my firstborn child to the devil," I admit, and he grins.

He unsheathes my knife, admiring it. "I'll guard it with my life."

"Don't use it," I warn, narrowing my eyes to slits. "I don't want some murder attributed to me while I'm gone."

"I'll try to refrain from murder and mayhem." He smirks, cocking his head to the side. "But I'll make no promises."

"Of course, you won't." I roll my eyes, taking in my surroundings as Saint eyes the locket around my neck.

"Where'd you get that?" His eyes burn with jealousy, and I'd love to tell him Diesel gave it to me, but it'll only end up smashed on the ground if I admit the truth.

"My dad gave it to me."

"You weren't wearing it at the warehouse."

Shit. The obvious lie would be to say I had it at the cabin, but I don't want the guys to know about that place.

"I thought I'd lost it, but apparently, I left it behind at training. The chain was broken so Diesel got it repaired. He just gave it back to me."

He opens his mouth, to ask more questions, I assume, and I need to shut this down. "I should head in." I gesture at the door. "They'll be wondering what's keeping me."

He looks like he wants to argue but thinks better of it, and I release the breath I was holding.

Saint moves around me, a slight suspicion clouding his features, as he removes my bag from the trunk. His instincts are sharp, but I doubt he suspects it's a tracker. He's probably questioning my explanation and wondering if Dad really was the one who gave it to me. Throwing one last look my way, Saint tosses my bag over his shoulder and walks toward the others. They are leaning against Caz's car, quietly conversing.

Turning my back on them, I check out my new temporary home. The property is huge and surprisingly modern, comprising a large two-story building made up of glass and wood, spread across a site that spans acres and acres of woodland. I can't see the infamous assault course from the front because the building is so wide.

"What do you think?" Theo asks, coming up alongside me.

"Crime pays," I deadpan.

"You thought it didn't?" Galen says, arching a brow.

"Who said you could speak?!" I bark, shooting daggers at him. "Just shut up and look pretty." I scan my eyes over his bruised, battered face, snorting. "You can't even do that anymore. You're a hot mess."

"I *have* looked in the mirror," he snaps.

I shove him in the shoulders, and he bites down hard on his lower lip, wincing. "What part of our conversation yesterday didn't you understand?" I shove him again. "You will fucking beg for my forgiveness. Anything less won't do."

"I said I'm fucking sorry!" he shouts.

"Words are meaningless!" I shout back. "And I'm sick of listening to the same pathetic crap coming out of your mouth. Unless you've something valuable to add, say nothing."

Caz slings his arm around my shoulders. "Nervous, babe?"

I roll my eyes. "Don't be ridiculous."

Caz and Saint share a look, and I see red. I slam to a halt, shoving Caz's arm off me. "You don't think I can do this."

"That's not it," Theo says, ever the peacemaker. "We know you're smart and you have obvious skills, but this is a whole other ballgame."

"Your lack of faith has been noted," I say, snatching my bag from Saint. "I've got this. You can all fuck off now."

I storm off, using my anger to propel me forward.

Pushing through the double glass doors, I enter the perfunctory lobby area, masking my surprise. A woman in a smart white blouse and gray pinstripe skirt sits behind the small reception desk, smiling at me as I approach. Small black leather couches, with glass coffee tables in front, are propped against the windows on either side of the entrance

It's surreal, business-like and professional, and not at all what I was expecting.

"Good afternoon, Ms. Westbrook," the woman says, placing an A4 envelope on the counter before me. "That's your welcome pack with your schedule, room assignment, and map of the facility." She hands me a black card, and I scowl at the familiar fiery emblem as I tuck it into the front pocket of my jeans.

I hate The Sainthood's logo because it reminds me of the mark etched on my skin and the destiny Sinner has mapped out for me.

"That will get you in and out of all the doorways," she continues, "and it doubles as a meal card in the cafeteria." She glances at the clock on the wall. "Your general skills test starts in forty minutes, so you must hurry. I've left training clothes in your room. Report to the assembly area in thirty minutes."

She points at the doorway on the right. "Go through there, and head for the inspection room. Once completed, go back to the corridor, and take the elevator to the first floor. Turn left for your accommodation."

"Thank you." I consider asking her exactly what the inspection room is but decide against it because it seems self-explanatory. I'm pressed for time, and I'll find out soon enough. I grab the envelope and take a step away when she calls out to me.

"You can't take that with you," she says, standing and pointing at my bag. "I'll store it, and it will be returned to you upon leaving."

I hand it over without argument, assuming I'll have everything I need in my room, and I have my two cells on me. She didn't specifically say anything about no phones, so I'm not mentioning it.

A thought lands in my head, and my fingers fly to my locket. If I'm undergoing some kind of inspection, I can't have this with me in case they identify the tracking device even though it pains me to remove it because I promised Diesel I wouldn't. It would be ideal to record shit while I'm here, but walking around a training facility with a locket around my neck would raise suspicion, so I have no choice. I console myself with the fact it will remain with my bag, so Diesel still has a lock on my location even if I don't have it on me until I walk back out the door. "I'd best leave this in my bag," I say, putting the envelope down so I can remove the chain. She nods in agreement, and I tuck it into the side pocket of my bag.

I snatch the envelope up again, glancing outside as I walk toward the side door, noting the guys are still there, leaning back against Caz's car, legs stretched out in front of them and arms folded. They stare at me through the window, and I flip them the bird.

Using the key card, I gain entry to the corridor and walk down the carpeted hallway until I come to a door with INSPECTION marked at the top of it. The door swings open before I can knock, and a man dressed all in black appears before me. He steps aside, motioning me in. The door closes behind me, and I look around the small square room. Apart from a bench, coat hooks on the wall, and a wooden unit with some technical devices on top, the room is empty.

"Remove your jacket, and stand with your legs spread wide and your arms out."

He takes my jacket, hanging it on a hook on the wall, and then, I adopt the position expected of me.

He pats me down thoroughly while I stare ahead, conveying no emotion.

"Strip down to your underwear," he says, giving me his back as he walks to the wooden unit. Panic whittles through me at the thought of what's coming. I guess they're not just checking for concealed weapons but for drugs too, and there's no way in hell that man is putting his fingers inside my ass or my pussy. I will fucking decimate him if he tries to touch me there.

Forcing myself to remain calm, I sit down on the bench and remove my boots and clothing while his eyes watch my every move. When I'm down to my underwear, I stand and walk into the center of the room. "Same stance," he instructs, his eyes dropping to my chest.

Using some type of digital scanner, he scans every part of my body. His fingers brush against me an inordinate amount of times, but I don't flinch even though I'm on edge and ready to take him down if he goes near my lady parts.

"You can get dressed now," he says, and I don't need to be told twice, breathing a quiet sigh of relief.

I hurry out of the room a few minutes later, take the elevator to the first floor, and quickly locate my room.

It's a small utilitarian room with a single cot and bedside table, compact wardrobe and matching dresser, and a small wall-mounted TV.

I grab the quickest shower in history, careful not to wet my hair, and I dress in the black training top and black combat pants left on the bed. I scowl at the fiery symbol on my shirt, wishing I could rip it off.

A quick inspection of the closet and dresser confirms other sets of the same clothes plus some underwear and plain black pajamas. Everything is in the right sizes, and that creeps me out more than anything else so far. The thought of that bastard Sinner rooting through my stuff to determine my clothes and underwear sizes makes me ill, but I don't dwell on it because I need to keep my head in the game.

The bathroom cabinet has all the essentials I need, and I remove a brush and a hair tie, quickly smoothing my hair into a high ponytail.

I open the envelope and skim through the documents, locating my schedule and the map, as I lace up my black boots. I'm to report to Assembly Area A, which is at the rear of the building, on the lower level. I memorize the way before folding the map and tucking it inside my bra.

I hide one cell under the mattress and one in the bathroom cabinet before heading out, making my way downstairs and walking along successive hallways toward my destination. I pass a few other trainees and staff, but there doesn't seem to be a huge amount of people milling around.

The sound of a booming voice talking up ahead has me quickening my pace. I'm obviously a little late, and it's not the best way to make a first impression.

Rounding the corner, I spot the correct door and step through it. A line of about ten people, all similarly attired to me, is facing a tall glass window that wraps around the entire room, offering impressive views of the rear of the property including the vast assault course we will shortly become acquainted with.

"How good of you to join us, Initiate Westbrook," the man with the booming voice says, slanting a displeased look my way.

He's in his forties, if I had to guess, of average height and strong build with wide shoulders and big arms. Ink creeps up over his shirt collar, up his neck, and onto one side of his face. His shaved head glistens as the bright overhead lights beat down on us, and the glare on his face almost matches it in intensity.

"Apologies, sir," I say, offering no explanation.

"Get in line," he snaps. "And don't make this a habit."

Asshole.

"Yes, sir."

I walk to the end of the line without looking at any of my fellow trainees. I stop beside a tall guy with shorn black hair as the instructor speaks again, explaining the process.

The guy beside me angles his head, risking a quick glance in my direction when the instructor looks away, and I stare into familiar hazel eyes with mounting horror. He shoots me a brief smile before facing frontward when the instructor's gaze swings this way. I conceal my shock and stare straight ahead, wondering what the actual fuck is going on, because I have no clue why Bryant Eccleston—an Arrows member and Darrow's number two—is undergoing The Sainthood's initiation.

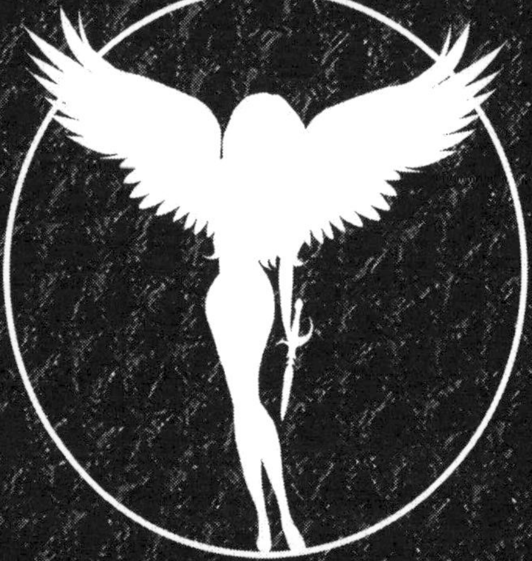

THE SAINTHOOD

CHAPTER 10

"Follow me," Instructor Corr says, marching toward the side exit. I've barely heard a word he said because I'm in a tailspin trying to figure out why Bryant is here. Bry smirks as we follow the line and head outside.

There's a distinct chill in the air, but the skies are clear, and the day is bright. We walk down a few flights of stairs, trailing the instructor as he leads us to a small wooden station, manned by the same man who was in the inspection room. "Get your time tracker from Instructor Tanner," our instructor commands, and we all comply.

Instructor Tanner fits the small round digital device to the pocket of my shirt, pressing in firmly against my chest, his fingers brushing my breast. A loud throat clearing captures our attention, and everyone looks up. My mouth hangs open as I spot the overhead walkway and the four assholes leaning against the side, staring at me.

Saint pins Instructor Tanner with a lethal look, one that conveys possessiveness and a clear threat, before his eyes move to my side. He stares at Bryant with the usual impassive face he wears, so I can't tell if his presence is a surprise to him or not.

"Listen up," Instructor Corr says, clapping his hands and reclaiming our attention. "You'll be split into two groups, but this isn't a team exercise. The purpose of the general skills test is to ascertain basic levels of fitness and coordination. After that, we'll assign you to a group for the duration of the week, based on matching skill sets."

He breaks the line into two even groups, which means I'm going out the same time as Bryant. The instructor is busy issuing commands to the first group, so I risk whispering to Bry. "Why are you here?"

"I'm beginning initiation," he coolly replies. "Same as you." He winks, and I narrow my eyes.

We both look straight ahead as we conduct a whispered conversation. "You're an Arrow." I state the obvious.

"Not anymore."

"Why?"

Bry glances sideways at the instructor. "I'll tell you later. Best not to get on that asshole's bad side."

I harrumph. "Since when do you care about shit like that?"

"Initiate Westbrook," the instructor barks. "Care to share with the group?"

"I was just telling Initiate Eccleston how excited I am for the training." I plaster a fake smile on my lips.

The instructor walks up to me, putting his face all up in mine. "There's a reason women don't belong in The Sainthood. Five seconds in your company isn't convincing me I'm wrong."

"You'll be eating your words by the end of the week, sir." I smile sweetly at him.

He laughs. "I highly doubt it."

I'll happily prove him wrong.

Tossing one last glance my way, he folds his hands behind his back and paces the ground by our small line.

The first group has already entered the assault course and begun their test.

"Your time will start in ten minutes, and every second counts.

The course has several obstacles to test various skills. The average completion time is thirty minutes. Once you cross the finish line, there will be a short instructional before you enter the maze—our simulated war zone. We'll be using paintball guns for that exercise." He drills a look at me. "What a shame."

Yeah, yeah. I get it. You hate women, and I'm already an annoying pain in your ass. I'll enjoy ripping his sexist manifesto to pieces this week.

I glance up at the guys, scowling at them. "Must we have an audience?"

Instructor Corr steps up to me, sneering. "Shut your goddamned mouth, or I'll shut it for you. You speak only when spoken to."

"It's a valid question," Bry says, coming to my defense.

Instructor Corr snorts. "Butt out of shit that doesn't concern you, and I suggest you quit trying to get in her panties because that one's nothing but trouble."

"That might be true," I agree, smiling at Bry. "But I'm the right kind of trouble."

"Don't I know it." Bry grins, and there's another loud throat clearing from above. I ignore Saint this time, slapping an amicable smile on my face as I address the instructor. "Permission to warm up, sir."

"Permission denied." His smile is tight.

"I might get injured if I don't warm up first."

"What a shame it'd be if we had to send you home early."

I take a step forward, eyeballing him. "I don't think you quite understand the situation, *sir*. Neo Lennox is soon to be my stepfather, and he chose me to be the first female member for a reason. Those assholes up there"—I point at the guys—"are the junior chapter in Prestwick and Lowell, and they are very protective of me. Especially Saint Lennox. I really don't think you want to cross them."

Or me, but I keep that thought to myself because the jerk has already proven he has little regard for women and I'm as insignificant as the dirt under his boot.

"Unless you have a death wish." I shrug. "And it's not like I'm asking for much."

He grabs me by the neck. "Listen here, you little cunt." He squeezes my throat harder. I could extract myself, but I'd rather let Saint prove my point and reserve showing my hand.

In my peripheral, I watch Saint jump off the walkway without fear or any regard for his safety, and fuck, if that doesn't seriously turn me on. He stalks toward us with his nostrils flaring and murder in his eyes. Instructor Corr's eyes widen in alarm when he hears the approaching footfall, and he twists his head around in time for Saint's punch to land on the side of his face.

His arms drop from my neck, and he staggers back as Saint hits him again, landing a powerful punch on his nose this time. Saint grabs him by the shirt, slamming him into the wooden post behind us. "Touch her again, and I'll fucking bury you alive in a cesspit of poisonous snakes." He slams him against the post once more. "Is that clear?"

Instructor Corr nods, and Saint lets him go. Corr swipes at the blood pumping from his nose, and naked anger oozes from every pore. I doubt he'll heed Saint's warning once the guys leave, but I'll take whatever he throws at me and throw it back with added venom.

"You okay, princess?" Saint probes my neck with his fingers, inspecting my skin for damage. It's hysterical because we both know he's not opposed to choking—if he's the one with his hands around my throat.

"I'm good, baby," I purr, snaking my arms around his neck and pressing my body into his. Figure I might as well play this up so the other assholes know I'm off limits. Especially Bryant, because he's entertained notions of us in the past. I want zero distractions this week, and holing me up in the middle of the woods with a bunch of violent, horny wannabe gangsters means guaranteed grabby hands and sleazy proposals.

Saint reels me into his arms, slamming his lips on mine in a domineering kiss I feel all the way to the tips of my toes. "She's ours," he growls when our lips separate, slicing a look through

Bryant.

He didn't say *mine*. That's progress.

Sliding his hand lower on my back, he palms my ass, and I roll my eyes. "Anyone lays a finger on Lo, we'll put a bullet in your skull." He glares over my shoulder in a pointed direction. "That especially applies to you."

"You find this shit attractive?" Bryant asks, blatantly ignoring Saint.

I twist around in Saint's arms, arching a brow. "What girl wouldn't?"

"A sane one?" some stupid guy with messy strawberry-blond hair says. Saint takes a step toward him, and hostility rains down on him from above. I don't need to look up to know the guys are shooting daggers at him. A burst of warmth spreads across my chest, and I can't deny how good it feels to have backup after so long going it alone.

"It's time to move," Instructor Corr says, saving the initiate from a Saint-style throat punch.

"We need to talk," Saint says, releasing me. "Don't wander off after the maze." He lifts his head up, piercing Bry with a look. "You too, asswipe."

"Fuck off. I'm not answerable to you."

"Like hell you're not." Saint takes a step toward him, but I push him back, cautioning him with my eyes. I'll handle Bry, I silently convey. A muscle ticks in Saint's jaw before he lowers his mouth to mine, pecking my lips as he eyeballs Bry with a dark glare.

"You're interfering with our schedules," Corr says to Saint. "I'll mark that on my report."

Saint scoffs. "Do I look like I give a fuck?"

"Go." I nudge Saint back. "I'll meet you afterward at the maze."

I feel Saint's eyes glued to my back as we follow Corr through the entrance and into the assault course.

My eyes scan the ground in front of me. There are a couple low walls at the start, then a rope wall, and a high wall beyond that, but that's as far as I can see. I purposely don't look up at the guys, even though I know they are there, because I can't afford to lose focus.

I cast a sneaky glance at the competition. The four guys in my group are strong and tall, but my smaller weight and height should work to my advantage with some of the obstacles.

Out of the corner of my eye, I spot Instructor Corr whispering in one of the initiate's ears—the same guy who mouthed off back there. As Corr's mouth works overtime, he shoots daggers in my direction. I hadn't intended to make enemies here, but it's obvious I'm not wanted, and I doubt if I keep silent and act like a Goody Two-Shoes that the outcome will be any different.

Being female is the biggest obstacle I must overcome this week.

The instructor blows a whistle. "Line up. On my count."

I block out everything around me, pressing one foot forward and stretching my other foot out behind me, poised and ready.

Corr counts, and when he gets to three, I bolt forward, jumping over the low walls with ease. Pounding feet keep pace with me, and while I need to keep aware of the other initiates, I won't let myself get distracted by their progress because that dilutes my focus. So, I keep my eyes ahead and concentrate on the tasks as they arise.

I climb the rope wall with skill, but the high wall proves more challenging because I have to stretch to reach the markers. When I pull myself over, Bry and the guy with the strawberry-blond hair, the one Corr was whispering to, are already on the ground and moving toward the row of tunnels.

Taking a risk, I jump down the bottom half of the wall instead of climbing down it, grateful when I land firmly on the ground. I scramble to the tunnel, entering mine a few seconds after the guys have entered theirs, crawling through it, using my elbows and my knees to propel me forward. I emerge like a bullet from a gun, adrenaline charging through my veins as I plunge headfirst into cold, muddy, brown water.

My eyes sting, and I swallow a mouthful of yucky water. I thrust up to the surface, and the instant my head is above water, a hand pushes me back down. Fighting instinct, I let the asshole hold me under the water while my hands move sluggishly in front of me. Grabbing hold of his dick through his pants, I twist hard. The pressure releases from my head, and I resurface, spitting out water and gasping for air.

"You fucking bitch," the guy with the reddish-blond hair says.

"Come at me again, and you'll know all about it."

Splashing sounds behind me alert me to the other two guys, and I forget the asshole cradling his sore dick and swim across the lake. Up ahead, Bry is hauling himself out of the water, heading for the balance beams and the hanging frame. I plow through the murky water, pushing my arms and kicking my legs as fast as I can.

Climbing up the muddy bank, I slip three times, shivering as my wet clothes plaster to my cold skin. Ignoring my discomfort, I race toward the balance beams, quickly traversing them, and then, I scale the side wall of the hanger using the rope, grabbing onto the bar and dropping down, using my arms to move along the frame, one bar at a time.

My arms throb, but I push on, completing that task and entering the wire crawl on my back. This was a tip Diesel gave me. It's easier to avoid getting trapped if you shimmy under the wire on your back rather than on your belly. Bry isn't in the know, because he's stuck a few feet from the end, wires tangled in the back of his shirt.

"Good luck getting out of that," I say, sliding out of the end on my back.

"I don't need luck," he says, gritting his teeth as he pushes forward, the wire ripping his shirt and scratching his skin.

I run toward the zip line, climbing the ladder with Bry hot on my heels. I clip myself onto the wire, grab hold of the handrails, and push off my feet, propelling my body forward as I glide over another lake. I glance to my left at the sound of pounding footsteps, grinning at Theo, Saint, and Caz as they race along the walkway, attempting to keep up with me. "You got this, princess," Caz roars before blowing me a kiss.

I almost miss my footing at the end because I'm distracted,

but I pull back before I face-plant into the wooden wall. I unclip myself and grab the rope swing just as Bry arrives. I swing forward, letting out a lusty animalistic cry as I let go of the rope, landing on the inflatable below. I crawl on all fours until I'm on solid ground, pushing damp tendrils of hair back off my face and sprinting toward the last section of the course.

It's a combination of low and high walls with a few more tunnels and wire crawls. I make my way through them, straining my aching limbs, panting and mentally encouraging my body to keep pushing through. Bry has caught up with me, and we are neck and neck until the last two hundred meters when I trip over a hidden log underfoot, crashing to the ground face-first, eating a mouthful of dead leaves and damp debris.

Silently cursing, I scramble to my feet and forge on, coming in thirty seconds after Bry.

Bry is bent over, exhaling heavily and grinning in my direction as he accepts a bottle of water from Instructor Tanner. I'm guessing there's another path on the other side of the course they used to get here before us.

Tanner hands me water without making eye contact, and I fight a grin. I uncap the bottle, sloshing water around my mouth and spitting it out on the ground.

"So ladylike," Corr says, and I shrug. If he thinks that'll offend me, he can think again.

"You did good out there," Bry says between panting. "I'm impressed."

"Thanks." I raise the bottle to my lips again, wondering what his gameplay is.

"Listen up," Corr shouts as the other three initiates arrive. We all finished so close together. "You have five minutes to regroup before we move to the maze." He gestures at the large military-type truck on the left. It has a cloth covering behind the cabin, and my lips curl into a smile of their own volition. I've always wanted to ride in one of those.

"You're liking this," Bry says, sidling right up next to me.

"I've always been a physical kind of girl." I smirk.

He grins down at me, and a burst of sunlight through the trees highlights the deep scar running from his left eye across his temple and into his hairline. I've often wondered how he got it, but I've never asked because scars tell a personal story, and that story should only be revealed if the person wishes to share it.

"So I hear."

I feel the daggers embedding in my back, but I don't look up.

Bry leans in closer, pressing his mouth to my ear. "I know what Galen and Dar tried to do. I'm sorry."

Panic swirls through my veins. "You tell Sinner?"

He shakes his head. "I'm not an idiot."

I breathe out a sigh of relief. "He's not to know."

"You and I have a lot to discuss," he whispers, as Tanner directs us toward the truck.

I peer into his hazel eyes, seeing the truth there. I've always liked Bryant. He was decent to me when I was with Dar, and he's got smarts. I never understood how Dar ended up leader of the junior chapter of The Arrows, because Bry was way more intelligent, and he's known for keeping a cool head under pressure, unlike hothead Darrow Knight.

Now, I'm wondering if Bry has been playing double agent all along, and if so, he could be a mine of useful information. Keeping him on my side seems like a smart plan, and I know he's got a thing for me, so using that to my advantage is a no-brainer. Saint and the guys will just have to suck it up.

I place my hand on his arm, smiling up at him. "I think we do."

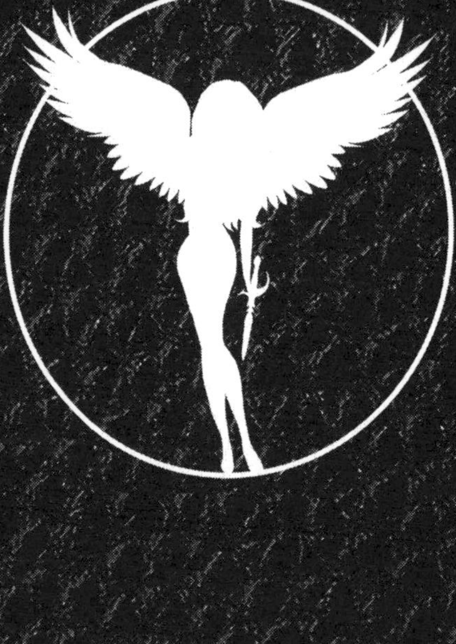

THE SAINTHOOD

CHAPTER 11

GALEN

Saint is about two seconds from full-blown detonation. Either he'll rip Bryant Eccleston's head off or fuck Lo senseless until she remembers who she belongs to.

"Calm down." Theo attempts to reason with my cousin.

"She's playing the game, dude," Caz says. "She knows Bryant could be useful to us. Chill out." He lights up a cigarette, leaning back against the wall in the small auditorium.

We've just watched Harlow Westbrook decimate the competition in the maze.

Every time I hear the word *maze*, it reminds me of the time I spent an afternoon chasing the pretty girl with the sad eyes and the haunted smile through the maze at the back of my grandma's house—now our house. Although this maze is different, because it's not outdoors and it's composed of a series of interlocking structures of different shapes and sizes, made to resemble a war-torn town.

All ten initiates went head to head using paintball guns, and Lo was the last one standing.

I can't deny how hard it made my cock watching her expertly

maneuver the course like a pro, taking down her opponents skillfully and with military precision. We know she's trained and skilled with a gun, but it's clear after today she is a freaking ninja wrapped up in a tempting, beguiling, confusing package.

It only makes me feel like a bigger asshole.

I fucked up so bad, and now, I risk losing everyone, because the guys are furious with me, and I doubt Lo will ever forgive me. Maybe, it's a blessing in disguise, because my feelings for her are a total clusterfuck.

I thought I had it all worked out, but now, I don't know what to think.

"He's fucking dead," Saint snarls, watching Bryant whisper in Lo's ear on the screen.

There are a handful of guys in the room with us, watching the action go down. Instructor Corr turns around, overhearing Saint's outburst, and grins in a way that lets him know he's not done messing with his girl.

"Drop it, Saint," Theo hisses. "You're only making things worse."

"She doesn't need us stepping in," Caz agrees. "Our badass beauty has got this in the bag."

"She's been holding out on us," Saint says.

"Would you blame her?" Theo sends a pointed look in my direction.

"Don't start blaming me for everything," I hiss. "I fucked up, and I will own that shit, but don't pin it all on me."

"Why not?" Saint whirls around on me, his eyes burning with anger. I can't remember any other time he's been this mad with me. Not even when I stuffed vegetables up the exhaust pipe of the first piece of shit truck he bought and the damn thing exploded minutes after he started the engine. Throwing himself out of the truck, he escaped relatively unscathed, but he was still pissed at me. However, he was over it the next day—even seeing the funny side.

This is different.

Because she's different.

I thought it was the hot sex and her fiery mouth, but it's way more than that. Whatever bond they formed at thirteen has my cousin tied into knots, and he's only falling harder. He's in deep with her, and he might never forgive me.

"Because I'm not responsible for everything," I reply, wincing as I shift on the seat and it feels like someone just stuck a red-hot poker in my ribs. "You've made mistakes too."

Saint punches me in the face, and my head whips back. "Fuck you," I snap. "I let you beat me because I deserved it, but I'm done being a punching bag."

"You're done when I say you're done."

"Don't you mean when *Lo* says you're done," I retort, reacting swiftly this time and deflecting his clenched fist with my raised palm.

"You're an idiot." Theo shakes his head.

"I thought we agreed on that already," I deadpan.

"Bigger idiot," Theo snaps, uncharacteristically. "If you think any of us will forget this in a hurry, you're sorely mistaken."

I know they have history, but I don't know the specifics. The thought gives me an idea, but I park it for a more opportune time.

Caz throws his cig on the ground, putting it out with his boot. "They're on the move. Let's go."

We file out of the auditorium, waiting outside the maze for Lo to emerge.

Initiates filter out, looking worse for wear, all in desperate need of showers. Lo spots us immediately, walking toward us with Bryant in tow. Saint vibrates with rage, and his level of possessiveness with this girl is off-the-charts crazy.

"Top marks, baby," Caz says, stepping forward and pulling her into his arms. "I worship at the altar of Queen Harlow."

I roll my eyes. Gag. Someone, pass the puke bucket.

"You were amazing, Lo." Theo kisses her cheek, pride evident in his smile.

Saint and Bryant are in an epic stare down. One Saint doesn't break as he reaches out, hauling Lo into his chest. He holds her close, and tightness spreads across my chest. I lean back against the wooden railing, holding my arm around my ribs as if that will heal my broken limbs and aching heart.

Saint finally pulls his eyes from our enemy, leaning down and kissing Lo with a tenderness I didn't think he was capable of. He whispers in her ear as I watch Bryant seethe. He balls his hands into fists at his sides, and his eyes burn with envy.

I'm not surprised he's into her.

Lo has this way about her that sucks all the red-blooded males in. And it's not because she's hot or smart or mouthy, which she is, but it goes deeper. She's like a magnetic force-field, drawing people to her with ease.

It's one reason I've been fighting her so hard.

The other is the past and a multitude of pent-up emotions where she's concerned.

"I don't have all fucking day," Bryant barks. "Say what you need to say, Lennox."

Lo slips out from under Saint's arm, cricking her neck from side to side. She's covered in mud, dirt, and sweat, and strands of hair are stuck to her brow, but she's still beautiful as fuck.

Girl is in a league of her own.

"How the fuck did my father win you to our side?" Saint demands to know.

"Wait!" Lo straightens up, planting her hands on her hips and leveling Saint with an evil eye. "You knew about this and didn't tell me?"

"Keep your panties on." Saint ruffles her hair, knowing how much it pisses her off. He leans in, whispering in her ear. I'm guessing he doesn't want Bryant to know Sinner neglected to tell any of us about his new spy-slash-recruit.

Lo calms down as Saint fills her in. "Why are you doing this?" she bluntly asks Bryant.

"Because I'm sick of Darrow and his bullshit. And everyone knows The Arrows will lose this war. I prefer to be on the winning side."

"That still doesn't answer my question," Saint says, folding his arms across his chest.

"How does Sinner win anyone to his side?" Bryant challenges, smoothing a hand over his hair.

"He has leverage on you," I say.

Bryant nods, his eyes narrowing at me. "I hope you're hurting, Lennox, because it's the least you deserve."

"What have you offered in return?" Saint asks, ignoring his comment.

"Ask your dad."

Saint glowers. "I'm asking you."

Lo steps between them before they throw punches. "Bry, cut the crap. You're one of us now, and that means we *all* need to work as a team." She levels both guys with a warning look.

A devilish glint appears in Bryant's eye. "If it means I finally get that sexy body underneath me, consider it done."

Saint swings for him, but Caz anticipates the move, pulling him back. "Dude. Chill." Caz points at Bryant. "Quit that shit. Lo is ours, and only ours."

"We've got serious issues to deal with." Lo jabs her finger in Saint's chest. "Like The Bulls wanting to nuke my ass and an impending bloody war. We cannot fight among ourselves. This bullshit ends now." She turns to Bryant. "I wasn't interested before, and that hasn't changed, but I respect you, and we'll be working together from now on. I'd prefer to do that as friends."

"I don't like you," Saint says.

"The feeling is mutual," Bryant agrees.

"But Lo is right," Saint adds, and I almost fall over in shock. "You must earn our trust," he continues.

"You can start by keeping our girl safe," Caz says, as Lo rolls her eyes, muttering under her breath.

Bryant scrubs a hand over his jaw, eyeballing each of us. He nods, wetting his lips before he speaks. "Sinner wants me to identify the rat," he admits.

"Can you?" Lo asks.

"I've heard nothing, but that's not unusual. We're only junior chapter and not privy to a lot of stuff. But I can press Darrow.

He has an in with the president. He might find out." Pressing Darrow is also our plan—an excuse for the lack of retaliation. But he won't know it's also Bryant's endgame because he doesn't know his number two is now a Sainthood spy, so our angle isn't compromised.

"You get a name, you tell us first," Saint says.

"Why?"

"The why isn't important right now."

Bryant looks to Lo, and she nods. Saint stiffens.

"Okay." Bryant looks over his shoulder to where the truck is getting ready to leave. "We need to go."

Caz grabs Lo to him, enveloping her in a bear hug. "Stay safe, badass."

She grins. "You betcha, sexy." She plants a kiss on him.

"If anything happens to Lo, I'm holding you accountable," Saint says to Bryant because he just can't resist going there.

Lo slaps his chest. "Just stop. I'm tiring of this." She pecks his lips. "I can take care of myself. You stick to your end of the bargain."

He swats her ass. "See you this weekend, princess."

Lo turns to Theo, looking unsure. They stare at one another, and Theo looks equally unsure. Tentatively, they step toward each other, and he kisses her on the cheek. "Mind yourself, Lo."

She nods, smiling, but it doesn't meet her eyes. Her gaze whips around to me, and I straighten up, grimacing as red-hot pain whittles through me. "Meet me in the lobby," she says, after a few beats of awkward silence, surprising me.

I open my mouth to ask why, but she's already leaving, running alongside Bryant in the truck's direction.

I'M SITTING ON a small black leather couch in the lobby area when Lo arrives. The guys are here too. She sets a white box down on the coffee table. "Take your shirt off," she commands, not looking at me as she removes a few things from the box.

"What?" I splutter.

She bores a hole in my head. "Do it before I change my mind."

With great difficulty, I remove my shirt, sweating with the exertion as splintering pain assaults my upper body. Cool fingers brush against mine as she helps lift it over my head.

Our eyes meet, and I drop my usual barrier, hoping she can see how sorry I am. I'm still confused over the past, and the lingering resentment I harbor toward her for the part she played, but I'm so fucking sorry for handing her to Darrow. It was a temporary lapse in judgment. I let that bastard manipulate me in a moment of weakness, and I'm better than that.

She deserves better than that.

And I don't deserve any show of kindness.

Hurt and anger and uncertainty are etched upon her face.

"Lo, I—"

"Don't speak!" Her harsh tone reminds me where we're at, and I swallow my apology.

It's not enough to say I'm sorry. I know words are cheap. And the only way I'll redeem myself in her eyes is through my actions.

I stay quiet and hold still as she applies arnica cream to my broken ribs before wrapping a bandage around them. Her touch is gentle, and she's careful not to hurt me, and I'm awash with confusing emotions. Despite the pain I'm in, her touch and her presence are doing funny things to me. My stomach flips, my skin heats, and I conduct a stern inner talk with my dick, urging him to stay the fuck down.

The guys watch her every move, looking as entranced as I feel, and it's obvious we're all under her spell.

Lo unwraps a couple of ice packs, holding them to my burning ribs. She takes my hand, keeping it pressed on top of the packs. "Keep them iced for a few days, and take regular pain meds." She looks over her shoulder at Caz. "Can you get me a cup of water from the cooler?"

He ambles off, returning a minute later.

"Open your mouth," she says, and I comply without protest, staring at her plump lips and the high angles of her cheekbones as she drops a couple tablets in my mouth before holding the cup to my lips. I drink, swallowing the tablets as I stare into her beautiful green eyes. She hands a box of pills to Theo. "Make sure he takes those."

Saint is watching with a frown, rubbing his hand back and forth across his chest. And I get it. I'm confused too. Growing up, both of us sustained more than our fair share of injuries and we got used to living with the pain, because neither of us had anyone, other than each other, to care.

Emotion bubbles up my throat, and tears sting the back of my eyes. I drop my mask, offering her a glimpse of the real me. "Thank you."

"I still hate you," she says, as if on autopilot, her voice devoid of feeling.

"I know."

"That's not changing anytime soon."

"I know that too."

"Good." She tips her chin up, adopting a determined look. "You'd do well to remember that and stay out of my way."

THE SAINTHOOD

CHAPTER 12

"Why'd she do that?" Saint asks from the driver's seat a half hour later, as we are on our way home. He insisted I ride with him though this is the first time he's spoken to me or even acknowledged my presence.

"Because she's a bigger person than me, and she has a good heart." I shift on my side, pressing the ice pack to my ribs as I stretch my legs out on the back seat. I prop my head against the door, because it's too painful to lie down flat.

He looks at me through the mirror. "Why'd you do it?"

"You know why."

"It's more than that."

I sigh. "Everything is changing, and that scares me."

His chest heaves. "I know, but it feels right. She feels right." His eyes meet mine in the mirror.

"You love her."

"Maybe."

"What about the others?"

"She's made her feelings clear." He barks out a laugh. "It serves me right for putting the sharing rule in place."

"You implemented that with good reason, and it's been for the best. Caz is tits over ass crazy for her, and her past with Theo sure seems complicated. She would've torn us apart if that rule wasn't there."

"Hasn't she done that already?" He stares me straight in the eye. "Isn't that what you were afraid of?"

"Yes, but I was wrong. I think—" I pause, because if I say this, there is no taking it back.

"What?" Saint prompts me to continue.

"I think she has the power to make us stronger, and she loves you too. I see it when she looks at you."

"And when she looks at you?"

I send him a scathing look. "She hates me."

Silence ensues for a few minutes. "You need to fix things with her."

"How? I want to, but I've no clue how to go about it."

He purses his lips, signaling as he takes the exit to the highway. "I don't know," he admits.

"Will it work?" I ask. "Because we're the product of our upbringing. How will we ever know?"

"She's easy to love," he replies, his tone low, his face soft.

"She's broken too."

"Because of us." The soft look vanishes from his face, replaced with a familiar cold expression that's in part directed at me. I don't need a look inside my cousin's head to know he reserves the other part for Sinner, because he was the one who broke her first. And he seems hell-bent on breaking her further.

"Because of me." I say what he's thinking, closing my eyes, wishing I could rewind time.

When I wake, we're back at the house—at Lo's house. Saint helps me from the car and into the house via the garage, and I know he's thawing, thanks to Lo. Her kindness and generosity have taken the edge off his anger. A layer of stress leaves my shoulders, but the knot of guilt inside me churns faster.

"Oh my God." Giana, Lo's mom, rushes across the kitchen toward me. "Galen, what happened?"

"I ran into an ambush Saturday night," I lie. "It's why we were lying low."

She bends down, checking my bandaged ribs, and it's only now I remember I'm shirtless. "Have you been taking meds?" she asks. "And icing it?"

"Lo gave me some stuff before we left." At the mention of her daughter, her eyes well up.

She glances over her shoulder before fixing her gaze on Saint. "Is she okay?"

"She's fine." None of us know what bullshit Sinner has fed his fiancée, so we're treading on eggshells here.

"I still can't believe she begged Sinner to join the ranks or that he agreed." Her eyes plead with Saint. "She's doing this for you, right?"

Saint shuffles awkwardly on his feet while I drag my aching body in the direction of the refrigerator. "She's not with me," Saint says.

Giana looks confused. "She isn't? I thought—"

"She's with all of us," Caz says, walking into the kitchen with Theo.

Wow, way to just drop it on her. And it's not even the truth. She's really only invested in Caz and my cousin.

Giana's cheeks flush. "You don't mean—"

"She's our girl, and we'll take care of her. You have our word, so you don't need to worry about anything," Saint adds.

"I… I… I don't know what to say," she blurts, as Sinner walks into the kitchen from the direction of the living room.

I grab cold water from the refrigerator and close the door.

"About what?" Sinner says, coming up behind her and sliding his hands around her waist.

She angles her head back. "Did you know about this? All of them being in a relationship?"

He kisses her cheek as his hands run across her flat stomach. "Not officially, but I've heard sounds of fucking coming from Lo's room. I assumed my son was sticking it to her, but knowing how much of a slut she is, I can't say I'm surprised to hear she's banging all of them."

Giana pushes her fiancé back, rounding on him. "How dare you talk about my daughter like that!"

Sinner slaps her face hard, and we all stiffen. "How dare you talk back to me in front of my son and his friends." He grips her chin hard. The pale skin on her cheek is red, and tears glisten in her angry eyes, but they don't fall. "Your daughter is a dirty slut who opens her legs for any cock. Don't hate me for stating the obvious." Sinner's gaze flits to Saint's. "But you need not worry. I have plans to discipline her."

I walk to Saint's side, my presence a warning to calm the fuck down, because this is how Sinner tortures his son. I know Saint tried to keep Lo at arm's length. To fight his attraction to her. Because it's the best way of keeping her safe. But Sinner isn't blind. He's seen the connection growing between all of us. And he'll use that to hurt his son. To hurt Lo. And to make a point.

I'm not letting it happen. I don't know how yet, but it's one thing I can do to make amends.

"You will not touch my daughter," Giana screams, knowing full and well what he's inferring.

Sinner drops her chin, lowering his hand to her crotch and cupping her pussy through her dress. Tension pours into the air. I don't want to bear witness to this, but to leave when he's mid-rant would incense him. Sinner will use Lo to punish Saint, and he'll use my mom against me, so I can't afford to piss him off.

"This pussy is mine," he snarls, gripping her cunt so tight I'm sure it must hurt. "And your daughter's pussy will be mine if I say so."

"Lo belongs to me," Saint says, adding, "To *us*. If you even look at her funny, I will gut you in your sleep."

Sinner stares at his son, and you could hear a pin drop in the room. Until he grins, breaking out in peals of laughter.

The guy is crazy unpredictable.

Another time, he'd pull a gun on his son for daring to publicly challenge him.

"About time you fucking manned up." He shoves Giana away

forcefully. She wobbles on her high heels, tumbling to the floor.

"The wedding's off!" she yells, propping up on her elbows on the floor.

Sinner bends over her, and she cowers. "The wedding will go ahead, or I'll put a gun up that treacherous cunt of yours and blow you to smithereens before I do the same to your precious daughter."

"I hate you."

"I love you." He presses a kiss to the top of her head, like he hasn't just slapped her and thrown her to the ground in front of us. Like it's normal to treat the person you profess to love in such a cruel manner.

He turns to me, waving his hand about my body. "The Bulls did this, you say."

"Yeah. Five of them jumped me when I was cleaning up the scene." Saint told him The Bulls killed Parker and then put the beatdown on me when I discovered her body.

"They need to pay. Arrows too, but I'm working on that."

"We will handle The Bulls," Saint says, this playing out perfectly for us. "You have enough on your plate. Let us deal with them." He extends his hand, helping Giana to her feet.

Sinner slaps Saint on the shoulder. "That's my boy. Future president." He looks at the three of us. "Nothing less than full annihilation will appease me. Wipe The Bulls from existence, and your initiation is complete."

"Lo too?" Theo asks, even though we all know it's futile.

"Lo will be set different initiation tasks." A gleeful look ghosts over his face, churning my stomach. Whatever he has planned for her will not be good.

Giana gulps, smoothing a hand down the front of her dress.

Sinner points a finger at Saint. "Do whatever you need to, and I want full progress reports." Sinner leans into Giana, kissing her on the cheek. "Get changed, babe. I'm taking you out." He strolls out of the kitchen without another word or glance.

Saint turns to Giana. "Can we do anything?"

Her answering smile is sad. "Not for me." She palms his face.

"You can't interfere between me and your father, but you can protect my daughter." Her gaze bounces between us. "Maybe, it's a good thing she has all of you to protect her. She's going to need it."

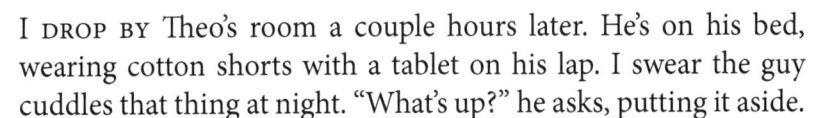

I drop by Theo's room a couple hours later. He's on his bed, wearing cotton shorts with a tablet on his lap. I swear the guy cuddles that thing at night. "What's up?" he asks, putting it aside.

I hobble into the room. "I wanted to ask you about Lo." He goes rigidly still. "Not about your history." I ease onto the bed beside him. "I need to make it up to her, but I have no clue how to do that. I thought you might have ideas."

"Wow." He grins. "The infamous Galen Lennox is asking the nerd for advice with the ladies. I need to note this moment for posterity."

I flip him the bird. "It's in all our interests for me to fix it. Can you help or not?" I'm pissy 'cause I'm in pain and I haven't been able to locate Mom in days, which can only mean one thing—she's high or passed out someplace. I knew this latest round of sobriety wouldn't last, but it's still a punch to the gut every time she falls off the wagon.

"Lo isn't like other girls, so buying her jewelry or flowers won't work," he says, tapping his fingers off his chin, "especially when the sin is so heinous."

"Thanks for the reminder," I growl. "It's not like I'm thinking about it every second of every day."

"Lo enjoys shooting and training, so maybe, buy her a gun. A collector's item, perhaps."

I stare at him. "Great idea. I'll buy her a gun so she has something to use on me when she remembers my betrayal."

"Or you could take her to the shooting range or one of those hunting weekend things. I bet she'll love that," he says, pretending he didn't hear my sarcasm.

"And how do you expect me to get her to agree to come

anywhere with me?"

"You need to earn her trust." He tucks his long blond hair behind his ears, looking contemplative. He pins earnest eyes on me. "You need to open up to her. Nothing is more appealing to Lo than honesty and vulnerability." He wets his lips, looking down at his lap. "Whatever it is you haven't told her, about the past, tell her now. Tell her everything."

"Like you have?"

His jaw tenses. "I have *tried* to tell her, which is more than you've done."

I raise a palm in surrender. "You're right, but I'm not sure it won't make things worse."

"I guess that's a risk you must take."

"I guess so," I say, swinging my legs around and leaving his room.

"You're an hour late," I hiss at Darrow Knight, scowling over the rim of my warm beer.

"Chill the fuck out. You've got beer and easy women." His eyes dart around the dimly lit, grungy biker's bar. "It's not much of a hardship."

"I'm trying to stay under the radar," I snap. "You've landed me in the shit. We had a fucking deal, asshole." I glare at him, really playing it up, because Lo will string me up by the balls if I mess this up. "And she's not dead." I slam my beer down for added effect.

"She's a fucking liability," Darrow says. "And now, she'll come after me."

"She won't. She's out of town for a while, and then, she'll be busy with her mom's wedding. I can keep her under control."

"How? Doesn't she want you dead too? And how are you still alive? I thought Saint was fucking her."

"He is," I sneer. "I didn't get these injuries walking into a door, but I've bought us some time."

A bottle blonde with big tits slides two fresh beers on the table. "Can I get you anything else, sweetheart?" She eye fucks Dar with zero shame.

"Keep your tight ass on ice, babe," he says, sliding his hand up her fleshy thigh. "I'll fuck you nice and hard before I leave." He swats her ass as she walks away, sashaying her hips. "We can tag team," he offers.

"Pass. Despite what's said about me, I'm fussy about who I stick my dick in." Contrary to popular belief, we all are, and tales of our conquests are much exaggerated. Within our crew, Saint and Caz are the ones who partake the most. I've been known to sit out, and Theo rarely pounds pussy, preferring blowies and the occasional anal fuck.

"You hitting Lo, too?" he inquires, sipping his beer.

"I hate that bitch, and I regret fucking her stupid cunt," I lie. "She still needs to be taken out," I add, eyeing his reaction.

He doesn't blink or show any emotion. "I agree. If she opens her pretty mouth to Sinner and more shit rains down on The Arrows, I'm a dead man."

You're a dead man, anyway.

"I have a new plan. A new deal. One which will give us both what we want."

He leans forward, grinning. "I'm all ears."

CHAPTER 13

HARLOW

A RAP ON my door signals Bry's arrival. "You ready?"

I swing the door open, stepping back, briefly looking up from my cell. "Almost. Just give me a few."

I tap out a short thank-you message to Galen, my chest heavy as I stare at today's pic from the hospital. Galen has been checking in daily with Sean, sending me updates on Sariah.

Unfortunately, my bestie is still in a coma, and with every passing day, it becomes more serious. If she doesn't wake up, I don't know what I'll do.

She can't die.

I need her, and she doesn't deserve to go out like this.

Why does God punish good, kind people over and over, yet evil pieces of shit like Sinner Lennox get to stroll around the place unencumbered by his sins and his many crimes? It makes no sense to me, and the unfairness reeks. It's one reason I gave up on any notion of a God years ago.

"Any change?" Bry asks, dropping onto the end of my bed.

"No." I sigh, opening the text from Saint next. "Sar's still in a coma."

"Those bitches need to pay for that."

"They will," I promise.

I read Saint's message, pleased the guys are taking care of business while I'm gone. They have a plan for The Bulls, which they'll share with me tomorrow. They are coming to watch the final challenge and then taking me home. Although I have quite enjoyed this week, I'm dying to get home, itching to put wheels in motion, and to put my plan for vengeance back on track.

Sliding my phone in my pants pocket, I slip my feet into my boots and stand. "Let's go."

It's Saturday night, and we're going to a bar off-site for dinner and a few beers. Several of the instructors will be there, and all the initiates, so it'll probably be lame ass, but the change of scenery is welcome.

"Gotten into her panties yet?" John says, sneering at Bry when we land in the lobby where the others are waiting.

"Go annoy some other sap." Bry folds his arms, threatening John with a dark look.

"When it's so much fun annoying you two?" He snorts. "Not likely."

I step right in front of him, clicking my fingers in his face. "You're an annoying gnat. One I'd enjoy crushing except you're not worthy of that investment of time." I shove his shoulders. "Fuck off, John. Run to your older brother, and plot more ways to take me down if you dare."

Turns out, John is Instructor Corr's younger brother. I would never have made the connection if he hadn't let that slip, because they look nothing alike. All week, they've tried to undermine me and make my life hell. John is doing the dirty work, but I know his older brother is the orchestrator. He's tried sabotaging me every step of the way, but I've handled everything he's thrown at me. It helps that Bry has my back, and the more time I spend with him, the more I realize him joining our ranks is a good thing.

Not sure I'll ever be able to sell that to Saint, but I'll try.

We pile into the truck, and Bry and I take seats in the back. We don't talk as the truck ambles over bumpy terrain, but the silence is comfortable.

The bar is your typical back-end-of-nowhere ramshackle hut, but the beers are flowing freely, the music isn't too cheesy, and the burger fills a hole in my belly. Bry and I are seated at the end of a long bench, as far away from the gnat as possible, talking quietly with our heads close together. "How did you and Dar meet?" I ask between sipping my beer.

"We met when we were ten. One of my older brothers was dating his sister Rita. He used to drag me to her place when he was babysitting me. Dar and I started hanging out in school after that, and a couple years later, he introduced me to The Arrows."

"How many siblings do you have?"

"Three older brothers, and I had a sister, but she died a few months before I was born."

"I'm sorry."

He shrugs, picking at the label on his beer. "It's cool. I never met her, so it was different for me. My eldest brother was super close to her, because there was only a year between them, and he's never gotten over it."

I want to ask him how she died, but I don't want to be rude. I know from experience how hard it is talking about the death of a loved one.

"I'm sorry about your dad," he says, shifting on the bench. His knee brushes against mine.

"Thanks." I quietly sip my beer.

"I didn't know that night at Galen's place. I wouldn't have let you see Dar with Tempest if I'd known."

I take a mouthful of beer. "I don't hold that against you. You did me a favor."

He gulps back some beer. "You were always far too good for him. I never understood how he grabbed your attention or kept it for so long."

"I was using him. I thought he might have intel I was after. When I found out he didn't, I should've broken it off, but the sex was great, so I let it go on longer than it should have."

"What intel?"

I shrug casually, like it's nothing, because I can't divulge the truth. Not until I know I can trust him. Sinner has just recruited him, and he seems firmly pro-Sainthood, but I know how easily that can be faked. If he discovered I only got with Darrow because he was the leader of the junior chapter of The Arrows and I was hoping he might have intel I could use to help take the Saints down, I'm not sure what he'd make of it.

The Arrows are known enemies of The Sainthood, and I felt sure they must have something on their rivals that would be of use, but I failed to understand how little sway Darrow has within the organization, and he was of fuck all use to me. "It doesn't matter now."

"I wanted to make a move on you," he admits, a cheeky grin spreading across his face.

"I thought Dar was your friend. Isn't there some bro code against that?"

"Dar and I barely tolerate one another these days." He knocks back his beer, his grin turning into a grimace.

"Why? What happened?"

"We went in two different directions. He's self-obsessed and selfish, and nothing or no one will stand in his way. I don't like the person he's become."

I nod. "I'm with you there. He makes decisions purely on how they'll impact him. How they'll further his agenda."

"I should've reached out to you after the party," he says. "Maybe I might've stood a chance back then. Now, I see it's too late."

Fuck. I don't want to hurt his feelings, but I won't lead him on either. "I'm flattered, Bry, and I think we'll be good friends. But it won't be anything more. I'm sorry."

He brushes a few stray hairs back off my face. "No need to apologize, Lo. You can't force yourself to feel something you don't. And the fact you're straight with me only makes me respect you more. Saint and the guys are lucky bastards. I'm not surprised you're the one who's caught their eye. You're pretty damn special, and they better make you feel like that because they're not worthy of you otherwise. Galen sure as fuck isn't."

I clasp his hands, squeezing. "You will make some girl so fucking happy one day because I think you're pretty damn special yourself." I let his hands go, curling my fingers around my beer bottle. "And this thing with the guys is new. We're all navigating choppy waters. I have history with Galen, Saint, and Theo, which complicates things."

"But not Caz?"

I smile as I think of my big, burly, sexy guy, who's all heart underneath that scary exterior.

"Wow."

"What?" I ask, quirking a brow.

"I hope someone looks like that when thinking of me someday."

His words prod at my heart, reminding me I'm not being careful. My smile slips a little. "Things are easy with Caz because there's no painful past, and he's laid-back, and he makes me laugh." My smile returns. "He's a good guy."

"I'm reserving judgment," he admits, and I appreciate his honesty.

"That's fair, and I know the guys are doing the same with you."

"No matter what I think of them, there's no doubting how much they care about you. They made that perfectly clear on Monday." He peers into my eyes. "They've got your back. Me too."

I'm still smiling at Bry's words as I emerge from the dingy bathroom a few minutes later. A hand wraps around my hair from behind, and I'm hauled back against a solid chest. My training kicks in, and I twist around, landing a punch in the guy's gut. I wrench my head free, ignoring the stinging pain ripping across my scalp as several strands of my hair are yanked out.

John comes at me, anger contorting his face as he lunges at me with a knife. I duck down, swiping his legs out from under him. He grabs hold of my shirt before I can step aside, and we crash to the floor with him on top of me. He brandishes the knife at my face, and I grip his forearms, holding him off as the knife dangles precariously close to my flesh. He presses his large body down on top of me, and every attempt to push him off fails. Sweat beads on my brow as we battle for control of his arms. I dig my nails into his skin, as his mouth pulls into an ugly grimace. "I will enjoy slitting that pretty throat," he threatens as pounding footsteps echo in the hallway.

He jerks his head up, and I use the distraction to my advantage, freeing one of my hands and scraping my nails across his cheek. He curses, pinning me with murderous eyes as he angles the knife, dragging it across my hand. I scream as Bry reaches us, lifting John up and slamming him against the wall. The knife falls to the floor with a loud clang. "You okay?" Bry asks from over his shoulder as he wedges John to the wall with his body.

I tear a strip off the bottom of the front of my shirt with my teeth, wrapping it around my bleeding hand. "I'm fine, but this asshole needs to be taught a valuable lesson."

Bry grins, showcasing a set of white teeth. "What'd you have in mind?"

We drag John out the back door and beat the shit out of him. I feel zero remorse as I kick him in the ribs and the head, knowing, in some twisted way, I'm saving him from a fate much worse, because if the guys find out about this, they won't hesitate to pull the trigger.

John is lying in the fetal position on the ground, bloodied and bruised, moaning and clutching his stomach, when I crouch down in front of him. "You will not breathe a word of this, or those will be the last words you ever say."

"Screw you," he pants, spitting blood at me.

I bury my fist in his broken ribs, and he yells out in pain. "I will call Saint Lennox right now and tell him you tried to kill me. They will come for you and you won't be breathing by the time they're finished." I stand, pulling my cell out. "So, what's it to be?"

"Okay, okay," he rasps. "I won't say anything."

"When your brother asks, you tell him you walked back and a group of local thugs jumped you."

"Understand, asshole?" Bry kicks him in the back.

"Yes," he sobs. "I got it."

We drag him a mile up the road, ditching him in an enclosed spot where he won't be seen, and jog back to the bar.

We scrub his blood off us in the bathroom, stopping in the hallway outside. "They'll be suspicious we've been gone so long," I say. No doubt, Instructor Corr thinks it's because his brother is taking care of us.

Isn't he in for a surprise?

I can't wait to wipe the smug look off that sexist asshole's face.

"We need them to think we were fucking back here. It's the only explanation that will work."

Bry grins as I unbutton a few buttons on his shirt before suctioning my mouth to his neck. I don't ask permission as I mark his skin, leaving noticeable bruising on his flesh. I pretend not to see the bulge tenting in his pants as I apply a fresh layer of lipstick, leaving clear lip marks on his jawline.

"I'll beat assholes up any day of the week if that's my reward," he quips while I mess up my hair, rub rouge into my cheeks, and leave the back of my shirt hanging out.

"Bry," I warn, and he holds up his hands.

"I'm joking, Lo. I heard you loud and clear."

"C'mon." I grab his hand, pulling him back toward the bar. "Time to put on a show."

THE SAINTHOOD

CHAPTER 14

"Fucking A," Bry says, holding out his hand when I emerge victorious from the showcase the next afternoon. "You owned the room."

I shake his hand, smiling. "We both did."

"But you had the faster times," Caz says, and I whip around, smiling as he swaggers toward me. Messy waves of brown hair tumble into his gorgeous eyes, and his lips are pulled into a lopsided grin as he approaches. He's wearing a black T-shirt that looks welded to his body, and holy hell, have his biceps gotten even bigger since we were apart? He lifts me up, and I fling my arms around his neck. "Missed you, princess," he says against my neck, slowly lowering me to the ground.

"I missed you too," I admit, accepting the truth because I can't deny what I've felt this past week.

I've missed them all.

Well, Galen, not so much. The pain of his betrayal has been simmering under the surface of my skin all week. Now, I've moved past the angry phase, and I'm hurt. There was a moment, a few weeks ago, when I thought Galen and I were connecting, but his actions have destroyed anything credible that was building between us.

Caz's lips descend on mine, and we kiss until I pull away. "I'm a sweaty mess."

"That's my favorite look on you," Saint says, capturing my attention as he approaches behind Caz.

I drink him in and note how that dirty-blond hair I love so much has grown a little longer, his eyes seem bluer, and the intensity that radiates from his every pore seems heavier but less oppressive. The urge to run into his arms rides me hard, but I play it cool.

He grabs my face in his hands, his eyes searching mine. "You good?"

"I'm good."

He lowers his face, planting his mouth against mine with no hesitation. His tongue prods at the seam of my lips, and I open for him, knowing it's futile to resist. His tongue swallows me whole, and I cling to him as I sway on my feet.

Damn, can this man kiss—branding me with the expert ministrations of his lips and his tongue, ruining me for all eternity.

I have to blink to clear my vision when we finally break apart, still clutching him because I don't trust my legs not to go out from under me.

"I think I got pregnant just watching that," Caz jokes.

Saint smirks, and I roll my eyes, walking to where Galen and Theo hang back. "Hey."

"Nicely played, Lo." Theo kisses my cheek, pinning me with a proud smile.

"Sinner was bragging to no end," Galen says, and I eye him warily. The bruises have faded, and the cuts are healing nicely, showcasing more of his pretty face. His green eyes plead with me, but he's not off the hook. Not by a long shot.

Ignoring him, I turn around, addressing Saint. "Is there time to grab a quick shower before I need to meet the board?" I knew Sinner and the other members of the board would watch our final test today and that my initiation tasks would be issued thereafter. To say I'm not scared would be a lie. I know he'll push me to extremes, in the hope I'll fail, but I won't give him the satisfaction.

Saint glances at his cell. "There's time."

"Cool." My eyes dart to Caz's. "You look a little dirty."

His lips kick up. "I'm more than a little dirty," he agrees, walking to me. He grabs the back of my neck, pulling me in to his face. "I'm positively filthy."

"It's settled then." I grab his hand, heading toward the exit, ignoring the dour look on Bry's face and the eyeballs glued to my back. Caz glances at me, fixing me with a pointed look, and I know what he's saying. Refusing to meet his eyes, I pull him out into the corridor.

Pain barrels up my throat, and I squeeze my eyes shut, slamming to a halt. "Damn it all to hell," I mutter, shaking my head and blinking my eyes open. "Stay here." I kiss the corner of Caz's mouth before rushing back into the room.

Saint lifts his gaze to mine, and he's not quick enough to shield his hurt. I stalk across the room and snag his hand. I stretch up, pressing my mouth to his ear. "I need you."

I need both of them.

Nothing gets my juices flowing like fighting and shooting, and I've been on a high all week and horny as fuck, resorting to fingering myself most nights to thoughts of my guys.

I just kicked ass at the showcase, and the adrenaline still flowing through my veins needs an outlet. I also need a distraction because I know what's coming next won't be pleasant. I need my guys to take the edge off.

Saint peers into my eyes, and I let him see all that.

"We'll meet you in the lobby," Saint says to the others, his eyes never leaving mine.

I avoid looking at any of them as I lead Saint out to the hallway where Caz is waiting with an exuberant smile.

We don't talk as we travel in the elevator to my room. I hold hands with Caz while my free hand runs up and down the side of Saint's leg.

The instant we are inside my room, they descend like vultures zeroing in on their prey. "We don't have much time," I rasp, as Saint tugs at my shirt while Caz unbuttons my pants.

"Not a problem, princess." Saint smirks, lifting my shirt up and tossing it to the floor.

We undress in record time, and I take turns kissing them before dropping to my knees. I grab hold of both their erect cocks, stroking them in long, firm tugs before I lean in, taking Saint's hard dick into my mouth. I continue stroking Caz as I suck Saint off, and then, I switch around, alternating back and forth between them.

"Enough." Saint yanks his dick from my mouth, lifting me up by the arms and throwing me down on the bed.

Caz spreads my legs wide, dipping two fingers inside me. "She's fucking drenched."

"I've been so fucking horny all week, and I can't wait any longer," I say over a low moan as Caz adds another finger, stretching me while Saint sucks my nipple into his hot mouth. I grab at Saint's neck and curl my fingers around his wide length with my other hand, swiping my thumb along the precum glistening at his crown. "Fuck me now. Both of you at once."

Saint's eyes darken with lust as his mouth slams down on mine. Caz removes his fingers from my pussy, parting my ass cheeks and sliding one finger inside my puckered hole. I arch off the bed as sensation consumes me. Caz uses my pussy juices to prepare my ass, spitting on his hand and running it along the length of his cock.

Saint lifts me up, sliding behind me and lying lengthways on the bed with his head slightly propped up against the headboard. I climb over him, holding his dick in my hand as I lower my pussy down onto him. We both groan as my heat envelops his throbbing length, and I close my eyes as contentment settles deep in my chest. I pop my eyes open a few seconds later, and he's watching me, his face betraying similar emotions. Leaning down, I kiss him passionately, because I can't get enough of his mouth, while Caz trails his fingers down my spine and over the curve of my butt before pressing two digits into my ass.

"Stay like that, baby," Caz says, sliding his fingers in and out. "And relax."

I rip my mouth from Saint's, glancing over my shoulder with a smirk. "You know this isn't my first rodeo."

"How could I forget?" He winks, lining his cock up with my ass.

I face Saint again, and we stare into each other's eyes as Caz slowly slides in my ass. My chest floods with warmth, and my heart swells, and I'm feeling so full—of D and heartfelt emotions I've no business feeling.

"Saint, I—" My voice cracks, and I'm on the verge of something monumental. Something I can't voice because I can't accept this. This isn't what I wanted, and I'm scared of losing control or, worse, handing it over to them.

But I seem powerless to stop this freight train of emotion, carrying my heart and my soul as it charges ahead, directionless, with little regard of the journey, only knowing it will stop where fate determines it to stop.

Saint winds his fingers in my hair, firmly grabbing my neck in a vise grip, knowing I need a rough touch. "I know, baby." He drags my lower lip between his teeth, biting hard and drawing blood. "We feel it too." His tongue darts out, licking the bead of blood on my lip. "And we've got you."

"Always," Caz adds, gently rocking in and out of my ass.

"Harder," Saint commands him, shoving me back until I'm only halfway bent over him. He grips my hips in a painful clutch, moving me up and down on his cock.

"Fuck," I moan, throwing my hair back and going with the flow, letting them take full control.

Caz leans forward, tugging my head back and claiming my lips in a half-upside-down kiss. His tongue swirls into my mouth as we fuck, and I'm in the middle of my own personal heaven.

Saint trails a hand up my body, rolling and flicking my nipples, one at a time, tweaking and twisting, and I whimper at the pleasure-pain sensations snaking through me.

Caz removes his lips from mine, groaning and cussing as he increases his pace, thrusting in and out of my ass. He nips and bites on my earlobe as he slams in and out of me, and I'm just riding the wave. Saint thrusts his hips up with force as I bounce on top of him, and I'm lost to sensation, ceasing to exist on this plane. There is only pleasure tinged with pain as they pluck and stroke my body like skilled magicians.

Caz slides a hand around my waist, dipping low, his expert fingers finding my clit. Lightning dances across my eyes as he vigorously rubs my bundle of nerves while thrusting inside my ass, in perfect sync with Saint's commanding pumps inside my pussy.

"Come for us, princess," Saint demands on a growl, and I self-destruct, screaming as a powerful orgasm whips through me, igniting every nerve ending and cell in my body.

Caz comes next, pulling out of my ass fast and moving around to my front, jerking his dick off over my tits. Ropes of warm cum coat my flushed breasts until Caz leans in, lapping up his own bodily fluids as he cleans me with a wicked glint in his eyes.

"Oh fuck. That is so hot." I tilt my mouth up toward him, seeking his lips on mine. He kisses me with his lips and his tongue as I bounce up and down on Saint, riding his hard cock with abandon.

"Fuck off, Evans," Saint snaps, breaking our reverie.

I wondered when Saintly would reach his limit. To be fair, he's trying, so I won't give him shit for this. I smirk at my territorial caveman as he flips me over, smashing my head into the pillow and thrusting in my pussy from behind. Caz wanders into the bathroom, and I hear the shower running a minute later. Saint picks up speed, rutting into me like a madman, fucking me raw, tearing strips off my heart, and shattering my defenses. "You're ours, Lo. *Mine. Ours.*" Saint has come a long way in a short distance, but his words prove he's still struggling inside. "I don't fucking care what the label is as long as you know you belong to us. With us."

"I know, Saintly. Trust me, I know." Part of me loves it. Part of me hates it.

How can they make me feel like I'm unraveling and being sewn back together at the same time? Perhaps, I'm being remade anew, but thoughts of the unknown terrify me, and putting my trust in them is still something I cannot fully do.

Saint digs his fingers into my hip bones, bruising me, and I can't get enough. I push my ass back against him, keeping time with his thrusts, and he comes with a deafening roar, shooting his load deep inside me, invading me body and soul. He slumps over my back, pulling us down on the bed. "Lo," he whispers, pressing his lips to my back. "What are you doing to me?"

"I could ask you the same question," I pant, trying to regulate my breathing.

He turns me around, cupping my face, and I gasp at the vulnerability in his eyes. "I don't do this, Lo. I've never given any part of myself to any woman."

"I haven't either, and I'm trusting more than just you."

He stares into my eyes, probing the truth, and his vulnerability takes on a new slant. His eyes darken, and his hold on my face tightens. "Do not fuck me over." He grips my cheeks tight. "I will fucking squeeze every breath from your body if you screw with me."

"How did you get that cut on your hand?" Saint asks as we make our way back downstairs. We have all showered—separately because the shower is small and none of us trusted we wouldn't go back for seconds if we attempted to shower together—but there was no time to dry our hair, so it'll be obvious as fuck when I rock up to the board.

I got Saint to grab my bag from reception when they first arrived, and my locket is securely fastened around my neck. It gives me some comfort walking into the lion's den, knowing the conversation is being recorded.

"I'm covered in cuts and scrapes from this week," I say, convincing myself it's not a lie if I evade the truth. "More now," I add, piercing them with a knowing look.

I will tell them what happened with John, and how his brother is pulling the strings, but only once we are away from here. Instructor Corr needs to pay, and losing his job will be good enough for me. Both men are sexist pigs, but I don't want their deaths on my conscience. I'm hoping to get away without mentioning how I staged things Saturday night so it looked like Bry and I had been fucking in the hallway, because I don't want Bry's death on my conscience either.

"I'll ask again." A muscle clenches in Saint's jaw. "How did that happen?" He grabs my wrist, holding my hand up, the long, thin cut evident under the clear Band-Aid.

"It doesn't matter. I handled it," I say, as the elevator pings and the doors slide open. Caz grabs my bag, and I storm out into the hallway.

Saint catches up to me, grabbing my elbow. "Who?"

"Forget it," I hiss. "He's not worth our time, or have you forgotten the shit we're dealing with?" I yank my elbow out of his hold. "Drop it, Saint. Bry and I dealt with it. End of story."

"Harlow. There you are." Sinner strides across the lobby toward me. Out of the corner of my eyes, I notice Theo, Bry, and Galen lounging on the couches. Theo is on his tablet, Galen looks bored, and Bry is scribbling on a notepad. "We've just finished with Bryant, so you're up." He slings his arm over my shoulders, tucking me into his side as he pins me with a sleazy look that sends unpleasant shivers tiptoeing up my spine. He slants a condescending look in Saint's direction. "Don't worry, son." He slaps him hard on the back. "We'll look after your girl."

"I thought I'd come with," Saint says, shoving his hands in his pockets and working hard to appear casual.

"That's not how this works." Sinner points at the couch. "Park your butt there. This won't take long." Discreetly, I press in on the locket, activating the recording device.

Sinner digs his nails into my upper arm as he walks me

through a set of glass doors at the rear of the lobby area and into a small conference room. "There," he barks, pointing at a chair in the middle of the floor. It's facing a row of chairs at the top of the room where the board members are waiting for me. Six assholes stare at me with blatant interest, and bile rises up my throat. Some of them I recognize from the basement in the warehouse and a couple from the engagement party at my house.

"Spread your legs and arms out," Sinner commands.

Acid lines the walls of my stomach, but I do as he says, biting on the inside of my mouth as he enthusiastically pats me down. A few guffaws ring out at the top of the room as Sinner cups my pussy through my pants and fondles my breasts through my shirt.

"You can have this back after," he says, removing my iPhone from my pocket. He checks the screen and eyeballs me, most likely wondering why I didn't have it set to record. "Sit," he barks, pushing me back on the seat.

He joins his despicable buddies, sinking into the empty chair in the middle of the line, leaning back, and gloating like the cat that got the cream.

"You've done us proud this week, Harlow. We've watched all your tapes, and your skill set is impressive."

I rest my hands on my lap, steadying my nerves and keeping a neutral expression on my face as I stare into the eyes of the devil. "Thank you for the opportunity. I've enjoyed it."

Sinner shares a grin with the man beside him, and I fight a shudder. The man has a shaved head, ink halfway up his face, and a dark, menacing look in his eyes that freaks me out like the first time I saw him in the basement. He tied me to the chair that time, his leering gaze upon me the entire time. "Your marksman skills at the warehouse didn't go unnoticed either." Sinner leans forward, pressing his arms on his knees. "I had plans for you, Lo, but this has exceeded our wildest dreams."

He gets up, eliminating the space between us, crouching down in front of me. "You remind me of your mother," he says, and that can't be anything good. "But an enhanced version. With all the qualities I wish she had." He runs his fingers along my cheek, and adrenaline pumps through my veins.

I want to throat punch him, kick him in the junk, and light cigarettes on his naked flesh before slashing at his chest, cutting into flesh and bone, and leaving him to bleed out on the floor.

But revenge takes time.

And I'm sowing the seeds.

So, I bite back my distaste and swallow the retorts begging to let loose on my tongue.

"I'm glad to see you're cooperating." He lowers his fingers to my neck, glancing at my chain, and I hold my breath. "This will work to both our advantages," he says, raising his eyes to my face, "if you don't fight me." His fingers brush against my chest, and I force bile back down my throat.

"What tasks are being set for me?" I ask, working hard to hide the disgust and fear from my face and my tone.

Sinner leans in, rubbing his nose along my neck, inhaling my scent, and a low growl escapes his throat, prickling the hairs on the back of my neck.

My heart pounds, and my palms turn sweaty, and the urge to flee is riding me hard, but I grip the edge of the chair, reminding myself of the endgame. Despite my bravado, he senses my unease, and a devilish grin spreads across his mouth as he kisses my cheek. My skin crawls like a thousand fire ants just dug their way into my flesh, and I need a scorching hot shower to remove all trace of his saliva and his touch from my skin.

He walks back to his seat, and I relax a smidgeon.

"We have three important jobs for you." He flashes me a wide grin. "Pass these, and I will induct you into the senior chapter along with the other junior chapter members upon high school graduation."

I nod. "I understand."

"While we have made progress into Lowell, controlling the supply chain in the public school and taking charge on the streets, the private academy remains a stumbling block. You will work with my son and his crew to rectify that."

"I can do that." Lowell Academy is my old school, and while I left under a cloud, this task shouldn't be too difficult to pull off with the guys' help. The girls will cream their panties when I rock up with The Sainthood, and I doubt it'll take much to convince anyone to buy from them. Look how easily they wiped the board with Finn at Lowell High.

"You will attend Sainthood HQ once a month, on a day of our choosing, to manage some *tasks* for myself and the other board members."

I'm guessing those tasks involve dropping to my knees and getting on all fours. My blood turns to ice at the thought of those assholes with their hands on me, and it won't happen, but arguing the point will feed their sick perversion, so I nod, smiling, pretending I'm naïve. Sinner won't buy it, but I'm not sure how much the others know about me.

"Of course." I nod, and Sinner almost glows.

"The third is more delicate, but it will prove your loyalty is with us."

His eyes turn cold, and isn't that the sign of a true psychopath? That he can flip the switch so easily?

"I'm sure I don't have to remind you of the consequences should you fail to deliver. As much as I love my fiancée, her comfort and her survival are in your hands. I will punish you and your mother if you displease me." The veins in his neck bulge as he knots his hands in front of him. "Deceive me, and I'll stab those *boys* you love through the heart without blinking."

Panic shuttles through me, and I'm losing the hold on my tenuous emotions. Potent fear slithers through my veins, and I'm on the verge of throwing up.

"What is the last task?" I ask, pleased my voice sounds level even though I'm shaking inside.

"You will kill Police Commissioner Leydon."

THE SAINTHOOD

CHAPTER 15

THE MEETING CONCLUDES with Sinner telling me he'll provide more details on the commissioner's execution in due course and he'll message me when I'm being summoned to HQ. Then, he escorts me out of the room.

Shouting and screaming greet our ears, growing louder when we enter the lobby. John is in a pool of blood on the floor, and Saint and Galen are taking turns kicking the shit out of him. Guess the cat's out of the bag. I never should've mentioned Bry because Saint must've gone straight to him and demanded answers.

"Do I want to know?" Sinner drawls, patting me on the ass before pushing me away. He's getting far too handsy for my liking. I lean against the desk, keeping quiet as I wait to see how this pans out.

"You should stick around," Saint says, as the side door opens with a slam and Caz and Theo emerge, dragging Instructor Corr with them.

"You won't get away with this," he shouts. "I'm a respected staff member and a long-standing member of The Sainthood."

"Then, you should know better," Saint says, punching him in

the face. "I warned you to leave her alone."

Sinner leans against the other side of the reception desk, crossing his ankles. He winks at the pretty receptionist, the same one who greeted me the day I arrived. "Hey, sweetheart."

Her cheeks flush, and from the way she's eye fucking him, I know she's screwed him. Probably recently, too. I knew that bastard wasn't faithful to Mom, and who knows what venereal diseases he's carrying. I should warn her, but I'm sure she knows exactly what kind of asshole her fiancé is.

"Women have no place in our world," the instructor says, appealing to Sinner with his eyes. "They are lower-class citizens for a reason, only good for sucking dick and spreading their legs."

Saint punches him in the face again, and blood spurts from his nose, spraying across Saint's white T-shirt. Saint looks down, scowling.

"Times are changing." Sinner loses the smirk, stepping toward him. "And every member needs to get behind our new philosophy."

"Of course!" Instructor Corr is sweating bullets now. "It was part of the strategy," he blurts, grasping at straws. "To toughen her up." His wild eyes dart around the men in the room. "She needs to have balls of steel to take a place beside The Sainthood men."

Even when arguing—with his survival hanging in the balance—he still comes off like a misogynist jerk.

And every smart man knows pussy beats balls every day of the week.

Caz and Theo tighten their hold on his arms as Saint punches him in the gut. "Lo has more balls than most guys I know. Like fuck, she needs toughening up." He punches him again, and the guy's knees buckle.

Galen drops another kick to the asshole writhing and crying on the floor while holding his ribs and clenching his jaw. I know he's on strong meds, but he must be in pain. He should sit this one out, but I guess he's keen to prove his loyalty. "Well, shit for brains. You ready to fess up?" he snarls.

"Okay. Okay." John blubbers, snot leaking from his nose, and I shudder. Ugh. "It wasn't my idea."

"Well, duh." I roll my eyes.

"My brother said—"

"Shut your mouth, John," the instructor hisses.

"They'll kill me!" John cries. "And this is all your fault!"

What a sniveling, pathetic idiot. I don't know why I tried to save him from this fate.

"It was The Bulls!" John shouts. "They made us do it. That slut he's fucking is connected to them." He jabs his finger in his brother's direction as I trade a look with Saint.

How did The Bulls even know I'd be here? And is there no end to their reach? I hate to say it, but I think the Saints have completely underestimated The Bulls.

"I had no choice," the instructor pleads as Sinner's eyes darken with rage. "And I didn't kill her like they asked," he adds, as if that will buy him any favors.

A shrill pop resonates around the room, and the receptionist screams, dropping to her knees behind the desk. Sinner's arm is extended, his gun pressed flushed to Instructor Corr's forehead, a hole in the center of Corr's brow where the bullet went through.

Holy fucking shit.

I wet my dry lips, sharing another look with Saint.

Sinner does not mess around.

Can't say I'm surprised.

He's an unpredictable psycho.

John roars, watching with horror as the guys let go of his brother and his lifeless body falls to the floor with a resounding thud.

Sinner places his gun on top of the counter, leaning over the edge. "Get up, you stupid bitch." The woman stands on wobbly legs, tears streaming down her face. "How long have you worked here?" he asks, and I guess there wasn't time for small talk when he was fucking her.

"Three weeks," she whispers.

Warm fingers wrap around mine, and I look up into Galen's

green eyes. He pulls me away, shoving me behind him just as Sinner grabs the gun and he pumps three bullets in the receptionist's chest. She slumps to the ground, blood oozing out of her wounds, her eyes unmoving, confirming she's dead.

John's screams ring out around the room, because he is just that stupid, and Sinner aims his gun in his direction.

"Wait." Saint's lethal tone bounces off the walls. "He might know something."

The glass doors at the rear of the space open, and two of the board members enter the lobby. "We heard shots," the creepy dude with the bald head and face ink says. "I'll call a cleanup crew," he adds, spotting the two dead bodies on the ground.

Sinner stabs Saint with a look. "Find out what he knows, then dispose of him." He glances out the front window. "Not here."

Saint nods as Caz and Bry lift a whimpering John off the floor. They move toward the side door, and Galen tugs me forward, his fingers still linked through mine. Warmth seeps into my bones, snaking up my arm, and I clasp his hand tighter before I snap out of it, remembering I'm holding hands with a traitor. Yanking my hand from his, I push forward, putting some distance between us, as I follow the three guys out into the corridor.

We end up in the inspection room, where they toss John to the floor. Saint removes my Strider from its holder, handing it to me. "You want to do the honors?"

"Gladly." I run the tip of my finger gently along the pointed end, delighted to have my weapon back in my hands. I've felt naked without it.

I straddle the asshole on the floor and lean down, pressing my knife to his throat. "Start talking, gnat. And please don't piss your pants because I'd hate to cut your dick off."

"That's all I know," he blurts, more snot flying from his nose.

I rear back, thoroughly repulsed. "You are so gross." I press my knife into his neck, nicking him.

His lip trembles. "Ask Taylor. She's the one he was screwing."

"Last name, asshole," Saint asks, kicking him in the side.

"Tamlin. Her name is Taylor Tamlin."

Bry curses, and we all turn to him. "You know her?" I ask.

"She's the blonde I was with at the party," he explains, looking me directly in the face. I remember her—she was gloating over what went down between Dar and me until Bry shoved her off his lap to chase me. "I'd no idea she had ties to The Bulls."

"Perhaps, she was the link who brought The Bulls and The Arrows together," Theo says, and he's already tapping away on his cell.

"Who is she?" Saint's gaze bounces between John and Bry.

"I know nothing about her," Bry says, "except she's a lousy lay." He glances at John. "Your brother had shit taste in women." He eyeballs Saint. "I can ask around. See who brought her to the party. Find out if Dar knows her."

"Be discreet," Saint warns.

"I am not a moron." Bry narrows his eyes to slits.

"Debatable," Galen pipes up.

"Focus!" I snap, pressing the knife to John's throat again. "Tell us everything you know about her."

"My brother was fucking her behind his wife's back, and the kill request came through her, but that is all I know. You'll have to ask her."

"This is a waste of time," Caz says, lighting up a cigarette. "You so fluke, man." He grins widely.

"Dude, no." Theo shakes his head, and I laugh.

"Trending today?" I guess, and Caz nods. "I want in on this," I add.

"It could be a competition," he replies, his eyes lighting up.

I get up, done with the douche on the floor. "I'm game." I waggle my brows. "Starting from tomorrow."

"Fuck my life." Saint groans, shaking his head as he presses his booted foot under John's chin, keeping him down on the floor. "Take princess to the car." He pulls out a gun, and his expression turns serious.

"Hell no." I tuck my knife in the back pocket of my jeans as Caz and Galen aid Saint in keeping John on the floor. Caz rips the bottom of John's shirt, stuffing his mouth with the torn strip, muffling his shouts and cries. "I'm going nowhere." I challenge Saint with my eyes, and he stares right through me. But his intimidation tactics don't work on me anymore. I prod my finger in his chest. "I'm one of you now. I won't be shielded."

"Very well." He holds my gaze for another few seconds before swinging his eyes in John's direction. "Don't bother saying a prayer, motherfucker." He points the gun at his head. "Because prayers don't work when your destination is hell." He pulls the trigger, pumping two rounds into his skull, and John dies instantly.

Saint cleans his gun, wiping it down, before tucking it into the back of his jeans. He looks at Galen. "Instruct the cleanup crew to take care of him." Galen nods before exiting the room.

"Let's get the fuck out of here." Grabbing my hand, Saint pulls me toward the door, and we get the hell out of Dodge.

"Are we going to your place?" I inquire after I've finished filling them in on my week. I'm waiting until we get back to tell them about my initiation tasks because shit will hit the fan when they find out what the psycho expects me to do.

"Nah," Caz puffs on a cigarette while I rest my head on his shoulder. Saint is driving, Galen is beside him in the passenger seat, and Theo is on the other side of me, nose buried in his tablet. "Not with dickhead Eccleston in tow."

Bry is driving behind us. Saint wants to hear about his initiation tasks, too. And he probably wants to rub his nose in it about me a little more.

"We're going back to the house," Saint confirms. "The oldies are out, doing menu tastings or some shit."

I sit up straighter, leaning my head through the gap in the front seats. "What's been happening since I've been gone?" Mom texted me a few times, but we haven't spoken.

Awkward silence filters into the air.

"What is it? Is Mom all right?"

Caz sighs, and Theo finally puts his tablet down, scooting forward to the edge of the seat. "She's okay," Theo confirms. "But the dynamic has shifted in their relationship."

"Meaning what exactly?"

"He's pushing her around a bit," Saint says. "When she told him the wedding was off, he threatened her." His eyes drill into mine through the mirror. "And you."

I slump back in the seat, air whooshing out of my mouth. "Fuck." I rub at my temples, still feeling so conflicted over the woman who gave me life.

"We won't let him hurt her or you," Saint says.

"Don't make promises you can't keep," I hiss.

"Don't fucking push me, princess," Saint snarls. "No one is hurting either of you on our watch, and that is one promise I fully intend to keep."

THE SAINTHOOD

CHAPTER 16

"Nice pad," Bry says, looking around as we walk through the house and downstairs to the basement.

"Thanks. Mom's anal about the house. She never stops decorating."

"This is a world away from where I grew up."

"Save your sob story for someone who cares," Saint says, stopping in the middle of the two couches and folding his arms. "Sit." He jerks his head toward the couch on the left. I flop down beside Bry, and Saint glares at me. "You." He jabs his finger at me. "Over there." He points at the opposite couch.

I flip him the bird. "You already pissed on me, and Bry knows where we stand, so lose the caveman act unless you plan to sleep alone for the rest of your life."

He stalks toward me, leaning down, caging me in with his arms. "I would like to see you try."

"Okay, enough." Theo grabs the back of Saint's shirt, and I gawk at him. "Lo is right. We're deep in shit, and we don't have time for this. She's yours. You don't need to remind her and everyone else of that every second of every day."

Saint straightens up, whirling around on Theo, ready to pummel him into yesterday. I jump up, grabbing Saint's face, and I kiss him hard, shoving my tongue in his mouth and shutting him the fuck up. He doesn't let me down, wrapping his arms around me and kissing me back with the same fervor. After a couple minutes, I pull back, cupping his cheek and staring into his eyes. "Okay?"

He nods, and I drop back onto the couch beside Bry. Saint perches his butt on the armchair beside me. "You're up first." He gestures at Bry. "What are your initiation tasks?"

Bry crosses one leg over his knee, leaning back with zero evidence of discomfort. The guy wasn't the brute force in Dar's operation for nothing. It takes a lot to rattle him. "It wasn't a surprise. Find the rat. Eliminate the rat. Help the Saints take The Arrows down."

"How fast can you find the informant?" Saint asks, and I'm glad he's lost the jealousy even though I'm sure it's only temporary.

"It will take time," Bry admits, scrubbing a hand over his prickly jawline. "And I'll need to lean on Dar."

Galen glances at Saint, and Saint gives him a curt nod. "That might be easier than you expect," Galen says. "He believes our deal is back on and it hinges on him identifying our traitor."

Bry smirks. "That's helpful, and I'll watch him, see if he intends to screw you over."

I bark out a laugh. "Of course, he's gonna screw him over. That's what Dar does."

I clear my throat, preparing to fess up. I've given this a lot of thought in the past week, and I can't keep the details of my deal with Darrow off the table any longer. There are too many moving pieces, and I don't trust that asshole not to rat me out to Galen, anyway.

Keeping shit from one another almost killed me last time.

Diesel will probably freak when he finds out, because he doesn't trust the Saints at all, but I'll deal with him when the time comes.

"There is something I need to tell you." All eyes swing to me.

"My escape didn't go down quite how I explained it."

Saint drills a hole in the side of my head, and his jaw locks up. Caz cusses, Galen sits up straighter, and Theo has his serious face on. Only Bry looks amused. "I know how to play Dar," I say, ignoring the hostile vibes emanating from Saint. "So, I manipulated him into letting me go."

"Stabbing him was to cover your tracks?" Theo asks.

"No, that was pure enjoyment." Caz chuckles, and Bry grins. Saint continues boring holes in my head. "It only occurred to me after I plunged the knife in his thigh that it gave him the alibi he needed to explain my escape."

"What did you agree to?" Saint asks, already racing ahead of the conversation.

"I agreed to spy for him and provide intel he could use to take The Sainthood down."

"Were you planning on delivering?" Bry asks.

"Dude," Caz intervenes. "Of course, she wasn't. It was all part of the plan."

I blow Caz a kiss, loving how confident he is in my motives and how easily and quickly he jumped to my defense. "Right. Playing both sides against one another feeds into our overall agenda."

Saint loudly clears his throat, sending a subtle glance in Bry's direction. And I get it. I don't trust him yet either. He must earn our honesty.

"Let's park that," Saint says, and Bry stares at him. "What?" Saint snaps.

"You don't trust me. I respect that."

Saint stares at him for a few beats before focusing on me. "What tasks were you set?"

I flick my gaze at Caz. "You might need to sit on him for this."

For once, Caz isn't laughing. "We're expecting the worst. Just tell us."

"I'm to help you get control of the drug supply in Lowell Academy, show up at HQ once a month to be gang-raped, and kill Commissioner Leydon," I reply in a level tone. No point in hysterics.

Saint explodes, as predicted, stomping around the basement, throwing shit at the walls, pacing, and cursing while we wait him out.

"Fuck," Galen murmurs. "That is messed up."

"No shit, Sherlock." Saint fumes, stalking to the couch and dropping beside me. He hauls me into his lap, circling his arms around my waist and holding me tight. He leans his chin on my shoulder, keeping me close, cocooning me in his protective embrace.

A messy ball of emotion clogs my throat as warmth spreads across my chest. I feel safe in his arms. Cherished and protected. And it's an unfamiliar feeling even though Dad and Diesel have gone to great lengths to keep me safe.

This feels different, and in this moment, I realize there is nothing I can do to shield my heart from this onslaught.

The guys have me, and my heart is already invested.

There's no way I can get out of this now without getting hurt.

"You can't murder the fucking commissioner," Bry says, looking genuinely shocked.

"Do I look dumb to you?" I ask, glaring at him, because that is a fucking given.

"I say we slaughter the board in their sleep," Caz suggests, and Saint whips his head up, warning him with his eyes. Then, he stares at Bry. "Get out."

"I can help. I—"

"Get the fuck out," Saint says, whipping his gun out and leveling it at Bry. "I don't care if you're one of us."

Bry smirks, grabbing the gun and moving it to his brow. "Go ahead, asshole. Do it."

I wrap my hand around the gun. "No one else is getting shot today." I turn my head, eyeballing Saint. "Put it away. Bry is leaving." Slowly, Saint pulls back. I stand. "I'll show you out." Saint opens his mouth to protest, but I clamp my hand over his lips. "Nope. Not listening to it. Switch your brain back on, and be ready for a serious conversation when I return."

I escort Bry outside and lean against the side of his truck. "We want to trust you, but it'll take time."

"It's smart, Lo, and what I would do. I've defected, and I need to prove my worth. I intend to follow through as fast as I can."

"That would be wise." I give him a quick hug. "Later, dude."

The air is heavy when I return, but Saint seems to have calmed down. I sit beside him, placing my hand on his knee. "For what it's worth, I don't think he has any loyalty to The Arrows anymore."

"I agree," Theo says.

"I don't think he has any loyalty to the Saints either," Galen supplies.

"I don't disagree," I say, "but our loyalty could be questioned too, for various reasons."

My words linger in the air, and no one can deny the truth.

"That doesn't mean we should trust him," Saint adds, circling his arm around my shoulders.

"Agreed, but I know Bry a little, and I think he'll deliver soon. Then, we can decide how much we tell him or whether we tell him anything at all."

"Have you found out anything on Taylor Tamlin yet?" Saint asks Theo.

"I'm working on it, but I'll hopefully have something later."

"The Bulls seem well connected," I admit.

"Better connected than we realized," Saint says.

"Parker was the link between Finn and The Bulls," Theo confirms. "We have footage of her entering their clubhouse a couple nights after we handed her ass to Ruben."

"Do you think Ruben already knew the truth that night?"

Saint toys with the ends of my hair. "None of us would've walked out of there alive that night if he knew."

I pull at my lips. "It makes little sense. If someone was watching the night I killed Luke McKenzie, why didn't they pass that tape off to Ruben immediately?"

Theo shrugs. "Who knows? I'm struggling to piece this all together."

"It's a fucking shitshow," Galen agrees.

"One you added to," I remind him, but my chastisement lacks bite because he knows what he's done and snapping at him continuously won't help anyone. While I'm still pissed over his betrayal, reminding him every five minutes only hurts me too. I'm trying to put it behind me, but it's difficult.

"I know." His face and his voice are resigned.

"What are we going to do about The Bulls? They won't stop until I'm dead."

"It's kill or be killed," Saint agrees. "Which is why we're taking them down." He explains that Sinner is on board.

"How is it going down?" I ask.

"Boy wonder has tracked down all the key players within the organization, and we'll eliminate them in a targeted attack," Saint says.

"I'm still finalizing the details," Theo says, "but we'll hit each of them at the same time, wiping the leadership out in one fell swoop."

"Will that be enough? Won't the other members seek revenge?"

"They'll be too busy scrambling to maintain their business," Saint says, grinning. "Because we already have men infiltrating their ranks, and we'll start picking off towns and taking ownership."

"They'll be too busy fighting to save their income to care," Galen says.

"Is it really that easy to take over their turf?"

"It is," Saint says. "I don't know what Ruben is thinking. He knows he owns his turf because we've let him have it. We've coexisted peacefully for years because there was a mutual understanding."

"And now, he's coming after Lo over a piece of shit like McKenzie," Caz shakes his head, lighting a cigarette.

I jump up, grabbing it and stomping it out with my foot. "You're smoking way too much. You're going cold turkey."

"Now, princess. You—"

I shut him up with a dark look. "You might not care about your lungs, but I do, and we're not done discussing this." He pins me with a moody pout, but underneath it, I think he secretly likes that I care. "So, when the new leadership realizes you're taking control of their territory, you'll do a deal to stop them from retaliating in exchange for the return of their turf, and the threat goes away," I surmise.

Saint tweaks my nose. "Top marks, princess."

I swat his hand away. "That's a good plan. When do we execute?"

"Hopefully, next week. We want our ducks in a row first. Ensure we've covered all bases," Saint says.

"Of course. That's smart." I tap my fingers off my chin.

"What?" Saint asks.

"There's something we're missing." My gaze dances between him and Theo. "What if Sinner isn't the only one to realize women can play a role?"

"You think Taylor is involved officially?" Theo asks.

"She's got to be. She relayed the info to Corr, and that must have come from within the ranks. And if she was sniffing around The Arrows back in April, maybe, there was a reason for that too."

"I think you're right," Saint says, looking at Theo. "Which is why we need that intel on Taylor ASAP."

"You'll have it," Theo assures him.

"Your deal with Darrow," Saint adds, gripping my chin. "Is there anything more to it?"

I shake my head. "I sold him on having a spy in the ranks to save my ass"—I purposely stare at Galen, and he averts his eyes—"and because it makes sense to feed him some intel. We can use this to our advantage. Get The Arrows to fuck with Sinner and distract him."

"And the rat can take all the blame," Theo adds.

"Exactly." I bob my head.

"There is something else."

I've debated this too, but I've got to put my trust in them. Galen is still on my shit list, but I believe the others are on my side. That they won't hurt me, and I've got to include them. I remove my locket from under my shirt. "This is a tracking device and an audio recording device. I got the whole conversation with the board on tape."

Saint narrows his eyes at me, and I poke him in the ribs. "Do *not* give me that look."

"That asshole gave you it, didn't he?"

I nod. "Yes, and before you rip me a new one, I didn't tell you because you would've destroyed it and I knew it would come in handy."

"Who has that recording, Lo?" Theo asks, and his troubled expression alarms me.

"It saves to the chip, and a copy uploads to the cloud. Diesel has access."

"Fuck!" Theo jumps up, pacing.

Saint sits up straighter, exchanging a look with Galen. "What don't we know?"

Theo stares at me, and I realize he'd intended on speaking to me alone, but events have overtaken things. I'm momentarily speechless, because I can't believe he would keep something from the guys, putting me above them. I don't know what to make of it, and I'm not about to decipher it now. "You know who he is." It's the only explanation for his reaction.

Theo nods.

I stand, walking to him. I place my hand on his arm. "Tell me."

"I had my suspicions when I saw the bullet from your gun. He gave that to you, right?"

I nod, and it's admitting I lied because I told them I got it from my dad's study after he died.

"The bullet had distinguishing markings on it, and I knew I'd come across that image on the darknet before. I've been trawling through shit trying to relocate it, and I finally did."

Tension is so thick the air is borderline claustrophobic.

"Who do the bullets belong to?" I ask.

"A mercenary group who operates on the fringes of society, hiding in the shadows. They're called VERO. For years, stories of their existence were like an urban legend because they left no trace. Until a couple years back and some bullet casings, like the one you had, were discovered at the scene of this massive explosion in Germany. Since then, I've read shit on the darknet. I'm not sure exactly what is truth and what is fiction, but it's said they are a global operation, composed of ex-CIA, ex-FBI, and ex-Homeland Security. Highly skilled individuals who lacked the discipline to remain in the employment of the US government."

"Who do they work for? Who owns it?" Saint asks.

"This is where it gets scary," he admits, and chills creep up my spine. "If the intel I've gathered is correct, they hide behind a shell corporation, so it looks like a legit multimillion-dollar global private security firm. But it's just a front. This organization carries out deadly and dangerous missions, the type no one wants anyone to know about. We are talking major shit here. And if it got out, it would be a global scandal. Enough to cause mass hysteria and mass damage."

"Who is behind it, Theo?" Saint barks, his patience finally snapping.

"The government," Theo admits, pinning his eyes on me. "Diesel is working for the US government's biggest secret."

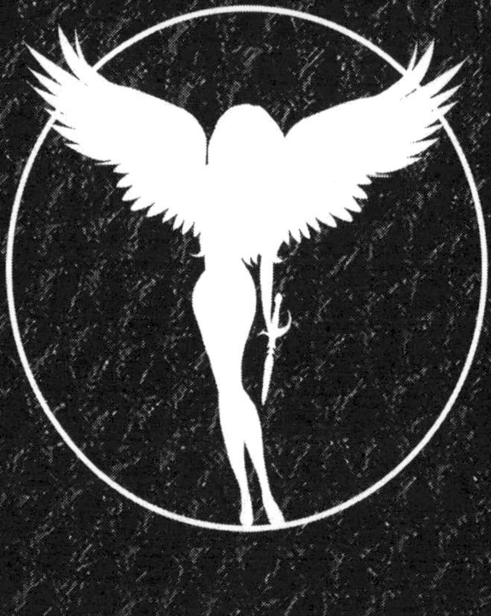

CHAPTER 17

I SIT IN stunned silence, unable to form a single coherent thought. I mean, it's not like I haven't considered the possibility Diesel was CIA or Homeland Security, but I always dismissed it because why on Earth would he get involved with me? And this revelation is so much bigger than that. *A secret government mercenary group up to shady shit?* I believe our government can establish such an operation, but the connection to me is what I can't wrap my head around. "It makes no sense," I blurt, my eyes fixing on Theo. "Why would Diesel train me if he's a part of such a dangerous, secret government organization?"

"That's what I'd like to know," Saint says.

"We should haul his ass in and demand answers," Galen supplies.

"No fucking way." Caz folds his arms around his chest. "We start asking questions about that kind of shit, and we all end up dead or imprisoned and tortured."

"Caz makes a valid point." Saint scrubs a hand back and forth across the top of his head. "We need to think this through." He glances at me. "He can't know we know."

I nod, still in a bit of a daze. "He may come to us first, anyway. If he listens to that recording."

"Then, we play dumb and say nothing about this." There is no mistaking the gravity of the situation. While I don't think Diesel would hurt me, he has no loyalty to the guys. It would be crazy stupid to ignore the threat, because who knows what his boss would do should he discover we know the truth?

"How did my dad cross paths with Diesel?" I murmur. My head jerks up as an idea lodges in my brain. My eyes meet Theo's. "Do you think my dad was working with them?" *Is that why there are coded files hidden in the floor in his office at the cabin?*

Saint rises, coming around the couch to walk to where Theo and I are standing. "We've got to assume it's a possibility."

"Then, there's something you need to know." We sit back down, and I tell them about the files.

"Where are they?" Theo asks. "I'd like to go through them. Maybe we could figure it out together?"

This is the shady part, because while I want to trust them fully, the cabin is my safe haven, and I'm reluctant to reveal it. It's my last closely guarded secret. The special place that holds so many precious memories of weekends with Dad. I'm not ready to share it yet.

"They are hidden for safekeeping," I admit. "But I'll retrieve them soon and bring them to your place in the forest. Then, maybe, we can crack the code together."

***

I'M GETTING CHANGED in my bedroom when there's a knock on my door. I left the guys downstairs, reeling from my revelation about the secret files, because my head is about to explode, and I've reached my limit today. Besides, I want to visit my bestie, and there is only a short window of opportunity as the hospital visiting hours end soon.

I push my feet into my sneakers and swing the door open. Galen stands there, propped against the doorway, looking anxious. "I'll give you a ride to the hospital."

"I'm driving myself." I swipe the keys to my Lexus off the bedside table and grab my jacket from the end of the bed.

"Until we deal with The Bulls, we feel it's best if one of us goes with you everywhere."

I whirl around, ready to lay into him, when Saint materializes behind his cousin. "Don't fight us on this." Air whooshes out of his mouth as he rubs a spot between his brows. "We know how fucking badass you are, but you can't have eyes and ears everywhere. You want to visit your friend and not look over your shoulder."

"Can't you ride with me?"

Galen's head drops, and I feel like a bit of a bitch. Which is ridic, because he's the one who tried to have me murdered. But it's getting harder and harder to hold on to that anger and resentment.

"No." Saint pushes between me and his cousin. "You two need to sort your shit."

I open my mouth to snap at him that attempted murder is not some *shit*, but he stops me with a hard kiss. When he pulls back, he weaves his hands through my hair. "He fucked up. He knows it, and he's genuinely sorry for his actions. Now, more than ever, we need unity. I won't ask you to forgive him, because I can't ask that of you, but I am asking if you could find a way of putting it behind you and work with Galen so it doesn't get in the way of what we need to do."

"Okay." He arches a brow, and I know he was expecting an argument. "I can't disagree with your logic, and my head is cluttered with all this stuff." I glance at Galen. "I know this has to happen, so I'll try, but I'm not making any promises."

"I can drive," Galen says a few minutes later when we land in the garage.

"You're injured," I say, opening the driver's side door. "You keep lookout."

I buckle my seat belt as he climbs into the passenger seat, hissing under his breath, his face contorting into a painful grimace. When he is finally settled, I pull out of the garage and along our driveway. "You still taking your meds and icing those ribs?" I inquire.

"Yeah. And I've seen a doc. Just have to wait for them to heal."

An awkward silence fills the space between us, and maybe, I should attempt to smooth things over, but I'm too exhausted to go there tonight. So, I hook my iPhone to the stereo system and pull up one of my more mellow playlists, cranking up the volume as music pours into the car.

The roads are quiet, and we make it to the hospital in good time.

We walk silently side by side to Sariah's room, and when we reach it, I rap gently on the door before poking my head inside.

Sean, Sar's boyfriend, and Emmett, his fellow football player and friend, are alone with my bestie, sitting on either side of her cot.

Emmett hops up, walking toward me and pulling me into a bear hug. I've missed my friends. Missed normal days at school, hanging out in the cafeteria at lunchtime, just shooting the shit. "Thank fuck, you're okay." He keeps me in his arms as he shoots daggers at Galen over my head.

"Why wouldn't I be? It was only the flu." I shuck out of his hold, offering him a lopsided smile. Saint had texted me on Tuesday to say they'd spread the word at school that I had the flu and was sick in bed with no visitors permitted on the doctor's orders.

"You were brief in your text messages, and that worried me." Emmett continues glaring at Galen, so I loop my arm through his, dragging him over to the bed. "Plus, that asshole said jack shit every day when he turned up." He jerks his head at Galen again, and I'm grateful he is in groveling mode, because otherwise, he'd most likely beat Emmett to a pulp for throwing shade.

"I slept most of the time, and I stayed away until the doc gave me the all clear because I didn't want to risk passing anything to Sar." I hate lying to my friends, but I must keep them out of this. "How has she been?" I bend down and kiss Sean on the cheek.

"The same." His voice is monotone and bereft of hope.

"What are the doctors saying?"

"Every day that she doesn't wake up lessens the possibility she will."

Emmett pulls the chair around the bed, placing it beside Sean, and I sit down. "That sucks, but I refuse to believe it. Sar is a fighter, and she won't give up. I bet she's listening to all of us, having a little chuckle at our expense, because she's healing herself, and she'll wake up when the time is right." I'm not sure I believe that, but after today, I need to cling to something positive, to believe there is hope and that good triumphs over evil sometimes.

"I want to believe that so bad," Sean says, taking my free hand and squeezing it. His other hand is placed over Sariah's hand on the bed. "But it's hard to hold on to hope day in, day out when there is no change."

"You've got to try, Sean, because Sar needs all of us to be strong for her."

He nods, turning to face me with a sad smile. "I'm glad you're here. We missed you."

"I'll be here as often as I can, but there's a lot of shit going on right now."

"Like what?" Emmett asks, folding his arms and staring at me.

"How's your sister?" I purposely ask because it seems he needs a reminder.

A muscle ticks in his jaw. "She's good," he says, following my lead. "Still asking when you're dropping by."

"I'll come by soon. I promise."

He nods. "That would really cheer her up."

"What happened with the school investigations?" I hadn't thought to ask the guys before now.

"No one will say a word, and the only witness is still missing," Sean says. I make a mental note to ask the guys where that freshman girl is and what they plan to do with her. I know they had sent her away so we could deal with the situation ourselves, but events have overtaken us, and I think it might be best now to let the authorities handle it.

Emmett eyeballs Galen. "As are Parker, Finn, and Brooklyn,

but I suspect you guys already know that."

It's obvious he's suspicious—and with good reason. "I wasn't aware they were MIA." I cast a glance at Galen over my shoulder, and his eyes warn me to say nothing. I'm not sure how much of a threat Finn represents now he's lost control to the Saints at school. His little rebellion at the warehouse backfired, so I presume he's running scared with Brooklyn. Or maybe, they've officially and permanently joined forces with The Bulls. I make a mental note to ask Saint.

"Beth is shitting her pants," Emmett says, but there's no humor in his tone. "We gave statements to the school and the police saying it was Beth, Parker, and some of their cronies, but we weren't there at the time of the attack, so our word doesn't mean much."

"I think the cops believe us," Sean adds. "But with no evidence or any witnesses, they can't do much."

"They're not getting away with this." I peer straight into Sean's eyes. "I promise you that. Just hold tight, and they will get what's coming to them."

I get twenty minutes with Sar before the nurse comes to confirm visiting hours are over. Sar's grandma arrives to stay the night, and we leave with Emmett and Sean.

When we reach outside, they head off in Sean's car, and we walk to mine. I open the passenger side door and Galen frowns. "You want me to drive?"

I shake my head. "I'll drive. Get in." I place my arms around his toned waist from behind, and he looks down at me, his gorgeous green eyes staring at me in confusion. He hasn't been styling his faux hawk lately, I've noticed, and though the sides are still shorn tight, the brown hair on top of his head is in a messy heap of tangled waves. It's every bit as sexy as the faux hawk, and I hate how much I'm attracted to him.

Guess that's another side to my perverse personality—feeling desire for the person who would sooner kill me than fuck me.

I help him into the car, and then, we drive home in silence.

When we get back to the house, Galen disappears into his

room while I go in search of the guys. Mom and the psycho are still out, thank fuck.

Saint is alone in the basement when I find him, shirtless, his back glistening with sweat as he punches the shit out of the punching bag hanging from the ceiling. I walk toward him, admiring his muscular form, as he keeps thrusting, his fists pounding the bag powerfully. I step around, holding the bag and urging him to continue.

"How's Sariah?" he pants, bouncing from foot to foot, as he jabs the bag.

"No change. That's what I want to talk to you about."

Beads of sweat dot his brow, and he swipes his arm along his forehead. "Talk."

"Are you still hiding that witness?" He nods, and my eyes zoom in on the muscles bulging in his arms as he hits the bag and the way his abs ripple and flex with the motion. The only clothes he's wearing are training shorts, and I'm having a hard time concentrating.

Saint is so freaking hot, and my attraction to him is only growing stronger.

He smirks as he watches me checking him out, and I shrug. He ogles me too, so he's not one to talk. "You need to bring her back," I say. "We don't have time to dig up dirt on Beth or the others, but I want them to pay for what they've done to my bestie. Let the witness give a statement, and then, the police can do their job."

"They might make looking for Parker a priority," he admits, stopping and dropping to his knees to grab the bottle of water at his feet.

"I've had a thought about that."

"I'm listening." He lifts the bottle to his lips, drinking greedily, and the way his throat works as he swallows is so sexy.

Fuck. I've got it bad.

I clear my throat and shake my head. "I know the guys buried her remains, but now, we know she had ties to The Bulls, would it not make more sense to pin her murder on them?"

I can almost see the wheels churning in his head. "We could dig her up and bury her in their backyard and then get a tip sent to the cops."

I nod. "There's no evidence linking me to her, so I think it'd be nice to set the cops crawling all over The Bulls. They'll be forced to lie low, and it buys us some time to plan our takedown."

"Your sharp mind gets my dick hard every bit as much as your hot body," he admits, smirking as he cups his crotch.

"Should I be flattered?"

"Come here." He holds out his hand, and I take it, letting him pull me into his sweat-soaked body. "Shower with me?"

"To get clean or dirty?" I tease, grabbing his ass cheeks and pulling his hard-on flush against my crotch.

"Both, princess," he says, licking a line up the side of my neck. "It's always both."

THE SAINTHOOD

CHAPTER 18

"Honey, it's so good you're home," Mom says the following morning as I'm standing in the kitchen at the window, looking out over the back lawn. Her heels click across the tile floor as she heads for the coffeepot.

I turn around, clasping my hands around the mug I'm holding. "I waited up for you last night."

Her spine stiffens. "We were out late." She busies herself making coffee.

I walk toward her, pressing my hip into the counter and facing her. "Are you okay?"

"I'm fine," she says, finally glancing at me, and I bite down hard on the inside of my cheek.

Gently, I turn her face toward me. She's wearing a ton of makeup, but it's still not enough to disguise the swelling on her left cheek, and there's no disguising the cut on her lip.

She pulls her face out of my grip. "Don't, honey."

"Why are you with him, Mom?"

"I love him." She's quick to reply as she removes bread from the breadbox.

"I'm not buying it."

She pops the bread in the toaster, still averting her gaze. "I know that, and I hope in time you'll warm to him."

I harrumph. "That will never happen. He's a monster."

I'd love to tell her what he expects of me. That he's salivating at the prospect of fucking me with his perverted buddies. But I won't expose her to those truths because it's not safe for her to know.

Doesn't mean I can't drop a few clues.

I shudder on purpose. "And I hate how he looks at me sometimes and how he's finding more and more opportunities to touch me."

Her face pales before she catches herself. "I'm sure you're imagining it. He's just trying to get closer to you, stepfather to stepdaughter."

I can't tell if she's trying to convince herself or me. "Yeah, I'm sure that's it." Sarcasm drips from my tone. "Not that he's a sick bastard with grabby hands and perverted ideas."

She rubs at her temples. "Harlow, you can't talk about him like that." She grabs my hands, her eyes pleading with me. "But if he makes you feel uncomfortable, perhaps, it's best you keep your distance and do nothing to upset him."

Her changing thoughts are giving me whiplash. "How about you give that pep talk to him, huh?"

Air whooshes out of her mouth, and she lets go of my hands, rubbing her temples again. "Can you please try? For my sake?"

"Why should I, Mom?" I top up my coffee as acid churns in my gut.

"Because you don't have much longer left in this house, and it'll be a much more pleasant experience for everyone if you act civil toward him."

I shake my head. Un-fucking-believable. He's using her as his punching bag, and she's trying to smooth things over so I don't upset him. She's so weak it makes me sick. "What happened to you? Or are you so blind you can't see what he's doing to you?"

Her shoulders straighten, and the softness in her features

evaporates. "My relationship is none of your business, Harlow. And all I ask is that you don't argue with him. Is that really too much for a mother to ask of her daughter?"

"Do you even know where I was this week?" I challenge, losing control of the tenuous hold on my emotions. "Or do you just not care?"

"Of course, I care." She reaches her hand out to touch me, and I take a step back. Her arm drops to her side as her face showcases resignation. "I know you were training and that you're an initiate. My fiancé doesn't keep secrets from me."

"And you're okay with that?"

"Learning how to defend yourself is not a bad thing, and it's an honor to be the first female member of The Sainthood."

I stare at her, wondering who the woman standing in front of me is. *Does she not hear herself? Have I wandered onto the set of some movie or show? How is she okay with this?* "You disgust me." I empty the rest of my coffee down the sink as Caz appears in the doorway.

"Hey, princess. You ready?"

"Yep." I throw a scathing look at my mother as Caz walks away, and I move to go after him.

"Harlow."

I stop and look at her over my shoulder.

"I was wrong about those boys. Stay close to them, both inside and outside of the house. They care about you."

"How about you butt out of my relationship, and I'll butt out of yours?"

"That sounds like a plan," she agrees, and I shake my head in disgust, walking out without another word.

SAINT PULLS INTO the parking lot right in front of the school, killing the engine. When I refused to get in his Land Rover, citing safety reasons and my desire to abide by my late father's wishes, I expected him to argue his point. But he surprised me, grabbing the keys to my Lexus and jumping in the driver's seat. "Theo and Caz will keep you company today," he says, grabbing the back of my head and pulling me in for a kiss.

"You're not coming?" I ask when he releases my mouth.

"Galen and I have stuff to attend to."

I remember our discussion last night and nod. "Okay. Be careful." I peck his lips before exiting the car the same time he does. Saint locks the car using the fob and then tosses the keys to me. Caz and Theo are already at the top of the steps, having arrived first, and Galen is waiting on the sidewalk in front of Saint's Land Rover, dangling the keys from the tips of his fingers.

I walk toward him as Saint steps onto the sidewalk behind me. Galen and I stare at one another, and there is so much unspoken between us.

"Be safe," he says.

I nod and walk away, joining the guys at the entrance doors and making my way inside.

Morning classes are boring in their normality, but there's something so refreshing about it.

When the bell chimes after the last class before lunch, I gather up my stuff and head out into the corridor. Caz and Theo are waiting against the lockers for me, and I walk toward them. "Hey, babe." Caz plants his lips on mine, kissing me in a way that screams possession. Imaginary daggers embed in my back from the various female bystanders.

"We're going out for lunch," Theo says. "Let's go."

Caz links his fingers in mine as we walk beside Theo, in the direction of the exit. "We're doing this, huh?" I ask, raising our conjoined hands, a smile teasing my lips.

Caz smirks, pulling our hands to his mouth, kissing my knuckles. "Everyone knows you are ours. This isn't a shock."

"You guys haven't done this before though, right?"

Caz squeezes my shoulder. "You're the first and the last." He lets go for a second, only to bring his hands to my hips, steering me out the door while Theo holds it open. Caz brushes his plump lips against my neck, and his warm breath raises goose bumps along my flesh. "Because we're keeping you." Caz removes my car keys from my pocket, throwing them at Theo. "You drive. I want to feel our princess up in the back seat."

I roll my eyes, but I don't protest as Caz leads me to the Lexus, helping me inside.

Theo hasn't even started up the engine when Caz pounces on me, pushing me down on the back seat and covering me with his large body. I sink into the seat, melting under the warmth of his toned torso and the feel of his lips grazing mine.

We make out like demons to the heavy metal backdrop Theo has playing in the car. Every so often, my gaze finds Theo's, and guilt slaps me in the face. We could always read one another like a book, and his hurt and pain slices me open, digging into flesh and bone, and I feel his agony as if it is my own.

Every time I catch him watching us through the mirror, I look away, because I don't want to confront the messy truth, and I'd rather drown in guilt.

Caz is a welcome distraction, and I cling to his easy loving, blocking everything else out. His lips explore mine with skilled finesse, his tongue diving into my mouth for a taste, and his wandering hands fuel the burn zinging through my body.

A few minutes later, we're at the grungy diner downtown, and I force my libido back in its box, urging my overheated lady parts to cool down. Theo removes two guns from a plastic bag one of them must have secretly stowed under the passenger seat, handing one to Caz. "You got any spares?" I ask, regretting not removing my Glock from my bedroom before we left for school this morning.

"No. I thought you had a gun?" Theo says, tucking the weapon in the back of his jeans.

"I do, but I left it at home."

"Probably best to have a second one in your car," Caz suggests.

"We'll organize that for you," Theo adds, climbing out, and I nod.

Caz helps me out of the car, and I straighten up, pulling my top down and smoothing my hair back off my face. Caz links our fingers as Theo shoves his hands in the pockets of his jeans while looking at the ground.

A sharp pang slices across my chest as his shoulders slump, and his long blond locks curtain his face. He's hurting, and I can't ignore it anymore. Especially when I just made it worse.

When we were together, one of my favorite things to do was run my fingers through Theo's hair. His head was usually in my lap, his eyes closed and his features soft as he quietly purred while I threaded my hands in his hair. The urge to wind my fingers through his hair is riding me hard, and I grip Caz's hand more firmly to stop myself from reaching for Theo.

Things with Theo were always complicated yet simple. Difficult yet as easy as breathing. Our relationship now is no less complex, but I know I need to fix things with him. It's no different from Galen in that regard. I can't cause a divide in the group with me, Caz, and Saint on one side and Galen and Theo being frozen out on the other side. But even if I do patch things up with them, I still don't see how it ends up working out. There are too many barriers to unity, especially with Theo.

I remove my hand from Caz's. "Hey, could you give us a minute?" I gesture toward Theo.

"Sure." He kisses my lips. "I'll grab us a table."

Theo lifts his head, his eyes finding mine, and I hate the anguish I discover there, because I know I'm partly responsible for it. I step toward him. "Hey." I peer into his beautiful hazel eyes. Green is most prominent today, but his pupils are ringed in a layer of brown and amber, and I could stare at his handsome face all day. Tentatively, I reach out, cupping one side of his face. "You doing okay?"

He shrugs, looking away, and I tilt his face around with my fingers. "Don't do that. Please."

"It hurts so much to look at you sometimes," he admits, his voice cracking a bit.

"I know." I press my forehead to his, and my heart beats wildly out of control. "I'm sorry if I hurt you with Caz in the car."

"It's not that," he says. "I just miss you, Lo. Miss the way we were." His hands land on my hips.

"I miss you so fucking much," I whisper. Tears sting my eyes, and I'm horrified. I pull back, because I can't break down here. "Can we go to the park tonight? Just you and me. Like old times?"

His eyes turn glassy, and a soft smile graces his lips. "I would like that. We are long overdue a talk."

I nod. "You hurt me, Theo, and I'm not sure I'm ready yet, but I want to try."

"I want to try too, because I want to fix things with us."

"Do you think we can?"

He shrugs. "I don't know. I think I'm even more confused than I was back then."

"Because of me or someone else?" I gently inquire.

His eyes pop wide. "Is it—"

I shake my head. "I don't think it's obvious."

The door opens, and Caz pops his head out. "You guys coming or what?"

"Always so impatient." Theo punches him in the arm, but he's smiling. "We're coming." He reaches back, and I take his hand, letting him lead me inside.

"So, why are we eating here and not in the cafeteria?" I ask once we are seated in a booth at the back and we've placed our orders.

Theo takes out his cell. "I've uncovered some background on Taylor Tamlin, and I wanted to update everyone without prying ears. Let me call the guys." He dials Galen and Saint in, and I sip my soda as I wait for him to begin.

"Taylor is a senior at Fenton High, and her old man is a member of The Bulls. He is also Parker's father. Seems her old man split on Parker's mom when she was a baby because he got Taylor's mom pregnant around the same time."

"What a stellar human being," I drawl, leaning back into Caz's side.

"He ended up marrying Taylor's mom, and they have two more kids. He had no contact with Parker until two years ago when he reached out and welcomed her into his new family with open arms."

"Parker didn't strike me as the forgiving type." I place my hand on Caz's thigh.

"I second that assessment," Saint says through the phone.

"I don't know how he swung it," Theo continues. "But she was a regular visitor to his home, and her and Taylor started hanging out together. Found a bunch of photos of them from various parties."

"Maybe, her old man helped her fund the drug supply at Lowell High, aiding Finn in ascending the throne," Caz suggests.

"That might be it," Saint agrees.

"Whatever the carrot was, at least, we know that's the connection between The Bulls and Finn's crew. But where's the link with The Arrows?" I ask. "Why was she invited to the party, and who invited her?"

"I think I've found that connection too," Theo says, just as the waitress appears with our food. We stop talking while she sets plates in front of us, only resuming the conversation after she's gone. "Taylor has a cousin who has an in with The Arrows. Most likely, she invited her there and, I assume, forged a connection."

"You have a name?"

"Tempest Higgins."

I pause with my fork halfway to my mouth. "You've got to be kidding me."

"She's Knight's girlfriend, right?" Saint says.

"Yep. She was the one he cheated on me with."

Theo shakes his head. "Dude's an idiot. You outshine that ho a million to one."

I beam at my ex, reaching under the table to squeeze his knee.

Perhaps, things *are* fixable, because every time he says something like this, I'm reminded he's a decent guy and I remember how good things were between us.

Caz presses a kiss to my temple. "Dar's fuckup was our gain."

"I can't believe Tempest was the conduit. Honestly, she has, like, three brain cells, and they're all in her vagina," I say.

Caz chuckles, running his hand up and down my arm as he

pops a fry in his mouth with his free hand.

"I think it's fair to say her cousin Taylor has far more intelligence. Most likely, she used Tempest to get her an introduction, and she ran with it from there," Theo surmises.

"Eccleston has to know more," Galen says. "He's Knight's number two. How was this going down without him being aware?"

"He lied to us," Saint says.

"Not necessarily," I say, and I'm not defending Bry per se. "The only loyalty Darrow has is to himself, and he keeps Bry on a pretty tight leash. Bry is the brute strength in the crew while Dar likes to handle the decision making on his own. They're not solid like you guys. The relationships are surface level, and everyone has their set roles, knowing not to overstep the mark. It's possible Tempest was using The Bulls connection to entice Dar into her bed, and if Taylor wanted it kept on the down low, then, it's not hard to believe Dar kept Bry out of the loop."

"What do The Bulls want with The Arrows and vice versa?" Saint says.

"I'd have thought that's obvious." I cut up my chicken. "They have a mutual enemy. Perhaps, they decided it was time to form an alliance and work to take The Sainthood down once and for all."

"Why did—"

The window on our right shatters explosively, raining glass on top of us. A bullet whizzes by my head, and Caz roars, grabbing me onto the floor with him. Shards of broken glass dig into my knees through my jeans and cut the skin on my hands, but I barely feel any pain. Adrenaline courses through my veins as I watch Theo and Caz remove their guns. A chorus of screams rings out in the diner as more bullets zing through the air, over our heads, embedding in the walls and the row of glass jars sitting on shelves behind the counter. The sound of breaking glass crashing to the floor mingles with the terrified cries of frightened customers and staff. "Stay down," I shout, lest any idiot decides to be a hero.

Theo and Caz exchange a look across the underside of our

table, nodding in silent agreement, before they hop up, firing back through the open window. They duck back down, as more bullets fly in our direction, and a pattern forms as both sides shoot at one another.

Sirens blare in the distance, and the guys jump up again. "They're getting away!" Caz shouts, grabbing my hand and hauling me to my feet. Theo throws a few hundred-dollar bills down on the table and snatches the keys and his cell, pressing it to his ear as he races toward the door.

"We were never here," Caz says to the waitress, drilling her with a deadly look I've never seen on his face before.

"They got away," Theo says, fuming, when we emerge outside. "Fuck!"

"Was it The Bulls?" I ask, because it's the obvious conclusion.

"They wore plain black hoodies with scarves pulled halfway up their faces, so it's hard to tell," Caz says. "But my money's on them."

"Theo!" Saint's gnarly tone emits from the cell in Theo's hand. Theo tosses the keys to Caz, and we get in the car.

Caz is concentrating on getting us out of there, and Theo is busy trying to calm Saint down on the phone, so neither of them is paying attention to the black SUV parked across the road with the tinted windows or the tall, dark-haired man who gets out, holding a long-lens camera in one hand, deliberately eye-checking me as we drive past.

I don't believe I've ever seen him before, but all the tiny hairs on my arms stand to attention, and blood rushes to my head as an ominous sense of foreboding washes over me. I turn around, locking eyes with him, as he watches us hightail it away from the scene of the crime, with a growing sense of trepidation.

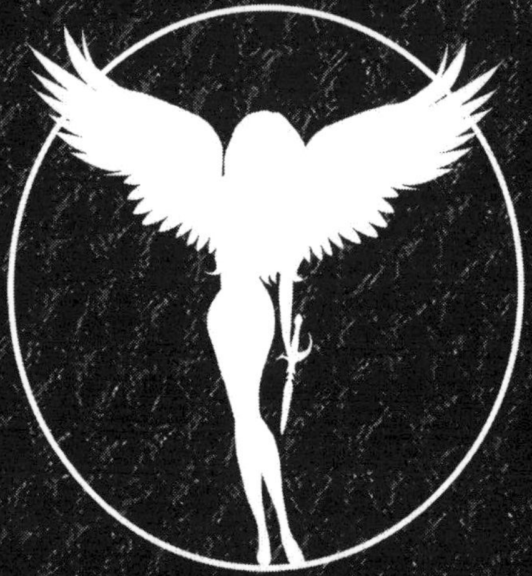

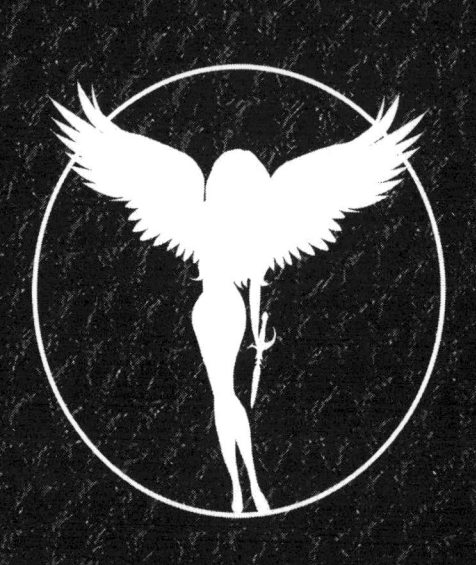

THE SAINTHOOD

CHAPTER 19

WE DON'T RETURN to school, heading for the guys' warehouse in Prestwick Forest to wait for Galen and Saint to arrive. They have picked up the freshman Parker paid to keep watch in the hallway while they assaulted Sariah, and they are dropping her off at home before swinging by here.

"The guy was shady as fuck. He had a camera, and I got the sense he wanted me to see him. To know he was watching us and that he caught what went down," I finish explaining to Theo and Caz.

"What the actual fuck is going on?" Caz asks, removing a pack of cigarettes. I whip them out of his hand, crushing them with my fingers. He scowls. "That wasn't nice, princess. I'm fucking stressed, and I need to let off steam."

"You don't get stressed," I say, as Theo powers up his tablet, taking a seat at the long table.

"I do when someone takes potshots at my girl."

I walk to him, wrapping my arms around his neck, just as Saint and Galen storm into the place. Saint exudes tension in spades, and Galen is feeding off his concern. Theo is freaking out over the guy I spotted, and Caz, my laid-back gruff yet gentle giant is stressed.

I need to lighten the atmosphere.

"Want me to vacuum your pork sword to relieve some stress?" I tease, fighting a grin.

Caz's eyes light up like it's Christmas morning. "Only if you let me flood the basement, babe," he adds, and I lose the battle, cracking up laughing. Caz joins in while the others stare at us in disbelief.

"How can you fucking joke at a time like this?" Saint seethes.

I sigh, my laughter dying off, removing my arms from Caz and walking to Saint. "Because everyone is so damn tense." I run my fingers along his taut jawline to prove my point.

"Some assholes just tried to take you out!" Saint yells. "And I want to fucking gut the bastards from head to toe."

I slam my lips on his, forcing my tongue into his mouth and grabbing his tight body against mine, until I feel him relaxing against me. With every sweep of my lips, his tension dials down a notch, and I feel the atmosphere lightening. I break our kiss, resting my hands on his shoulders. "Better now, Saintly?"

"Dat is true talent," Caz says, chuckling.

"Please tell me you got something on camera," Galen says, dropping into the seat across from Theo.

"I'm hacking into the street cam across from the diner now," Theo confirms, and I wander off to make some drinks and snacks while he works.

"Hey." Saint comes up behind me, pressing the length of his body against mine. "Are you okay?"

"I'm fine," I truthfully admit as I dump a large bag of chips into a bowl.

"You're bleeding." He lifts one of my hands to inspect it.

I swivel around so I'm looking at him. "It's nothing. Surface scratches."

"Let me see." Galen approaches with a first aid kit in hand.

Saint lifts me up by the hips, placing me on the counter. His eyes lower to my ripped, torn jeans and the dried blood sticking to my skin. "You're fucking injured. Take them off," he growls.

I know not to pick a battle with him when he's like this, so I slide off the counter and shimmy out of my jeans. I pull myself back up on the counter, only wearing my sweater and lace panties. Both guys pretend not to notice my state of undress, but a charge of electricity ignites the surrounding space.

The damage to my legs is worse than it felt, although the various cuts all appear shallow, and I doubt I need any stitches.

Saint mutters under his breath as he makes sandwiches, and I avoid eye contact with Galen as he cleans the wounds on my hands first, applying a few Band-Aids. I grip the edge of the counter when he raises one of my legs, placing my foot flat against his chest as he examines the wounds on my leg. His fingers are cool against my skin as he gently probes the damaged area around my knee and on my shin.

He has singular focus, cleaning the cuts with rubbing alcohol and applying cream to the smaller cuts and Band-Aids to the larger ones. His touch is tender, his concern obvious, and it's doing funny things to my insides. Saint watches us as he cuts sandwiches in half, placing them on a large plate. I tilt my head up and look at the ceiling, anything to avoid looking at either guy.

Electricity crackles in the air again, and my mind wanders to the gutter.

Images flit across my mind's eye, of dual touches and caresses as they both worship my body, and I squirm on the counter while my core throbs with need. I wonder what it would be like to be ravaged by the Lennox cousins at the same time, and I thank my lucky stars that neither of them is mind readers, because there's no way I want them privy to my present fantasy.

Yet, when I look at Saint, he has a knowing expression on his face, and I hate how keen his observational skills are.

"What?" I snap.

He walks toward me and brushes my hair to one side as Galen lowers one leg and raises the other one. Saint presses his lips to that sensitive spot just under my ear. "What were you thinking about just now?" he rasps, his warm breath fanning over my sensitive skin.

"Nothing." A shiver overtakes me, and I close my eyes as his lips trail up and down my neck.

"Liar," he whispers. "Were you imagining both of us with our hands on you?" He nips at my earlobe. "Both of us fucking you at the same time?"

Screw him and his ability to delve into my head. There's little point denying it now. "What if I was?"

"That can be arranged." He slides his hand under my sweater, running his fingers up my tummy and over my rib cage.

"You've forgotten one very important thing," I pant.

Galen is pretending not to listen, diligently attending to the cuts on my leg, but from the rigid way he's holding his shoulders, I know he's hearing every word.

"You two should fuck your way to forgiveness," Saint says. "It's the perfect solution."

I slap his hand away as his fingers brush the side of my breast. "Sex is not the solution to everything."

"Says who?" Saint smirks, and I cock my head to the side.

"I use sex for a whole heap of reasons," I admit, "but this is one occasion where sex is not enough. Fucking me is not going to magically make me forget how he tried to have me killed."

"Then, what will?" Galen asks, gently placing my leg back down and standing. "Because I'm at a loss here."

I jump down off the counter. "Me telling you how to fix it isn't the fucking solution, that's for sure. You're a smart guy, Galen. I'm sure you'll figure it out."

"I've got something," Theo calls out, and it's the perfect moment to break up the sudden heavy atmosphere.

We all crowd around him, watching the film roll across the screen on his tablet. We see the white van with missing plates pull up to the curb across from the diner, the two assholes jumping out and immediately opening fire. It's as the guys said: they are wearing indistinguishable clothing, and there is nothing that confirms their identity.

"That's him," I say, pointing at the guy with the camera a couple minutes later when he appears on the screen.

"Can you zoom in on the plates?" Saint asks.

"Not from this angle," Theo says.

"He doesn't look like crew," Galen says.

"He doesn't look like a cop either," Caz adds.

Saint and I share a look. "You thinking what I'm thinking?" I ask.

"Only one way to find out," he replies. "Message Diesel, and ask for a meet."

Diesel messages a short while later to say he's out of the country and he can't meet for a couple days. I have to reassure him I'm fine to stop him from sending a colleague to check up on me. This conversation needs to happen with Diesel and only Diesel. I tell him it can wait until he returns, and we make alternative plans.

The guys leave just before dark to stake out The Bulls' clubhouse. They already have Parker's charred remains wrapped up in the trunk of Saint's Land Rover, so it's a matter of watching and waiting for the right moment to plant them on the enemy.

Theo agrees to come along with me. I'm stopping by Ashley Shaw's house on the off chance I might catch her at home. She's head cheerleader at Lowell Academy, and her palatial home functions as party central for the crème de la crème of academy society most weekends, because her parents are absentee rents and rarely at home. We were never friends, but we weren't enemies either. So, I'm hoping she won't slam the door in my face when I rock up uninvited.

We make a quick stop at my house so I can ditch the sweats I borrowed from Theo, and I change into a new pair of ripped jeans, a lacy black tank, and a clean hoodie before we head out.

An hour later, Theo and I leave Ashley's home with an invitation to her party Friday night. Having Theo with me helped, and making the request on behalf of The Sainthood worked like a charm. I'm sure the guys won't have to do much to take over the supply chain at my former school.

"The guys won't be back for hours," Theo confirms. "You want to have that talk?"

I swivel in the passenger seat and look at him. "Yeah. I think we need to have it."

"The park is too risky with someone gunning for your ass. Are you okay to talk at our place?"

"That's cool."

We stop at a local store in Prestwick on our way to stock up on beer, chips, and some other supplies before heading to the barn. Thank fuck for fake ID and a bored cashier who ignored the obvious fact we're underage, because I really need alcohol for this conversation.

"How is it so warm in here?" I ask as we step inside and a blast of heat hits me in the face.

"We replaced the heating system with a remote-controlled system," Theo explains. "It's hooked up to all our cells. I switched the heating on when we were at the store. This place can get hella chilly with the high ceilings."

"You were always thoughtful," I admit, opening the door to nostalgia.

"Until I wasn't." His lips pinch tight.

Our eyes connect across the kitchen counter. "It almost killed me when you cut me out of your life," I admit.

"It almost killed me too."

I believe him. I see the honesty written all over his face. I just don't understand it.

"I want to get out of these clothes," he says, backing up toward the stairs.

"Take your time. I'll grab us some beers." It's past dinnertime, and we should probably eat, but I'm not hungry for food. Only answers.

I grab some cold beers from the refrigerator and slide the twelve-pack we just bought on a shelf to cool. Then, I pad into the sitting room, kick off my boots, and sit cross-legged on the couch, sipping from my beer as I wait for Theo.

He arrives downstairs a couple minutes later wearing gray

sweats and a long-sleeved white Henley that clings to his lean muscles. His feet are bare, his hair is hanging loose around his neck, and he has never looked more gorgeous to me.

But my attraction to Theo is more than skin deep.

I've always been equally attracted to his intelligent mind, his kind heart, and his spiritual soul.

When I lost him, it was akin to losing half of myself. I have never found another soul on this planet I connect to in the way I connect to Theo. We could sit and talk for hours, about everything and anything, and he understands me on a level no one else does. I used to think it was the same for him, but the way he cut me so efficiently from his life seemed to confirm that bond was more one-sided than I'd thought. And that hurt so fucking much.

Theo kneels in front of the fireplace, tossing some logs in before setting it alight. I watch him work, silently admiring the steadiness he brings just by his presence. He stands and walks toward me as flames lick the walls of the fireplace, casting faint shadows across the room.

Outside, nightfall is creeping across the skyline, adding to the overall surreal quality of the moment.

I never thought Theo and I would ever recover what we've lost, and now, we're on the cusp of a second chance.

Theo sits at the other end of the couch, adopting my pose, and the tips of our toes meet in the middle.

"Who goes first?" I ask, handing him a beer.

"Me." There is no hesitation in his voice. Our fingers brush when he takes the bottle from me, sending a rush of fiery tingles shooting up my arm. "I'm the one who fucked up, so I'm the one who needs to explain."

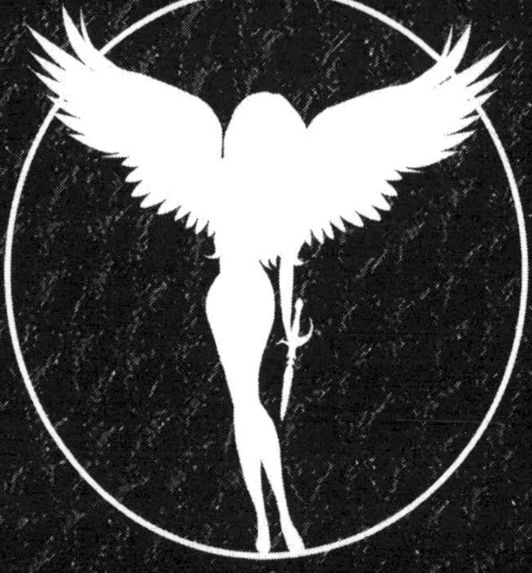

THE SAINTHOOD

CHAPTER 20

THEO

"To this day, I still don't know how my father found out your father was mixed up with The Sainthood," I say, pausing to taste my beer. "He went ballistic." I remember it as vividly as if it was yesterday. "You know how he likes to be in control and how everything is legit and aboveboard. When he discovered his lawyer was on The Sainthood's payroll, he damn near had a coronary." My father gives anal retentive new meaning.

"I didn't know why our parents had fallen out," Lo says, tossing her long dark hair over her shoulder. "And it only added to my confusion."

"I only discovered the truth because I eavesdropped on my parents arguing the night before that horrible Thanksgiving dinner," I admit. My parents had still gone ahead with the dinner, only because my father wanted to confront Trey Westbrook face to face. Naturally, the dinner was cut short after my father leveled his accusation at Lo's father. I had taken Lo to my room the minute they arrived, wanting to shield her from the argument I knew was about to go down.

"I wish you'd told me." She stares me straight in the eye.

thing I admire about Lo is her direct approach. She wasn't always like that. At least not, in the beginning, when she was broken and scared to trust anyone. But as we grew closer, she opened up to me the same way I opened up to her.

"I wasn't sure it was the full truth, and I didn't want to hurt you."

"But you ended up doing that anyway." She pulls her legs in to her chest, resting her chin on her knees. "Why did you break up with me, Theo? We still could've found a way to be together."

"At first, it was because my father put me under pressure to do it. He threatened to pull my college fund if I didn't cut all ties with you."

She snorts. "And I used to think it was your mother who didn't like me."

I rub my hand across my stomach. "Mom liked you well enough. She just wanted me to marry into old wealth. To find a sweet, wholesome girl from a well-established family."

She shakes her head. "It's so ridiculous. You were fourteen, fifteen, and she was already trying to map your whole life out."

Pain pierces me in the chest. "I know, but it's how she was brought up. Mom's family is one of the oldest in the state, and she grew up in this monstrous mansion being courted from a young age. The most ironic thing is, she eloped with my dad when she got pregnant with me."

"I never knew that," Lo says, swigging from her beer. "What a hypocrite."

"Her parents still berate her for the choices she made," I admit.

"Your father owns a multimillion-dollar medical supplies company, and he has provided adequately for his family. What the hell is wrong with these people?"

"It's nuts, and I gave up trying to understand it a long time ago. All I knew is, Mom was trying to make amends with her parents through me." I rip the corner off the label of my beer. "They would all freak the fuck out if they knew the truth."

She scoots forward on her knees, moving closer to me. "They still don't know?"

I shake my head. "I severed ties with my family the day I became a member of The Sainthood. Dad threw me out of the house."

"What?" Shock splays across her face. "You don't talk to them?"

"Nope. I meet Ria on the down low, but the twins are too young. I doubt they even remember me." My younger sisters are only six, and I've been estranged from my family for two and a half years. My sister Ria is the only one I speak to on the regular. She's fifteen, and we were close growing up.

"I'm so sorry. I had no idea." Lo tilts her head to the side, scrutinizing my face.

"He threatened to disown me, but I never thought he'd actually do it for joining the Saints." I rip another corner off the label. "Not that it really matters. We both know it was gonna happen sometime, anyway."

"Is that why you did it? It was an easier pill to swallow if he disowned you for being a member of the Saints?" Her knee brushes against my leg, and warmth invades my bones.

"I wanted to take back control. I was sick of my parents dictating what I could and couldn't do. After they forced me to break things off with you, I swore that was the last time they were interfering in my life. I'd met the guys at this point, but my parents weren't aware of our friendship. I already knew they wouldn't approve. Saint was eager for me to join his crew, but I'd been resisting. After our relationship ended, I felt lost." Taking a risk, I reach out, threading my fingers through hers, delighted when she doesn't resist, curling her fingers around mine tightly.

"Me too," she whispers. "I never knew the heart could hurt so much. I thought I'd protected myself, learned to block out my emotions, but the heartbreak I felt when you shut me out proved I was wrong. And I felt like such an idiot, because it wasn't even real. Trust me to catch feelings for the guy I was in a fake relationship with. A guy who would never, could never, reciprocate."

"You're wrong, Lo." I put my beer down and lift her on my lap.

"It might have started out fake, as a means to an end for both of us, but it was the most real thing I've ever known."

Placing her hands on my shoulders, she peers into my face, frowning. "What are you saying, Theo?"

"It was real, Lo. Everything we shared." I press my lips to her smooth cheek. "It was too late when I realized the truth. I had already cut you loose and ruined everything, and I believed you were better off without me, because there was a part of me that always felt wrong about it. That felt like I used you."

"I didn't do anything with you I didn't want to," she says, running her fingers through my hair. "I felt guilty," she adds in a soft whisper. "Because I fell in love with you and you'd made it very clear from the beginning you could never love me."

I circle my arms around her back. "Not you. Any girl," I say, needing to clarify. "And that's what I believed back then."

"But not anymore?" Her brow creases. "I don't understand."

"That makes two of us." I smooth a hand up and down her back, loving the feeling of her in my arms again. "I was confused over my sexuality when we first agreed to fake date to keep our parents off our backs, but that was nothing compared to how confused I was after I let you go."

"Are you saying you're into women now too?" she asks, repositioning herself on my lap so she's straddling me.

The sultry, spicy perfume she wears wraps around me like a comfort blanket, and my cock swells in my pants. "I'm saying I'm into *you*."

She blinks profusely. "How?"

I lift my hips, pressing my hard-on against her. "Feel that?" She nods. "That's what you do to me. No other woman has ever turned me on like you, and it took me letting you go to realize it."

"But you're still into guys."

There is no judgment in her statement. She has always accepted me as I am.

I was honest with her, pretty much from the start.

That first night we met, at my house, because Dad had just hired his lawyer's wife to work on a new advertising campaign, we got drunk on a stolen bottle of Mom's gin and ended up making out. I thought about her a lot over the next few weeks, and when we next met, and ended up kissing again, I blurted out that I was gay. She was cool about it, and the fake relationship was her suggestion. One I latched on to because it would get Mom off my case. She'd started arranging dates for me, and it was making me ill. Lo wanted to get her parents off her case too. They were worried about her after the traumatic experience she'd been through. Having me as a boyfriend helped alleviate some of their fears.

"Yes, but I've never acted on it."

"But you've fucked other girls," she says. "With the guys."

"Two," I admit. "And there were a few I let suck my dick, but that's it. None of them got my juices flowing."

She grabs both sides of my face, tilting my head up to her. "It was seeing the guys that did it."

Heat creeps up my neck and on to my cheeks. She knows me so well.

"Or was it just him?"

I gulp over the messy ball of emotion clogging my throat. "I should've known you'd figure it out."

"Does he know?"

I vigorously shake my head. "No, and that's the way I want to keep it."

"He won't hear it from me."

"I don't know how to tell them," I admit. "I don't know how they'll react. I can't lose the only family I've got."

"Do you think they suspect?" she asks.

I shrug. "I think I've hidden it well. It's the only reason I've gone near any of those girls."

She looks off into space. "I think they might surprise you." She turns to me with a soft smile. "You should tell them. You *need* to tell them. The longer you keep it secret, the harder it will get, and the more they might feel like it's a betrayal."

"I'm scared," I admit. "I don't want them to look at me any differently."

"You really think they would?"

"I don't think so, but if they do, I stand to lose everything." She worries her lower lip between her teeth. "I'm sorry, Theo."

"For what?" I arch a brow. "You've nothing to be sorry for. I'm the one who needs to apologize. I should never have pushed you away." I close my eyes as her fingers wind through my hair, and I'm in heaven.

I have always loved the feel of her hands running through my hair.

I have always loved her touch.

Period.

I can't begin to explain it, because she's the only woman I'm attracted to. The only woman I've ever wanted.

"I spent years torturing myself over being gay," I admit, and this is nothing new, because Harlow is the only other person on this planet who knows the truth about me. "And now, I don't know what label to apply."

"You're bi," she says, and my eyes pop open.

I run my hands up each side of her neck. "I'm not. I'm into guys. And you."

"Then, maybe, you're…" She halts mid-sentence, a look of fierce determination washing over her beautiful face. "You know what? I fucking hate labels, and I'm not attaching one to you. You are *you*." She cups my face. "And you are beautifully, perfectly imperfect. Never change, and never apologize or feel bad for who you are."

"I am not worthy of you." I skim my thumbs along the elegant column of her neck, my eyes dropping to her lips. "Do you have any idea how deeply I care about you? How badly my heart and soul has ached for you?"

"Theo." Her tone is barely louder than a whisper, her voice choked. "I spent years missing you. Believing my feelings were unrequited. If I'd known…"

"I did it for you, Lo." I move my hands up, clasping her face in my palms. "The main reason I joined The Sainthood was for you. I knew if your father was caught up with them it wasn't by choice. Dad was freaking out too badly to stop and realize that truth. Your father was a good man, and he worshiped the ground you and Giana walked on. My gut told me he was mixed up with them out of force, not free will."

I pull her face to mine, resting my forehead against hers. Her alluring scent swirls around me, and I never want to let her go. "I didn't know they were behind your kidnapping, but I knew somehow, instinctively, that your dad's involvement with them was connected to you. I was terrified you'd get dragged into it, and I knew if I could make it up to you I had to protect you. And what better way to do that than from the inside? It's all been for you Lo, because you are everything to me."

"Oh my God, Theo," she cries, planting a firm kiss on my lips. "You crazy, stupid idiot. I never wanted you to get involved with them, certainly not on my account. All you had to do was tell me the truth." She flings her arms around me, smushing my face all up in her tits.

Not that I'm complaining. They are bigger than they were when we were dating, even though she was already well developed, but I've been itching to put my hands on her from the moment she reentered my life. I bury my head in her chest, and a satisfied sigh escapes my lips.

"Do you know how much I love you?" she whispers, her voice trembling. I lift my head. A single tear rolls down her face. "Or how hard it is to admit that even to myself?" Another tear slides out of her eye. "There were so many nights I berated myself over yearning for you, knowing you could never love me back because I had the wrong body parts."

Silent tears continue to cascade down her face, and I wipe them away with my thumbs. "You don't, baby," I whisper, pressing my lips to hers and closing my eyes, reveling in the feel of her hot mouth against mine. "That's where we were both wrong." I open my eyes, placing my hand over her tit, in the spot where her heart is thudding wildly. "It was never about that. Not with us. Not when your soul speaks to mine in the way it does. Not with the connection we have. I know you're scared. Fuck it, I'm scared too. I never want to hurt you again, but I'm done feeling like half a person. I lost half my soul the day I let you go, and I was an idiot for not chasing after you."

I kiss the wetness on her cheeks. "I'm not making the same mistake again. I love you, Lo. I love you, and I want you, and I will wait for however long you take to be okay with that, but mark my words, I am going nowhere. I won't lose you again. I *can't* lose you again. And more than that, I won't ever fail you again. I will never, ever, let you down again. That is a promise I will take to the grave."

CHAPTER 21

HARLOW

I CLING TO him, pressing my body flush against his, and I never want to let go. Holding Theo like this brings back a host of memories.

Mostly good.

Some not so much.

I can't stop crying, and it hasn't escaped my notice that, after all these years, Theo is the one to crack through my veneer. I don't know why I'm all that surprised. Theo is the only one I have ever been able to open up to. He knows some of my deepest, darkest secrets, like I know his.

But this.

This has thrown me for a loop.

His admission, his profession of love, has burrowed through the walls I've built around my heart. They were already wobbling, weakened by the strength of my growing feelings for these guys.

But this revelation is everything.

Everything.

Theo's hard underneath me, not that I need it to prove his words. Theo wouldn't lie to me about something like this.

We dated for roughly a year, from the time I was fourteen and a half to fifteen and a half, and that whole time, I believed he was gay. He was so troubled and upset over it, and together we found a safe place to explore our sexual desires. We watched gay porn together, and he shared some of his fantasies with me. I used sex toys on him, and my fingers, and while I was never the right sex, we derived great pleasure from one another.

At a time when we were both confused, alone, and struggling to make our way in this sick world, we found a way to comfort one another. We lost our virginity to one another, and he took my anal virginity too. In fact, a lot of times we fucked, he took me from behind, and I always believed he imagined I was some guy. I didn't care at first, because I was enjoying it too much for it to matter. But after a while, it started upsetting me because I wanted him to want me for *me*.

Now, I'm rethinking everything, and my head and my heart are on overload. It's no wonder my emotional dam broke and I'm crying.

Because the connection I share with Theo is way more than sex. He was my best friend. The person I told everything to. We shared our dreams and aspirations for the future and made plans to always be in each other's lives. Which is why it hurt so much when he cut all contact dead after our parents' relationship imploded.

It was as if I hadn't mattered.

Like everything was a lie.

And I had been convenient and an outlet for channeling his hidden desires.

But he was holding out on me. Not admitting his feelings were real. *Can I blame him for that? Especially when I held a part of myself back too?* Afraid to tell him for fear of rejection. And I never disclosed the snooping I did for The Sainthood because I was ashamed, and I didn't want him thinking less of me.

"Why didn't you attempt to explain it?" I ask. "If I'd had one letter or a text, just *something* to make sense of it instead of cutting me off dead like that. You almost broke me for good."

"I wanted to," he admits, clasping my face in his hands and peering deep into my eyes. "But I couldn't find the right words. And I convinced myself you were better off without me."

"Not knowing tore me apart. I blamed myself for all the things I could've done differently."

He wraps his arms tightly around me, dotting kisses into my hair. "I'm so sorry, Lo. You deserved better, and if I could go back, I'd do it all differently."

We have both made mistakes. We were kids, and he was doing what he thought was the best thing for me, no matter how misguided and flawed his decision-making process was.

I've been keeping him at arm's length to protect my heart, but all I've done is waste more precious time.

That ends now.

"Theo." I lift my face, grab fistfuls of his hair, and yank his head back. "I forgive you, and I want to leave the past in the past and start over."

"Nothing would make me happier."

"Make love to me," I say, rocking my hips gently against his erection. "I need you."

"It would be my pleasure. I love you, Harlow Westbrook," he says, stripping my hoodie and tank top off me and throwing them aside. "I love you so fucking much." He unclasps my bra, letting it slide down my arms as he sucks one puckered nipple into his mouth, pulling on it hard. His fingers roll my other nipple, playfully teasing my sensitive flesh, and his familiar touch is a lot like coming home after an extended vacation.

I throw my head back, whimpering. It's as if all the nerve endings in my body are on one continuous loop, because every time he touches my nipples with his mouth or his expert fingers, a shot of liquid lust darts straight to my pussy, drenching me in desire.

We stand, slowly undressing one another, as our lips collide in a slew of unhurried kisses. When we're naked, we fall against one another, and he angles his head, taking our kiss deeper, until I'm swimming in euphoria, bathing in bliss, my body, heart, and soul claimed anew.

He lays me down on the couch and parts my legs, sliding two fingers inside me. I grab his head down to mine, kissing him deeply as he finger-fucks me in slow, precise movements planned to take me to a pinnacle where heaven waits. His fingers work my pussy perfectly. He remembers exactly how I like to be touched, and I feel his careful caresses soul deep, in a place I've only ever reserved for him.

When I shatter, it's a languid, lazy kind of bliss but one I feel all the way to the tips of my toes. Wasting no more time, Theo slides inside my pussy, and my eyes flit to his, a little surprised. Despite what he's said, I still expected him to flip me over and fuck my ass.

He thrusts in and out of me slowly, like I might break, and it's such a contrast to the way the other guys fuck me, but I love it every bit as much.

His eyes are endless pools of emotion as he makes love to me, never losing that intimate contact, and my heart is full to bursting point. "I can't believe I wasted so long not enjoying it like this," he admits, pressing a line of tender kisses along my neck. "The way you feel is indescribable, Lo, and I'll never deprive either of us of this again."

I drag my fingers through his hair, softly digging my nails into his scalp in a way I know he loves. "I love every way you fuck me, Theo." I kiss him once on the lips before purposely pulling back. "I have regretted many things over the years, and cursed you more times than I can count, but I have never, ever, regretted giving you my virginity or all the ways we enjoyed our bodies. I'm confident in my sexuality because you helped me to explore it in a safe environment and you helped me learn to listen to my body."

I run my hands up and down his back as he picks up his pace, fucking me harder. Light sweat pearls his smooth, tan skin, and I press a kiss to his collarbone. "That's all I ever wanted for you too," I truthfully admit. I hate that he hasn't quite reached the same place, and I'm determined to help him find his nirvana.

"Lo." He lifts my left leg up to his shoulder, tilting his hips and pounding into me harder. His fingers rub my clit, and I feel another orgasm climbing. "You have already given me so much." He presses his lips to mine, swirling his tongue around my mouth, as he rocks into me, over and over, until we're both sweating, panting, and crying out in release.

We collapse against one another, and he twists us around so we're side to side, facing one another. He holds me close, our bodies perfectly aligned, our breathing in sync. He clasps my face, leaning down to kiss me. When the kiss ends, we smile at one another, and it's been a long time since I've felt such deep-seated contentment.

My eyes flutter closed, and a yawn slips out of my mouth. "Good talk," I whisper, my lips curving into a smile.

His chest rumbles in silent laughter as his warm lips press against my brow. "Sleep, my love. I've got you. Always."

I STIR SOMETIME later, conscious of soft voices talking and the feel of light cotton over my skin. My cheek is pressed to Theo's chest, and I'm comforted by the steady beat of his heart.

"You love her," Saint says, and I squeeze my eyes tight to keep them closed.

"More than I ever realized," Theo admits, pulling me in even closer.

"It's good now?" Saint asks.

"Yeah. We've cleared the air." Theo plants a kiss in my hair. "You okay with this?"

Silence rings out in the dark room. "Yeah, man," he says after a few awkward beats. "Can't promise I won't get jealous, because she brings out a side of me I wasn't aware I was hiding, but you're my brother. Caz and Galen too. I don't want to fight with any of you. You might need to be patient."

"It's cool, brother, and I'll need to get used to sharing her too. Last time, she was all mine, and I know how good that feels."

Warmth blossoms in my chest, and my heart swells.

"You need her, and she needs you too," Saint says, and I'm so proud of him for his selflessness. "You offer her something we can't, and we can't be selfish. This is all about her."

"It is," Theo whispers. "Lo is all that matters."

"You hear that, princess?" Saint says, and I hear the amusement lacing his tone. "You can stop pretending you're asleep now."

"I wasn't pretending," I say over a yawn. "I just didn't want to interrupt. Seemed rude." I open my eyes, staring into Theo's gorgeous amber-hued gaze.

The couch dips at the end, and I glance down at Saint. He slides his hand under the cotton sheet someone draped over us, finding my feet. "It's only three a.m. You should go back to sleep." His warm hands rub up and down my legs.

"Come here," I demand, not feeling sleepy anymore. "I need to kiss you."

He gets up, dropping to his knees on the ground before me, and I twist around and kiss him. Theo stirs, and I hold on to his arm, keeping him in place. I tear my lips from Saint's, angling around to softly kiss Theo. "Now I've confirmation it's all about me," I say, my gaze alternating between the two guys, "I'd like to make a request." My lips kick up as Saint rolls his eyes.

"I have a feeling we'll never hear the end of this," Saint drawls.

"I want you both sleeping in my bed tonight."

"Whatever you need, baby," Theo says, kissing my cheek.

Saint stands, sliding his arms underneath my naked body, as Theo peels the cover back. Saint scoops me into his arms, and I curl into him, burying my nose in his neck, ingesting the scent that is uniquely Saint Lennox as he carries me upstairs with Theo following close behind.

"Morning." Caz drops a kiss on the end of my nose when I amble into the kitchen the next morning. "Sleep well?" he teases.

I wink as I pour myself a cup of coffee. "I slept perfectly

snuggled between Theo and Saint."

"Someone sounds loved up." He waggles his brows before biting into a slice of buttery toast.

"Stop giving her a hard time," Theo says, coming up behind me and snaking his arms around my waist. "You should be pleased we've patched up our differences."

"Is that what we're calling it now?" Caz jokes. "I think your dick was still inside her when we got home."

Theo locks up, his body tense behind me, and I draw soft circles on the back of his hand, urging him to relax.

"Stop teasing." I pour a coffee for Theo, and he reluctantly breaks our embrace.

Saint arrives in the kitchen, yawning and scratching the back of his head. His hair is damp from the shower, and little droplets of water cling to the scruff on his cheeks. I pour him a coffee, walking toward him with a smile. I stretch up and peck his lips. "Morning, Saintly."

"Are you ever going to quit with that Saintly shit?"

"You gonna stop calling me princess?"

A hint of a smile ghosts over his lips as he rolls his eyes.

"Do we need to stop by the house, or are we heading straight to school?" Galen asks in a clipped tone, and we all turn around. His butt is perched on the edge of the table, and his arms are softly folded across his chest. His face is a mask, hiding all emotion, but from the rigid way he's holding himself, I can tell he's unhappy.

"Princess, you need anything from the house?" Saint asks, maintaining eye contact with his cousin.

"Nah. I'll manage although I should probably start keeping a bag here."

"That's a good idea," Theo says, handing me a bowl of chopped fruit. It's got a plastic lid on it, and he's included a fork and paper towel. "For later, when you get hungry."

My features soften. "You remember I don't like breakfast first thing."

He kisses me tenderly, his adoring gaze pinning me in place. "I remember everything."

Caz snorts. "You are so fucking pussy-whipped. I can't decide if I want to puke, laugh, or swoon."

Theo flips him the bird, and Saint smirks.

"I'm gonna take my truck," Galen says, striding toward the door.

"You don't have to—"

"I want to get it thoroughly cleaned, in case there's any trace evidence from last night," he says, cutting across whatever Saint was about to say. "I'll see you at school," he adds without looking at any of us.

The door slams violently behind him, and I flinch.

"Fuck." Saint runs a hand over his hair, his eyes finding mine.

And I know what he's not saying.

We're at risk of losing Galen.

He probably feels like more of an outsider now than ever.

"I'll fix it," I promise, feeling more charitable today. And I'm more hopeful too. I didn't think I could repair things with Theo, but we're on the right road, and I can't deny how much happier it's made me.

It's time to repair things with Galen too. If I need to be the bigger person, I'll do it, because this needs to happen.

Saint nods, gulping down coffee, and I see the worry building behind his eyes.

"What happened last night?" I ask. "Did you plant the remains?"

"Yeppers," Caz says over a mouthful of toast. "And one of our guys called in an anonymous tip."

"Cops should be crawling up Ruben's butt right about now," Saint says, grinning widely, showcasing a set of perfectly straight, white teeth.

"Good. Maybe, he'll forget about murdering me for five minutes."

"We'll move to stage two of our plan now," Saint says, drawing me to his side and slinging his arm around my neck. He kisses my temple. "Don't worry about The Bulls. We've got it in hand. Where they're going, they won't be able to touch you."

    I'll believe it when I see it.

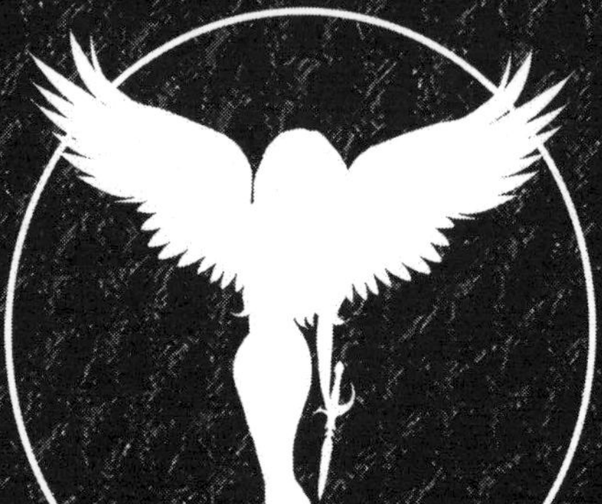

CHAPTER 22

By WEDNESDAY, NEWS of Parker's murder is all over school and splashed across the airwaves. The media speculation over Finn's and Brooklyn's disappearance is a bonus as they debate the possibility they've fled the scene of their crime.

I dump my keys on the kitchen counter when I arrive home after visiting Sariah at the hospital, rubbing my sore temples. A dull ache has taken up residence in my skull all day, and I can't shake the sense of impending doom. Caz removes two beers from the refrigerator, handing one to me as he slings his arm around my shoulders. "You hanging in there, babe?"

I shrug, feeling sadder every day that passes when my bestie doesn't wake up. Even news of Beth McCoy's arrest has done little to help my depressed mood. Two other girls were arrested too, and they are all being detained for further questioning, pending assault charges.

The guys look up as our footsteps thud on the basement stairs. Theo strides toward us, pulling me into his comforting arms when I reach the last step. "I take it there's no change?"

I shake my head against his chest.

"Unfortunately, not," Caz confirms. "Sean is totally messed up."

Theo steers me to the couch, placing me beside Saint, before sitting down on my other side. I rest my head against Saint's shoulder as his hand lands on my knee. "Do we have any clue where Finn and Brooklyn are, and should we be worried?" I ask, because right now, I need to focus on something else.

"We don't know is the answer to both questions," Saint admits, caressing my thigh.

"I have their images uploaded to the facial recognition software system I use, but it's like they've disappeared off the face of the Earth," Theo admits. "I've messaged Diesel in our private chat room to see if he can help. I don't like not having eyes on all the moving parts."

"He respond?" Saint asks, leaning his head back so he's looking at Theo.

Theo shakes his head. "He's been offline the past few days."

"I got a message from him an hour ago," I say. "He can meet Sunday, but he wants me to come alone."

Saint harrumphs. "Yeah, so not happening." He tilts my head around to his. "Tell him we all meet at the barn or we don't meet at all."

I press a kiss to the underside of his jaw. "Already done."

He squeezes my thigh as a genuine smile lifts the corners of his mouth.

"What are we going to do about Taylor Tamlin?" Galen asks, sitting up straighter on the other couch.

"We need to find out what she knows," Theo says.

"Maybe our princess should befriend her," Caz suggests.

I shake my head. "That won't work. She's Tempest's cousin, and Tempest hates my guts. Besides, it's pretty much common knowledge I'm your girl. She'll instantly smell a rat."

"We need someone she won't know," Galen says.

"Emmett," Saint supplies.

I tilt my face up to his. "No way. We do not involve him in any of this. And he won't do shit for you after you threatened his sister."

Saint smirks. "He'd jump off a cliff for you."

"It's too risky. Dar might remember him from a party we were at a while back. I won't put Emmett in harm's way."

"We're low on options," Theo says.

"No, we're not." I drag my lower lip between my teeth as I think about it. "She's important to The Bulls because she's the connection between them and The Arrows and she had an in with The Sainthood, something she is probably reworking now she's lost her puppet." I stand, pacing as my mind works through it. "She's not some inconsequential hoodrat. She successfully feeds intel among the different crews, and that is not something that can be easily replicated, so let's make things harder for them."

"I like where this is going," Saint says. "What exactly do you have in mind?"

"Let's kidnap the bitch's ass and torture her until we get answers."

Caz whistles under his breath, crossing one leg over his knee, as he lights up a joint. "Sign me up if you're doing the torturing." He grabs his crotch. "I'm already hard thinking about it."

I hop up and grab the joint from Caz's lips, stubbing it out. "I didn't say quit cigarettes so you could smoke this shit every day."

"Aw, c'mon, princess." He sends me puppy dog eyes. "A man's got to have some vices."

I plonk myself on his lap, lacing my arms around his neck. "You've already got two. Beer and me." I lean down, licking a path up the side of his neck. "Trust me, that's more than enough for any guy to handle."

"You might have to convince me." Caz's wicked gaze is seductive in the extreme.

"Deal." I purposely rub my ass over the growing bulge in his jeans. "I'll start convincing you later." I press a kiss to the corner of his lips. "I'm claiming you in my bed tonight."

"Hell yeah, baby." He nuzzles his nose in my neck.

My eyes meet Galen's troubled green ones, and we share a lingering stare before he breaks eye contact, looking at Theo.

"What about the rat?" Galen asks. "Any progress with those background checks?"

"Not so far, and I've had no luck getting past the firewall at Sainthood HQ."

"Meaning what?" I ask, swiveling on Caz's lap to face Theo.

"I can't infiltrate their security system or get into their cameras."

"Maybe, I could do it whenever I'm summoned there," I say.

"Your pretty ass is not stepping foot in that place," Saint growls.

"I thought you attended monthly junior chapter meetings?"

"We do, but you won't be there." Saint runs his fingers over his cropped blond hair. "I don't trust any of those bastards with you."

"That won't cut it, and you know it."

"I don't fucking care!" he roars. "He's not getting his dirty hands on you."

I get off Caz, walk over to Saint, and sink down on to his lap. I tip his face up. "Agreed. But we can't be stupid. We need access to those cameras, to watch things and to check logs for any evidence of the rat. Me getting summoned to HQ might help, and I'll figure out a way to avoid being gang-raped by Sinner and his buddies." A shudder crawls its way up my spine.

"I don't see how," Theo says. "And that's another problem to solve. But we haven't exhausted all options yet. I bet Diesel could get us what we need."

I nod slowly. "Yeah, with what we've learned, I'm sure he could. We'll ask him on Sunday."

"There is another option we haven't considered in relation to Taylor," Galen says, and we all direct our attention his way. "Eccleston. He hooked up with her before, so maybe Bryant reaches out, wanting round two?"

"I should've thought of that," I murmur.

"I still don't trust that guy," Saint says, and the others nod. "But he's supposedly on our side now."

"Supposedly?" I inquire.

"I don't trust it. It feels like there is more we don't know," Saint says, running his hand up and down my back.

"We're due an update from him," Galen reminds us.

Saint eyeballs his cousin. "Set up a meet. Let's get him to do this, and if his dick doesn't get us the answers we need, we try the princess's suggestion and kidnap the bitch."

After the convo ends, I head to my room and take a long, hot shower. When I emerge, followed by a trail of cloudy steam, Galen is sitting on the edge of my bed. "I knocked," he blurts, averting his eyes as I tuck my towel in tighter under my arms.

"What's up?" I ask, picking up my hairbrush and running it through my damp hair.

"I have something for you." He holds out a rectangular black box.

I walk to the bed, holding his gaze as I sit down beside him, taking the offering. I unclip the small lock on the side of the box and pull the lid back to reveal the contents.

My heart pounds in my chest as I inspect the five small, silver daggers. Removing one from the silk bed it rests on, I examine the exquisite workmanship with a lump in my throat. The handle of each dagger contains an image of an avenging angel etched into the ornate metal.

"They're beautiful," I whisper, holding the dagger in the palm of my hand, testing its weight, as I lift my eyes to Galen's.

Something close to relief flares in his eyes. "The minute I saw them I thought of you."

My lips kick up. Most guys buy girls chocolate or flowers, but Galen knows me better than I realized. It's a thoughtful gesture and the perfect icebreaker.

But if we're truly going to get past this, I need to know he's all in.

"I wonder how sharp they are," I muse, keeping my eyes locked on his gorgeous green ones.

"Sharp enough to inflict pain," he coolly replies.

I look down at the thin, raised scars covering both parts of my upper arms. "I still remember how much it hurt," I admit. "I had this one recurring nightmare, the first couple years after the kidnapping, where my kidnappers broke into my bedroom and sliced open my wounds repeatedly." I lift my eyes to his face. "Their faces were blacked out. All except Sinner's, although I didn't know who he was back then. His face haunted me in my sleep for so long."

A heavy weight sits on my chest, compressing my air supply. "I used to wake up screaming," I continue, "holding on to my arms because they throbbed like a bitch. It wasn't imaginary pain because it felt so real." I shoot him a sad smile. "The mind is such a powerful organ. So susceptible to suggestion."

I lift the dagger, staring at Galen as I press the tip of the dagger against the topmost mark on my left arm, maintaining eye contact as I cut a line across the existing scar. Blood rushes to the surface immediately, pooling along my skin and trickling down my arm.

"Jesus. Fuck." Galen drags his hands through his hair, staring at me wide-eyed.

"The hypnosis therapy I underwent helped me heal. The nightmares reduced in regularity until they disappeared completely. It took me a long time to realize it isn't physical pain I'm scared of. It's emotional." I drill him with a determined look as blood flows down my arm. "I could cut through every one of these scars, opening old wounds, and it wouldn't hurt me. Not the way you did when you handed me off to the enemy to kill."

"Lo, I—"

I clamp my free hand over his mouth. "Don't interrupt me." His nostrils flare, and I smile as a glimpse of the real Galen peeks through. "If I'm to forgive you, it means exposing my heart, making myself vulnerable to you, and that's a far scarier prospect. How do I know I can trust you? How do I know you're worthy of that?" Taking his hand, I flip it palm up before placing the dagger coated with my blood on it. "Would you bleed for me, Galen?" I wrap his fingers around the knife. "Would you cut yourself open for me?" I lean into his face, pressing my lips to his ear. "Would you trust me to take that knife and slice into your skin?"

He takes my hand and places the bloody dagger in it. "Yes, I would bleed for you, Lo." A muscle clenches in his jaw. "I would die for you."

"Why?"

"Because you are the reason everything makes sense. You are the only truth amid all the secrets and lies. The glue that binds us together. The substance to our purpose." He gulps, reaching up to cup my face with bloody fingertips. "You're not the only one scared of emotional pain. Why do you think I went to such lengths to push you away? I'm not talking about what went down with Dar. I mean everything that came before that made me vulnerable to his manipulation. I've seen what you can do. I've known how that would change our dynamic, and it fucking terrified me."

He rubs his thumb along my cheek. "I was a coward, and I took the coward's way out." He drops his hand from my face, wrapping my fingers around the handle of the dagger. "No one would blame you for retaliating, but I know you won't do that because you are better than me. You confront your pain head-on while I bury mine deep in my blackened soul."

"Oh, Galen." I kiss his cheek. "Your soul isn't black. It's every shade of gray. And that's something I understand."

"I don't deserve a second chance, but I'm asking for one," he says. "I was afraid you'd tear us apart, but I was wrong because you're bringing us together in a way that is making us stronger. You're the center of my brothers' universe, and I want you to be the center of mine." He clasps my cheeks in his palms, and his face radiates sincerity.

"Are you ready to give me your full truth? To commit to always being honest with me?"

"I am, Lo. I desperately want a second chance, and I'm asking for forgiveness if you can find it in your heart." He glances at the dagger. "Does that answer your questions?"

"Take your hoodie off," I instruct.

He stands, removing his hoodie and yanking his T-shirt up over his head, throwing both items of clothing on the floor. Bruises cover his ribs—a very real reminder of his shame and his pain.

I rise with blood pouring down my arm, dripping onto the carpet. I stand directly in front of him, looking up at his stunning face. He is shielding nothing now, and I have hope this will be all right. "I think you and I are the most alike, Galen. It's one of the reasons we butt heads so much."

It's true even with the connection I share with the others.

Saint knows pain but he doesn't bury it—he lashes out, and he vents in a physical way. Theo knows pain too, but he throws himself into his work to alleviate his feelings of failure. If Caz is in any pain, he does a fantastic job hiding it behind his legendary humor.

But Galen has succumbed to his pain, and it's eating him alive in a way the pain used to eat me alive until I learned to control it.

They all need me, but in this moment, I acknowledge Galen needs me more.

I'm not sure I can be who he needs me to be, but I want to try, and that is a huge step forward.

As for forgiveness?

That remains to be seen.

"Ready to bleed for me now, Galen?" I brush my fingers along the upper side of his right arm.

He doesn't flinch, just stares into my eyes, placing all his trust in me. "Yes. I'm ready to live for you, Lo."

It's beautifully poetic and the most perfect thing he could say to me in this moment. I press my lips to his cheek, lingering for a few beats, bathing in his presence. When I ease back, his eyes lock on mine, and we stare at one another, on the precipice of a new beginning.

He nods, and I clasp his arm more firmly, watching his reaction as I bring the dagger to his arm, breaking skin. I feel his intense gaze on me as I dip my head, concentrating while I drag my dagger across his arm, in a diagonal line, marking him in the exact same spot as my arm. Blood spills from the cut, flowing down his arm much like it did mine.

I dip my fingers in his blood, smudging my fingertips as I raise them to my mouth. I stare into his eyes as I place my fingers in my mouth, sucking his blood. His eyes darken, and the air charges around us. My eyes lower to his lips, and I'm tempted to dive in.

Tingles shoot up my arm when his fingers dip into my blood. Watching him bring them to his lips, licking my blood clean off his skin, is sexy as hell.

I smile, and for the first time in ages, it feels like I'm back where I should be.

With my family, my crew.

Like things are finally falling into place.

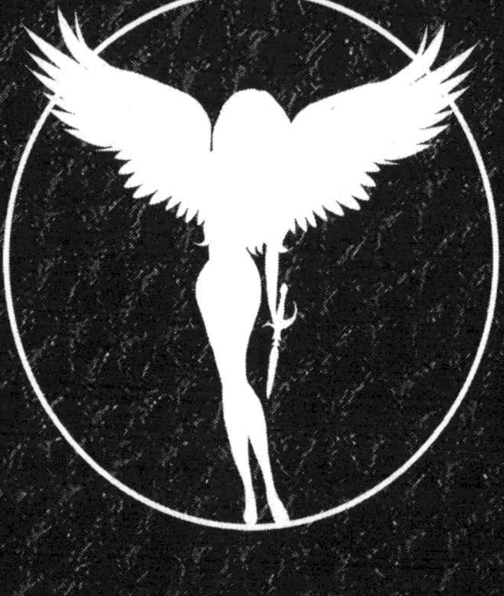

CHAPTER 23

"Wow," Caz says as we pull up to Ashley Shaw's house late Friday night. "This is definitely how the other half live."

Music blares from the open double doors and windows, and partygoers occupy every spare space of the upper-level balcony that extends along the front of the house and around to the side. Girls and guys from my old school are laughing, chatting, drinking, and dancing under the starless night sky as if they haven't a care in the world, but I know better.

Everyone has shit to deal with.

Some are just better at hiding it than others.

Galen kills the engine on my Lexus, parking it to one side of the driveway behind a yellow Maserati.

I've requested we use my car as much as possible, because Dad and Diesel asked that of me and the safety features are second to none. The guys readily agreed without protest.

Their genuine concern for my safety pricks more holes in the wall around my heart, but I've accepted the inevitable—that I'm a lost cause when it comes to my Saints—and I've thrown caution to the wind.

The chips will fall where they fall, and there's no backing out now.

"What kind of asswipe ruins a Maserati by ordering it in yellow?" Saint shakes his head in disgust when we climb out of the car.

"The kind of new-money asswipe you need to win over tonight," I reply, looping my arm through his. "I suggest you keep such thoughts to yourself. These people will press all your buttons. Just let their shit go over your head."

"Is that how you did it?" Galen asks, tucking the keys in the pocket of his jeans as we walk toward the front door.

"Pretty much," I agree. "Also, my rep preceded me. I was 'that girl,' the one who'd been kidnapped and cut up, and most people at the academy kept a healthy distance from me."

"People suck." Theo threads his fingers through my free hand.

"I figured that out many years ago." I shoot him an appreciative smile. His hair is smoothed back off his face and styled into a sexy man bun on top of his head. He's wearing a Muse T-Shirt over faded, ripped skinny jeans with untied boots on his feet, and he looks good enough to eat. "You look hot as fuck."

Caz snorts from behind, and I glance over my shoulder. "You look hot too."

They all do tonight.

Caz is wearing a leather jacket over a tight black T-shirt with grayish-black jeans and biker boots. He's got his eyebrow piercing and lip ring in, and his hair is an artfully messy mess.

Saint's Supreme T-shirt is molded to his impressive abs, and he's also wearing ripped jeans and boots.

Galen has a fitted black shirt on, rolled up to the sleeves, showcasing his muscular arms, and his ass looks delectable in tight black jeans. His hair is back in a faux hawk, the tips edged in green.

"I wasn't fishing for compliments," Caz says, winking at me. "You two are just too stinking cute for words." He waves his hand at me and Theo.

"Cute is not the word I'd use to describe our girl tonight." Theo leans in, kissing my cheek. "You're straight fire, babe."

"I think we all scrub up good." I smooth a hand down over my black glitter minidress. It's a sleeveless, choker-style bodycon dress that leaves zero to the imagination. I've teamed it with skyscraper black stilettos that have spiky silver studs all over them. My hair is pulled back in a slick ponytail, and I went heavy on the makeup.

I used body paint to paint the bandage around the cut on my arm in black so now it looks like part of my outfit. Not that I'm ever embarrassed by any of my scars, but I don't want to invite questions.

Saint, Caz, and Theo noticed the matching bandages on our arms, but none of them asked about it. At least, they didn't ask me. Not sure if Saint interrogated Galen or decided to trust that I'm handling shit in my own way.

"Why else do you think I'm hanging back here?" Caz says, waggling his brows at Theo. "Your ass is smokin' hot in that dress, babe," he adds, flattening his palm over my butt. He moves his lips to my ear. "I want to slide between those cheeks before the night is over."

"Play your cards right, and you just might," I retort, leaning back to peck his lips.

"Lead the way, princess," Saint says when we reach the front doors, and I untangle my limbs from my guys and push inside Ashley's extravagant mansion.

I stride through the crowd lining the hallway, heading toward the kitchen at the back of the house, noticing the hush that settles over the space as we advance. My lips twitch as I catch all the lingering glances sent my guys' way. I knew all the rich bitches would be lusting after them tonight. There's nothing like the promise of a foul-mouthed, sexy-as-fuck bad boy from the wrong side of the tracks to send hearts racing and dampen panties.

Too bad for them I don't share.

I reach my arm back, grabbing the nearest hand and tugging.

"Jealous, princess?" Saint whispers in my ear, wrapping his arm around me from behind as we continue walking.

"Don't play dumb, babe." I squeeze his hand. "There's a difference between jealousy and possessiveness." I angle my head so I'm meeting his eyes. "You're mine, and those greedy bitches need to know it."

Grabbing me by the hips, he slams me up against the wall. He cages me in with his muscular arms, leaning down to trail his nose along the underside of my jaw. "Fuck, princess. I love it when your claws come out." I smirk, sliding my hand around his toned waist and palming his ass. "I know this shit turns you on," he adds, dropping one arm. He clasps my thigh roughly, and his fingers slide up my skin. "I'm betting you're so fucking wet for us right now."

"No betting required." I push my chest into his. "I'm horny as shit, and you're definitely taking care of me when we get home."

Saint arches a brow as his fingers creep under the hem of my dress. "Who said anything about waiting till we get home?"

I kiss his mouth quickly. "I like the way you think," I purr over his lips, pinning him with a sultry look. "Let's get this shit done so we can get to the sexy times."

He presses his body flush against mine, grasping my chin and tilting my face up to his. "So." He kisses one corner of my mouth. "Fucking." He kisses the other side. "Perfect." He cups my pussy under my dress the same time his mouth descends on mine in a greedy kiss that screams possession.

I have zero complaints.

"Oh my God! Harlow Westbrook!" A shrill voice explodes in my ear, forcing my lips from Saint's.

Saint lets me go, removing his hand from under my dress while sending daggers at the gorgeous airhead invading our private time.

"Julia." I plaster a smarmy smile on my lips. "Great to see you."

Not.

Julia is Ashley's bestie in life and on the cheer squad. But where Ashley has charisma by the bucketful, her sidekick lacks even basic social skills.

Julia is heir to the Manford throne, a global, multibillion-dollar media corporation, and she thinks Daddy's money buys her a golden ticket for life. She's one of the most revered *and* reviled girls at Lowell Academy, but everyone sucks up to her because they're just that shallow.

"Aren't you going to introduce me?" Julia says, blatantly eye fucking Saint.

I spot the others leaning against the doorway to the kitchen behind her. Caz is smirking. Galen is inspecting his nails and avoiding the amorous glances being sent his way, while Theo shakes his head, smiling.

Julia places her hands on Saint's chest, batting her fake eyelashes at him. "I'm Julia, and you've just made all my dreams come true."

"Word to the wise," I say, squaring up to her as I shove her hands off Saint. "The last bitch that tried that shit with my man didn't fare so well." I tilt my head to the side. "But be my guest. Let's see how stupid you really are."

"Harlow!" She gasps, holding a hand to her chest. "There's no need to be rude."

"There's every need to be rude," Saint replies, sliding his arm around my waist and pulling me in close. "Don't touch what doesn't belong to you." He fixes her with one of his legendary sneers, and she physically cowers. "Now, if you'll excuse us, *Julia*. Some of us have shit to do."

"Great catching up," I drawl, shoving her aside and pushing past her.

She stomps her foot, folds her arms across her inflated chest, and screams, "Jason!" at the top of her voice. "Where the fuck are you, Jase?"

Caz covers his ears, Galen rolls his eyes, and Theo smiles as he steps forward, taking my hand and leading me into the kitchen.

"This way," I say, spotting Ashley in the corner, talking to some guy I don't know. I march toward her. "Cool party. Thanks for the invite."

"You're welcome." Her eyes pop wide when they land on my guys. Her gaze homes in on where my fingers are linked with

Theo's and where Saint's hand is resting on my hip. "I'm glad you could come," she adds, smiling at the guys.

"We haven't yet," Caz quips, grinning at me.

"You know I'll always take care of you," I reply, blowing him a kiss.

"We'll grab some beers," Galen says, grabbing Caz, and they head outside to the bar.

"So, it's true," Ashley says, dismissing the guy she was talking to with a less-than-gentle push. "You're fucking all of them."

I shrug. "Pretty much."

"Lucky bitch."

"I am, aren't I?" I can't keep the smug smile off my face. "You still dating Chad and fucking Jase on the side?"

She grabs onto my elbow, eyes darting around the room. "How the hell do you know that?"

"Most everyone knows," I admit, accepting a cold beer from Galen. I take a sip. "Except Julia. I'm curious. How the hell are you two best friends?"

She casts another glance around. "I can't stand her, but our parents are best friends, and I got lumped with her as a freshman. I know what everyone thinks at the academy, but I barely hang out with her unless I have to."

Saint rubs a hand along my stomach, and I know it's a signal to move this along.

"Speaking of Chad and Jase, are they here, and can you take us to them?"

She stares into my face. "Figured that's why you wanted an invite. They're expecting you." She jerks her head outside. "They're in the pool house."

We make our way outside with Saint's arm wrapped around me. Ashley walks on my other side while Caz, Galen, and Theo keep step behind us. Several heads turn in our direction, but this time, they're all male, and the attention is firmly fixed on me. Predictably, Saint snarls at a few of them and Caz throws a couple punches.

Ashley leans into me, grinning. "Like I said, lucky bitch."

I'm wondering why we were never friends.

"It seems like you've got your own good thing going," I murmur.

"I do," she agrees, winking conspiratorially at me. "We're the type of girls that need multiple men."

"Amen, sister." I clink my beer bottle against hers.

Ashley enters the pool house, and the sound of loud conversation from the next room pricks my ears. She holds the door open while we all step inside, locking it behind us. At the sound of the door locking, the voices quiet and the TV mutes.

Ashley guides us into the large living room where Chad, Jase, and a bunch of their football buddies are sprawled across two large leather couches, game controllers in hand.

All eyes are on us, and tension bleeds into the air.

"You guys! Stop that!" Ashley slides onto Jase's lap, slapping his chest, and it's my turn to sport the deer-in-a-headlights look. When I mentioned she had a good thing going, I assumed she was fucking Jase behind her boyfriend's back, as well as her bestie's. But by the casual way she's flaunting herself on Jase's lap, it's obvious her boyfriend is in the know, where Julia clearly isn't. *I wonder if she turns a blind eye on purpose? Or is she so arrogant she believes no one would cheat on her? Or is she just that stupid?*

Ashley flashes me a blinding smile, and I raise my beer to her, grinning. *Good for you, girl.* Jase and Chad are hot if you're into the whole jock look.

Which I'm not.

Because I prefer my men rough and reckless with a side of danger.

"Harlow Westbrook," Chad says, giving me a long once-over. "It's been a while. You look good."

"Thanks, but we're not here for chitchat."

He scrubs a hand along his smooth jaw. "Yeah, didn't think you were." He stands, jerking his head up at Saint. "I heard The Sainthood rolled into town. Took you long enough to show up here."

"We've been busy," Saint says, releasing his hold on me. "You the guy I need to talk with?" Chad nods. "Let's get down to business."

Drinks are poured, and Caz, Theo, and I join Ashley and the others on the couch, taking turns enjoying a few rounds of COD on Xbox while Jase, Chad, Galen, and Saint discuss business.

When they finish their conversation, and rejoin the main group, I can't make out anything on Saint's or Galen's faces, but they're not throwing punches, so I'm hoping that means it was a productive meeting.

"Stay, have a beer," Chad says, lifting Ashley and sliding onto the couch underneath her. She settles on his lap, circling her arm around his neck.

"Thanks, man, but we've got plans," Caz says, answering before Saint can. Caz jumps up, pulling me with him and sliding his arms around my waist from behind. He presses his lips to my neck. "Plans that can't wait," he murmurs against my skin.

Chad and Jase grin, and Ashley smiles. "Feel free to use any of the guest bedrooms. Upstairs is closed off to the assholes."

Laughter bubbles up my throat. "Thanks for the offer, but I think we'll split." I clasp Caz's hands joined at my waist. "What I have in mind requires the privacy of our own space."

A chorus of whoops and hollers ring out, and Saint smirks, yanking me from Caz's embrace. I've noticed he gets extra possessive in a crowd.

I briefly debate dragging the guys into the living room as we pass through the main house. A lively crowd is dancing to beats blaring from loudspeakers, and I'm tempted, but my need to get them under and over me is stronger, so I say nothing, and we leave the party behind to attend our own private one.

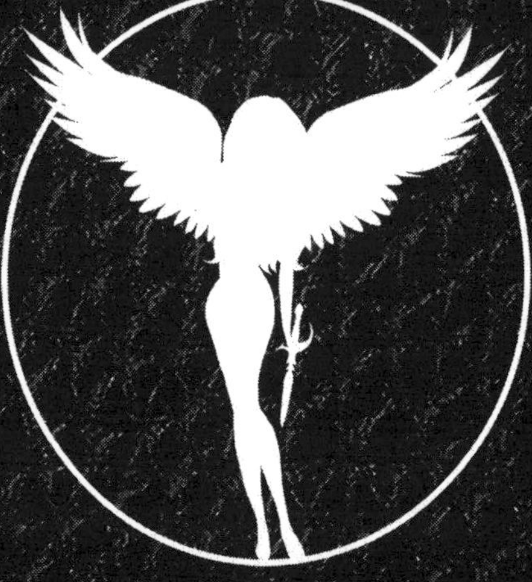

THE SAINTHOOD

CHAPTER 24

I WAKE THE next morning as soft lips press against my cheek. I stir, blinking my eyes open, and my limbs ache deliciously. "Sorry, babe," Theo whispers. "I didn't mean to wake you."

"'Sokay," I murmur over a yawn.

A deep snore rumbles from Caz's chest, and I turn my head, smiling at my Sleeping Beauty. He is still out for the count, and he looks like a giant, cuddly, teddy bear under the light comforter.

We came back to the barn last night, because we wanted privacy and Prestwick is closer to Fenton, so it was nearer. Galen immediately disappeared into the smaller outbuilding—their workout area—and I debated going after him, but, ultimately, I decided against it. Even though I hate the thought of him feeling left out, we're not in that space yet. Theo confirmed they have a hammock out there Galen sometimes sleeps in, and that helped to lessen my guilt.

"I'll cook breakfast. Saint has gone to check on Galen," Theo says.

I nod, puckering my lips up for a kiss. My mouth probably tastes like salty cum, but Theo doesn't hesitate, sliding his between my lips and kissing me like I'm the oxygen he needs to survive.

"Love you," he whispers, rubbing his nose against mine.

"Love you too," I whisper back, not wanting to wake the sleeping giant.

Theo glances at Caz when his chest inflates as another snore slices through the quiet, his eyes flooded with emotion. I pull Theo's hand to my lips, kissing his knuckle. He kisses the top of my head before making his escape.

I snuggle into the crook of Caz's arm, inhaling his masculine scent as I sigh contentedly.

"Did you just sniff my armpit?" he asks, his voice drenched with sleep.

I giggle softly. "I'm a lot of things," I admit. "But a sniffer of armpits is not my kink. I was sniffing your manly chest." My tongue darts out, and I lick a line across his chest. "And that was me licking your chest, not your hairy armpit, in case you're still confused."

His arms come around me. "Last night was hot."

"It was," I agree, wrapping my arm around his waist as images flash across my retina.

Saint taking me against the wall as Caz and Theo lay naked on the bed, stroking their cocks.

Riding Theo while Caz fucked my ass, and then, they swapped positions.

Theo shaking as he came deep inside my ass before pulling out and letting Saint take over.

Caz's roars as he came hard, bringing me along for the ride and giving me my third orgasm of the night.

Collapsing sweaty and sated on the bed with Caz on one side, Saint on my other, and Theo at my feet.

"We need a bigger bed," I blurt after my brain has finished replaying our hot foursome.

"That we do," he agrees, running his hand along my hipbone. "I'll get boy wonder on the case."

I trace circles with my finger along his chest. "Can I ask you something?"

"Sure." He kisses the tip of my nose. "You can ask me anything."

"Have you ever had sex with a guy?"

He eases back, scanning my face. "Why'd you ask?"

I shrug. "You like a little ass play, so I'm just curious."

"Would it shock you if I said yes?"

Shock me? Hell no. Excite me? Fuck, yeah. But I keep those thoughts to myself, because this requires delicate handling. "No. It wouldn't shock me. To be honest, the thought turns me on."

"I explored a bit in my early teens. I fucked a couple guys, and I've taken it up the ass a few times." He smirks. "I liked it, but I love fucking pussy." He licks my cheek. "I love fucking *you*." He waggles his brows, grabbing his cell and checking the time. "How about a quickie?" His grin turns downright wicked.

Pushing him flat on his back, I crawl on top of him. "Do you need to ask?"

"Hey." Galen is waiting for me when I emerge from my shower after consuming my body weight in eggs and bacon.

"This is becoming a habit." I smile as I gesture toward my towel-clad body and his butt seated on the edge of my bed.

"Does it bother you?"

"No." I drop my towel and proceed to get dressed in front of him.

His eyes skate over my naked body, and he doesn't disguise the tent situation in his jeans. "You need me to change the bandage?" he asks after a couple of tense, electrically charged beats, his eyes lowering to the cut on my arm.

"Actually, yeah. I had to throw the other one out."

He walks to the bathroom while I put my bra on. When he returns, he points to the bed, and I sit down in my underwear. He sits beside me, placing supplies on his lap. His fingers are like hot embers on my skin as he dresses my wound.

Every few seconds, his eyes fly to mine, and the undercurrent that has always existed between us is back in full force. My nipples harden, the tips jutting through the cups of my red lace bra. His hand stalls on my arm when his eyes lock on my tits, and the air is so heavy with lust I struggle to draw a breath.

He gulps before clearing his throat and returning his focus to my arm. I try not to squirm on the bed as desire pools low in my belly, and my pussy aches with fresh need.

His hair is back to messy today, and damp strands fall into his eyes. Without thinking, I lift my free hand, weaving my fingers through his hair. He stalls again, sucking in a soft gasp he probably thinks I can't hear. "I love your hair like this," I murmur, leaning forward and pressing my nose into the tangled waves. "So soft."

He turns his head, and our noses brush as I straighten up. There is barely an inch between our mouths, and my eyes drop to his plump lips the same time his gaze lowers to mine. My heart is pounding, and butterflies are running amok in my chest. Every part of my body is acutely aware of Galen Lennox's proximity, and my fingers itch with a craving to touch him.

He tried to murder you. That nasty inner devil cackles on my shoulder, effectively breaking the spell we're under. I sit back and look away, feeling heartsick and confused. After a few seconds, he resumes his ministrations on my arm, fixing the new bandage securely in place.

He stands, shoving his hands deep in the pocket of his jeans as he eyeballs me. "I need to check on my mom. I want you to come. The others have stuff to do."

"Okay," I say before I've had time to second-guess myself. Galen and I need to spend time alone to start healing, and he's extended an olive branch.

His eyes land on mine. "Okay. I'll wait outside. Take your time."

I rummage through the bag I brought with me last night, finding a wrinkled green knee-length jersey dress. I pair it with black-and-white-striped leggings, my white Vans, and my black leather jacket. Letting my damp hair hang in soft waves, I slick some gloss on my lips and apply a light layer of blush to my cheeks and a thick layer of mascara to my lashes. I grab my purse and cell just as it vibrates.

I curse as I read the message from Dar, slipping my cell in my purse and bounding down the stairs.

The lower level is empty, so the guys must be either in the workout barn or they've gone someplace. I walk to the wall with the framed posters, taking a few quick pics of the naked women, smirking as I head outside to meet Galen.

He's already behind the wheel of my Lexus, so I slide in the passenger seat. "You sure you're okay to drive?"

"I'm fine." His eyes rake over my body in appreciation. "I barely register the pain in my ribs anymore," he adds, starting the engine.

"Darrow just messaged me," I say, bringing my knees up to my chest.

"Shit. When does he want to meet?"

"Later today, but I told him midweek."

He smirks. "Bet that went down well."

"I really don't give a fuck. I'm not at his beck and call, and he needs to remember that." I glance out the window as we approach the gate that hides their place from prying eyes. Galen pops out, and I slide into the driver's seat, maneuvering the car out onto the road. Galen secures the gate and sets the alarm through his cell before climbing back in the car. I crawl into the passenger seat, and we head out.

"Has Dar reached out to you since you met with him?" I ask, and he shakes his head.

"Nope, but I'm not surprised. I fully expect him to drag this out now that he thinks you're going to feed him intel." He punches a button on his cell. "We should update the others."

I nod, listening as Galen tells Saint Dar has reached out.

"I need something to give him," I say.

"We have it covered." Saint's deep tone does funny things to me even through the phone. "Sinner has a truck coming from Mexico next Wednesday."

"Since when?" Galen asks, frowning.

"I overheard him on the phone just now."

"You're at the house?" I ask.

"Yeah. He summoned me."

"For what?" I sit up straighter.

"Probably an update on the Lowell Academy situation. He's eager to lock Lowell down tight. Jase and Chad gave up their supplier. This is the guy we've been trying to find. He's the only other dealer on the street, so we'll get the academy and sole ownership of the town as soon as we take him out."

"Why'd they give up their supplier?"

"Idiot raised his prices in some misguided notion that he has a monopoly," Galen says, smirking.

"Your jock buddies don't like being ripped off, so he's delivered his turf right into our hands."

"What will you tell Sinner?" I ask.

"I'll feed him a few nuggets to get him off our back but not enough that he'll be pushing you to complete your other two initiation tasks."

"What about this truck?" Galen asks. "And why is he bringing supply in from Mexico?"

"That's not usual?" I ask, my interest instantly piqued.

"No. We get guns from the Irish and drugs from the Italians, but he's always looking for cheaper options, and I guess he found it."

"Weird he didn't tell us," Galen says, taking a turn that leads us to the rougher part of Prestwick. My brow creases as I stare at him. I assumed we were going to his house in Thornton Heights, but this is in the opposite direction.

"I know." Saint sounds tense.

"You think he suspects something?" I inquire, tucking my hair behind my ears.

"Maybe. Maybe not. Anyway, you can give the intel to Darrow, and that way, we'll find out exactly what's going on, Dar will have a win over the Saints, albeit a small one, and Sinner will shit a brick," Saint says.

"Sounds like a plan," I agree. "I'll still make Dar stew until Monday."

"Gotta go, man," Galen says, pulling up to the curb across from a neglected three-story townhouse. It sits on its own plot of land, surrounded by forest at the rear and a boarded up corrugated fence in front. We're parked in front of the fence, and I peer at the old, weathered sign hanging overhead, noting it was once a gas station and car repair workshop. Apart from a couple houses we passed a mile back, this place is isolated and creepy as fuck. It's giving me a major case of the heebie-jeebies.

"Call if you need backup," Saint says. "Watch your back, princess," he adds before cutting the call.

"Where are we?" I inquire as Galen kills the engine and leans his forearms on the steering wheel.

A different kind of tension bleeds into the air.

He looks up at the dilapidated building across the street. Shutters are hanging off the cracked windows, the grass at the front of the house is waist high, and paint peels off the wooden façade. Crumpled cans, cigarette butts, candy wrappers, and other trash rolls around the sidewalk in front of the property.

"What's going on?" I ask, angling my body so I'm facing him.

"This won't be pleasant," he admits, turning to look at me. "The new housekeeper I hired to keep an eye on Mom called me this morning. She never came home last night." He sighs, looking back up at the house again. "This is usually where I find her."

Understanding washes over me. "It's a drug house?"

He nods, pulling a gun out of the glove compartment. "I shouldn't be too long." He hands me the gun. "Keep alert. Don't hesitate to use it if you need to."

I roll my eyes, checking to make sure the safety is on before placing the small handgun in the inside pocket of my jacket. "Don't insult my fucking intelligence, Lennox." I place my hand on the door handle. "I'm coming in with you, and don't even attempt to argue with me."

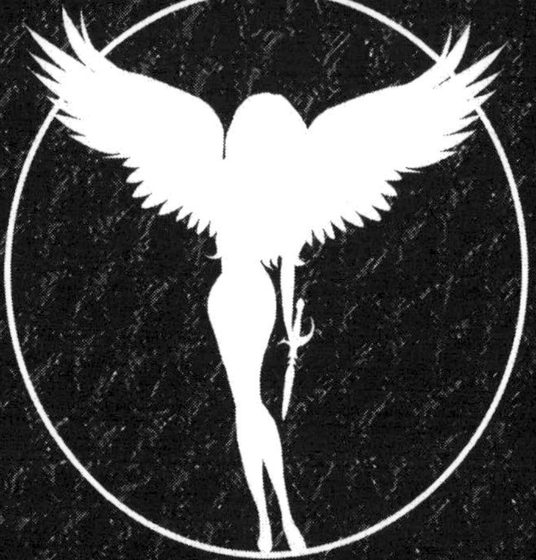

THE SAINTHOOD

CHAPTER 25

THE DOOR CREAKS as Galen pushes it in, and I'm instantly assaulted with an abundance of noxious odors the second I step into the dark hallway. My nose wrinkles as the smell of piss and sweat assaults my nostrils. I keep close to Galen while we climb the stairs.

"Watch out for the broken step third from the top," he whispers, glancing over his shoulder at me. I nod, carefully sidestepping the large hole in the stairs, landing safely on the first floor.

Galen's shoulders are locked tight as he walks past a few doorways. The bare floorboards threaten to give way underfoot despite how softly we tread. A couple of doors are open as we pass, but I don't look too closely, avoiding the vacuous eyes of the woman with the greasy red hair slumped against the floor in one of the rooms as they follow our path.

Galen stops in front of the last door, and his shoulders lift as his heavy breaths filter through the eerie silence. I can see how much of a toll this is taking on him.

How often has he had to do this? And how long has it been

going on?

I take his hand, squeezing it in a show of support. His fingers thread through mine, and I lean into him, gently laying my head against his back. Every muscle and sinew in his body is corded into knots, his body strung tight with stress. We stay like this for a minute, before he moves, releasing my hand. "Stay right beside me, and keep your wits about you," he cautions in a low tone.

"I'll be okay," I whisper back. "Just focus on your mom."

He opens the door, and we step inside. The room is long and wide with high ceilings and peeling wallpaper on the walls. An old-fashioned fireplace is boarded up on one side of the room. A bunch of dirty, torn mattresses are strewn around the exposed wooden floorboards, most occupied with prone bodies. I almost gag over the putrid stench of vomit, piss, and shit. Someone has nailed dark cotton sheets over the two windows, blocking out the real world. The only light comes from slivers of daylight creeping through the side of both windows.

I squint as my eyes adjust to the gloomy room.

"Get the fuck out," a hoarse voice shouts, and some of the people on the mattresses stir, mumbling and groaning.

I step over drug paraphernalia on the floor as I follow Galen to where the man who spoke sits at the far end of the room.

"I'm looking for Alisha Lennox," Galen says, approaching the man. "Is she here?" His gaze flips side to side as he checks people out.

Nausea churns in my gut as I walk past men and women of all ages and races. Most are sprawled across the filthy mattresses. Some are slumped against the walls with their eyes closed. Others are passed out on the floor. The only thing they have in common is pale skin, sunken eyeballs, gaunt cheeks, and an addiction that is worth more to them than life.

I'm not naïve.

I've seen and experienced more than my fair share of dark shit in this world, but there is something so heart-wrenchingly devastating about this scene that is almost worse.

They should take pictures of this room and show it in schools.

Maybe then, kids would take drugs more seriously. I smoke weed on occasion, but this right here is exactly why I never dabble in drugs. I never want to lose control of myself or lose my will to live. I've experienced both, and I swore to myself it would never happen again. I hate I had to go through such a traumatic experience to toughen me up, but I'd rather experience that than go through this living hell day in, day out.

My eyes dart to the skinny woman in the dirty dress lying on her side on a mattress to my right. Her hands are under her head, and clumps of matted hair cover part of her face, but I still recognize her.

I'm shocked at how much she's deteriorated since I last saw her four years ago. "Galen. Over here." I bend down in front of her once beautiful face, and she barely resembles the woman I remember. My eyes lower to the strap tied around her arm and the empty needle still stuck in her vein, and I'm overwhelmed with sadness for her and her son.

Galen hovers over his mom on the other side, pulling plastic gloves from his pocket and handing a pair to me. I watch him gloving up with a heavy ache in my heart. His tormented eyes find mine, and I just want to take away his pain. I put my gloves on as he presses his fingers to her neck, closing his eyes, his shoulders visibly relaxing when he finds a pulse.

"Should we wake her?" I ask, wanting to help but not knowing how.

"We can try." He shakes her shoulders gently. "Mom. It's Galen. Wake up." She arches her back, mumbling in her sleep. "C'mon, Mom. Let's go home." She squirms again, but her eyes still don't open. "This is useless." He sighs, walking around to me, and I straighten up and step aside to let him by. My heart lodges in my throat, and tears prick my eyes as he gently removes the needle from her vein and unties the strap from her arm. I kick both away, letting them join the myriad of other shit on the floor.

Galen scoops his mom up, cradling her to his chest. I walk toward the door, opening it wide for him to step through.

We don't talk as we walk back down the stairs, out the front door, and over to the Lexus.

I open the passenger side back door, only noticing the blanket draped across the leather interior for the first time. A couple plastic bags and a couple bottles of water are in the side pocket. Galen moves to put his Mom in, but I hold his elbow, stalling him. "Do you want me to drive so you can sit with her?"

"No, I … Yeah. Would that be okay?"

"Of course. Whatever you need."

I help them get situated in the back. Alisha is still out cold with her head on Galen's lap as I drag the second blanket over her thin frame.

"Thanks," Galen says.

"I need the keys," I remind him, and he lifts his hips, attempting to extract them from his pocket.

"Let me." He sits his butt back down, and I dig into his jeans pocket, ignoring how my fingers brush against the side of his cock, fishing out the keys.

Our eyes meet, and a lick of red-hot lust ignites the space between us.

"She might get sick," he whispers. "I'll try to keep your car clean."

I grin. "It's okay. I'm not Saint." His lips twitch. "We can clean up later. You take care of your mom." I lean in, kissing his cheek. "You're a great son."

His smile fades. "She wouldn't be like this if that were true."

I climb behind the wheel and close the door, wanting to get the fuck out of here. "You're not responsible for her actions," I say, as I turn the car around, driving back the way we came. "She's an adult, and she should've been the one taking care of you."

"I've never known anything different." He brushes matted hair back off her face. "Although it wasn't quite this bad when Dad and Mya were alive."

"I'm sorry you lost your dad and your sister. I know how horrible it is to lose someone you love." A muscle ticks in his jaw, and a familiar hard glaze glints in his eyes. I frown as I look at him through the mirror. "Did I say something wrong?"

He forcibly relaxes his facial muscles. "Mya is a touchy subject for me," he admits after a few beats of tense silence.

"Why?" I ask, turning onto the road that leads to Thornton Heights, because I'm sensing this is more than just grief.

"I'll tell you later. After we get Mom settled."

I nod, wetting my lips, my mouth suddenly feeling dry. "Do the guys know how bad this is?"

"Yeah. They are usually with me when I'm hauling her out of places. Believe it or not, that place is one of the better ones."

A shudder works its way through me. "No one should have to live like that."

"Mom has always battled demons, but after Dad died, she just gave up." He looks out the window, his Adam's apple jumping in his throat. "Apparently, her life means that little to her and I'm not enough for her to fight to live."

"You *are* enough," I say in a soft voice, as so many things make sense now. "Addiction is selfish, but that's all on her. Not you. From what I'm seeing, you are doing everything you can for her." I knew Alisha was a junkie, but I never properly stopped to think about what that meant for Galen. No wonder, he's bitter and lashes out. He's in so much pain. At some point, he'll have to start prioritizing self-love and self-care before his mom's addictions ruin his life for good.

"Except I'm part of the very organization supplying the drugs on the street." A look of disgust crosses his face. "I go to great lengths to keep drugs out of the house, only throwing parties when she's not there and making sure there is no cash lying around, but she always gets her hands on it. I've threatened dealers, and Sinner has helped me handle a few, but she's fucking resourceful."

Addicts usually are.

"Can't you get out?" I ask, already half-knowing the truth.

"I wish I could, angel." He leans his head against the side of the window, looking at me through the mirror as I turn into his driveway. "But I need the money to take care of us because we don't have money coming from any other source. And, besides, this is a life choice. One decided for me before I was born." He glances down at his mother, his features softening as he caresses her gaunt cheek. "The best we can hope for is to gain control of The Sainthood in the future and make changes. Quit with the illegal shit and set up legitimate businesses." A ghost of a smile graces his lips. "We need more guys like Theo with the smarts to bring us to the next level."

It's a tall order because you don't change an organization as twisted as The Sainthood so easily, but I admire his determination and the inherent goodness that exists in all of them.

It's quite miraculous when you think about it. Especially for Saint and Galen because they had shitty upbringings and no one or nothing to guide them except for the thread of decency and morality that resides inside them. I can only imagine how conflicted they must be. Because some of this is in their blood, and it's all they've ever known, and it would be so much easier to just go with the flow. My admiration for them increases ten-fold because they are battling for what is right even though it's the harder road to travel.

I pull up in front of the neglected mansion, killing the engine.

Between us, we get Alisha into the house.

She has only made it through the front door when she wakes up, vomiting all over the tile floor. An older lady, with gray hair tied up in a bun, wearing an austere navy dress and tights, rushes to meet us. "I'll clean this up if you want to take her upstairs," she says.

Galen nods, waiting for Alisha to finish dry heaving on the floor. Her dress has ridden up her ass, displaying the black thong she's wearing. I pull her dress back down, and Galen shoots me an appreciative look.

Alisha falls in and out of consciousness as we carry her upstairs.

Galen holds her upright as I undress her to her bra and thong and wash her in the shower. We are all drenched when we get out, but I don't complain, stripping out of my wet clothes and accepting the hoodie, T-shirt, and leggings he hands me.

The shirt and hoodie are a little on the big side, so I'm guessing they belong to Galen and the leggings are too short so I figure they are Alisha's, but I can't complain because I'm warm and dry. I slip my feet into my Vans, thankful I remembered to remove them in time. I tie my wet hair up into a messy bun and return my attention to Alisha.

Galen looks up at the ceiling while I remove his mom's wet undies, pat her skeletal body dry, and help her floppy limbs into pajamas.

Galen carries her to the master suite, carefully laying her on the bed, propping her up against the headboard.

I look around, noting the freshly painted walls, luxurious, heavy velvet drapes, and the mahogany king-sized bed dressed in a plush gray, pink, and white comforter.

Galen takes such good care of his mother, only I'm not sure she deserves it.

I stand in front of the window, eyeing the overgrown maze outside with a new lump in my throat.

"Giana?" Alisha calls out, and I turn around as Galen stills, his hand clutching a comb as he drags it through her hair.

My chest tightens, and the lump in my throat grows bigger. "It's Harlow," I say, forcing the words out. I perch on the edge of the bed. "Giana's daughter."

Her dull green eyes skim my face. "You look so much like her." Her voice lowers. "Like him too."

Galen stiffens, and it confirms my suspicions. Whatever Galen's issue is with me, it's got something to do with my father. I'd stake my life on it.

Galen promised he'd give me his full truth, and I'm not leaving this house until I know it all.

THE SAINTHOOD

CHAPTER 26

AFTER WE DRY Alisha's hair and tuck her in bed, I watch Galen hook a drip up to her arm with a heavy heart for all he's had to endure. She looks so frail in the big bed, curled into a fetal position as she sleeps. A raspy wheezy noise rumbles from her chest that doesn't sound good. Galen presses a kiss to the top of her head before we quietly slip out of her bedroom.

He leads me downstairs into the kitchen. "Hungry?" he asks, moving toward the refrigerator.

"Not especially," I admit, because, honestly, the events of this morning have cost me my appetite. Not to mention I'm still quite full from the delicious late breakfast Theo prepared.

"Shoo, boy," the kindly gray-haired woman says, rushing into the kitchen. I assume she's the housekeeper he mentioned. She pulls on his elbow, and his head pops out of the refrigerator. "It's a lovely day. Take your girlfriend out to the garden. I'll call you when lunch is ready."

"She's not—"

"That sounds wonderful," I say, cutting across Galen. "And I'm Harlow. Pleased to meet you."

"I'm Mrs. Murphy, but you can call me Maureen." She squeezes my hand. "And it's lovely to meet you too, dear."

Galen snatches my hand. "Come on."

We walk hand in hand outside, and I swat my anxiety aside. If we're going to confront the ghosts of our past, there is no better place to do this. "Can we talk in the maze?" I ask, and he slams to a halt, his eyes drilling into mine.

"Why would you want to go in there?"

"Seems fitting." I hold his gaze confidently.

"Okay." He grips my hand more firmly as we change direction, heading for the other side of the garden. "It's overgrown now. I can't afford to pay for a groundskeeper."

"Didn't your grandmother leave an inheritance?"

"My parents shot that in their veins."

"I still think about the day of the party. The last time I was here with my parents," I say, wanting to change the subject.

"Me too," he admits, stopping at the entrance to the maze. "I wanted to kiss you so bad that day."

I tug on his hand, moving forward, taking a step into our past. Tall, unkempt shrubs tower over us, on all sides, as we walk, blocking out much of the light. The temp is cooler in here and I shiver.

"Over here," he says, walking to the worn wooden bench off to the side. He sweeps some leaves and debris off it before sitting down, pulling me in close to his side. His arm goes around me. "Steal some of my body warmth." He shoots me a lopsided grin. "Is this okay?"

I turn my head to face him, smiling softly. "Yes." I examine his eyes. "I want to know everything, Galen. No matter how painful it might be to hear, I want to leave here with all the facts."

He tucks a few stray strands of hair behind my ears. "I promise I will hold nothing back."

I nod, seeing the truth in his eyes. "I wanted to kiss you too," I admit, deciding to showcase my vulnerability first so he knows I'm in this with him. "But I was so broken, Galen. It was only a few months after the kidnapping, and I couldn't bear even the slightest touch. Mom couldn't kiss me good night and Dad couldn't hold my hand without me freaking out." Pressure settles on my chest as I remember how scared I was in the aftermath of my ordeal.

"I didn't know."

"How would you? You were a kid too, and I didn't say shit to anyone."

"Your rejection hurt," he admits. "Because you'd been the only bright spot that entire day." He smiles as he looks around. "I can still hear your giggles as I chased you through here."

I smile back at him, snuggling in closer to his side, siphoning some of his warmth as I look up at him. "That was the first time in ages I'd laughed like that, and I remember feeling happy."

"Until I had to go and ruin it." He shoots me another lopsided grin.

I roll my eyes. "Like a typical boy."

"Is it egotistical if I say I'm glad I was the one to make you laugh?"

"No." I nudge him playfully in the ribs. "Typical guy sentiment." I waggle my brows, and his smile returns, lighting up his whole face.

I know I've teased Galen about being pretty, but it's no word of a lie.

Galen is a stunning man.

He could be a model with that mass of dark hair, piercing green eyes, thick, lush lips and high angular cheekbones I'd kill for.

"Keep looking at me like that, angel, and we won't be doing much talking." His husky voice penetrates skin, lodging bone deep, and a flurry of shivers skips through my veins.

I cup his face. "You're beautiful, Galen. Hot as fuck, and I won't deny I want you, but I'm not ready to take it there yet."

He gulps, nodding. "It's okay. I understand, and I can be patient." His lips lift. "At least, I'll try to be." He brushes his thumbs across my cheeks as my hands drop to my lap. "And so there's no confusion, I'm fucking hot for you, Lo, and I'm done pretending otherwise."

"I'm glad we got that cleared up," I joke, pressing a soft kiss to the underside of his jaw. "But now, you need to explain why you hated me so much."

He tightens his hold on my arm. "It wasn't so much you I hated as—"

"My father." I finish for him.

He nods.

"Why? What did he do? Is this something to do with those pictures of your mom we found in his office?"

He grinds his teeth, and anger flashes in his eyes. "Yes."

"Where did those boxes come from?"

"Your mom had them."

"What? Why?"

"All I know is, she gave them to Sinner when he asked about your father's paperwork. And we're getting off point."

I nod, urging him to continue with my eyes, parking that little nugget of information in the back of my mind to think about later.

I patiently wait for him to continue, and the longer he remains silent, battling an invisible enemy, the more anxious I become. "Galen, please. Just spit it out. I need to know."

He looks at me, the hardness softening a smidgeon. "This is going to hurt you, Lo, and I promised I wouldn't do that again."

"Don't hide behind that! This only works if we get it all out. I'm a big girl. I'll handle it."

"Your father had an affair with my mother, and it set off a whole fucked-up chain of events," he blurts.

Okay, wait. What?

I shake my head. "No. No way. My father wouldn't do that! He worshiped the ground my mother walked on!"

"I saw them myself!"

"What?" I whisper as pain slices across my chest.

"That same day. You'd run off on me after I tried to kiss you. I sulked out here for a while, and then, I went looking for you. I stumbled across your dad kissing my mom."

Tears sting my eyes, but I refuse to let them fall. "Are you sure it was him?"

"One hundred percent."

"Maybe they were drunk, and it was only a onetime thing and—"

"He knocked her up," Galen says, pursing his lips.

"What?" Tears pool in my eyes this time. I can't believe what I'm hearing. "No!"

He presses his forehead to mine. "I'm sorry, Lo, but it's true."

I pull back from him. "How do you know?"

"I heard my parents arguing about it."

Shock splays across my face. "Your father *knew*?" *What kind of new sick, twisted shit is this?*

"It seems so. He was fucking furious until Mom told him your dad gave her fifty grand for an abortion and her silence."

I shuck out of Galen's arm, standing and clutching my stomach as I double over. "This isn't happening."

"He didn't want your mom to know. I watched my parents sign NDAs after they stopped bickering."

Tears spill down my cheeks. *Did I know my father at all? Has absolutely everything been a lie?*

Galen stands, reaching for me, but I swat his arms away. "You blamed me for this?" I wave my arms in the air as my voice elevates a few notches. "How the fuck was any of this my fault?"

"It wasn't," he says, tucking his hands in the pocket of his jeans. "But after my sister died, the anger inside me mushroomed and mushroomed until I hated your dad and you."

"Not my mom?"

"She was the innocent party in all of it. Her and Mya."

"I was a fucking innocent party too!" I yell before frowning. "What did your sister have to do with it?"

He starts pacing, grabbing fistfuls of his hair. "Mya was born with a congenital heart defect. She'd had multiple surgeries over the years. Around this time, she started having problems. Was in and out of the hospital. She had a mini-stroke a few months before she died." He drops down onto the bench, leaning his elbows on his knees and burying his face in his hands. His shoulders heave. I calm myself down, rejoining him on the bench, although I'm careful to keep a distance between us, because I'm fucking mad at him. And furious at my father.

"I'm sorry for how you lost your sister. Genuinely, I am, Galen, but how is it connected?"

"They neglected her!" he yells, lifting his face to mine. His nostrils flare, and a splash of red creeps up his neck. "Your dad gave my mom fifty grand and it was like Mardi fucking Gras for my parents. They took that money and partied hard, leaving me and Mya to fend for ourselves. I was fourteen. She was ten. Grandma was sick, dying, and I didn't want to burden her, so I tried my best. Took Mya to her appointments, made sure she ate and took her meds, but she was growing weaker, and my parents just weren't there." His voice cracks, and he buries his head in his hands.

His body shakes, and I let go of my anger, scooting over beside him, wrapping my arm around his back. "It's not your fault. You were a kid, and your parents should've cared for their daughter better."

"She died in my arms," he mumbles, lifting his head and slumping against my body. "She had a massive heart attack. I called nine-one-one, but they got to us too late. I couldn't save her," he adds in a whisper, as a tear sneaks out of one eye.

Now, I get why saving his pathetic excuse of a mother means so much to him.

"Oh, Galen." I hold him tighter. "No kid should have to go through that."

He turns red-rimmed eyes on me. "Like no little girl should have to go through what you went through."

Silent tears roll down his face. "It haunts me, Lo. I see Mya every night when I close my eyes, and I miss her so fucking much. Most little sisters annoy their older brothers, but Mya was never that for me. I loved everything about her. She had so much spirit, and she never complained even though her life was curtailed in so many ways because of her illness. She always saw the positive in every situation. My parents never deserved her."

"They didn't deserve either of you." I rub my hand up and down his back, and he leans into me, pressing his forehead to my shoulder. I hold on to him as he clings to me, my mind churning with all I've learned. I still don't understand why he hated me for this, but I'm not going to press him while he's so upset.

Galen and I have already suffered enough for the sins of our parents, so I'm letting go of my anger, for both our sakes.

"The night I heard my parents fighting," he continues, lifting his head but still keeping his arms around me, "Mom mentioned how much Trey loved you. She said everything revolved around you." He has the decency to look ashamed. "I latched on to that. I made it all about you. In my head, you were the reason your dad started an affair with my mom and got her knocked up. And you were the reason he bought her silence, and in doing so, he set everything in motion. When Mya died, I have never felt so lost or alone. Saint and the guys were all I had. Then Dad overdosed, and Mom stopped trying. That anger burning in my veins fueled my vengeance. That was the reason I got up every day. I swore I would get revenge on your father."

"And then Sinner killed him," I say, fitting the pieces together.

"And I transferred my anger to you. It wasn't that hard because you had my brothers in a tailspin."

"This is so fucked up." I sigh, letting my hands drop away from his body.

"You want to know what's really fucked up?" He raises his hands to my neck, rubbing his thumbs up and down my skin, eliciting a rake of fiery tremors. "They say there's a fine line between love and hate."

I stop breathing for a second, eyes locked on his. "Don't you dare say it," I hiss after a few seconds. "I can't hear that right now."

His expression is contrite. "Doesn't make it not true." He removes his hands from my face, propping his elbows on his knees, and resting his chin in his hands. "I told you I'm fucked up."

"Don't turn this into a pity party, because you're stronger than that."

"Am I?" he turns toward me. "It feels like I'm running on empty these past few weeks."

My anger dissipates again. "There is only one truth I know that matters anymore."

He stares at me with an intense lens, waiting for me to elaborate.

"We've got to stick together. We've got to trust in each other and believe that together we can make this all right, because otherwise we're doomed to lead lives we don't want." Fierce determination surges through me. "And I fucking refuse to accept that's my destiny."

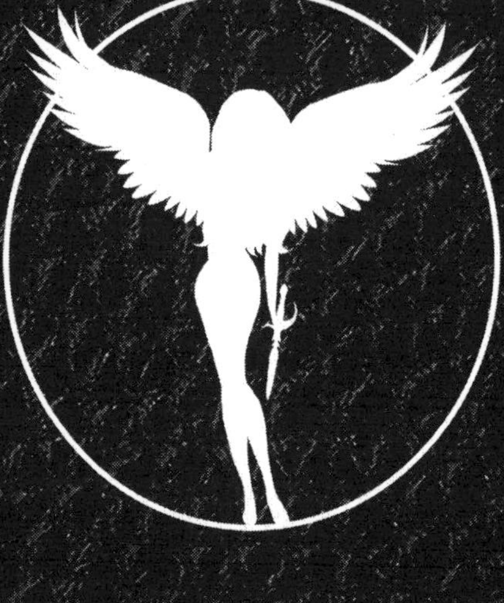

THE SAINTHOOD

CHAPTER 27

"No! PLEASE NO!" Galen thrashes about in the bed, crying out in his sleep, rousing me from my own troubled slumber. "You're not dead! You're not dead!" he whimpers, and that ache is back in my chest.

"Shush, babe." I sit up, resting my back against the headboard as I reach out for him. The second my hands land on his back, he scoots forward, snuggling into me with his head in my lap. "It's okay. I'm here. Go back to sleep," I murmur.

His arm wraps around my thighs, and he whimpers again. My fingers thread through his hair and I lean down, dotting kisses on his cheek. I continue stroking his hair as I lean my head back and close my eyes.

It's been an exhausting day, which seems to be the pattern of my life now.

When Galen asked me to stay here tonight, so he could keep a close eye on his mother, I wanted to tell him no. To explain I wanted to run a million miles from him and his horrid mother and this house full of terrible memories.

And that's precisely why I stayed.

There is no point coming here, moving into this in-between space with Galen and then running off half-assed before it's resolved. Best to confront it all head on.

I open my eyes as a slight breeze enters the room. I shiver and Galen's arm clutches my thigh harder as he cuddles into me. I smile as I run my fingers over his hair, watching, as his murmurs fade and his breathing evens out, until he's in a deep sleep. I'm happy one of us is. His long lashes fan out over his cheekbones, and air whooshes out of his gorgeous mouth in gentle puffs, and I could stare at him all night.

What a complex, broken soul he is. And so tortured. I'm happy I stayed now because this is what we both need. We didn't have sex, and I doubt it was on his mind either. He seemed content to go to sleep wrapped around me, and it didn't feel weird.

It felt right.

I lean down and press a kiss to his head.

I can't hold on to my anger because Galen doesn't deserve it. I'm going to offer him my forgiveness because it's right and it's what I feel in my heart.

It's not pity.

It's compassion.

He has been through so much, and even though he was misguided and so cruel to blame me for something I knew nothing about, and had no control over, he was so broken at the time, grieving his sister and drowning in responsibility.

And I get how afraid he was of me messing up the crew dynamic. The guys are all he has. When I waltzed into their lives, I shook everything up, bringing it all back to the present. Take that, and all this shit he's going through with his mom, and Dar preying on his vulnerability at the perfect moment, and I see how it happened.

The brain can't cope when it's overloaded, and it's exactly those moments when we make poor decisions.

At least, I understand it all now.

Movement at the door captures my attention, and I look up into Alisha Lennox's pale-green eyes. I wonder how long she's been standing there watching us. From the tears clinging to her lashes, I'd say it's been a while.

"Stay, sweetheart," she whispers when I move to lift Galen's head from my lap. "Look after my boy." She closes the door, careful not to make a sound.

I don't want to leave Galen, but he's sound asleep now, and I hope he won't wake again, because I can't waste this opportunity. I may not get another one where Alisha seems clearheaded, and I fucking want answers. Answers her son can't give.

Very slowly and carefully, I slide out from under Galen, shoving a pillow under his head and another one in front of his torso. He curls around the pillow, and he looks so young even with his long muscular body, ink creeping up his arms, and the ring in his nose. I press a kiss to his temple before I pull on the hoodie and leggings I removed before bed and slip my feet into my Vans.

I try Alisha's bedroom first, but the master suite is empty, so I pad downstairs to the kitchen.

She's sitting at the long wooden table, nursing a bottle of water when I arrive. She looks up, not surprised to see me. "I imagine you have questions."

"I do." I walk to the coffeepot, filling it with water and switching it on. "I think I'll need coffee for this conversation." We don't talk as I wait for the coffee to fill. We just stare at one another, sizing each other up.

"Want one?" I ask, holding up a mug.

She shakes her head. "I'm good with water."

"Is it safe to talk?" I inquire while pouring myself a black coffee.

"I disabled the camera in here. It's safe."

I take the seat across from her.

"How much do you know?"

"What Galen knows," I admit.

"Which is?"

"You had an affair with my father. You got pregnant with his baby. Took his money to abort it and kept it a secret from my mom, your former best friend." I glare at her, wanting her to see how much disdain I hold her in. "Used the money to fuel your party lifestyle, leaving your kids to fend for themselves. Your daughter died in your son's arms, and he hasn't stopped beating himself up over not saving her ever since. That about sums it up."

"How did Galen find out? Did Sinner tell him?" she asks. The glass shakes in her hand, and her body trembles.

"Why would Sinner tell him?" I narrow my eyes, immediately suspicious.

"Because he set the whole thing up, and I feared one day he'd tell my son everything."

"Which is?" I hiss, setting my mug down and straining forward. "What did that asshole do?"

"What hasn't he done might be an easier question to answer."

I drill her with a look, and she cracks a slight smile.

"You have her spirit you know. Giana is a fighter too."

She clearly doesn't know my mom as well as she thinks she does. "I didn't come down here for compliments. I want answers." I slam my hand down on the table. "I want to know why my father, the man I adored above all men, turned out to be a liar and a cheat. I need to know if any of it was real. And I need to know all the ways that bastard Sinner tried to ruin my family."

"I will tell you what I know, but my son can't hear this."

"Why?"

"Because he doesn't know the half of it, and if he finds out, I'm afraid of what he might do." She reaches across the table, and her bony hand lands on top of mine. Her palm is sweaty, her fingers trembling.

"I can't promise I won't tell him because we have a rule about not keeping secrets, but I can promise I will keep him safe. I will stop him from doing anything that might endanger his life. We will stop him. Sinner will not harm a hair on Galen's head."

"Do you love my son, Harlow?"

"I … I don't know," I honestly admit. "I have strong feelings for him, but things are complicated between us, and we're still working it out."

"Nothing can happen to him." Tears fill her eyes. "He is all I have left."

My eyes probe hers for the truth, and I see it there and the love shining brightly for him. "Then fight harder! If you die, it will break him for good. Don't you see that?"

"I want to," she sobs. "I want to so much, but you don't understand. These thoughts in my head, these voices whispering in my ear, they *never* stop, they never leave me alone, and I'm haunted by all my failings, and I just need to make it stop." She reclaims her hand, rubbing it back and forth across her chest. "It's never been about not loving my son enough, because if that was all it took, I would be clean and sober."

"You're right. I don't understand. And I want to help you, only because that helps your son, but I will never understand how a mother can selfishly choose to block out life rather than helping her own flesh and blood, but maybe, I'm the warped one."

If she thought she'd gain my sympathy, she can think again. I know what it's like to have voices and thoughts screaming in your head. I've often wondered what would've happened if Dad hadn't been there, supporting and helping me every step of the way. I think Alisha has just given me my first answer.

No amount of support and help works unless the person is willing to support and help themselves.

Alisha has Galen's love and support, but it wasn't enough because she didn't want to help herself.

I know now I would've been okay without Dad. The journey would've been tougher, but I would've come through it in the end because I didn't want to be a victim.

I'm a survivor, and I will always choose to live.

"Sinner forced your father to have an affair with me," she says, seemingly deciding I can be trusted. "It was a few months after your kidnapping," she adds, confirming she knew who had taken me, and my regard for her sinks even lower. "He threatened to kill you if he didn't do it."

"And this was all about my mom? Some fucked-up plan to get her back?"

She bobs her head, taking a sip of water. It dribbles down her chin, slipping under her pajama top. "It has always been about Giana. Sinner has loved her with this obsessive need from the moment they met. It was always unhealthy, and I tried to warn her so many times, but she was in love, and she couldn't see what the rest of us could see. That he was batshit crazy and a loose cannon but so fucking smart, and that scared me."

"Did you meet Galen's dad through my mom?"

She smiles sadly. "I did. Nix was nothing like his younger brother. He had a good heart. At least, before Neo stuck his claws in." Her features harden. "It was Neo who introduced Nix and me to drugs. He rarely partook, and he forbid your mom from touching the stuff. We were idiots to not see the writing on the wall. By the time I realized, it was too late."

She scrubs at her eyes, sniffing. "Anyway, with your dad, Sinner had him over a barrel. No one takes anything from Neo Lennox and lives to tell the tale. If he was insane before he lost your mom, he was completely psychotic after she married Trey. He threatened Trey from the very start. Told him he'd kill Giana. Forced your father to work for The Sainthood and then used that to threaten his career and his family. Trey tried to walk away, and they kidnapped you as a warning."

I gulp my lukewarm coffee, waiting for her to continue.

"But Sinner wasn't done punishing Trey. He told him to start an affair with me or he'd kill you next time."

"Why?"

"Because he wanted to prove to Giana that she'd chosen the wrong man, and he wanted to hurt Nix."

"Why would you agree to that?" She looks down at the table, and I swallow back bile. "For money," I surmise.

"For drugs," she whispers.

I shake my head, utterly disgusted. "And your husband knew?"

"Not at first, but I had to tell him when I got pregnant. That shouldn't have happened because Trey always used condoms."

I slam my coffee down and count to ten in my head. I do *not* want to hear this.

This fucking woman.

"What happened next?" I clip out, barely keeping it together.

"I got money from your dad, and Sinner trotted off to Giana to break up her marriage."

I sit up straighter, jerking my head up. "Wait? My mom *knew*?"

"Of course, she did. That was the whole point of Neo's plan. He thought she'd leave Trey and run straight back into his arms, but your mom is smart, Harlow. She knew Sinner was blackmailing your father."

"Does she know Sinner kidnapped me?"

"I don't know, sweetie. You'd have to ask her."

"Why did my father have pictures of you high, fucking different men?"

Her face pales, and her lower lip wobbles. "I don't know." She brings the glass to her lips, but her hands are shaking so bad she can't even swallow the water, and it trickles down her chin, down her pajamas, and on the table.

I move over beside her, holding the glass to her mouth, encouraging her to drink.

"You must think I'm terrible."

She really doesn't want to know what I think. "What I think doesn't matter."

"Sinner makes me do it!" she cries. "Drugs me up and pimps me out. It's been going on for years although he hasn't called on me lately."

No surprise there. I'm betting the market for strung-out washed-up junkies is nonexistent.

Perhaps, that's why she does it—dopes herself up to the eyeballs so she forgets. Damn, if I don't feel guilty for my earlier uncharitable thoughts. This is way more messed up than I could ever have imagined.

Fucking hell. Sinner is the devil hiding in human form.

And my mom is fucking engaged to be married to him.

Acid crawls up my throat at the thought of what he has planned for her, and I can't stand by and let it happen. I need to have an honest conversation with Mom.

I wrap my arm around Alisha's back as she quietly sobs, and pity flows through me. What a mess she has made of her life. And Sinner has fed off her every weakness, snatched every opportunity to dig the hole deeper and wider.

How many families has Sinner fucked up? I'm even more determined to stop him now.

"I want it to stop, Harlow, but I don't have any choice. If I don't do what he says, he'll kill Galen. He already took his father from me. I can't lose my son too."

Blood turns to ice in my veins. "What does that mean, Alisha?"

Her skeletal frame heaves as she cries. "I was the one who found Nix, and I always believed it was an accidental overdose until Neo told me he staged it to look like that. It seems Nix was stealing from him, saving money to take us overseas so we could finally get away from his poisonous brother, but Neo found out, because Neo *always* finds out, and he killed him for it." Her tearstained eyes meet mine. "Neo killed his own brother, and he had no qualms about doing it. So, everything I do, I do for my son because hell will freeze before I let that bastard take my son's life too."

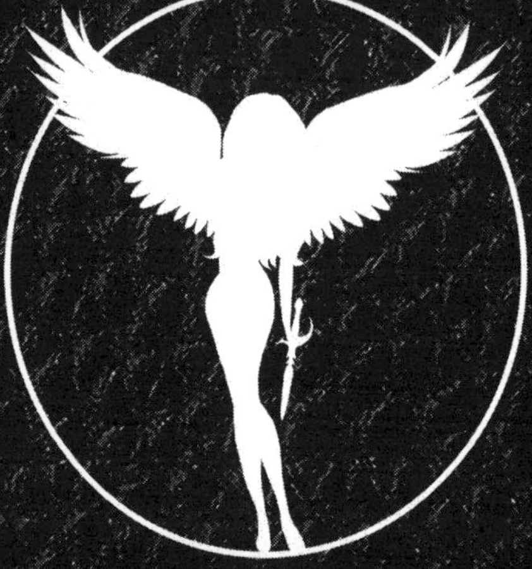

THE SAINTHOOD

CHAPTER 28

A LOUD CRASH from the hallway has us jumping from our seats and racing out of the kitchen to investigate. An ornate mahogany lamp table, most likely one of the few family heirlooms left, lies in pieces on the floor behind Galen. He's slamming his fists into the wall, over and over, screaming obscenities.

"Oh no!" Alisha rushes to her son's side. "How much did you hear?"

He ignores her, continuing to beat his fists into the wall, his knuckles already torn and bleeding.

"Galen, please stop. Talk to me!" Alisha pleads.

"Now, you want to talk?!" he roars, spinning around, and the expression on his face is one of lethal rage. "That fucking psycho bastard murdered my father, and you didn't think I should know that?!" His nostrils flare, and his entire body trembles and shakes as fury oozes from every pore.

"This is why," Alisha sobs, clutching his arm. "You can't go after him, Galen. He'll kill you!"

"Not if I fucking kill him first," he shouts. "Aaaggh." He races to the spot where the broken table lies, lifting his leg and slamming it up and down on the jagged wooden pile, breaking it into smaller pieces, as he takes his aggression out on the ancient wood.

"Galen, please." Alisha cries, wrapping her arms around herself.

"Go away, Mom. I can't be around you right now."

She hesitates, and I step up to her, urging her with my eyes. Her eyes beg me to help, and I reassure her as best I can because I'm not sure I can tame the storm inside her son. This has been an emotional day, and he's reached his breaking point.

Alisha walks off, her shoulders slumped, her cries bouncing off the creepy dark-green walls.

"Galen." I cautiously step up to him. "Stop."

"Don't fucking tell me what to do, Lo." He slams his foot down on the splintered wooden pile, and I grab the back of his shirt, pulling him back.

He stumbles a little on his feet, and I use it to my advantage, pushing him across the hallway and up against the wall. Rage burns in his eyes, and I do the only thing I can think of—I slam my lips down firmly on his. He reacts immediately, slanting his mouth harshly over mine, tugging my lip into his mouth and biting down hard, drawing blood.

Our lips and tongues battle for supremacy while our bodies thrust against one another, against the wall. I sink my teeth into his neck, breaking skin, and a guttural growl escapes his mouth. "I'll bleed for you now, Galen. We can bleed together." I shove his sweatpants down his legs without waiting for a response. He's not wearing boxers, and his cock springs up. He's long and thick, and his angry head leaks precum. He kicks his sweats away, spreading his thighs, as he glares at me, channeling all his anger in my direction.

I slide to my knees, looking up at him as my hand wraps around his erection, pumping his shaft in quick strokes. "Give it all to me. Unleash the storm. I can handle it." I don't wait for him to reply, lowering my mouth to his cock and sucking him deep.

He's the biggest of all the guys, and I can't take him all the way in my mouth without triggering my gag reflex, but I stretch my mouth and take as much of him as I can, fisting the base of his cock as he rolls his hips, thrusting savagely into my mouth.

He winds my hair around his hand, using it to control his movements, as he yanks my head back a little, angling his hips and shoving deeper into my mouth. Tears leak from my eyes, and I graze my teeth along his length. He hisses, yanking my hair harder, and stinging pain rips across my scalp. My panties are soaked, and my core pulses with need as he continues to fuck my mouth with abandon. His face is contorted in angry slashes, and he's lost to the moment as he violently thrusts in and out.

Without warning, he pulls me up by my hair, slinging me over his shoulder and slapping my ass. Liquid desire leaks from my pussy, and I moan while admiring his fine ass from this upside-down angle. He drops me on the table, pushing me down by my chest, and my head thuds off the hardwood, but I barely register the pain because my entire body is on fire and all I can think about is having his cock buried deep inside me.

He pulls my sneakers off and rips my leggings down my legs. I remove my hoodie and T-shirt as he whips his shirt over his head.

The bruises on his torso are faded, but I'm guessing he's still in pain. Yet I don't question it.

He needs this, and he'll fuck through his pain.

Forcing my legs apart, he shoves his face between the apex of my thighs, and his tongue plunges into my heat while he pushes two fingers into my ass.

"Fuck!" I squirm on the table as scorching-hot flames lick at my skin and charge every nerve ending in my body. I'm lost to sensation as he works my body like a pro.

Grabbing his hair, I jerk my hips up as he eats me out, and I'm drowning in a sea of bliss, dancing on the edge of pleasure and pain. His fingers are rough in my ass, his tongue fierce, as he brings me to orgasm in record time. I'm screaming out his name as he flips me over, my hips banging painfully against the edge of the table, with stars still blurring my vision when he thrusts inside my cunt without warning.

I cry out as he fucks me without restraint, slamming into me so deep it feels like he's invading my womb. His fingers dig into my hips and the top of my ass as he ruts into me like an out-of-control, wild savage.

And I am seriously fucked in the head, because I fucking love it.

"Harder," I demand, gripping the edge of the table for support.

He lays his whole body down on top of me, pressing me into the table as his cock pounds in and out of my pussy. He bites my earlobe before trailing his teeth up and down my neck. He sucks and bites, and I cry out as a second climax crashes over me from nowhere. His hands wrap around my throat from behind, and he squeezes. "You like pain," he grits out. "And I've got plenty of that to go around."

When it feels like I might pass out from lack of oxygen and the crushing weight of his body, he eases off me, his hands gliding more gently down my back. "Fucking beautiful," he rasps, viciously jamming his cock inside me, while moving his fingers around to the front of my body, finding my clit and rubbing it hard. "My beautiful avenging angel." He bites my lower back, right where my ink covers the logo I hate so much. "We are going to destroy the world together."

"Damn fucking straight," I rasp just as he roars out his release, spilling inside me, branding me for eternity.

We stay like that for a couple minutes, and the only sound in the kitchen is our joint ragged breathing. His hands roam my back, his fingers exploring the tattoo covering my skin.

"He's fucking dead," he says in a low tone, pulling out of me and helping me to straighten up.

I prop my butt against the table, watching as he walks to the hallway to retrieve his sweatpants. He snatches my clothes off the floor, along with this T-shirt, and hands them to me. "You can't go after him now," I say as I dress, watching him closely. Our angry fuck has only sliced the corners off his fury. "It needs to be planned."

He slams his bloodied fist on the table. "How the fuck do you expect me to look at that fucking bastard without wanting to kill him?" He shakes his head. "I can't do it."

I slide off the table and grab his cheeks in my hands. "You can, and you will."

"Fuck off, Lo. He was my father!" He pushes me away.

"He murdered mine too!" I yell. "And he's playing some sick game with Mom and me, just like he's doing to you and your mom. He kidnapped and tortured me, and I have to live with him!"

I reclaim the distance, placing my hands on his chest. "I hate him so much, Galen, and I cannot bear to look at his face, but I withstand it because I know he's a smart fucker and he's not killing any more Westbrooks." I press a hard kiss to his lips. "Or Lennoxes," I add in a softer tone. "I know you're hurting. That you want him to pay, and he will. But we've got to be smart about this."

"This will fuck with Saint's head too," he admits, pulling me in closer, and I'm relieved to see him regaining his control.

"Undoubtedly."

Racing footsteps greet us from the hallway, and we turn in time to witness a frantic Alisha bounding through the door. "You need to get out of here!" she screeches. "They're coming!" She shoves us toward the door at the far end of the kitchen, thrusting the Lexus keys at Galen. "You can't be here. You're not supposed to know about this. He'll kill us all." She glances over her shoulder, shrieking as the glare from multiple headlights filters through the kitchen window. Tears stream down her face. "Go, please. Take Harlow to safety."

That snaps Galen out of it. "What's going on?"

"No time to explain." She continues pushing us. "Use the back entrance to leave so they don't see you."

"What about you?" I ask.

"I'll be fine. I'll crawl back into bed, and they won't come near me. They never do anymore."

"Mom." Galen's voice cracks.

"I know, son. We'll talk again. Soon." She stretches up, kissing his cheek. "I love you so much, honey, and I need you to be safe, or else, it's all been for nothing!" Her voice elevates a few notches again. She gives us another push. "So, go!"

I grab Galen's arm, and we run out the side door as Alisha flees back out into the hallway. We race through the garage toward the SUV, and I thank our lucky stars Galen moved the car from the front of the house before we headed to bed. "Wait," Galen whispers when we reach the Lexus. His eyes narrow, and I can almost see the wheels churning in his head.

My mind instantly syncs with his. "Good plan," I say. "Let's find out what they're up to."

He clasps my hand. "Keep behind me, and stay low. We can't be spotted, so we'll go around the back. There are no cameras there."

I zip my hoodie up and creep out of the garage behind Galen. It's still dark out as it's the middle of the night, and the only illumination is the crescent moon high in the sky and the odd flickering outside light. We stay close to the wall, keeping our eyes and ears peeled, as we walk around the back of the property and past the empty pool and the pool house.

"Down," Galen hisses as lights flood one of the rooms at the rear, spilling through the naked windows, casting a dim glow on the patio a few meters ahead. "They're in the ballroom," he whispers, and I hear the unspoken curiosity behind his words. There is nothing in that space anymore. Just an empty room with old chandeliers and heavy drapes. We crouch down, crawling until we reach the first ballroom window. "Stay down," Galen whispers, popping his head up a little so he can see inside the room. "Holy fucking shit."

"What?"

He crouches down. "See for yourself. Be careful and be quick 'cause they have a guy going around the room closing the curtains."

We trade places, and I inch my head up until I can see into the room. The middle section of the floor is wide-open, revealing a hidden room underneath. It's not a huge space, but it's deep enough that steps are mounted on either side to access it. Men, wearing The Sainthood's leather cut, traipse into the room from outside, carrying boxes of various sizes down into the compartment.

Galen fists my hoodie, yanking me down just as a man approaches the window. We stare at one another, barely breathing, only relaxing once everything goes dark and the light fades. "Fucking hell," I whisper. "Guess now we know how your mom gets access to drugs."

"It wasn't just drugs," he whispers back. "Judging from the size of some boxes, they're hiding weapons there too."

"I wonder how long it's been going on?"

"He installed the cameras two years ago. Said it was for mom's protection because I was often gone for days at a time, but that was bullshit. He fitted cameras to protect his investment." His jaw stiffens, and anger burns in his eyes again.

I need to get him away before he loses control. I squeeze his hand. "Let's get the fuck out of here."

Even though the curtains are now drawn, we take no chances, bending down low until we pass the ballroom, and then, we race back the way we came.

I round the corner first, slamming into a hard chest. I open my mouth to scream when Galen's hand wraps around my mouth from behind, stalling me. "It's Saint!" he whispers. "Chill."

I look up into the foreboding face of Saint Lennox. He's dressed all in black, and he has a hood over his head, cloaking his features. "What the actual fuck is going on? I've been blowing up your cells. Why did neither of you pick up?" he snaps. His blue eyes pin me in place, and anger bleeds into the air on all sides of me.

"We left our cells upstairs, and there wasn't time to go back for them," Galen explains. "What's wrong?"

"We've got a problem to solve."

"At four a.m.?" I ask.

"The Bulls have been set free, and they'll be coming for us. We need to strike first."

"You have a plan?" Galen asks.

"Of course, we do." I hear the smirk in his tone. "Let's get the fuck out of Dodge. You can update me on the way to meet the others."

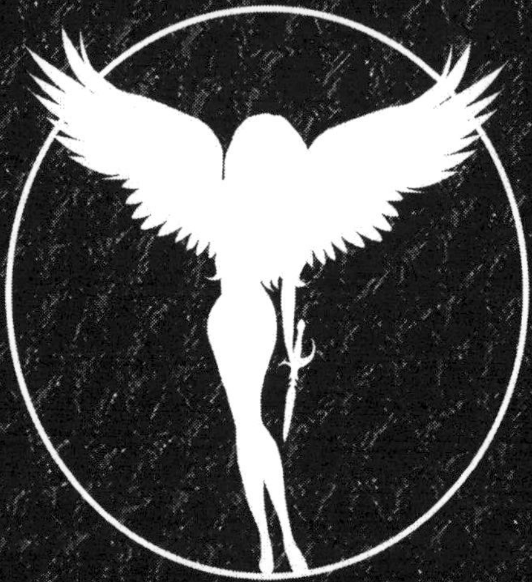

THE SAINTHOOD

CHAPTER 29

"I'M SO FUCKING sorry, man," Saint says after Galen has given him the cliff notes version of my convo with Alisha. He didn't miss much, confirming he wasn't in such a deep sleep after all. We also explained what we saw going down in the ballroom. "Fuck that bastard!" Saint slams his hands down on the steering wheel as aggression rolls off him in waves. The car swerves on the road, and it's a good thing it's empty this time of night.

"Pull over, and let me drive." I poke my head through the gap in the two front seats.

"I'm fucking driving." Saint barks, rubbing the back of his neck.

"I wasn't fucking asking," I snap. "Pull the goddamn car over now."

The brakes screech, and I'm jolted forward as Saint slams on the brakes in the middle of the road. I don't know why I'm surprised. He thinks he owns the fucking streets.

"Jesus Christ. Was breaking my ribs not good enough?" Galen asks. "Now, you want to give me whiplash?"

"Blame the princess," Saint growls, getting out of the driver's side door.

I climb out from the back seat, walking up to him and prodding my finger in his chest. "Listen, asshole. You don't have the monopoly on murderous rage. We're all fucking pissed, but getting us killed on this road tonight won't serve any good purpose." I jab my finger in his chest again. "And in case you've forgotten, my dad died in a car crash, so shut your fucking face."

Gripping my hips, he pulls me into his body and kisses the shit out of me.

I'm smirking as I pull back. "Is this our thing now?"

"I don't know, baby." He grabs handfuls of my ass. "Is it?"

I palm the bulge in his jeans. "Your body speaks for itself."

His hands drift to my waist, as his expression turns serious. "You fix shit with my cousin?"

"I did. We did."

"Thank fuck." He presses a kiss to my forehead, and it's a tender sweep of his lips, one that almost unravels me. I love Saint's alpha possessiveness, but every so often he shows me a softer side, and I love it just as much. "He's going to need you now more than ever," he murmurs, his lips lingering on my skin.

I tilt my head back so I'm looking up at him. "We all need each other." I place my hands on his rock-hard chest. "Just when I think things can't get any more fucked up, they do."

"We need to keep the others focused and on track."

I reach up and kiss him softly. "We will. Now, get your sexy ass in the back seat, and tell us what's going down."

"THAT'S THEIR CLUBHOUSE?" I ask, peeking around the corner to catch a glimpse.

"You don't sound impressed." Caz chuckles.

"I'm not. It's like some giant bloated silver box. I was expecting something grander, more like The Sainthood's training facility."

The warehouse in front of us is rudimentary, at least from the outside. It's a big corrugated iron warehouse with a flat roof and a few token windows on both sides. It's nestled between a couple of local businesses. A place that sells hardware and other DIY supplies. A carpet store, and a kitchen and bathroom showroom. It's in a quiet part of Fenton though, off the beaten track.

"Don't let that exterior fool you," Theo says, tapping away on his iPad while Saint and Galen scan the structure with binoculars. "It's a lot more sophisticated inside. The outside is mostly a front."

"How are we getting in?" I whisper though there's no need.

Theo lifts his head briefly, smiling at me. "I've just disabled their security system and all the cameras in the area."

I dart forward and kiss him quickly. "You're fucking amazing. Sometime, when we're not trying to save my ass, you've got to tell me how you developed such mad skills." Theo was always super handy with technology, but the stuff he can do now is on a whole other level.

"He's a genius," Caz agrees. "There's no way we could pull off half the shit we do without him."

Theo returns his gaze to his screen, but I spot the telltale bloom on his cheeks and the slight tilt of his lips.

Caz and I share a look, and I wonder.

"Have you run the heat scan?" Saint asks, lowering his binoculars and crouching down, unzipping his black duffel bag.

"On it now, boss."

"You mean boss man," Caz says, winking at me. "As opposed to boss lady."

"That has a nice ring to it." I grin at Caz, and I fucking love how he can effortlessly reduce tension and lighten the mood. I blow him a kiss, and his grin expands as he slides his hand into his boxers, cupping his junk.

"Later, babe," I mouth. While it's good to defuse tension, I don't want to distract the guys either. Blowing up the enemy's clubhouse is serious business—especially if we are to get in and out without detection.

"How do we know they aren't in there?" I ask. "And what happened to our original plan?"

"The original plan of attack was to target all the main players' homes at once, but that takes coordinated effort. After we got word the authorities had let The Bulls go earlier tonight, and they weren't pressing charges, we needed a plan we could implement quickly," Saint explains.

"How the fuck did they pull that off?" Galen inquires, scanning the area back and forth with his binoculars.

"How does anyone?" Saint says, shrugging.

"They have the cops in their pocket," I surmise, holding out my hand as Saint drops a couple things into my palm.

"The cops or someone with authority," Saint says. "Except it doesn't add up because it's well known the Fenton cops have been trying to pin something on The Bulls for years. They have a major drug problem in the area, and the police chief has put the blame squarely on Ruben and his crew. This should have been open and shut."

"The coast is clear," Theo says, handing Saint his tablet. "The decoy fire at the warehouse worked like a charm."

I guess that answers my second question. I turn the mask Saint handed me over in the palm of my hands, smiling. "Angel masks? Really?" I giggle as I trace my finger over the wings on either side of the black mask. They meet at the top of the mask with a fine silver dagger dissecting them.

"We are *saintly* after all," Galen says, grinning, and I'm glad this is distracting him from tonight's bombshell revelations.

"Let's get this show on the road." Saint hands Caz a set of pliers before zipping the bag up and slinging it over his shoulder. We all put our masks and gloves on and pull our hoods up over our heads before sprinting across the road toward The Bulls' clubhouse.

My heart is thumping wildly, and my veins are buzzing with excitement. There's nothing like a little retribution to get the juices flowing.

Caz snaps the padlock on the front door, and I step forward, snatching the lock pick from his hands. Sliding it carefully into the lock, I narrow my eyes and peer into the hole, giving it a little wiggle in the right place. The clicking, pinging sound is music to my ears, and I'm gloating behind my mask as I push the door in.

"I think you might be out of a job," Theo says to Caz, and Caz chuckles.

"Stay focused," Saint snaps as we step into The Bulls' domain. "Keep alert." He comes up behind me. "Princess, you're with me." He distributes guns and flashlights, handing a Glock to me. I unlock the safety and curl my hand around the trigger, lifting my head and scanning the dark hallway. Saint keeps the bag, leading us forward with the aid of a flashlight.

We emerge from the hallway into a wide-open space. Saint and Galen move their flashlights around, illuminating the room a bit at a time. There's a fully stocked bar on the right-hand side and two pool tables on the left. A myriad of couches, tables, and chairs are dotted around the space. Club paraphernalia hangs on the walls.

Saint dumps the duffel bag on one of the pool tables while the guys head out into the back corridor. "What's back there?" I ask, knowing Theo has already inspected the floorplans.

"Kitchen, bathrooms, and bedrooms," Saint says, carefully removing two cans of gasoline.

"Old school?" I arch a brow as my lips tug up.

"There wasn't time to make a bomb," Saint says. "And we don't want to damage the adjacent properties. A bomb would blow the whole street apart."

"All clear," Galen says, coming back into the room. He grabs one of the cans from Saint and starts throwing it over the furniture and floor.

"Let me," I say, putting the safety on the gun and slipping it into the pocket of my hoodie. "I'm the one they're trying to kill."

"Have at it, princess." Saint hands the second can to me, and I move to the other side of the room, tossing gasoline over everything I come across.

When we're done, we throw the cans away, backing up to the front hallway. Theo and Caz walk backward, holding a long rope. They drape it along the ground all the way to the front door.

"Outside, princess," Saint demands, holding the door open for me.

I pout, wanting to watch, but Galen stretches his arm back inside, pulling me out. "We need to get the car." I run with him around the corner, hopping in the passenger seat as he slides behind the wheel. He powers up the engine, and the brakes squeal as we peel out of there.

Saint, Caz, and Theo are racing toward us when we round the bend, and a loud pop pierces the still nighttime air as they open the back doors and scramble inside. "Woo-hoo, motherfuckers!" Caz shouts, pumping his fists in the air. "Take that up the ass!"

"Fuck you, Ruben," Saint says, flipping his fingers up at the burning building as we take off.

"Oh my God," I say when we are back at the barn in Prestwick Forest. "That was such an adrenaline rush." I finish bandaging Galen's torn knuckles, smiling up at him. "You're done."

"Thanks." He hesitates for a brief second before planting a soft kiss on my lips.

"Our princess has a hard-on for danger," Caz says, winking. He's sprawled across the large leather recliner, his bare feet hanging over the arm.

"Damn straight, but that's nothing new." I grin at him.

"It sends a clear message," Saint says, still in business mode. He pulls my feet up on his lap as we sit at opposite ends of the couch.

We've all showered and changed. I'm in sleep shorts and a long-sleeved sleep top, and the guys are all bare-chested and in sweats. If I wasn't so dead on my feet, I would be crawling all over their sexy asses, but I desperately need sleep. It's after six now, and daylight is breaking.

"But they won't stop coming for you." Saint rubs his hands up and down my legs, and warmth penetrates bone deep.

"We need to find some dirt on them. Something that is irrefutable, that no damn connections can get them out of," I suggest.

"I hate to say this," Theo says, pressing a kiss to the top of my head as he hands me a mug of hot chocolate. My heart swells at the gesture. All the small things he does tells me how much he remembers and how deeply he cares. "But we need Diesel's help." He sinks onto the smaller couch beside Galen.

"We don't need granddad," Saint growls. "We're capable of dealing with this problem on our own."

"I'm with Theo on this," Caz says. "Lo's life is at stake, and we don't have the time or the right resources to really nail their asses."

"We should explore all options," Galen agrees. "And personal shit has to stay at the front door." He drills a look at his cousin.

Saint scowls as he brings a bottle of beer to his lips. Putting my mug down, I crawl up the couch, nestling between his legs with my back to his chest. His arms automatically circle my waist, and I angle my head and look up, touching his face. "He isn't a threat to what we have. He and I were a thing for five seconds, and it was over before we got together. You need to let it go. He can help, and we'd be stupid to turn that down."

Everyone waits for Saint's response, and I run my fingers back and forth across the underside of his prickly jaw while I wait for him to process his shit.

"I'll try," he admits after a minute. "But I hate that fucking guy."

Caz snorts. "You hate any guy who's been inside the princess."

I send a glare in Caz's direction. "Not exactly helpful and not entirely true considering everyone in this room has been inside me."

"He has access to stuff I can only dream about," Theo says, appealing to Saint's strategic side as he refocuses the conversation. He hands me my hot chocolate again, and I smile over the rim of the mug. "We'll get things done much faster with his help." I drink the chocolate goodness while Saint thinks about it.

"All right," Saint concedes, fastening his arms more tightly around my waist. "But I'm not promising I won't hit him."

I shake my head, yawning as my eyes fight to stay open.

I guess I nodded off sometime after that because the next thing I know I'm being shaken awake. "Babe." Warm fingers brush hair off my face. "You need to get up."

"Go away." I swat at Saint's hands, pulling the pillow down over my face. Soft snoring and heat from another body confirms I'm not the only one having trouble waking up.

"Theo has found something important. He needs us all downstairs."

The covers are whipped off me, and I groan, yanking the pillow off my head, sitting up and scowling. Saint is perched on the edge of the bed, smirking at the state of the bird's nest on top of my head. I was too tired to dry it last night, so I just pulled it into a bun, and I'm sure it's a hot mess. I look over my shoulder at Galen. He's still passed out, and he actually looks peaceful in sleep. "Do we really have to wake him?"

Saint pulls me into his lap, nuzzling his nose in my shoulder. "I don't want to, but we have to."

I rest my head on his shoulder, yawning. "Did you sleep here too?"

"I did. You were practically comatose, so I carried you to bed. Galen followed, and I didn't think you'd mind if he joined us."

"I don't mind although we do need to buy a bigger bed."

"Truth." Saint pecks my lips before leaning across and slapping Galen across the cheek.

I jerk my head up, glaring at Saint. "Was that fucking necessary?"

"Jesus, man." Galen sits up, rubbing his reddened cheek. "You're a raving asshole."

"Tell us something we don't know." I slide off Saint's lap, crawling to Galen. "I'll kiss your boo-boo better," I tease, leaning forward and pressing my lips to his cheek. He pulls me down against him, wrapping his arms around me. I rest my head carefully on his shoulder, not wanting to press on his sore ribs.

"Touching as this is, we need to get our butts downstairs before Theo loses his shit." Saint stands, and I can't ignore the monster erection in his pants. I lick my lips as heat swamps my lower regions. "You are such a naughty, naughty princess." Saint smirks at me, adjusting himself in his sweatpants. "If you're a good girl, I'll let you suck my dick after breakfast."

I flip him the bird. "I'd rather choke on my own vomit."

"Wow. What a lovely visual," Caz says, his head appearing at the top of the stairs. "You need to get down here stat."

When Caz wears a serious face, you know it's about to get very real, so we get out of bed and follow him downstairs.

"What's going on?" Saint asks as we all take seats at the table.

"I've got a lead on our mystery dude with the camera," Theo confirms. "I ran him through facial recognition software, and when I didn't get any hits, I put out a few feelers among some contacts. One of them just came through." His eyes lock on Saint's. "It's not good, dude."

"Who is he?"

"He's with the DEA," he says, and a litany of curses rips through the air.

Honestly, I'm not surprised the Drug Enforcement Agency is sniffing around, but it seemed like he was following *us* when I'd expect him to follow Sinner and the senior chapter members.

"But that's not the worst of it," Theo adds, turning his laptop around, showing us the image on the screen.

All the color leaches from my face as I stare in shock at the photo of the DEA guy with Ruben. They're smiling as they shake hands, looking like smug assholes.

"Holy motherfucker," Caz says. "We're so fucked."

THE SAINTHOOD

CHAPTER 30

CAZ

"Want some help?" I ask, coming up behind Lo in the kitchen. She's making an early dinner because she wants to have it ready before the old man arrives. I think she thinks if we're all eating it'll be more civilized. Fat chance a mouthful of food will stop Saint from going postal on Diesel's ass.

"Could you cut the bread?" She gestures toward the chopping board on her right as she slides the lasagna in the oven.

"That smells delicious," I admit, sniffing the aromatic scent of garlic, tomato, and fresh herbs as it wafts around our small kitchen.

"Thanks. It's about the only thing I can cook." She washes lettuce in the sink. "Mom's a great cook, as I'm sure you've all noticed, but I didn't inherit her passion or talent."

"Sounds to me like you didn't have much downtime to learn." I slice through the baguette. "And you definitely have other talents." I waggle my brows suggestively, and she laughs.

"What about your family?" She looks over at me as she pats the salad leaves dry with some paper towels.

Bile swims up my throat. "Not much to tell. My sister Nelia

ten, and my brother Jake is six. Mom works at a grocery store, and Dad's a mechanic when he's not pulling shit for The Sainthood."

She stops what she's doing, her eyes popping wide. "Your dad's a member?" She absently drops lettuce in a glass bowl while she watches me.

"Yep. And he's your typical prick. Drinks too much. Likes to slap my mom around. And he's a proverbial cheater."

"Shit. I'm sorry."

I shrug. "It is what it is. I've tried to help Mom. I have enough money saved so she could move out and get her own place, but she won't leave him." I shake my head. "I don't get it."

Lo moves to my side, sliding her arms around my neck. "Can I do anything to help?"

I bury my head in her neck. "You help just by being here. Helping to take my mind off it."

She dots kisses all over my cheeks, and I wrap my arms around her waist, holding her close.

This girl. She slays me. Slays all of us. I'm never letting her go.

"Heads-up," Saint says, sauntering into the kitchen. "The pedo's here. I just sent him the code for the gate."

Until recently, no visitors had ever been here. It was our private domain, locked off from the world. But Diesel followed Lo the last time, so he knows where we live and how to get in. Saint and Theo installed a new automatic mechanism to the gate last night, before all that shit went down at Galen's house and at The Bulls' clubhouse. Access is now via a hidden keypad and only those with the code can get in.

Saint sends Galen a pointed look, and Galen nods. Lo will throw a hissy fit when she finds out what we've done, but all is fair in love and war, and we're not taking chances.

Lo sighs, removing herself from my embrace to swat the back of Saint's head. "He's early. And be nice to him, or no sex for a week."

I burst out laughing, slapping Saint on the shoulder. "It's cool, man. Go apeshit on his ass. We'll look after our girl." I pull her back into me, thrusting my hips against her body, my cock swelling behind my boxers.

Saint flips me the bird before his serious mask comes down. "Remember what we discussed. We don't mention anything about last night or that we know he's employed by VERO. We see if he's found out anything about Ruben and if he can help us take him down for good."

"Agreed," Galen and Theo say, coming up behind us.

"Get the drinks," Lo instructs. "I'll head outside to greet him."

Galen heads to the refrigerator while I dump the sliced bread on a plate. Theo is setting the table as Saint starts opening cupboards. "What are you looking for?" I ask.

"Anything we can use to poison him." He says it so matter-of-factly, and I know how batshit crazy the guy can be, so I'm not altogether sure he's joking.

Galen smirks, placing some beers down on the counter. "You kill him, the princess will cockblock you for life."

"More sexy time for us." I waggle my brows. "Have at it, Saintly."

He stabs me with an irritated look, and I chuckle. Lo has really ruffled his feathers. It's awesome to see, because if ever a guy needs to loosen up, it's our supreme leader. Don't get me wrong, I don't want him turning pussy-whipped like my man Theo, but he rarely drops his guard—he rarely relaxes or lets go. Not until our sexy goddess showed up and made mincemeat of our hearts.

"I'm not trying to kill him," Saint says, pulling out a bottle of bleach. "At least not yet." He pins us with a blinding smile as he closes the cupboard door. "I just want to make him a little ill."

Theo swipes the bleach from Saint's hand. "You're not putting anything in his drink. She's not into him. Get over yourself." He turns to me, thrusting the bleach into my hand. "Hide that someplace the lunatic can't reach it."

"Your wish is my command." I wink at him, and he quickly looks away.

I wonder when he'll fess up and whether his new closeness with the princess will help or hinder. I'm curious and more than a little excited by the possibilities, but I can't make a move. He's got to put himself out there and make himself vulnerable.

"For the last time, Diesel," Lo says, barreling into the house like a whirlwind, clutching an envelope in her hand. "I'm not running away!"

Galen slips out the back door while everyone's distracted.

"Who the fuck said anything about running away?" Saint steps out, grabbing Lo and pulling her in front of him. His hands land possessively on her hips as he glowers at Diesel.

"I want her to leave for a while until things have calmed down," Diesel says, standing confidently in front of Lo and Saint. We join in—me on their right and Theo on the left, forming a formidable line of defense. "You can all go with her. But getting out of the country is the safest plan of action."

"According to you," Saint says.

"What's changed?" Theo asks.

Diesel runs a hand over his head, and the guy looks tired as fuck as he eyeballs us. "Can we sit and discuss this calmly? We all want what's best for Lo, and we can't afford to disregard any option."

"Fine." Lo huffs. "We can sit, but I'm not leaving the country."

Saint smirks, kissing the top of her head before taking her hand and walking her to the table.

"Where's Galen?" Lo asks, glancing around with a frown, once we're all seated.

"Here," Galen says, coming in the back door. "I was just putting the trash out."

None of us look at him—not with the beady-eyed VERO assassin sitting across the table.

"I've got lasagna in the oven," Lo says, trying to defuse the stifling atmosphere, "but you're early, so it's not ready yet."

Diesel smiles at her in a way I'm familiar with. Dude definitely has a hard-on for our girl, but I don't think he's stupid enough to try anything.

Not because of us.

Because of Lo.

She's made her feelings pretty clear, and if he overstepped, he'd risk losing her forever.

"That was thoughtful, and you know how much I love your lasagna," Diesel says, his lips twitching as Saint stiffens. I kick Lennox under the table. He's so fucking obvious when it comes to Lo. It's hysterical because any other time Saint is an unreadable wall. But come after his girl, and it all rushes to the surface. "But something has come up, and I can't stay long."

"Get to the point then," Saint says in a clipped tone.

"I gather Lo has told you she's wearing a tracker and audio recording device around her neck," he says, shooting her a look of displeasure. "I listened to the initiation meeting, and it's obvious Lo is in a precarious situation. She can't take out Commissioner Leydon, and if your psycho father lays a finger on her again, I will slaughter him and the entire board in cold blood."

"We'd be right by your side," I admit, because that's exactly how we feel too.

"Then, you agree that disappearing for a few months makes the most sense."

I snort out a laugh. "Fuck, no. We're The Sainthood."

"We don't hide from our problems," Saint adds. "We run straight at them."

Diesel exhales heavily. "This is a fucking waste of my time. It's like negotiating with a bunch of kindergarteners."

"Diesel, I know you're scared for me, and I'm appreciative of your concern, but running away is not an option. We already discussed this, and there's no point going over old ground," Lo says. "Please drop it so we can discuss more pressing problems."

"There is so much you don't know, Lo." Diesel reaches for her hand, but she whips it off the table before he can touch her, shooting him an apologetic look.

"Then tell us," Theo says.

"I wish I could, but I can't."

Silence engulfs us, and tension slithers into the air like thick, black smoke.

"What *can* you tell us?" Lo asks. "Did you find out how Ruben got his hands on the video of me killing Luke McKenzie?"

"I'm narrowing it down," he cryptically says, looking cagey.

"I'm calling bullshit." Saint drums his fingers on the table.

Diesel ignores him, concentrating on Lo. "I'm sorry to hit and run, but I've somewhere to be. Just hold tight for another couple days. I'll have intel then and a way for you to end The Bulls."

"How?" Theo sits up straighter.

Diesel stands. "All in good time, Theo."

"You expect us to trust you when you're obviously hiding stuff? Intel that could keep Lo safe?" Saint says.

"Listen, punk." Diesel lunges across the table at Saint, but Lo pulls him back.

"Quit that shit, Diesel. Why can't you tell us now?"

He rubs his temples. "I know a lot of this doesn't make sense, but I'm keeping stuff back for a reason. Please trust me. I have your best interests at heart, and I'm putting myself on the line to do that. I'm working on an angle, and I promise I'll tell you everything when it's fully lined up." His gaze bounces around the room. "Until then, lay low. Keep Harlow away from your father and those perverted bastards." His teeth grind as he eyeballs Saint.

We all look to our leader. Even Lo. And I silently beseech Saint to do the right thing because she's looking to him to do that. Not that she can't or won't make that call. She needs to see him do it.

"Okay," Saint says after a few beats of awkward silence. "But if you're screwing us, we'll screw you back."

"That's not how I roll," Diesel says, kissing the top of Lo's head. "Stay safe."

"You too," she says.

We watch as he strides toward the door like he owns the fucking air we breathe. He turns around at the last second, his hand curled around the door handle. "One final thing. No more stunts like last night. I can't help you if the cops are breathing down your necks."

Saint flips him off. "We know how to cover our tracks."

Diesel rolls his eyes. "Evidently not." He fixes one final glance in Lo's direction before walking outside.

"What the fuck does that mean?" I ask.

"That he's watching our every move," Theo says, frowning, and I know he'll take this personally. Like he's somehow failed us because he can't stop Diesel from following our trail.

"It's time we repaid the favor," Saint says, standing. "Come on. We're leaving now."

"To go where?" Lo asks, jumping up.

Chairs scrape as we all stand.

"We're following the old man. Let's see what's so important he had to leave."

THE SAINTHOOD

CHAPTER 31

HARLOW

I TURN OFF the stove and leave the envelope with the fake IDs Diesel gave me on the kitchen counter. It seems his influence knows no bounds and, somehow, he forced Johnny into handing over my new identification. How simple that plan seems now, and it's so far removed from my current reality it's almost laughable.

I won't run, because my enemies will only chase after me. I don't doubt Diesel has the resources to hide me, but I refuse to spend the rest of my life looking over my shoulder and jumping at my own shadow.

"I'm still pissed you added a tracker to his car without telling me," I say when we're all safely inside the Lexus and on the move. Theo is frantically stabbing buttons on his iPad, doing what he does best.

"And that's why we didn't tell you," Saint replies, and I flip him off. He smirks at me over the console. "Babe, I know you trust him, but he's keeping shit from us, and we need to know what."

"He's a dangerous fucker," Caz says, and I narrow my eyes at him through the mirror. "Hey." He holds up his hands from the back seat. "Don't shoot the messenger. I'm telling it like it is.

He's a highly trained mercenary who kills people for a living. We know he'd never hurt you, but the jury's out on our asses."

"Especially since Saintly is determined to piss him off any chance he gets," Theo notes without lifting his head from his tablet.

"You can all fuck off with your Saintly," Saint says, and a smile lifts the corners of my mouth.

"Done," Theo says, and I glance over my shoulder, lifting a brow. "I've synced the tracking device to the GPS system in the car." He sits back in the seat. "I also changed the code on the gate. I've messaged you the new one." He pins me with a warning look. "Diesel is not to know that."

I hate that they don't trust him, but I can't really blame them, which is why I didn't go postal on their asses when they told me what Galen had done. I nod at Theo, and he smiles back at me, knowing he doesn't need to confirm where my loyalty lies.

Saint fiddles with a few buttons, grinning like a madman, as he stares at the red dot moving on the map when it loads. "Looks like he's heading out of Prestwick," he adds.

"Keep a safe distance behind him," Theo says. "He might recognize the car."

Saint rolls his eyes, before glancing at me. "Did he say anything outside that was helpful?"

"No. He just flipped his lid over the initiation tasks and begged me to skip town."

"What was in the envelope?" Galen asks.

"A fake driver's license and passport."

"They might come in handy," Saint says.

"Only if we get some for all of you, because I'm not going anywhere without you."

A different kind of heaviness settles in the air, and I wonder if I've said too much, but fuck it, I'm not hiding behind an emotionless wall anymore. They might be afraid to confront their feelings, but I've scaled that beast and come out the other side. I'm still scared, because I'm navigating new terrain, but I'm done pretending.

"I can make that happen," Theo says. "Because we're not letting you out of our sight."

"Ever," Saint adds, stretching his arm across the console to squeeze my hand.

Tears prick my eyes, but for once, they are happy tears.

Nothing else is said, but that's okay, because nothing else needs to be said.

"He's slowing down," Saint says ten minutes later when we reach the large public park and woodland on the outskirts of Fenton.

Saint follows his route through the park, pulling into the far end of the parking lot and killing the engine. It's late afternoon, and the sun is starting to set, but there are still a ton of people around. Families taking young kids to the playground. Couples out walking dogs. Joggers and cyclists. But it's the dark-haired man sitting on the bench beside Diesel who has claimed our interest.

Acid churns in my gut as I watch Diesel discreetly chatting with the DEA agent.

"I fucking knew we couldn't trust that motherfucker," Saint says, anger simmering in his tone.

"We don't know what this is." I'm not defending him per se—I just don't want to jump to the obvious conclusion. "He said he was working an angle. This could be it."

"We need fucking answers," Saint says. "And we're getting them tonight." He looks into the back seat. "Reschedule the meet with Bry to tomorrow night. This can't wait."

We sit in silence for another few minutes, watching the two men talking, their faces changing as the conversation grows heated.

What I wouldn't give to hear what they are saying.

The DEA dude jumps up, stalking off and getting into a blacked-out SUV. We all duck down in our seats, waiting for his car to pass. Saint has his hand on the door handle when I tug on his elbow. "I'll go. You two will just end up punching one another." I don't wait for his reply, hopping out and jogging toward Diesel's

Land Rover.

He's about to drive off when he spots me. He rests his head on the steering wheel, his lips moving as I walk around the car and climb into the passenger seat.

"I bet this was that asshole's idea," he supplies, but his voice is resigned, not angry. I'm guessing that is more to do with the bruising shadows under his eyes and his pale pallor.

"When did you last sleep, Diesel? Last eat a proper meal?"

He shrugs. "I've a lot on my plate right now," he admits.

"And I'm only adding to your burden."

"You're not a burden, Harlow. You never could be. You're my priority."

"Why, Diesel? You've got to give me, *us*, some answers." I make a split-second decision, hoping I'm making the right call. "I know you work for VERO."

"Shit." He closes his eyes briefly, and air escapes his mouth. "Theo is more talented than I've given him credit for."

"My man has mad skills." Pride seeps into my tone, and Diesel picks up on it.

"You're in love with him."

I confirm it with my eyes.

"With all of them?" he inquires.

I don't answer that question because I haven't told the guys yet. "It doesn't matter. What matters is, we're supposed to be working as a team and we're not. We need to know it all, Diesel." I touch his arm. "I know you don't trust them, but you trust me, and I trust them, so, please, come back to the barn, have a shower, eat some lasagna, have a beer, and just tell us what the fuck is going on."

"Where do you want me to start?" Diesel asks an hour later after we've all eaten. Theo has lit a fire, and we're all sitting around it, sipping beers. Diesel is drinking coffee, because he insists he needs to head home later, and it's probably for the best even though I offered him a room for the night.

There's no guarantee Saint wouldn't try to slit his throat while he slept.

"How did my father find you?" I ask, curling my hands around my beer.

"Through my brother Lincoln."

I sit up straighter. "Lincoln from the law firm is your brother?" He nods. "Huh. You look nothing alike."

"We were both adopted," he confirms, drinking from his mug.

"Lincoln never mentioned a word."

"He wouldn't. He's been sworn to secrecy. Anyone who knows the identity of my employer is at risk, so I tend to limit the people I tell."

I'm guessing it's a lonely lifestyle and not one conducive to marriage and family life. My heart aches for Diesel for all he's missing out on.

"How did you end up working for VERO?" Theo asks, idly threading his fingers through my hair. Saint is on the other side of me on the couch while Caz and Galen share the smaller couch and Diesel occupies the chair.

"I was recruited by the FBI straight from college. Spent a few years working for them, but the regimented structure went against my nature, so I quit. A couple months after I left, I was approached to join VERO. It sounded a better fit, so I took the job, and here I am."

"How did Lincoln convince you to train Lo?" Saint asks, and I'm pleased he's behaving himself now. When we first got back here, I thought he was going to put a bullet in Diesel's skull.

"I only signed up for a few weeks. No offense, Lo," he says, smiling at me. "But training a feisty thirteen-year-old wasn't exactly on my bucket list."

"What changed?" Galen asks.

"I met her," he softly says, and all the guys stare at him.

My heart thumps behind my rib cage.

He turns to me. "You were so lost, but you had this fiery determination and this inner strength, and I'd never seen anything like it before. I knew you were special, and I also knew you were vulnerable. Your father was a shrewd player. He knew as soon as I met you I would change my mind, and he told me what'd happened and explained about the continuous threat, and that was all it took to confirm my commitment to a more permanent arrangement."

"I'm taking it your employer doesn't know."

His jaw clenches. "They didn't at first. But they found out."

I shift uncomfortably, and the guys turn rigidly still.

"Explain that," Saint grits out.

"I kept Lo a secret, fitting training sessions around my missions. I called in favors and built up a small, loyal team I could call on to go head to head in combat, but otherwise, I kept it on the down low. But one of the guys in the team ratted me out to my superiors a year ago. I expected a couple of potential outcomes, but the one they presented me with was not on my list."

"What went down?" I ask, chewing on the corner of my nail.

"I'm guessing you weren't able to dig up much intel on the VERO board of directors," he says to Theo.

Theo shakes his head. "It's all sealed, but there is a lot of speculation on the darknet."

"About it being government funded and led?" Diesel asks.

"Yeah."

"And it is, but it's way bigger than that. The board is made up of powerful figures in business and government. All these guys stand to lose everything should their involvement in VERO ever come out."

I notice he hasn't mentioned what his missions entail, and I've no desire to pry. I know this is dangerous for him, and the less we know, the better. I want to keep our questions focused on how this impacts us.

"How is this connected to Lo and us?" Galen asks.

"When my superiors pulled me in, they told me I could continue training Lo and they'd let my disobedience slide provided Trey worked with the FBI to take down The Sainthood."

"What?" I yell, completely taken by surprise.

"Are the FBI involved with VERO?" Theo asks.

Diesel shakes his head. "They are aware of VERO's existence, but they operate as completely separate entities. VERO wanted to supply intel to the FBI in a way that couldn't tie back to them. When they found out about Trey's connection to Neo "Sinner" Lennox, they knew they'd hit pay dirt."

"Do they want to take The Sainthood down, or is this part of a personal agenda?" I ask.

"Honestly, your guess is as good as mine. I don't know if it's Sinner they want to take down, or the entire criminal organization, or it's about the Leydon murder, or maybe, it's a combination." He rubs his hands together. "They wanted Trey to spy for the FBI, and they specifically asked him to find the evidence connecting The Sainthood to Daphne Leydon's murder."

"Holy hell," Caz says, toying with his lip ring. "This gets more complicated by the minute."

"Everything seems to be connected to that poor woman's death." I bite down on my lip, needing to ask a question but wishing I didn't. "Did you know about the false intel?"

He shoots me a soft smile. "I did. I do." I avert my eyes, shame washing over me. "You were a kid, Lo, and I've always known they blackmailed you into it."

"Dad told you?" I ask, and he bobs his head. Another question forms in my mind. "Was the FBI supplying the reports Dad was leaving for me to pass to Sinner?" Diesel nods. "And do you think Sinner knew it was them? Is that why Dad was killed? Because he was working for the FBI and trying to find that evidence? Have they known all along he didn't have it?"

"I think it's possible they found out about the FBI connection, and your father's murder was a warning to them to back off. But Sinner's actions since Trey was killed seems to confirm the evidence is missing and he's desperately trying to find it. Everything hinges on that evidence. We need to locate it."

"We're coming up empty so far," I say.

"There are various entities seeking the evidence, so we don't have time to waste. Especially when Sinner is asking you to take out the commissioner. That makes me suspicious as fuck."

"You think he's involved?" Galen asks.

"Yes." Diesel doesn't falter. "I'm not sure how, but I think he's up to his neck in this, and Sinner took Daphne to threaten him into silence."

I'm beginning to suspect the ramifications extend even farther than we think.

"Why were you meeting the DEA agent?" Saint asks.

"He's the one who gave Ruben the recording," Diesel confirms.

"They've been watching me?"

"Not you." Diesel glances at the guys. "The Sainthood. I was meeting with him to find out why and to see if I could get my hands on it."

"And?" Saint asks, growing impatient.

"And he's a fucking asshole."

Caz chuckles, and I smile.

"He's DEA," Saint drawls. "That's basically a mandatory requirement if you wanna work for them."

"He doesn't care that he's made you a target, Lo. All he cares about is fucking with the Saints and taking Sinner down." Saint opens his mouth to ask the obvious question but Diesel holds up a hand. "He fed me the usual bullshit about wanting to remove the biggest player from the streets, but it was fucking lies. I don't have any facts yet, but this is personal for that guy, and I get a sense he'd trample over everyone and anyone to achieve his goal."

"He was the one who got them set free," I say.

"Yep, and the local cops are spitting blood. But The Bulls are his informants, and he got the powers that be to let them go."

"They're overlooking the murder of a nobody because taking down one of the largest criminal organizations is worth way more," I surmise.

"We need to make The Bulls go away," Saint says, plucking at his lips with his fingers. "They're getting in the way of what we need to do."

"Agreed," Diesel says. "And this is where I can help." He takes a folded sheet of paper out of his back pocket and hands it to Saint. "That is a shipment of drugs and weapons The Bulls are taking possession of on Thursday. The cargo ship is due to arrive at the docks at four thirty a.m. Ruben will have a few vans waiting. Get that intel handed to the Fenton police chief. He's a decent guy, and he'll do what needs to be done. Make sure the message is handed only to him. And use someone reliable."

"What if the DEA steps in again?" Theo asks.

"They won't be able to make this go away. I have a few media contacts. I'll get them there. The DEA won't be able to turn a blind eye to millions of dollars of seized weapons and drugs. They'll have no choice but to prosecute."

"Meaning The Bulls go to jail, the target is gone from my back, and we get to focus on finding that evidence and nailing Sinner to the wall."

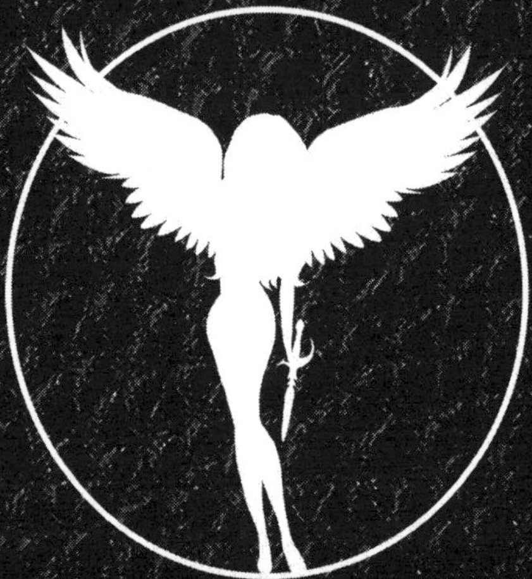

CHAPTER 32

School Monday is totally anticlimactic after the weekend we've had. I'm tired too, because I didn't sleep well last night after everything Diesel revealed. Theo and I ended up cuddling in bed and talking until the early hours, and then, I slept fitfully until it was time to get up.

"Any change?" Saint asks when I climb in the car after leaving the hospital.

I shake my head. I can't form words over the lump in my throat. *Why isn't she waking up?* It feels like forever since I last heard Sariah's laugh.

"Maybe, we should reschedule this," Theo says.

"No," I croak. "The meet with Darrow is going ahead."

"You have your knife?" Saint asks as Galen peels out of the parking lot.

I tap the side of my calf and then hold out the inside of my leather jacket. "I have my gun too."

"And you have the locket, right?" Caz says.

I nod. "Relax, guys. This is one thing you don't have to worry about. In my current mood, I'll gut Dar if he even looks at me funny."

Galen pulls the car off the road a mile from the biker bar, in front of an abandoned store, and I let them out. They duck inside to wait for me. I slide into the driver's seat and head to the bar, pressing down on my locket to activate the audio recorder before I step foot in the seedy establishment.

Darrow isn't here yet, so I order a bag of chips and a bottle of water and wait in a booth for him. He arrives ten minutes later, swaggering in like he owns the place. The tetchy blonde who was behind the counter when I visited Johnny flies across the room like she's got a bee up her butt. "Hey, Dar." She leans her elbows on the table, pushing her tits up and practically shoving them in his face. "What can I get ya?" She blatantly eye fucks him, and an amused grin spreads across my mouth.

"Tempest is gonna kick your cheating ass, Dar."

"I never promised her exclusivity," he says, winking at the bottle blonde. "I only ever gave that to you," he adds, earning me a venomous look from the waitress.

He's clearly forgotten he cheated on me with that redheaded witch, but I have zero fucks to give. "Relax, babe," I say, leaning back in the booth. "I've no interest in fucking him. He's all yours."

Dar scowls, yanking the blonde to him and slamming his lips down on hers.

I sip my water as I sext Caz, grinning at his equally dirty reply.

"Who the fuck are you texting?" Dar spits, yanking his mouth from the blonde.

"One of my boyfriends," I say, repocketing my cell.

"One?" the girl inquires, losing the dour face.

"Yep." I tilt my head to the side. "I have four, and they're all hot as fuck." I'd love to show her some pics, to really rile Dar up, but the guys are well-known, and I don't want word getting out that I was meeting the enemy for fear it ends up getting back to the psycho. This is already risky enough as it is.

"Well, damn, girl." She plants her hands on her hips. "Where can I get me some of that?"

"I don't have all day," Dar snaps. "Get me a beer." He dismisses her with a flip of his hand.

"Neither do I." I slide the piece of paper across the table to him.

"What's this?"

"Details of a shipment The Sainthood has coming up from Mexico Wednesday night."

"Mexico?" He rubs at his brow. "I thought they got their supplies from Europe?"

"They're testing a new supplier." I pop a chip in my mouth. He grins as he unfolds the paper, reading the details. "You're welcome."

"This is good, Lo."

"I know." I stand. "Don't fuck it up. I can't wait to see the look on Sinner's face when he finds out you ambushed his delivery."

"I'll need more," he adds. "If you want me to keep quiet about your betrayal."

"Like I said," I say, slipping out of the booth and taking my knife from where I placed it on the seat beside me, "I want to see them taken down." I lean into his face, deliberately lowering my gaze to his mouth and licking my lips. "You don't need to threaten me." I press the tip of my knife to his cock. "Or next time, I'll stab you in the balls."

I walk off toward the counter, smiling like it's my birthday, because I just fucking love it when a plan comes together. I hand the blonde a twenty, smirking. "Keep the change, and take my advice—make sure he wraps it before he taps it."

We've just finished eating our takeout in the basement when Bry shows up at the house a little after nine. "Hey." I greet him at the door with a quick hug. "It's good to see you."

"You too." He eyes the marks around my neck with suspicion. "You doing okay?"

"I've never been better." I shoot him a cheeky wink as I lead him downstairs to the guys.

"Sit your ass down," Saint says, gruffly, pointing at the couch across from us. I smirk, because he's such a grumpy shit.

But he's *my* grumpy shit.

Saint pulls me down on the couch between him and Galen, slapping a possessive hand on my thigh. I barely resist the urge to roll my eyes.

Bry casually flips Saint off before dropping onto the couch beside Theo. He leans back, crossing one leg over his knee and smirking. Caz hands him a beer, with a matching smirk, before plonking his butt on the arm of the couch. "Thanks, man." Bry nods.

"What's the update?" Saint asks.

"Not a lot," Bry admits. "Whoever the rat is, he's well protected. I've dropped a couple hints, put out a few feelers, but no one seems to know anything, or if they do, they're not saying."

"How can we move this forward?" I ask.

"I suggest we install some cameras and break in to the prez's office. Nothing goes down without Archer Quinn knowing."

"You think the rat approached him and he's dealing with him directly?" Galen asks.

Bry nods.

"It would explain why no one seems to know anything," Theo supplies.

"Get the cameras set up," Saint says. "And we'll plan a B&E after all the shit goes down this week."

"What shit?" Bry inquires, his brows climbing to his hairline.

"Things that don't concern you," Saint says. Until we know exactly where Bry's loyalties lie, we can't let him know our true agenda.

"Did Dar mention anything about his deal with me or Galen?" I ask.

"Sly fucker hasn't said a word to me." Bry swallows a mouthful of beer. "But he's shitting bricks. He's on edge and snapping at everyone and anything. It's clear he's rattled."

"You heard anything about the DEA sniffing around?" Saint asks, and Bry almost chokes on his beer.

"Shit," he says when he's composed himself. "No, but that's not good."

He won't meet my eyes, and all the tiny hairs lift on the back of my neck.

Saint bores a hole in his skull, and they enter into a silent face-off for a few beats. "You sure you don't want to amend your answer?"

The vein in Bry's neck pulses, but outwardly, he looks unfazed. "I'm sure," he coolly replies. "I'll let you know if I hear anything."

Silence slices through the air, and everyone feels the tension.

"We have something else for you to do," Saint says, breaking up the heavy atmosphere.

"Taylor Tamlin," Theo adds. "We need you to hook up with her again and drill her for intel."

"Pun intended," Caz cuts in, wearing a goofy smile.

"We want to know what part she's played and what she knows," Galen says.

"Consider it done." Bry finishes the rest of his beer in one go and stands. "Anything else? I need to get home."

"We're good. For now." Saint says. "Lo will see you out." Saint sends me a knowing look, and I rise, lifting my shoulder and gesturing at Bry to follow me.

I step out into the cool night air. "If there's more you know, you need to spit it out," I say as he throws his leg over his Harley.

"You still don't trust me." It's a statement, not a question. He watches me carefully as he straps his helmet on.

"I get the feeling you're not telling us everything."

He places his hands on the handlebars, and his feet are on the ground. He looks me straight in the eye. "Let's say I wasn't but the reason is justified, and I believe our goals are aligned, would you still trust me?"

"It's hard to trust someone who keeps secrets. You know how I feel about that."

He kick-starts his bike. "I'm not the only one keeping secrets, though, am I, Lo?" he says, staring pointedly at me before taking off and disappearing down the driveway.

We stay at the house again on Wednesday after my hospital visit. Things are going to hit the fan tonight, provided Dar comes through. We want to be here to watch Sinner's reaction when he gets the news.

"It's good to have you all home," Mom says, sliding the pot roast to the middle of the table. She's cooked up a delicious feast, and there's enough food here to feed an army. But the swelling on her cheeks, cut on her lip, bruising on her neck and arms, and the way she's hobbling around the kitchen has vanquished my appetite. She hasn't texted me since I've been staying at the barn, and I haven't made the effort to reach out to her either, and now, I feel guilty for abandoning her to a fate I wouldn't wish on my worst enemy.

Watching her play the perfect Stepford wife aggravates me, and I'm already in a pissy mood because there's no change in Sariah's condition, and the doctors aren't holding out much hope. "Maybe, now we're home, your fiancé will stop beating the shit out of you," I snap, unable to hold the words back.

Sinner stands, lifting the carving knife and pinning me with an evil grin. He starts to cut slices of beef as he talks. "Don't act naïve, Lo." His eyes zoom in on my neck, landing on the faded fingermarks and bruises Galen left behind. "Is it so hard to imagine your mother enjoys rough sex too?"

"Her face is beaten to a pulp, and she's walking with a limp!" I snap, as Giana stands, her chair scraping in the process. Her fists are clenched at her sides as she glares at me, as if I'm the one who inflicted her injuries. "My sex life is none of your business, Harlow, and I'm getting sick of telling you to butt out of things that don't concern you." She walks up behind Sinner, draping herself around him. "I love Neo, and I'm happy. Why can't you be happy for me?"

I jump up, knocking my chair to the floor. "Maybe because you look fucking miserable all the time." I swallow over the lump in my throat. "I can't do this." I storm off to my bedroom, stride into my closet, open my lungs, and let loose the scream that's trapped inside me. I pound my fists into the wall as I scream, venting all the frustration that's been building for weeks.

Strong arms wrap around me from behind a couple minutes later. "Let it out, baby," Theo says, and I scream and scream and scream until my throat feels scraped raw.

I drop to the ground, sitting cross-legged on the floor, my shoulders slumping. Theo sits down across from me, mirroring my position. "What is she doing with him, Theo? Is she that stupid, or is she playing him?"

He runs his fingers through his gorgeous hair. He's been wearing it down a lot more lately, because he knows how much I love threading my hands through it. "Giana is smart, Lo."

"You think she *is* playing him?"

He scoots forward, taking my hands in his. "I think she's protecting you the only way she knows how."

"I need to talk to her." I hop up.

Theo climbs to his feet, reeling me gently into his arms. "You need to put your emotions aside and think about this logically. If she *is* playing some angle, she clearly doesn't want you involved, and we've got to assume that's the safest way of handling the situation."

"I think Theo is right," Saint says, leaning against the door to my closet. "It's better if you don't know. Trust her to manage it."

"She's not managing it!" I cry. "He's beating the crap out of her!" A sob escapes my throat. "I'm a shitty daughter. All this time, I've been hating on her and she's been trying to protect me."

"You're not." Theo brushes his lips against my cheek. "You're trying to protect her too. Taking Sinner down is the only way to save your mom at this point."

"You've got to focus on the endgame," Saint agrees. "No matter how hard that is."

"Maybe, if I talked to her, and she knows all the stuff I know, we can work together? Surely, it makes sense to team up? Alisha confirmed she knows a lot more than either Dad or I realized."

Saint's expression softens as he walks toward me. "You can't trust Galen's mom, Lo. She's fucked in the head from years of drug abuse. She might've dreamed up half of it."

"We know she had an affair with my dad because Galen saw them together and he overheard his parents arguing about it when she got knocked up," I say.

"But we don't know if Giana knows, because we only have Alisha's word for that," Saint protests.

"And if you talk to your mom, if you tell her everything," Theo says, "you might find out she doesn't know the half of it."

Saint pulls me out of Theo's arms and into his. "If she doesn't know about the affair and the baby, do you really want her to know? Is that the memory she should be left with of your dad?"

"No," I quietly admit. "Because it's shaken me to the core and has me questioning my belief in my father." The bags under my eyes attest to that. I've had trouble sleeping ever since I found out the man I've always held on a pedestal wasn't so perfect after all. I get he was coerced into it, but I can't help wondering how the hell he let Sinner trap him in the first place, and now, I'll never find out.

"If she's working something, this could distract her and cause her to lose focus," Theo says.

"And if she's working this hard to protect you, we can't undermine that in any way." Saint wipes the moisture from my cheeks, and I hadn't even realized I was crying. Fuck. I'm turning into a basket case, and I've always prided myself on my ability to shut my emotions down.

"How do I sit back and watch this happening?" I squeeze my eyes shut, leaning my head on Saint's chest. "How do I turn my back on her?"

"You do it because it's what she wants and you have to trust her." Theo smooths a hand up and down my back.

"I've just hired a guy to do some work around the house," Saint adds. "It's an excuse to have someone watching over her. I'd trust this guy with my life, and while he's around, Dad will be more careful."

I cup his beautiful face. "I appreciate that, but let's not pretend like he won't just beat her behind closed doors."

"This guy will find a way to intervene," Saint says, and I want to believe it, but we all know no one can stop Sinner when he's hell-bent on something.

It all kicks off a few hours later when we're down in the basement attempting to watch a movie. We've been on edge all night waiting for it to go down.

Footsteps thud on the stairs and we share knowing glances.

We all swing our gaze in Sinner's direction when he storms into the room like a raging tornado. His body is wired tight, his eyes almost demonic in their madness. His hands are in balls at his side, and he looks two seconds away from ripping someone apart. "You two!" he snaps, pointing at Galen and Saint. "You're with me."

"What's going on?" Saint asks, standing.

"The Arrows are fucking dead!" Sinner shouts. "That's what's going on, and we're about to send them that message."

"How?" Galen asks, also standing.

"Don't fucking question me, boy." Sinner grabs him by the shoulders, shoving him in the direction of the stairs. "If I say I need you, that's all you need to know."

"We're with you, Dad," Saint says, his voice calm, cautioning Galen with his eyes. "Let's go."

"You three!" Sinner points at Caz, me, and Theo. "Protect Giana, and keep a watch outside. I can't guarantee The Arrows haven't planned other shit for tonight."

"We've got it," Caz says.

Saint casts a wary glance over his shoulder before they follow Sinner upstairs.

"Sweet." Caz grins. "Dar came through."

"Speak of the devil," I murmur, pulling my cell out of my pocket as it vibrates with an incoming call. Dar's name flashes on the screen. I swipe my finger to accept the call, opening my mouth to speak, but before I can utter a word, he is shouting obscenities at me, threatening to stick a gun in my mouth, a knife in my pussy, and a bat up my ass.

Theo stiffens and Caz snarls as they hear him shouting his threats through the phone even before I've put it on speaker.

I wait for Darrow to exhaust himself, and when he's finally stopped spewing venom, I clear my throat. "Are you done?"

"I'm fucking done, all right!" he yells. "You fucking screwed me over big time."

"I have no idea what you're talking about, and I'm confused because Sinner just hightailed it out of here in a murderous rage. What happened? Where is the shipment?"

"Spilling out of the back of the semi as we speak," Dar says. "Fucking hell!" he shouts. "Archer will cut my fucking balls off for this!"

"Calm your shit, and tell me what went down." I am quickly losing patience with the dick.

"The truck was exactly where you said it would be, and it took little effort to ambush it because they were not expecting us, but they weren't the only ones surprised. Are you saying you didn't know?"

"Know what, Dar?" I bark. "You're not making sense." I exchange a concerned look with Theo and Caz.

"The shipment wasn't drugs, Lo. It was fucking girls. What the fuck are we supposed to do with that?"

THE SAINTHOOD

THE SAINTHOOD

CHAPTER 33

"THIS MEANS ALL-out war," Sinner seethes the following morning at breakfast, pacing the kitchen like the batshit crazy psycho he is.

We stayed up half the night waiting for the guys to return, and then, we had a hushed, shocked conversation at four a.m. before crawling into bed for a few hours' sleep.

Judging from Sinner's whiskey breath and bloodshot eyes, I'd say he didn't get to bed at all. "I'm putting a man on you," he tells Mom the second she steps into the kitchen in a fitted skirt suit. "Things are going to get ugly now."

I'll say. After they failed to retrieve the "shipment," they attacked three of The Arrows' warehouses, burning them to the ground. War has most definitely arrived in Lowell now.

"Is it really necessary?" Mom asks, pouring a cup of coffee.

Sinner flies across the kitchen, grabbing her by the throat.

I move to stand, but Saint yanks me back down, warning me with his eyes. I dig my nails into my thighs as Saint wraps his arm around my waist, keeping me in place. I don't know how much longer I can stay in this house and not do something. Mom as hot coffee spills down the front of her blouse, and a sickening feeling swirls in my gut. "It's necessary if I say it's necessary," Sinner hisses, his spittle landing on her face.

"Okay." She gulps. "Fine."

He pins manic eyes on her, and I seriously consider embedding my knife in his back. I'm a good shot. I could easily do it from here.

As if he's heard my thoughts, Galen shakes his head at me from across the table. I'm reminded of our conversation when we were in his house, and I know this is as hard for him as it is for me, yet he's keeping it together.

I nod, forcing myself to think about the endgame.

"I need to get changed," Mom says when Sinner eventually backs away. She leans in, kissing his cheek. "I'll talk to you later, darling." If she's acting, she deserves a fucking Oscar for her stellar performance.

"Chapter meeting tonight at HQ. Everyone is to be there," Sinner barks, his lips pulling into a sly sneer when he looks at me. "You too, *princess*. We might find some of those tasks for you after everyone has gone."

Blood turns to ice in my veins, but I school my features into a neutral mask.

"When were you going to tell us?" Saint clips out, removing his arm from my waist and glaring at his father.

"When we'd successfully trafficked our first shipment." Sinner dumps a load of whiskey in his cup.

"Now that the authorities have the girls, what will you do?" Saint inquires, and I can tell how hard it is for him to keep his voice calm. Every muscle and sinew in his body is locked tight, and I'm guessing he's having similar murderous thoughts about his father.

After I ended my call with Dar, I contacted Saint, and he agreed to organize an anonymous tip to be sent to the cops. They showed up minutes before Sinner and his crew, and, according to the guys, Sinner went apeshit that they missed out on reclaiming the girls he's already paid for.

The Arrows had fled the scene by then, narrowly avoiding arrest. From what Darrow said, Archer Quinn, The Arrows president, wants nothing to do with sex trafficking and he's out for my blood, because he thinks I set them up.

Nice of Dar to throw me to the wolves, and isn't it just my luck to take care of one enemy and gain a new one at the same time.

"Wait until the heat cools down, and then, try again," Sinner says.

"We don't traffic women," Galen supplies, his voice strained. "You honestly think members will vote this in?"

Sinner snorts. "They'll fucking do what I say, and the profits speak for themselves. With Luke McKenzie out of the way, that business is wide-open for the taking. It's worth millions, billions." His eyes glint greedily, and my stomach churns.

"What's McKenzie got to do with it?" Theo asks.

"He was The Bulls liaison with the supplier in Mexico. Dude doesn't trust Ruben, thanks to some past history and bad blood. He didn't realize he was supplying The Bulls until I informed him. We have a way in now, provided I can spin last night and not fucking ruin everything before it's begun." His nostrils flare as he slams his hands on the table.

"This should help," Caz says, turning on the TV and tilting his head to the side.

Sinner's eyes pop wide, and his fury turns to quick delight as we watch the news report confirming a large shipment of drugs and weapons were seized in an early morning raid on the docks in Fenton. Pictures show Ruben and a line of guys in cuts being frog-marched into police vans.

Saint has already sent spies out onto the streets to start taking control of the Fenton supply, because we don't know if the cops will arrest everyone. In the event they don't, the remaining members should be too busy trying to hold on to their turf to bother about me.

Sinner grins, rubbing his hands together. "At least, something good has come from this shitshow." He jabs his finger at Saint. "Get guys on the street. I want that supply locked up tight before other greedy assholes try to take the territory."

"I'm on it," Saint says, his fingers flying over his phone.

Sinner slaps him on the back. "That's my boy." He leers at me, peering down the front of my shirt, and nausea swims up my throat. "I just might be in the mood for celebrating tonight after all."

"Knock it off, Dad." Saint slings his arm around my shoulders, glaring at his dad. "Lo is ours."

"Sharing is caring, son." Sinner smirks, slapping him extra hard on the back. "And I don't take orders from you." He swats the back of his head, and the urge to stab him is riding me hard again. "Have a good day at school." He laughs, walking off with a half-empty whiskey bottle clutched in one hand.

"I say we implement a new plan," Galen growls. Our gazes swing to his. "Let's kill the asshole. I don't know how much more of his shit I can stomach."

"I'm down with that plan." I remove my knife, running my finger along the tip.

"We stick to the original plan," Saint says. He looks down at me. "Put that away."

"You're no fun." I pout, tucking my knife away.

"And there's no fucking way you're coming to the meeting tonight."

"I can't just not show up." I crick my head from side to side, loosening my tense shoulder muscles.

"You fucking can, and you will. I'll think of some excuse," Saint promises.

"Can you think of it later," Theo says, standing and knocking back the last of his orange juice. "We need to get to school."

It's the second-to-last class of the day, and I'm staring out the window, yawning and trying to keep my eyes open. I'm not listening to a word Batshit Branning is saying because I'm too fucking tired to concentrate.

"Ms. Westbrook!" she screeches in my ear. I turn my head, surprised to find the teacher standing at my desk. "The vice principal has requested your attendance in her office immediately."

"What's this about?" I ask, gathering my books.

"You'll find out when you get there," she retorts before returning to the front of the class. None of the guys are in this class, so I pop off a quick group text as I follow the secretary to Vice Principal Pierson's office.

"Harlow." The small, curvy woman pins me with a soft smile. "Have a seat, dear."

"What's going on? Am I in trouble?" I thought the guys fixed it so the week I was absent was not an issue, but maybe, they didn't. I plop into the seat across from her, dropping my bag on the ground by my feet.

"No." She shakes her head, reaching across the desk to pat my hand. "There's no easy way to say this. I just received a call from the hospital."

My heart stops beating, and panic sluices into my veins. I gulp. "Tell me," I croak.

"The doctor has confirmed there is no brain activity. They're waiting for you to say goodbye to Sariah before switching off the life support machine."

Tears prick my eyes, and I drag my lower lip between my teeth. I can hardly breathe over the messy ball of emotion clogging my throat. *No! This can't be happening. Not to my bestie. She's a fighter. The best of them.*

Her eyes fill up, and she squeezes my hand. "I'm so sorry, Harlow."

"Does Sean know?"

"My understanding is he's already at the hospital. What can I do?"

I stare straight through her. I can't force myself to say anything, and I can't make myself move either. I'm adrift at sea without a life vest.

"Can I call someone for you?" she asks. "Saint Lennox?"

"No need," Saint says, as the door swings open, slamming

against the wall. He stalks toward me. "We've got it from here, Mrs. P."

"Princess." Saint crouches down in front of me while Theo speaks in hushed tones with the vice principal. Saint's warm hand palms my face. "You're scaring me, babe." His concerned blue eyes meet my green ones.

"Saint," I rasp, placing my hand over his as tears spill down my face. "Say it's not real. It can't be real. Make it not be real." Theo whispers in his ear, and Saint's Adam's apple jumps in his throat.

"C'mere, babe." With more tenderness than he's ever exhibited, Saint helps me from my chair. He pulls me into his chest while Theo takes my hand, Galen presses a kiss to the top of my head, and Caz rubs my back.

I rest my head on Saint's chest while silent tears cascade down my cheeks, and the pain in my heart is so intense it feels like it might explode behind my rib cage. My eyes meet the vice principal's and she's looking at all of us with a curious smile. I'm imagining what it must look like to her—these four inked, pierced, towering bad boys, showering affection on the same girl, and I bet she never thought behind those rough, tough exteriors lie the biggest hearts with the greatest capacity for love.

"I'm okay," I say, straightening up and wiping my tears with the arm of my sweater. "I need to get to the hospital before it's too late."

I rest my head on Theo's shoulder, and he presses a kiss to my cheek, keeping a firm hold of my hand as we make our way out of the office. I assume someone has taken my bag. Galen comes up on my other side, threading his fingers through mine while Saint and Caz take up the rear. The hallways are empty as we make our way past classrooms and head outside.

"Theo." Saint calls out.

Theo tosses the car keys into Galen's hand before kissing me softly on the lips. "Go with Galen, babe."

Galen squeezes my hand as we walk off, leaving the other three quietly talking on top of the steps. "I'm so sorry, Lo," Galen says as we walk toward the Lexus. Theo parked it in the first row, directly in front of the school building, a few spots down on the right.

"Everyone I love dies," I say, feeling a strange combination of numb and emotionally crippled.

"Not us, angel." He kisses the top of my head, unlocking the car with the key fob. It makes a distinct pinging sound as we approach. "We're going nowhere."

My hand curls around the door handle as movement off to the left captures my attention.

"Lo! No!" Galen roars, yanking my arm back just as the door opens.

A flash of blonde hair meets the corner of my eye as Galen swings me around.

"Run!" he yells, pushing me forward, his body pressed up against my back.

My legs swing into action, but everything else slows down, and my brain registers several things at once as if I'm drifting high above the sky, watching it all go down.

Saint, Caz, and Theo are racing toward us, their mouths open, lips moving, but I can't hear the words.

A high-pitched laugh tickles my eardrums just as a loud explosion pierces the air, cracking through the haze I'm in, ripping through the silence, and unmuting the shouts of the guys as they run toward us.

Heat blasts me from behind, and I'm thrown forward with force as another booming pop detonates around us.

"Lo!" Galen screams from somewhere close by, as I soar through the air, legs and arms flailing uncontrollably.

My body slams into the asphalt, face-first, and splintering pain whips through me as a crushing weight lands on my back.

Then, the world turns black.

TO BE CONTINUED

Reign, the third and final book in The Sainthood series, is AVAILABLE NOW in e-book, paperback, and audiobook format.

ABOUT THE AUTHOR

USA Today bestselling author **Siobhan Davis** writes emotionally intense young adult and new adult fiction with swoon-worthy romance, complex characters, and tons of unexpected plot twists and turns that will have you flipping the pages beyond bedtime!

Siobhan's family will tell you she's a little bit obsessive when it comes to reading and writing, and they aren't wrong. She can rarely be found without her trusty Kindle, a paperback book, or her laptop somewhere close at hand.

Prior to becoming a full-time writer, Siobhan forged a successful corporate career in human resource management.

She resides in the Garden County of Ireland with her husband and two sons.

You can connect with Siobhan in the following ways:

Website: www.siobhandavis.com
Blog: myyanabookobsession.com
Facebook: AuthorSiobhanDavis
Twitter: @siobhandavis
Instagram: @siobhandavisauthor
Email: siobhan@siobhandavis.com

BOOKS BY SIOBHAN DAVIS

KENNEDY BOYS SERIES
Upper Young Adult/New Adult Contemporary Romance

Finding Kyler
Losing Kyler
Keeping Kyler
The Irish Getaway
Loving Kalvin
Saving Brad
Seducing Kaden
Forgiving Keven
Summer in Nantucket
Releasing Keanu
Adoring Keaton
Reforming Kent

STANDALONES
New Adult Contemporary Romance

Inseparable
Incognito
When Forever Changes
Only Ever You
No Feelings Involved
Second Chances Box Set

Reverse Harem Contemporary Romance

Surviving Amber Springs

RYDEVILLE ELITE SERIES
Dark High School Romance

Cruel Intentions
Twisted Betrayal
Sweet Retribution
Charlie
Jackson
*Sawyer^*
*Drew^*

THE SAINTHOOD (BOYS OF LOWELL HIGH)
Dark HS Reverse Harem Romance

Resurrection
Rebellion
Reign
The Sainthood: The Complete Series

ALL OF ME DUET
Angsty New Adult Romance

Say I'm The One ^
*Let Me Love You^*

ALINTHIA SERIES
Upper YA/NA Paranormal Romance/Reverse Harem

The Lost Savior
The Secret Heir
The Warrior Princess

The Chosen One
The Rightful Queen

TRUE CALLING SERIES
Young Adult Science Fiction/Dystopian Romance

True Calling
Lovestruck
Beyond Reach
Light of a Thousand Stars
Destiny Rising

Short Story Collection
True Calling Series Collection

SAVEN SERIES
Young Adult Science Fiction/Paranormal Romance

Saven Deception
Logan
Saven Disclosure
Saven Denial
Saven Defiance
Axton
Saven Deliverance
Saven: The Complete Series

^**Release date to be confirmed**

Printed in Great Britain
by Amazon